FULL
METAL
MOON

Richard Sullivan

FULL METAL MOON

A Novel of the Vietnam War

Deering & Hardin / Los Angeles

A special thanks to Stephanie, for early review of the ms. and encouragement.

Cover Design by Brad Fraunfelter http: bfillustration.com
Interior Artwork by Romy Muirhead http://romymuirhead.com
Interior Design by Ghislain Viau http://www.creativepublishingdesign.com

ISBN Paperback: 978-0-9978775-0-2
ISBN Hardcover: 978-0-9978775-1-9

Printed in the United States of America

FOR
the 0300s and the 11Bravos

In Memory Of

JAMES DONNIE HOWE, USMC, CMOH
December 17, 1948 – May 6, 1970

Semper Fi

AUTHOR'S NOTE

There are many words used in this novel that a reader would not be expected to have ever encountered. These include military jargon and abbreviations (already present in previous pages), the names and characteristics of weapons, slang expressions peculiar to a long-ago war, even the names of artists, personalities and cultural phenomena now as historical to most people as a half-century old battle in a country that no longer exists. Hopeful that you will complete a four hundred page journey that begins throwing roadblocks of unfamiliar language right away, I have added a Glossary at the back to help a writer's cause, which, aside from paying the rent, as far as I can tell is primarily that his readers find out what happens to his heroes. And in this case, his heroines. They are, after all, hopelessly flawed or impossibly beautiful, his children.

I tried writing this story and omitting the obscenity. I saw no reason it couldn't be done. Language in war is no less vulgar than war itself, but that was far from any point to my story. I sought the high road but fell face down. Again and again. And again and again I picked myself up and carried the torch for purity and restraint, only to watch in horror as scandalous words and imagery grew in volume, frequency and detail. Far from succeeding, I found I had written instead as concentrated an outpouring of obscenity as may have appeared in print on a single page, at least in my own reading experience. I realized finally that it was *their* story now and the language was no longer mine. It belonged to *them*, the characters I was subjecting to every form of abuse and indignity, and despite my every furious typing assault at revision or even compromise, they stubbornly refused to let it go. My sincere apologies in advance. If you can get past the second chapter, you should find, for instance, Maurice Debro's stormy diatribes downgraded to a much less offensive pattern of scattered showers, with only the occasional further monsoon downpour. Maybe you'll just become numb to it, as I did. But I hope you can make it to the end. I think that despite all the roadblocks, carnage and possibly tedium (also a part of war) en route, you will arrive unscathed.

An early reviewer had a great deal of trouble with the middle of the book and strongly suggested I consider making deep cuts to this part of the story. I agreed in principle if not wholeheartedly and got out the hatchet. But when the blade fell from my exhausted arm and the blood and dust settled, much like my characters' unrepentant vocabulary, the middle part had grown instead. The characters from that part of the tale would have nothing to do with it, staged a palace coup, and ran me out of town, inflating themselves in the bargain. Again, my apologies. If you find that half a novel spent describing the firing of eight shots from a rifle is just too much to demand of a reader's patience, you can put these loose-cannon figments of imagination in their place by simply skipping the middle sections. Turn right to "IV" from "I". You'll still find out what happens to my heroes and heroines, and despite all the abuse and indignity I meted out—hopefully tempered by some measure of redemption—they won't have lived, or died, in vain.

Nor, for that matter, will have their author.

Richard Sullivan
Winter's night
Los Angeles, California

A people cannot be debased in a single generation…no nation is ever so formidable to its neighbors for a time, as a nation which, after being trained up in self-government, passes suddenly under a despotic ruler. The energy of democratic institutions survives for a few generations, and to it are added the decision and certainty which are the attributes of government when all its powers are directed by a single mind. It is true that this preternatural vigor is short-lived: national corruption and debasement gradually follow the loss of the national liberties; but there is an interval before their workings are felt, and in that interval the most ambitious schemes of foreign conquest are often successfully undertaken.

—Edward Shepherd Creasy, 1851
Fifteen Decisive Battles of the Western World

But I suggest, gentlemen, that the difficulty is not so much to escape death; the real difficulty is to escape from doing wrong, an adversary far more fleet of foot.

—Socrates,
in the *Apology*

"Tell brave deeds of war."

Then they recounted tales,—
"There were stern stands
"And bitter runs for glory."

Ah, I think there were braver tales.

—Stephen Crane, 1895
The Black Riders and Other Lines

CONTENTS

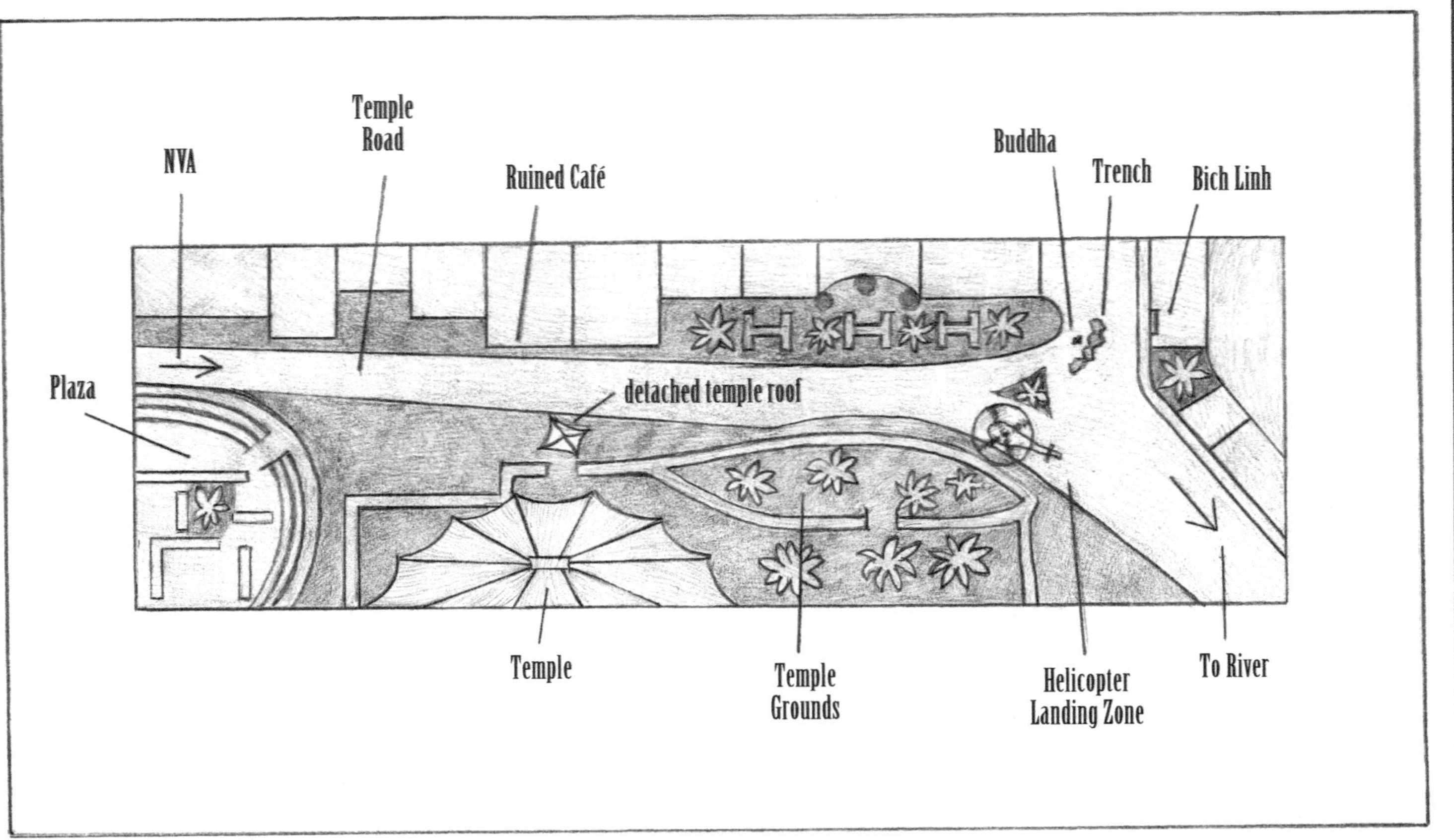
Temple
Road
NVA
Ruined Café
Buddha
Trench
Bich Linh
Plaza
detached temple roof
Temple
Temple
Grounds
Helicopter
Landing Zone
To River

Prologue

ON HER ARRIVAL she would speak to no one save to ask for Thanh, refusing to sleep until he came. When Thanh heard, he left the fighting in the mountains and descended with reckless skill along trails thick with enemy patrols and buried explosives. He found her settled inside the old hut in the hidden village, lying on the aluminum cot he had won in combat against Americans at Dak To. He sat on the earthen floor beside the cot while her two companions rested outside and took turns sleeping. Once she began her story he listened without interruption, asking no questions, refusing to distract her even by offering food or water. Occasionally he looked down to scribble something in his notebook. The hours passed. It was dark inside the summer evening when she finished, drained more by the telling than the rigors of which she told. The sleep she resisted finally overcame her but before it did Thanh knelt and placed his hand gently on her ruined face and said, *I will write the story of your life and mine in the words of a single breath and however many years pass and whatever happens for ill or good there will be nothing left to add.*

When she awoke she was alone in the hut. She could hear the little lizards that mocked the noise of crickets and the crickets too. These were the sounds of deepest night. Had only a few hours passed to restore her strength so? On the crude writing stool by the cot Thanh had left his notebook open, the one with the blood-stained bullet hole that held all his poetry. She picked it up, rose and went to the doorway, her solitary eye blinking awake before it recognized the total darkness of the hours before dawn. She realized that she must have slept a full day and a night, something she had never done before. As Thanh had never before left behind the little notebook, his life's sole constant companion. Was she awake, or dreaming where she stood?

The moon was down but she could still read in the starlight streaming from horizon to horizon like shattered glass. Wind from the fan of a distant storm washed over her and in the tiny breeze the tips of her hair twitched like separate living things. The edges of the notebook fluttered as though living too. In the artwork of his tiny impeccable script Thanh had written:

The rooftops smolder after days of air strikes. Bich Linh leaps across them casting exactly the same shadow as fire. Her sandals are a pair of little wings, a gift of one god stolen from another, that she might outrace the fire of evil days. The single flame of a dual passion drives her as relentlessly as American jets above split the sky into black fragments and cover the holy city in ashes.

Love and hate, lust and vengeance: no other purpose so bright, no understanding so pure, one no less a part of the other than any knife plunged into a human heart.

To own all the thought of a lover, to break the body of an enemy. These and these alone, forever, until all things remaining merge one day at the end of time, whether in doom or in triumph, godhead or oblivion.

Beneath these few paragraphs, lines of poetry sprawled across two full pages despite the miniscule writing. But now she knew she was awake. And alone. Thanh was gone, and she could not bring herself to read further.

I

Tomlin

HUE CITY, Republic of South Vietnam, February, 1968

1

THE ROOFTOPS STILL SMOLDERED after days of air strikes. Bich Linh leapt across them casting exactly the same shadow as fire, her sandals a pair of little wings. The flame of conflicting passion drove her as relentlessly as American jets and artillery split the sky into black fragments and covered the city in ashes.

Love and hate drove her. The lust for vengeance sustained her. No other purpose so bright, no understanding so pure. To own all the thought of a lover, to break the body of an enemy. This and this alone, forever, until all things merged one day at the end of time, whether in doom or in triumph, heaven or hell, godhead or oblivion.

Devils were loose. Above her a full moon in daylight leered down upon the earth, its malice shimmering through broken clouds. Devils were loose, so let the enemy tremble. She feared nothing. No demons could catch her, no witches slipping from their warrens a match for her protection under the gods.

As far as she knew, of her cadre she alone was left, the others deserted or dead, victims of their own pale fears or the wine-soaked bravado of the days before the assault began. Many had fought well, but as always the bravest died first, leaving only the timid and self-absorbed, the thin shell of their courage shattered by American air power. These half-dead huddled beneath crumbled archways and walls and whispered their doubts and furtive conspiracies, as though lives spared by defeat remained worth living. To shame them she had twice stood and returned fire against strafing Phantom F-4s. But to no avail. They avoided her gaze and fired blindly at enemy they couldn't see.

And then they were no more. As Thanh would have said, *Praise Buddha*.

For three days Linh had fought alone and run, and hidden and fought, and fought and killed until her senses scouted prey in front of her and shielded her while she slept. She had not eaten since the white devils entered the city in force, subsisting on hallucination, drinking water from canteens of the dead on both sides. She wondered where the strength in her body came from. Was the need for food a myth, or had she been absent at her own death and now lived unknowing in another world?

Alive or dead, in this world or any other, wherever she could she approached the Americans she killed and compared them to the Hated One in the photograph. *Not you*, she would say to the corpse, and drop the bloodied or disfigured or purpling head back into the rubble. And then think again of Thanh, his bare feet skimming rocks and trails of the Que Son mountains, coolness and shade all around him, a universe distant, safe from her broodings. His mind fixed on his god, the wooden icon around his neck bound in leather and soaked in his sweat. *His* mind empty of *her*, curse all that was shallow, neglectful, beautiful.

She was mid-air.

In the narrow gulf below her, she smelled, then saw, a pair of enemy soldiers throwing themselves about, staggering from doorway to doorway, weapons jabbing about in ragged little motions, shouting at each other over the city's constant explosions and rifle fire, as if the fragile bond of words could bind them together tighter than her

Dragunov could rend them apart. She imagined she heard singing, strange and high-pitched, the way a man in a woman's body might sing. Or did she truly hear it? A startled cry rose up to greet her; one of the soldiers below even managed a burst of automatic fire. She felt scorn, landed lightly on an intact wall and kept running, her destination already chosen. Not ten strides further on, a barrage of mortars rained stone and metal in all directions, filling the air with molten death. If she lived, and the gods favored her, there might be time to return and kill these she left behind. If the mortars hadn't robbed her of the privilege.

In the Old City, before its destruction, the buildings had climbed over each other the way highland trees wrestled for sunlight. Now their blackened remains smoked from the constant artillery and bombings. They lay in twisted heaps or stood in broken and solitary walls, jagged structures with senseless arms of plaster and wood dangling from tendons of exposed timbers. The skyline was a shattered bowl. Broken buildings were the turning wheels in death's machine, grinding life from the wounded, burying prostrate figures in green or brown beneath outbursts of sudden collapse. The death they brought was indiscriminate, but to Linh they had become as intimate as family, she who had no other, made a widow and childless by the Hated One.

The twisted ruins of the city built her nests, gave her fortresses, sheltered her in depths where she could sleep soundly inside the bowels of war, as she had once deep in mountain caves beneath the pounding of American bombers. Often she awakened to the chatter and strange odor of Americans so close to her she could have shot them with her pistol. Instead she lay still and went back to sleep, to kill later, rested, with her rifle. When the mornings came, the Americans would be gone, the sun a heathen red behind a veil of dust and cloud as she rose to hunt them again.

Yet even the solace of spent and black exhaustion, wrapped in the arms of the broken city, could not keep the dream at bay. Under her blankets of stone she still crossed the River at the fords, something still moved inside the shallows. The serpents rose and she stood as always transfixed and helpless as they leered and ripped the flesh from the bodies of her husband and children.

When the largest one had consumed her son he came and swayed beside her.

"Cry no more," he said, and sank his fangs into her eye.

Always when she awoke from the dream, she expected continued darkness. Her sorrow boundless, she expected to cry. But only one eye had been crushed to pulp, and though she could still see, no tears would flow, even from the sighted eye. The serpent had left her vision, but stolen her tears. The River in the dream roared away full of its wetness, mocking the orphaned eye that could not weep.

And so she had died and been born the second time, become who she was and vowed to remain. And always in search of Him, the Hated One.

At the end of the street, and then two streets west, below the strangely intact multiple roofs of a holy building, a furious firefight was in progress. This she thought was good fortune, near as it seemed to her current hideaway. She bounded westward, soaring above little alleyways, aware suddenly of a rhythmic slap of bullet strikes around her. The shooting came from her blind side. Without turning her head to look, she sensed the American machine gun on its platform of destroyed roof to the east. Instinctively she adjusted her route and flew lightly along a shattered parapet wall to drop from the gunner's view down steps of broken columns, the following wave of enemy bullets passing harmlessly overhead.

In the street below, landslides of disintegrated walls lay in frozen eddies around fallen building facades and smashed and burning vehicles. Red dust and shards of clay tile coated everything like dried blood. Unmoved, she noted the numbers of brown-clad bodies everywhere. More of her countrymen sacrificed by generals who imagined their battlefield from parade ground windows and sent armies to move in daylight while enemy jets owned the sky.

Behold their genius.

Some of the soldiers clutched weapons in death, some of them still writhed in death's farewell. Against a wall a nameless wretch cried soundlessly, as though the bomb that ruined his legs and took his arm had carried off his voice as well.

She was a warrior, not a nurse. Ignoring the wounded, she chose her path through the ruins and raced toward a flight of stairs set back inside the deformed maw of a pagoda's skull. Once past the first corner she sprang easily over heaps of mangled timbers and stone, vigilant for enemy patrols. Passing so closely to him that she didn't need to aim, she shot a kneeling American between the eyes before he could do more than look up in anguish over a fallen comrade.

Close enough to see he wasn't the Hated One.

Not you either, she concluded of the second dead American, sailing over both bodies onto the clutter of a broken sidewalk and into the building, mindful that where one American was, there were others close by.

The stairway was destroyed but she ran without pause up its remnants, onto a second story floor with sky for a ceiling. Effortlessly, even gracefully, she dodged gaping holes and hanging rafters and vaulted up and down higher and lower walls from steps exploded into shape by American artillery. She flew through skeleton frames of windows and skewed doorways and passed along roof lines from building to building crowded so closely together that the spaces of their separation were clogged to the brim with pulverized dust and fist-sized fragments of mortar and cinder block.

Invulnerable, Thanh had written her. *Be invulnerable. You cannot be killed without your own submission. Conceive that you are wrapped in an armor not of mineral but of vengeance, forged not on earth but in heaven, on the anvil of the gods. Your cause is holy or none would oppose it.*

The air strikes had momentarily cleared the skies of helicopters, which was why she was moving now, inside the holes of their absence. The army's rocket launchers were so long since used up or their operators killed that the American pilots in their Hueys and gunships roamed the ruined city with impunity. Resupply was impossible. Days before, she had peeled a bloody RPG launcher from the grip of a dying soldier and stored it deep in her lair. For all she knew she represented all the remaining artillery available to the army.

Bich Linh knew the battle to hold the city was lost, but she had never believed the childish rantings of the political officers anyway. She knew also that the army had won regardless of what were obviously its final hours. Dying themselves in uncounted numbers, they had yet inflicted tremendous casualties among the enemy. The grief of American mothers would shackle the enemy's war machine in chains forged of their children's blood, sapping the will of the fathers and shaking the foundations of their nation. And she knew, too, that this had been the strategy all along.

She was fighting to the end with her one eye wide open. The brief victories of the early days a fool could have seen were futile delaying actions against the inevitable. Linh sneered at the cruelty and cowardice of purging Western sympathizers from the city walls, many with crimes no greater than taking a coin from the enemy to keep their children alive. She had heard the tales of barbarism and atrocities. When an officer commanded her to spare no woman or child, she sneered long and hard and turned the Dragunov in his direction. The man had paled and hastened on his way. Easy to massacre frightened and pitiful sheep, hard to fight the enemy. She scorned the commissars with their pamphlets and their bullhorns and awaited her own death at any time.

Oblivious to the fury of the skies above her, and heedless of the peril of being seen by any of the jets' pilots, she cleared one last alley and disappeared inside her haven in its tumble of destroyed rooftop. Overhead the Phantoms streaked and plunged, then rolled and spiraled like vain peacocks, bombs separating from their wings in a flash of silver. Rising from below the horizon they banked in wide circles and returned in 20 mm strafing runs, coating the world in a wash of engine roar, cannon fire and disintegrating city. Then abruptly, though hours of daylight remained, they turned eastward toward the ocean and disappeared. In their wake a silence louder than the city's eternal gunfire.

The walls of her fortress leaned and the ceiling was a skein of wrecked and shattered rafters, open to the sky. Broken sections of fallen wood beams served as a ladder and led down to her sleeping quarters, a straw mat inside a triangle of collapsed masonry. The timbers that remained above were cracked and bowed but afforded solid protection against enemy rifle fire. It was a perfect sanctuary, more bounty from her mother the destroyed city. At her fortress's walls she had a clear field of fire into the street behind the temple. From here, receding to darkness on the ebb tide of hunger and thirst, asking and expecting no quarter, and with none to give, she intended to make her final stand.

She leaned against a shattered masonry column, catching her breath and listening to the firefight in the little plaza in front of the temple. Farther away, but headed in her direction, she recognized a larger battle approaching. Devils were loose, and the end was at hand. But she didn't care. She the Invulnerable. She whom even Death in the illusion of its victory could not vanquish.

Each hour of her continued life had become a further unexpected gift to kill more white devils. Where there was still fighting on earth and sun in the sky, and breath in her body, there was still opportunity.

It was not a gift to be wasted.

2

DEBRO WAS IN RARE FORM EVEN FOR DEBRO. It wasn't just the cursing, it was the *feeling* he put into it, wear you out just to listen. *Where* he unloaded the artillery of his swearing didn't matter to Debro, or who sat front row in the audience: privates or generals, television cameramen or water buffaloes, pot-bellied pigs startled from the shade or platoon sergeants doing the dirty work. *Especially* the platoon sergeants, condemned as they were to hand out work parties back in the rear or night ambush duty after a long day's grind. Whatever the occasion, Debro could make you feel like a sinner in the hands of an angry God. No difference to him, whether over C-rations gone rancid, heat-stroke inducing humps up godforsaken mountain trails, in the exhausted hush before night dropped a curtain over the bush, or, as moments ago, in the middle of a firefight: *Where that motherfucker go took that cheap fuckin shot out that fuckin window bout 2 o'clock you see that prick? you see im? You do you rain some serious shit down his position that gotta be the motherfucker nailed Bender and Doc you hear that single shot sniper shit back all them AKs? That's him in that window got Swede too I know it this fuckin war I hate this fuckin war fuckin shitforbrains politicians got this cheapass fuckin war goin not a fuckin reason in the world oughta be drowned in a fifty five gallon barrel of shit ever last one of em hauled out dried out paraded in front of ever schoolhouse in Washington DC fuckin body bags hangin from flagpoles in front of em show ever schoolkid thinkin of votin in trash like that what in store for anyone believin their lyin shitcovered asses president goin on television sayin he aint gonna send no American boys to die for no Asian boys in no foreign fuckin war my ass they say one thing do the other all they want is the fuckin money I say send em all to hell and afuckinmen to ever fuckin one of em!*

When even Debro had to pause for air Tomlin shouted No! over the rampaging of Debro's M16. I don't know nothin about politics but I know the squad! Bender's best I seen at findin cover! No way Swede's gonna get himself shot, dead man gets no coffee! Doc and the rest of em gone back the way we came! And damn it, D-brother, God bless America!

That's for you motherfucker! Debro's bolt locked open on an empty magazine. He dumped the empty, reloaded and turned to Tomlin. What fuckin way's back the way we came, white boy? Your damn compass shot to shit it's blind leadin the blind ever street lookin like ever other street and I'm tellin you there's a bolt action up there displacin along them rooftops killin everythin fuckin movin and them's dead I said was dead and we better haul ass most riki-tik other side this fuckin street or we dead too movin or sittin behind these fuckin walls either fuckin way it don't fuckin matter!

Tomlin ducked back behind cover and swapped out his own magazine, small arms fire and bullet strikes everywhere, clusters of plaster and stone and wood raining down on them inside a nebula of billowing dust gloriously backlit by the morning sun. At the top of his lungs he shouted, And what I'm always tellin you about that foul language, D-brother? You keep that shit up we aint gettin invited nowhere!

Debro emptied another magazine, tore it out and slapped in a fresh one in the same motion and was back at it, arcing the M16 this way and that, firing in short bursts, pausing only to yell back at Tomlin, Foul language, white boy? Aint this war one big fuckin obscenity? Aint them politicians back home aint they the ones got the foul mouth? Wearin them fine coats and ties and puffed up hair and dresses and pukin up all them fine words Daddy sent em to school to learn so they can preach that bullshit how we need this fuckin war how we need all these fuckin wars you tell me what language your D-brother be usin be fuckin foul as that? And you wanna talk bout language? Here I am got what's left a squad full of Texas cowboys talkin redneck so thick man who speaks fuckin English can't hardly tell what fuckin language they usin! Now swap out your mag and let's didifuckinmau!

Debro shot his rifle empty, changed out his own magazine, and dove from behind the disintegrating cover of the shattered fountain, Tomlin following Debro, AK fire following them both.

Things started badly that morning and didn't get much better.

Tomlin was squad leader but that was a formality lost on Debro, who made it clear every day that Tomlin's flip-a-coin promotion was strictly a laughing matter and at best a spittoon for lip service. Telling Debro to knock off the narrative of his every displeasure was like asking the wind to blow back the way it came. And besides, Debro's cursing was the least of their troubles. Just the two of them left and both of them lost on a mission that made no sense.

They just said get a team up there, LT said and shrugged.

Who's they? Tomlin asked.

Who the hell really knows?

Where's there?

A temple. Here. LT tapping on the map.

Hell we do when we get there?

Nobody knows nothin. Somebody tells me, I tell you. Find the temple, find some cover and hang tight.

Tomlin figured Debro must have shot Webster's Third International Dictionary of Invective empty in the last full-auto diatribe and forgotten to reload. Over five minutes now and not a single four-letter word. Maybe even Debro had to shut up and pay attention sometimes.

He followed faithfully and from long practice as Debro dashed from behind another doorway, made a running left turn off the remains of another shattered boulevard and somehow managed to leave the AK fire behind. Vocabulary aside, Debro was good in a tight spot. Ten yards more, though, and Debro suddenly threw up an arm like a man shot dead in mid-air. Tomlin dove into the deck. It hurt.

"Look at that, white boy!"

Debro wasn't shot, he was pointing.

Tomlin was scanning windows, rooftops and doorways fast enough to throw his neck out, lying on his back and shooting into black holes of buildings, at banisters on second story patios, into already disintegrated windows, at anything resembling a stick figure. Debro took a knee behind a mound of rubble and looked back at him.

"You see it? You see it?" Debro jabbing away at the sky like a lunatic.

"See *what?* Damn it!"

Tomlin spat out a piece of cobblestone and kept shooting in the direction Debro pointed. He scrambled out of the open street, firing as he ran, then threw himself down and crowded Debro behind the pile of broken concrete. His elbow was bleeding again, debris clinging in the green and red stew that used to be skin. Doc kept telling him *Say hello to gangrene you don't stop hammerin that elbow.* When the bolt locked back on his rifle he twisted and squirmed to get another magazine from a utility pocket, cursing as it hung up on the pocket flaps the way it always did when he needed it in a hurry, trying his best to keep his body behind the cover of the low broken wall.

"Hell you shootin at?" Debro shouted in his ear, dropping his arm. "It's a *bird,* white boy. I seen a bird, swear to God. First I seen. A bird in this city. *Shee-it.* Mortars and RPGs, Phantoms and Cobras unloadin everywhere and right there a *bird.* Sparrow, had to be. Black and brown and I seen some grey. *Ballsy* little Oriental bird, man, hangin around a city got this kinda high explosive rainin down night and day.

Even the fuckin birds in this country hard corps." Debro shook his head. "What kind a sparrow got *that* kind a mustard?"

"I'm gonna need a transfusion you keep bird-watchin," Tomlin said, changing magazines in the M16 as he twisted onto his knees. "And I'll take the damn point." Still crouched, he ran into the street.

Without a word Debro fell in behind Tomlin like it was his idea. Maybe he was just bored with swearing. Instead he selected the little white girl tune from his repertoire and began singing in his melodic falsetto.

...it's my party and I'll cry if I want to...

Two blocks this way, a block that way, down this landslide of ruins, up this crater turn another corner, cross a street make a left make a right and there it was whatever it was and wherever they were: it had to be, couldn't be but one temple-looking thing wherever the LT was sending them. Wherever *that* was. *Told you we'd find a big-ass temple we keep goin,* Debro gloated, then got nervous, cursed and opened up full auto at the sky at nothing Tomlin could see, his M16 right next to Tomlin's head. Maybe that's why he never heard the mortar tubes. Bells still ringing in his ears, one minute Tomlin was dashing from the cover of a tangled building facade, diagonally toward a doorway in the courtyard wall encircling the Buddhist temple, Debro right behind him, Debro singing as he ran *...cry if I want to...* and in the next instant Tomlin was half-buried under dust and buckets of stone, half-deaf, blood gushing from behind his ear and pooling in the crater formed by his face in the rubble, an ocean of sound louder than a Jimi Hendrix concert reverberating inside his skull.

Then he was back in his west Texas cowtown, out in a distant corner of his pa's ranch, still a kid, his pa beside him prodding some half-dried cow turd with a stick, pointing and saying, *See that off-color round the edges, boy? Animal's sick. That shit aint right.*

It sure aint, came the thought now, over the bellow of Jimi's guitar, followed by a thought he just might be dead and beyond feeling, because for all the noise he didn't otherwise hurt.

Turn down those damn amps, he screamed at the stage. But Jimi didn't relent. Eyes heavenward he just went on holding that note while a legion of hippie girls screamed and pawed at his golden sneakers. Tomlin could only hope the fire marshal was in the building somewhere and would shut the place down.

Next he was in his brother's trailer watching the Sansui receiver pulsating bands of magenta, yellow and electric blue. Flames rolled up the fiberboard wall panels like they were on wheels. A girl's face appeared in a window, hair on fire and wreathed in sorrow, or was that marijuana smoke? The guitar collected its sound from all corners of the stadium, centered itself above Jimi's afro and got sucked straight up into the black night. What was left was whatever music played when water ran in a bathtub.

Thank God for the fire marshal.

Something like memory returned, but not under his control. Brief flashes of color in large gaps of black. There had been a letter. He remembered fetching the week-old letter from his cargo pocket. Reading it. That morning, in the pale gloom of dawn, too tired and cramped and sore in his joints from a bed of stone to eke out fifteen minutes more sleep. The truth was, he had a hard time with letters. Reading them, writing back. His long-distance communication skills had gone dysfunctional; he couldn't say why. It made no sense. He carried letters from his girlfriend like some people wore amulets. Yet opening them seemed to risk their protection, as if the gray light of day or war's foul air could break their spell. Where would he be then?

But in the dim glow of sunrise, and hearing Phineas' perfect armed forces radio imitation in his head—*Goo-ooo-od mooo-oooo-rning, VietNAM!!!!*—he had opened the letter from his mother and learned the pool was out of level, the feral cat in the alley had another litter and the neighbor's kid came home one night in a police car. Billy called from his dorm in Berkeley, you could hear that degenerate music in the background. From being a candidate for Juilliard now he was playing *rock and roll* in some *long-haired* band—her constant inflections audible as he read—the more he played that *electric* violin the worse his grades got. When he talked he was *incomprehensible*. She blamed hippies and Marxist professors. Bad enough he turned down the conservatory, couldn't his brother find a college in *Texas*? Hadn't she already lost an infant in its crib, a husband to booze and one child to drugs? Was her *baby* going down the same road?

And *You aren't swearing now, are you, Tommy*? The letters always worked that one in. Not was he getting any sleep, getting shot at, carrying dead friends, eating canned food from the Korean War, gone down with malaria a third hallucinatory time. *Obscenity is the air in a grunt's lungs*, he might have written. And added: *And you should hear my good friend Debro sometime.* But when it came to his mother, a lost woman stalking the remains of a life reduced to a balancing act between grief and rage, Tomlin the good son chose restraint and a route that still bore some semblance to honesty: *I swear less than most. Never for fun and usually only when nothing else does any good. And never in the name of our heavenly Father.*

Amen and True Enough. He was superstitious about invoking the Deity. What if He weren't a Loving God after all? His patience worn thin after so many millennia of human imperfection? Was the good Lord good or not-so-good, all-seeing, all-knowing or not? Maybe up there somewhere sitting on a cloud paring his celestial nails? Or was He keeping a ledger on mankind after all, like Santa Claus did with kids but using brimstone for ink? So many questions, so few answers. There could be truth, there could be penalties beyond the reach even of imagination.

Blasphemy did not occur to him. There were truly no atheists in fighting holes. But the bush had made him more honest, more conscious of his limitations. Humble as a beggar, he followed every trail his mind wandered across, looking for crumbs of truth. But however he looked and however he cogitated, all the trails led not to more celestial reflection but to the wisest men he knew. The ones who stayed alive. And their mantra was man to man the same, when they would confide it at all: *Nobody knows nothin.*

Lying in the street beside the temple he tried breathing through his mouth and choked on dust and blood. As he convulsed, there were more Technicolor snapshots of that morning...Swede firing up the coffee at daybreak, complaining they needed more sugar, Debro tossing pebble-sized shards of concrete at Swede's helmet saying *Here's your sugar white boy,* C-4 sending flames up the sides of Swede's C-ration stove…LT calling them up forward, Swede duck-walking half upright when he should be running, risking his life to keep from spilling the precious brew…maps draped all over a fifty-five gallon drum…*They need a team up there and hell you doin comin in here no coffee for your LT…* Swede begrudgingly handing over the cup, badgering in retaliation: *Hey LT all this is over let's get down to China Beach get out in them waves, you so fond of the ocean and all, hell, maybe they give you some sea duty…*LT the aquaphobe getting payback by a second long swig before returning the cup, then motioning them over to the map, where they clustered around his moving finger…Kestermont and his maps, this one a maze of city streets, fluttering like a giant butterfly's wings in the wash of Phantoms flying so close to the deck that debris vibrated from rooftops and bounced off the helmets of grunts hugging walls for dear life.

That was this morning.

In the Now—was it afternoon yet? Getting on to evening? Hadn't he seen a moon in broad daylight? Was Time wounded too? In the Now his head was pounding. Details grew hazier the closer he came to Now and the closer to Now the more his head pounded. In the general confusion he'd been running, Debro singing...*cry if I want to…* but then?...Again his memory was all gap, no color.

Tomlin shook rocks from his back and rose to his knees coughing powder and snot just as another mortar round crashed overhead into the side of the temple. His fists were death-clenched around the gas guards of his M16 and wouldn't unclench as he instinctively threw his arms up to protect his face, only to clobber himself with his own rifle barrel and fall over backward. Twisting in mid-flight, he hit the ground face down. Another mortar round exploded and another mule kicked him in the back of the head. This one hard.

Plenty of color now, but not from memory. And not Jimi this time. In his place on the same stage stood a clown in a striped suit with hair like Leon Russell. A piano in the background. The clown wore a purple carnation and laughed and pointed at Tomlin. He brought something from his pocket and cupped it in both hands, making a big show of guarding it from Tomlin's view. Then he peeked at whatever he was hiding, vaulted the arch of his eyebrows half a foot above the red ball of his nose and whistled dramatically. Shuffling closer to Tomlin, he pretended to offer the object for inspection, but when Tomlin leaned forward, he withdrew it haughtily, crinkling his powdered face in a frown.

Tomlin persisted, his forehead knotted into its own frown, his finger stabbing at the cavern formed by the clown's hands, at the something sparkling darkly inside. Conquering his own inner conflicts, Leon the clown relented with a sigh and opened his hands like a book, revealing a C-ration can. Tomlin couldn't help himself, consumed as though on the verge of the Rapture. Which ration was it? He craned his neck to see. Was it HAM AND EGGS? SPAGHETTI WITH MEATBALLS? BEANS WITH FRANKS? Maybe HAM AND LIMA BEANS, WITH WATER, ADDED? or even his personal staple, that manna of the grunt's existence, unloved by all but the savvy few and easily won in a trade for a four-pack of ration cigarettes—FRUIT CAKE? The lettering was upside down. Tomlin's curiosity was beer overflowing a mug. He had to know. He had a right to know. This was the stuff they fed him, for chrissakes. (And he could *think* the name of the Lord in vain, even if he couldn't say it. *By God!)*

The clown didn't resist when Tomlin reached over, righted the can and spun it around. The print on the can flickered against the olive drab cylinder like blue snow on a television set after sign-off. HEADS, TALKING, the label read. WITH BULLSHIT, ADDED. If there had been a lid on the can it was missing now. Tomlin looked inside. The odor was ghastly. Where was this HEAD? Oh, *head*. The front page of *The Times* swirled in a disgusting cascade imploding inside a miniature toilet bowl. For all the motion and diminution he read the tiny headlines easily: SCIENCE: WAR VITAL TO HUMANITY! MILLIONS DIE IN RESEARCH BUT NOT IN VAIN!

The clown dropped the can, slapped a knee and sang...*cry if I want to*...in a shrill falsetto, then threw his head back and lolled it around on his neck the way heads moved on plastic dogs stuck to car dashboards. Laughing hysterically, the clown took to stomping around the stage with his hands under his armpits, flapping his elbows like Red Skelton doing a seagull impression, his ridiculous hair flapping in unison, the purple carnation pulsating in bright flashes and making a noise like flatulence.

Tomlin stared at himself in a mirror suddenly appearing before him. Behind him in the same mirror, Leon the clown sat down on a piano stool, grinned and pointed his fists at Tomlin, both thumbs up. Only, one of the thumbs was missing. Infinitely pleased with himself, the clown slapped his knee again, broke out in more howls of laughter and spun around on his stool. He composed himself, poised his hands dramatically over the piano, then dropped them like thunderbolts and hammered the opening chords to Beethoven's Fifth (in C Minor). *Ummpumpumpaaaamb!* Paused suddenly, gave Tomlin a wink and a nod and launched into a raucous boogie-woogie, feet dive-bombing the pedals, elbows alternating with hands to pound the keys, flatulence providing percussion. A mangy Cheshire cat leapt onto the piano and flashed a piano-white grin. Fleas dove from its war-torn fur. The cat bowed, stood on its hind legs and mewed horribly in the wrong key, interrupting its performance only long enough to scratch behind one and then the other ear.

That shit aint right, Tomlin the poor sport complained to his face in the mirror. The image shrugged at him. Tomlin shrugged back. Another mortar round exploded against the side of the temple and both of him went unconscious again beneath a meteorite shower of dust and stone.

3

SOMEONE WAS CALLING HIS NAME from a long way off. A *long* way off. He only blinked himself back from the nether world because he seemed to recognize the voice.

"Wake up, *damnit*, you aint dead!"

The familiar voice was shouting, *must* have been shouting if sound travelled as deep as the bottom of *this* black pit.

"You might be thinkin you *half* dead, but you damn sure gonna be *all* dead you don't get up!"

The voice sounded so *certain* of itself, so *right*. It annoyed him.

Now something had him by the collar and was throttling him. He couldn't breathe. How was asphyxiation going to rectify things? Sound was returning from a distant journey and then express trains were flying past his ears. Another sound like air sucking up into the sky and the bathtub faucet was running again.

"Got to *move*, man!"

It was Debro, after all. So *dramatic*, he wanted to say, but the bridge was down between mind and mouth.

"Cowboy that shit up, Texas! Get them wheels turnin!"

He felt himself dragged forward in ragged, bone-jarring halts, exquisitely massaged in transit by the broken rock between skin and flak jacket. There were intermittent mortar rounds and then rifle fire in the breaks between mortar rounds but Tomlin didn't care. Debro was inflicting more pain than shrapnel or any AK round ever could.

"I got legs, damn it!" There, mind-to-mouth bridge back up.

"Then use em, white boy!"

Well, in all honesty he couldn't. Another bridge was down. Funny thing about his legs. No response under orders to move. Little more than ballast just then, conspirators engaged in outright mutiny.

"Hell's everybody else!" he managed to yell. "Where's Bender and the damn radio? Who's doin the shootin!"

"I told you about Bender! A *damn radio* don't stop no sniper round! And don't nobody know *nothin*!"

Something heavy crashed into the street nearby, something different, different and close but not a mortar round. The ground shook and more debris rained down, but nothing went *bang*. Then there were more mortars and *bang* enough to set his teeth to clattering. Debro kept dragging him by the flak jacket, jerking him forward on his butt, yelling over renewed mortar strikes to *Come on, white boy! Aint you from Texas? Aint you the Lone Ranger? Cowboy that shit up! Crank that damn motor and turn them college boy wheels! Get on that horse, white boy!* Tomlin tried to twist himself right-end-to, but each time that he got just so far around, his body uncoiled like a spring, flipping him face-up again. From this recurring perspective Tomlin got a glimpse of what had smashed into the street, the thing that was different. A small church, or something like one, stood against the sky, rocking from the impact of mortar fragments as he watched it, its roof pointing to heaven when it wasn't gone sideways with his constant rotation. It grew larger as Debro dragged him onward, Tomlin flailing his way along, his gorge rising and falling with every horizontal pirouette.

It seemed so unfair. Here he was cooperating and only nausea to show for it.

Tomlin complained as loudly as he could, the mouth working fine now, but Debro wasn't listening. He just kept pulling Tomlin through a cascade of dust and debris and explosions and the whine of metal fragments *Crank on it, white boy, crank on it!* while the mortars just kept pounding, pounding the temple roof and walls, pounding what must have been a courtyard at one time, pounding the street in front, pounding the street behind, pounding what world there was in his narrow little universe, the only universe that mattered just then. Hordes of steel insects whipped past Tomlin's face and a hundred Jimis were headlining concerts in full swing up and down Haight-Ashbury and out into the Avenues.

Somehow Tomlin got to his knees and half-crawled and half-stumbled, Debro still coordinating his monotone *Come on, white boy!* with each jerk on Tomlin's flak jacket, yanking him along and hammering his head into Debro's canteen, the .45 pistol in Debro's holster slapping his face with infuriating rhythm. When Debro finally dropped him Tomlin had no skin left on his forearms, as if they were hell-bent on matching his elbows. *Keep it up don't matter to me I aint medevacin no one for jungle rot,* Doc was saying inside the noise in his head. The noise inside his head was annoying him more than the blood running down his arms and even the whole world suddenly going dark.

Dark, it took an eternity to recognize, because Debro had finally dumped him inside the section of pagoda roof that had just arrived in the middle of the street with such fanfare. Pieces of clay tiles overhead popped and exploded in small red flowers beneath the onslaught of shrapnel. Lying face down on a pillow of broken street, breathing hard and inhaling clay dust, Tomlin went on a road trip. *Here I can't remember my boot size, I get prehistory.* There was no accounting for memory.

At ten years old his father had taken him north, out of the mesquite ocean of west Texas into a sea of deep forest in western New York, to a home for disabled veterans. His uncle was a double amputee courtesy of German machine gun fire in the last weeks of the war. *War almost over,* his father told him as they bounced along the wasted grounds, the ruined curve of driveway asphalt going back to dirt, the acres of lawn brown and scraggly and embarrassed, impatient for winter snows to come and cover them from view. Tomlin the kid looked up and watched the mildewed buildings sliding past, black holes for windows, the darkness inside broken here and there by pale reflections from tight-lipped faces so unmoving they could have been miniatures painted on a canvas of shadows. Everywhere, rotted storm shutters at crazy angles or long since fallen and leaning against foundations like drunks against urine-steeped walls.

Four years on the ground, his father said, braking and slamming the transmission of the old Buick into Park the way he always did, the car never quite stopped, internal parts crying out from the constant impact. *Brother fought in Sicily, North Africa, Normandy, a year under that crazy bastard Patton. Single-handed put two tanks out of action. Walked into and out of the Bulge, not a scratch. One week and the war's over. Most Germans just throwin down their rifles, lookin hard to escape them damn Russians, find some American to surrender to. Not this one Kraut bastard. Always someone never gets the word.*

The years had not been healing ones. In appearance his father's brother could have been his father's father.

The old man old before his time stared out of the single window in his small room the whole time they were there. There was an ancient pink radio set on a dresser but no one had bothered to plug it in. The window sill was scorched and blackened and overflowed cigarette butts against the rusty screen and onto the buckled plank floor. The room smelled like an ashtray, walls gone amber from the cinders of dreams and nicotine. His uncle sat in the wooden wheelchair and barely acknowledged their presence, staring into the hillside with his back to them, every other breath a drag on a cigarette, the ashes at his cigarette's end longer than the imploding white cylinder and defying gravity before falling into his lap on the slightest stirring of his head to regard the two of them for a moment as if greeting frequent but unwelcome guests who though so informed return to visit nevertheless. In such stillness the sudden strike with the back of his three-fingered hand to flick the ashes from his trousers seemed like the opening salvo of a cannonade between opposed armies. *Will my hands ever look like that?* the ten-year old Tomlin asked himself. When his uncle finally spoke Tomlin felt the words travel over his head and out the half-open door, back through the cold reaches of Time, onto frozen ground, blood-filled boots, night without end and daybreak without sunlight, agony in every corner of being. His uncle said *Bears at night under them trees on that hill. Ever night they come. Black bears, black as midnight. You see them by the light of the moon, that moon just drippin silver all over their black hides. Ever night, you hear? One day they'll be comin for me, bust me out of this goddamn prison. You won't find me sittin here next time you come draggin your yellow asses outta the rear. Nossir, I'll be gone over that hill, ridin one of them big blackass bears, bitch or male it don't matter.*

On the way back to the car his father changed course and insisted on walking up the hill. Tomlin felt conscious of his uncle's grey eyes on them the whole time. While his father looked he stood at the crest and exuded apology for which his fledgling conscience knew no penance would ever be enough.

No droppings, no markings on the trees, his father said. Ground's untouched. Aint no bears nowhere except in his mind.

When they left, his uncle never said goodbye in response. They just closed the door to his room, trapping his words and his agony inside, leaving him looking out the window up at the hill. Where he said the bears came but there was no bear sign.

It was late afternoon as they drove in silence through forest so deep and shaded it felt like night rose from the ground. His father slowed for a curve, then accelerated out of it as something broke from the bushes right alongside their front fender. There was nothing his father could do.

Tomlin twisted and peered through the window. The bear seemed to pace them for just a moment, its black eye lit by purpose and including Tomlin in its gaze. And then bear and car collided. Just a quick bump against the rear passenger door, but the old Buick shook. His father found a turnout up the road nearby and they drove back slowly, looking on both sides. There was no sign of the bear.

They stopped where they had seen the bear leave the roadside brush. Got out and looked around. There was a sizable dent in the passenger door. No blood anywhere. There was no bear sign. None in the roadside brush, none on the road.

They drove again in silence a long time and then his father said, I reckon that big male's okay. Can't say the same about my car door.

In its twisting the road looked like a giant snake fleeing their headlights, seeking refuge in the purple clouds that skirted the horizon. The road snaked on and on and the clouds turned to indigo. Tomlin watched for the phosphorescence of wild eyes among the trees, expecting another ambush. The snake dipped and rose and dipped and rose and when it dipped again a round flat moon flashed in the sky, washing them in silver.

There's bears on that hill, Tomlin said. His father didn't say anything. You don't believe it, that's why that bear come and knocked into your car.

He heard his uncle's voice again, passing overhead on its return from the past, a sound like steam wrestling inside a winter wind. A sound unheard by his father, who drove silently but cast an occasional sidelong glance at him. Not knowing that Tomlin was looking away already, into the future, maybe to that night at midnight, when the bears came to rescue his uncle. Tomlin imagined himself in his uncle's room looking out the window up at the hill, where a troop of black bears topped the crest, headed deep into the forest under that same silver moon. There on the back of the biggest bear rode his uncle, his remaining arm held high above him, a lone finger caught in a shaft of moonlight and extended in farewell to this world as he disappeared into another.

Fourteen years later, Tomlin pushed himself to his knees and looked through a large gap in splintered timbers and red tile at a world that brooked no disappearance from anyone save through annihilation. Heard himself say out loud: *Wars and more wars.* His voice steam inside a winter wind.

Red spittle dripped from his chin. He wiped his chin but only reddened it. Something like focus returned, then dissipated. The world spun. Stopped. Vibrated. Spun again and stopped again. Out of control. No pattern. No *center.*

It annoyed him to be so confused. But he was due some slack. After all, it was his first head wound. He was in virgin territory.

4

AFTER A FEW MOMENTS the world coalesced. Tomlin had the sensation of waking from a long sleep in a room he didn't recognize. Bullets whined and ricocheted, a firefight raged nearby. All familiar sounds, but where was he? He was sinking. Or floating away, he couldn't tell which. He needed an anchor.

A hand seemed to be opening and closing on the base of his skull. He was surprised to find his own hand still clasped around the triangular gas guards of his rifle. He ignored the pulsing and ran the charging handle of the M16 to make sure the bolt was working. A cartridge sprang out of the chamber like a soul released and clinked against his helmet. The bolt cycled normally and seated a new round. Still light-headed. Where was his anchor? Another wave of nausea. A sudden pain shot through the back of his head and he tore his helmet off and flung it to the ground. The pain receded, but no anchor arrived.

Then a curious thing happened. Without an anchor his thoughts came loose.

They stretched and elongated and began their migration.

Were they escaping through the hole in his head? It was only logical. He watched as his thoughts floated above him, thoughts disconnected but not disrelated, as though the laminate of punctuation had dissolved and meaning had sloughed the skin of syntax to rise in a harmony of perfect spheres, primordial integers of a language that was the only language the first language if only one spoke the language but no one did anymore certainly not him. He struggled to follow the globes of his thoughts as they shifted through iridescent tones and rose higher and higher until they slipped away into space forever diminished and irrecoverable the way a balloon slips from a child's fledgling grasp and leaves the sadness of a lost companion in the child's heart as boundless as the child's heart which was more boundless than the sky wherein he watched his loss moving to its unknown and unknowable limits if such limits to sorrow exist the child's heart calling it back the whole time.

In the wake of those thoughts lost and risen and vanished, a kaleidoscope of grey light dripped through the same holes in the pagoda roof the thoughts had exited. Somehow his body had relocated and was leaned back against the timber walls. But now he had to hold it steady, in case one more right or wrong thought at the right or wrong moment should unmoor the fragile ropes of his docking and cast the rest of him off to follow his thoughts into the sky. It was one thing to lose your thoughts, another to lose the mind entire. He pushed his head back against the wall. The pain helped. He tried focusing on the holes, why not? A drunken geometry of holes calling him back. Holes everywhere. A hole in his head, yes, but holes in the walls too. In the ceiling. Holes he could see through. Windows on the world. Apertures in time. Larger even than the one in his head.

There was a comforting thought.

A vision took form in front of him. Debro peering through his own hole, his M16 resting on a splintered and cracked wood beam, the light falling chiaroscuro across his face, helmet fabric ripped and unraveled and falling down his neck. His woodland camo sleeves in

reverse, falling up above his elbows. Debro motionless as a canvas on a museum wall, as though he gazed unflinching at a future that strode mercilessly toward them slashing left and right the sword of the End of Days. Debro in a Dutch master's painting without aura of bravado and none of retreat. Good old Debro. In the moment's hush that scene was the ballast he sought, the anchor he attached to his foundering vessel. It held him fast, snapped him back as he threatened to float weightless away.

And then the sound of bathtub water running again.

Restored to a semblance of Now, Tomlin felt alert enough to leave care of the front to Debro and revived enough to assign himself rear security. Fortunately the sides of the structure were mostly intact—sides that must have been short walls detached by high explosive from other framing members on some near or distant part of the temple roof. He twisted to watch for movement at the temple windows above or in the wrecks of buildings behind them. Something wasn't right with his hearing. Or his eyesight. And how *did* the 18-wheeler that ploughed him in the head ever fit on this tiny street?

It was time to ask some questions.

"Hell those mortars coming from?" Tomlin yelled over a renewed barrage of sound, the mortars now joined by a more furious exchange of small arms fire up at the front of the temple. He felt a small exultation at the certainty of his own voice again. Hey, *something* was working. And his head didn't *hurt* particularly, but it was curious how the blood kept running into his flak jacket and pooling behind his belt buckle while that fist kept opening and closing on his neck like a heartbeat.

"They gotta be ours," Debro yelled without looking back. "Didn't get the word we got sent up. I get back I'm gonna kick ass on every one of them useless pogues in weapons platoon."

Debro took a breath intended for a new round of swearing but suddenly paused. "You hear a chopper?"

Besides Debro, all Tomlin could hear was the surf crashing inside his head. Before he could answer, a stray mortar round blew cobblestone into the air half a football field up the street, near the end of the temple courtyard. He heard that. The mortar barrage abruptly came to a halt. The stray mortar round seemed a little too far away to have been part of the ongoing barrage. But a bit *too* stray to be a stray round.

It had all the feel of a gunner working up his next coordinates.

"That a spotting round, we dead men," Debro said, thinking like Tomlin was thinking, but probably talking to himself, staring through his splintered opening, his cheek gray in the spill of daylight. Tomlin was long used to Debro's habit of looking anywhere but at you when he spoke to you. If he were speaking to you. It made conversation hard sometimes.

"They drop fifty and fire for effect, we are," Tomlin agreed.

"Now why you gotta say somethin stupid?"

"*You* brought it up."

"Wasn't *talkin* to you. And *you* ain't gotta comment on every damn thing comes out my mouth." Debro got annoyed enough to glance at him.

Tough to win an argument with Debro.

"Well, maybe they'll add fifty instead," Tomlin said.

Debro didn't look consoled and turned away.

Tomlin looked behind him through the hole in the side of their cavern. There was a flash of black in a window high above where the stray mortar landed, but it was gone before he could center it up with his rifle. The mortars went quiet. Now just the sporadic rifle fire around the temple plaza to the front.

"Who's doin the shootin up there?" Tomlin asked.

"I look like the Asia almanac? Aint I lookin out the same windows on the same train you ridin?"

"Phantoms gonna be burnin this place down. We better *didi* the hell outta here."

"Now you sayin more stupid shit. Hell you gonna didi *to*? Lookit them fuckin buildins, they're fallin in. Besides, Air Wing musta missed chow and gone home, they aint been unloadin since mornin. *Somebody* knows there's friendlies this neck of the woods, even if that damn mortar section don't. LT squared away, he woulda had that FO tell them fast movers he sent a squad out this way. He don't screw up on that kind of shit. And I heard a chopper round here somewhere and aint a chopper pilot *nowhere* be flyin a bird where Phantoms are unloadin."

But for all Debro's logic Tomlin saw him scanning the heavens for any sign of approaching jets. Tomlin did the same. Debro said something but it was lost in the turbine rush of a helicopter suddenly appearing over the mangled skyline, howling past them fifty yards above the ground toward the firefight at the temple plaza. Daylight blinked as the helicopter's muted shadow passed them.

"*Told* you I heard choppers, white boy!" Debro exulted over the clatter of the helicopter. Paused. "There goes one *dinky-dau* pilot. That's a damn Huey. Aint no *YU-Ess* Marine chopper. Hell's a army Huey doin in these parts? Place hotter'n hell look how low he is. One RPG and that a *beaucoup* hunk of taxpayer money in little green pieces all *over* the parkin lot."

Tomlin said, "They're outta RPGs around here, man. When's the last time you saw one come callin?"

"What, you gonna bet your life on that? I wouldn't be takin no chances. Besides, one AK round in a rotor hose put that thing on the ground."

The helicopter blew over the temple and banked northward, out of sight, its guns scanning the earth below but silent, not pausing to lend any assistance to whatever marines were under fire at the temple plaza.

Tomlin watched Debro looking him over. He turned to one side, moving his bloody chest out of Debro's line of sight. What now? Debro got unhappy, out came that critical streak.

"You can stop bleedin from your ear. I'm not usin up my last battle dressin. You a damn mess, college boy. Ever since I know you."

Tomlin felt like a broken record but he really did want to know.

"Where's everybody else?" he asked again. "Where's Doc? Bender?"

With a carousel of intermittent electrical spasms coursing through his head, it didn't seem unreasonable that Debro might have a better store of immediate knowledge available. But Debro was in a philosophical mood.

"I already *told* you where everybody is. You hear what you want. But I tell you somethin and you listen up, college boy. This a *half-ass* war. Everythin bout it half-ass. Half-ass president, half-ass congress, half-ass army general. All they got is a half-ass plan for half-ass grunts to get they half-asses blown off. And I tell you somethin else. *You* the biggest half-ass I ever know. Maybe someday I tell your half-ass why."

"You keep promisin," Tomlin said, determined not to throw up all over his flak jacket. "Suspense gonna kill me this war don't first."

5

DEBRO IGNORED HIM and went back to watching the front of the temple, where both distinctive voices of opposing rifle fire had momentarily fallen mute. Another silence where silence shouldn't be.

Tomlin openly admired the virtuosity and musicality in Debro's tirades. This one jarred more memory loose.

O happy morning...

...says Phineas joking and slapping the point man on the helmet and walking back to take his place. Phineas seven months on the point himself, not once shot or blown up or missing an ambush causing others to die or lose arms, legs, eyes or testicles. Then kicked up to squad leader to fill another sudden vacancy, now third man back on patrol, as far back as Phineas was ever willing to concede the point, this morning grinning and running the bolt of his rifle, leaving the ejected round to sparkle primer up along the trail the way he always did. Thus led by example and superstitious as a second baseman, Tomlin adopted the loaded weapon ritual for his own. Between him and the rest of his squad cases of wasted ammo traced their passage through the countryside, a bread-crumb trail for the enemy to follow.

O happy morning, Phineas says again, the smile ear to ear, the phrase his trademark invocation to the Fates before every patrol into booby-trapped, ambush-infested, sniper-laden reaches of the bush, his challenge to the roulette wheel, a conscious mocking of the impulse that led Cortez to stare dumbfounded at yet another endless body of killing water and as superstitious himself as he was serial murderer, bow before his enabling god and name a merciless ocean the Pacific.

In the train wreck of Tomlin's memory freight car after freight car slammed into imagery, scrambled heaps of time and space. Another boxcar rolled from the carnage on the tracks and caromed into view.

Weeks of endless rain, everyone miserable to the bone. The blur of a resupply chopper hovering and inching toward them over a rice paddy, feeling its way inside cloud cover that rose from tree top level, following as best it could the yellow wisps of a smoke grenade struggling to provide guidance. All of them watching through breaks in the grey ether, no one caring about the food, the ammo, the letters or even a rumor of beer and soda, standing solemnly as stone outcrops as LT swore again that bird carried the crown jewel. A grunt's monsoon treasure stuffed somewhere inside the suspended cargo net. Debro didn't believe it and made it known loudly. *Ain't gonna be no dry socks. They say mail on board, you get boots don't fit nobody. They say beer, you get No. 10 cans tomato juice. Dry socks your ass!* Danny Hardin had bought the rumor as fact and thrown caution to the wind. He sat on his pack, boots already off, face locked tight against the pain lest a grimace mar his manhood, cutting away the rotted remains of filthy blood-browned socks with his bayonet and exposing clots of raw flesh ankle to toe just turning from red to green with jungle rot. The rest of them waiting silently in the rain with the pilot light of hope burning in their granite souls. They watched no less silently as the rope failed and the net separated from the chopper a hundred feet above the paddy, hit the surface with a muted handclap and burrowed into a fathom of mud, disappearing without a trace, taking even the rope with it, extinguishing their collective flame. Waves lapped the rice paddy dike, diminished and disappeared, leaving nothing but a flat sheet of rain-pricked surface. On cue the clouds seamed themselves back together and the chopper vanished too. *Thanks for fuckin nothin!* someone yelled from the mist. But for the sound of the rotors it had all been a dream. The dream shattered as Phineas broke out laughing, welcome as a reveler at a graveside.

Now ain't that a joke on Danny Hardin, he said and walked over to where Danny sat numbly on his pack, feet bare, sores opened and bleeding, socks cut to ribbons. Phineas kicked Danny's boots at him. *Shoe fits, wear it, cowboy. What am I always tellin you bout rumors?* Then reached in his cargo pocket, laughed again and dropped a pair of fresh socks wrapped in protective plastic inside one of the boots, the equivalent, in the moment, of any god's sacrifice of his only begotten son.

In the Now, though, Phineas was gone and Tomlin was squad leader. LT gave Tomlin the job after Phineas rotated because Debro, same rank but with time in grade above him, flatly refused it.

I aint doin it, Debro said. *Did it last three months my first tour and I aint writin no more goddam letters tellin pure fuckin lies about boneheaded kids I aint said ten words to don't know better than to step on a booby trap stand up in an ambush or get shot off a paddy dike. I aint doin it, that's all. There it is. Don't want your fuckin promotion. Hell you gonna do, LT, bust me and send me to Nam?*

No, but I aint givin you no pound cake neither, LT said.

LT flipped the can to Tomlin, caught him off guard. The can caromed off his forehead. Debro laughed and slapped his thigh.

Laugh while it's funny, LT said. He jerked a thumb in Tomlin's direction. *Butterfingers is your squad leader now.*

Tomlin picked up the can and pried it open with his P38.

And I aint sharin the party favors with either of you.

Halfway through he relented and tossed the can to Debro, who already had his spoon out. After a ragged attack on the contents Debro offered the remains to LT.

What, after you two been in it? Rather eat a can of bubonic plague.

Now a week in the city and Tomlin had six marines left, sent forward with his ragtag, half-strength squad to recon the temple, no one told them why.

More boxcars from his mangled memory righted themselves for inspection.

There was LT hunched over his maps, the angry white crater dividing the back of his close-cropped head in half. Shaking the scarred head, saying, *They just said get a team up there*.

Death waiting minutes away and Swede leaning against a wall and still bitching about the morning's coffee—*Who's bogartin the damn sugar?*—bitching worse as they saddled up and headed out without finishing it, saying, *Plenty of time to get fuckin wasted but aint got five minutes to finish a cup of fuckin joe.*

Bender saying *Hey, man, wasn't sweetened to your taste hell does it matter?*

Doc saying *Sugar rots your teeth Swede darlin nine out of ten dentists recommend ladymuffin*.

Fuck all you, Swede said in Nordic with the logic that ended half the arguments in world history. Swede needed his coffee like vampires needed blood.

Tomlin wondered where Swede was. Wily Swede. Coffee addict Swede. Dead as self-predicted?...*Plenty of time to get fuckin wasted...* No. Tomlin knew better. Swede, wily Swede, hunkered behind some shot-up masonry, maybe wandering up his own street oblivious to the war and still fuming. Not dead. Not wily Swede. But in spite of himself Tomlin's mood offered up the picture of Swede face down in ancient cobblestone, shot through the chest and writhing in agony, cursing the uncaffeinated death as he slid down the unsweetened slope to oblivion.

O *happy morning.*

Not Swede. Not dead. Only thing dead was how dead wrong Debro was about that.

Another train came off the tracks and the morning reeled itself off.

Whole streets and landmarks obliterated by air strikes and artillery, making it pointless to look at his own map. Flying blind within three blocks. Guilt and self-disgust over his incompetent navigation moved him up to take the point. In ten yards the world exploded with mortars dropping out of nowhere and small arms coming from every black hole in every shattered building. Doc took shrapnel in his own leg and bandaged it himself, waving Tomlin off when Tomlin started in his direction. Then the mortars went quiet. They picked themselves up, moved ten yards and took AK fire from half a dozen rooftops. Tomlin and Bender went back down in a tossed salad of concrete yards apart, AK rounds whistling and ricocheting past in cartoon quantities, shattering the compass in Tomlin's cargo pocket but missing his leg, arteries, kneecap and the two grenades. Bender couldn't move to him so he low-crawled over to Bender lying there rigid against the storm of bullets like he was sleeping in a train tunnel and found the handset and called the LT to get the Phantoms on the horn. LT went right to work but nary a bird would come down and play, LT cursing the FOs over the radio *where the fuck is the air support* and making it clear he didn't care if *the brass of three fuckin battalions and every fuckin general naked in the* China Sea were witness to his insubordination *I got men out there fuckin dyin you hear me?* Tomlin knew they had to move if they were going to live and he sent the squad scattering to whatever cover they could find while he ran from concrete molehill to molehill dumping magazine after magazine into every window and doorway he could see in any direction his legs would carry him. For once he hadn't carried too much ammo. When the AKs finally lost interest for reasons that certainly had nothing to do with his pitiful lone rifle he looked back and he was alone and more disgusted with himself. Debro and the rest of the squad and his radioman, gone. Doc, Swede and Bender vanished. The new guy, too. He'd been where new guys go, second to last, where everybody but Tail End Charlie—a pissed-off Swede on this morning—could forget about him. Just then he wasn't surprised he couldn't even remember the new guy's name. Kid from Minnesota. If there was only one KIA in a firefight it was usually the new guy. The nameless guy. *Hey, you, Minnesota,* they'd say. *Hump this can of 7.62. Kansas, get your ass saddled up. Eyes outboard, Bakersfield, you're in the bush not at the fuckin high school prom.* The guy's birthplace was his name the first few weeks of his audition, a designation useful only as a chain to be pulled or a place for his remains to be shipped. Get through a month and get a real name. Until then why remember today what you hope to forget tomorrow? The dead were ghosts that wandered in and out of twilight memory, ghosts to be forgotten if you could. Not so easy. For a grunt's ghost there was no death after death, and for the living no defense against a bad dream.

But Bender had been *right there.* How do you lose your own damn radioman? *Some squad leader you are.* He backtracked, turned two corners and found Debro, who'd been as lost as he was. There was fighting in front of them and fighting behind them. Tomlin led Debro along wreckage that might have once been a street, maybe back the way they came and maybe not and then more AKs from more directions. Where the hell was his squad? A couple of jets screamed low in strafing runs taking fire from every rooftop they passed but didn't unload and then disappeared. *They on vacation?* Debro yelled. They came to a crossroads that led to Hanoi or Houston for all he knew. A sibilance from overhead and cobblestone and shrapnel geysered in the center of the street. Again and again, each time they set a foot outside their cover in that direction. No crossing that intersection.

What to do? Waiting for gunners to make their adjustments and mortars to fall into handshake distance didn't appeal at all and better just lost than dead too, so the two of them turned back around and kept going, maybe the right way and maybe not. *Ought to be able to find a goddamn big-ass temple,* Debro said, *compass or no damn compass,* taking the point, and while they bobbed and weaved and stumbled and lurched from doorway to broken doorway Debro launched into the state of the war, the white fools that started it, the black fools fighting in it and the yellow fools that kept dying in it, with particular emphasis on his and Tomlin's—particularly Tomlin's—uselessness in it all. It was a relief when he started singing.

Back in Now, inside his skewed piece of pagoda roof, Tomlin had no idea how he'd misplaced his squad, who took what turn where, or what unit was engaged in the firefight up at the front of the temple. Or where the hell his whole damn company had got to. Couldn't be closer than ten blocks away and probably had its own hands full, from the sounds in the rest of the city. And what the hell was a chopper doing this low to the ground, in this hot a piece of Uncle Ho's real estate, when even the Phantoms were having second thoughts?

Didn't nobody know nothing, least of all him.

6

THE HUEY RETURNED OUT OF NOWHERE in a fury, south from north in an exactly reverse route, and now its twin M60s opened up on the temple plaza. A little too indiscriminately, Tomlin thought. Debro yelled, *Aint we got friendlies up there?* As the chopper braked, hovered and then slid backwards on a wall of air, both door gunners visible, the gunner facing their side suddenly swiveled the gun in its mount to concentrate long bursts on the temple roof and windows, sending shards of clay and clouds of red dust into the sky. The other gunner kept working the remains of the formerly manicured little plaza in front of the temple.

"Hell they beatin down on the temple for?" Debro yelled again. "That bird gotta be takin AK rounds. And they wreckin the only pretty thing left standin in this city!"

The chopper's two machine guns showered the earth in a rain of black metal links from M60 belts and copper from spent cartridges. They watched, fascinated. Neither of them had ever witnessed a chopper sit above a firefight and exchange small arms fire with ground troops.

Tomlin cursed and ducked as two more mortar rounds exploded, one in the temple courtyard and one in the street, close enough that fragments hammered the sides of the broken hunk of pagoda roof shielding them. Some of the shrapnel penetrated, showering them with splinters and bits of tile. A direct hit and they were pink mist.

"Hell is it with those *mortars*?" Debro said. "Got a bird right up there, us here?"

Tomlin mulled that one over. The fog parted for an instant, long enough for him to say, "Maybe they aint ours."

Tomlin got no response from Debro, then swore again as another mortar exploded. He couldn't hold a point of focus. The world blurred, regained contours, blurred again. He felt kind of malarial, without the chills. Was it malaria after all and not the horseshoe in the back of his head? Malaria had fooled him before.

The ruins of buildings beneath the chopper ghosted through the grit kicked up by the rotor wash. Scraps of newspapers and scores of political pamphlets from both sides flailed around in the wind currents as cartridges from the two M-60s kept tumbling, spinning and glinting in the weak sunlight. The chopper bucked erratically, slipping forward and sliding backward, rocking side to side, the pilot doing what he could to present a moving target.

"Look at wild man up there," Debro said. "Comes in outta nowhere middle a firefight. No markings. Shoots up the whole goddamn place and everybody in it. You see any markings? That aint no Marine Air Wing chopper. That's a damn Huey. Air Wing don't get no Huey slicks that I ever seen."

"Army, then," Tomlin said. Debro ignored him.

Tomlin turned to watch the high windows again behind them. Reached up and shoved against the crumpled section of pagoda roof. Immediately a blackened tile slipped out of position and smacked against his knee. It should have hurt, but he barely felt it.

"We're in a bad spot here, man. We need to think about displacin. Strong wind's gonna blow this place down."

A flick in the corner of Tomlin's eye. Something kept moving up in that window.

Debro ignored him again. Tomlin was used to it. Debro had no more use for the world when something got his attention. Now he stared up at the chopper as though unconvinced he observed reality.

"No markings, man. A chopper sittin there takin AK rounds, world all gone to hell, just don't make no sense. You ask me, nothin bout nothin makes no sense in this *champion* of all stupid half-ass wars."

When he spat the word *champion* his unstrapped helmet slipped to one side. He straightened it and finally considered what Tomlin had said. "White boy, what the hell would a damn *army* chopper be doin in jarhead country?"

"Don't nobody know nothin," Tomlin replied, taking his turn at repeating the pet wisdom of a grunt's shared experience. If you said it three times a day, you could count on it being truer each time.

The door gunners kept up their fire as the chopper suddenly froze in place and five ropes fell from the Huey. These were instantly followed by five figures with bush hats and carbines slung across their chests. On gloved hands they were half way down the ropes before the ropes hit the ground. The second they landed, the ropes fell from the Huey and it rose vertically, went nose down, banked and howled off, guns still blaring. Tomlin and Debro had orchestra-seat views of the proceedings, watching spellbound as the figures first made contact with the street and immediately went into eerily rhythmic motion, shooting as they moved, now going to a knee, now shifting to cover each other with near-ballet precision, changing magazines in a blur of hand speed. As their carbines flashed Tomlin could see khaki figures in the courtyard spinning and flailing, as though part of the choreography. In a final flourish, without losing a man though totally exposed, they disappeared behind the temple walls.

Tomlin resented the admiration he felt. He thought *he* was good with an M16. He thought *he* could move under fire. His squad out there would have been dead to a man. Hell, they would have been dead before they hit the ground.

"Never seen nothin like that," he said. "Ropin in middle of a firefight, takin rounds the whole time. Maybe Force Recon."

"I already damn *told* you that wasn't no Marine Air Wing chopper. Them boys wearin army fatigues. Recon wears camo. Recon rides in Sea Stallions and Jolly Greens. Recon don't rappel outta unmarked Huey slicks."

"Didn't look like any soldiers I ever seen."

"Not even. Special Forces, maybe. Them boys squared away."

"That's for damn sure."

"Damn quiet all a sudden," Debro said.

In the wake of the chopper's departure the rifle fire had diminished. They could hear shouted orders and responses in English and Vietnamese above agonized cries for help from the wounded in both languages. It troubled Tomlin that he hadn't heard any American voices until the chopper unloaded.

The quiet in the wake of the fury was eerie. Tomlin felt further displaced.

Fighting flared, diminished, and flared again in other parts of the city. To their ears it could have been a continent away. From somewhere closer a burst of AK-47 automatic fire. M16s in response, then the *thump-crunch* of a grenade launcher. Silence. The AK-47 again, in parting. Thrust and parry.

Debro was staring through another gap in the boards of their cave, straight ahead, but upward.

"*Shee-it,*" he said.

Tomlin came alert. After nearly a year of Debro's company in the bush Tomlin knew when Debro said *shee-it,* exactly the way he just said it, something bad was approaching, usually something really bad, maybe just a notch above certain death. Tomlin sat up straight and to be doing *something* removed the magazine from his rifle, dug in his pocket and was still pressing loose five-five-six rounds into the magazine when Debro spoke so quietly Tomlin could barely hear him.

"What?"

"I said, got us a interval moon out there."

Tomlin felt dizzy, as though Debro's words had started his head spinning. He slipped the full magazine, a regulation two rounds short of twenty, back into his rifle.

"A what?" he managed, the nausea rising.

"*Interval moon,* college boy. That moon you see hangin up there right now. I guess nothin they teach you in half a year of med school."

Tomlin fought his gorge down and tried to make himself more comfortable. Something was poking him in the back. Or neck. Or head. Somewhere in that region. A sudden convulsion in his gut and he nearly puked. The moment passed.

"I learned about bodies. Learned they don't stand up to hot metal worth a damn."

"I didn't finish high school I coulda told you that. And aint no doctor nowhere got a cure for interval moon."

Tomlin felt himself spinning. He twisted his back to try and relieve the pressure in his head, slow down the rotation. Just then Debro turned, stared for a moment at Tomlin's bloody helmet on the ground, then looked up and got a good look at Tomlin.

"You *damn* white boys," he said in disgust. "You bleedin like a stuck pig no wonder you aint actin so college boy smart. Even ol Debro beat hell out of you in a spellin bee right now."

He reached up and pulled a battle dressing from the black rubber band around his helmet and tore it open with his teeth. "My last one. You gonna owe me big time come I need one and I aint got one."

Debro examined Tomlin's wound more closely and tried to look unimpressed. He removed the dressing from its cover and pressed it on the hole in the back of Tomlin's head, behind his bleeding ear, doing his best not to jar or put undue pressure on the piece of shrapnel he saw embedded inside the exposed skull. He ran one end of the cloth bindings below Tomlin's chin and joined and knotted both ends together at the back of his head, gently as he could and still have any hope of stopping the bleeding he saw. Circled the ends around the forehead and tried tucking them into the folds under the chin. The ends of the bandages didn't want to stay put. Tomlin winced.

"Shut the hell up," Debro said.

Tomlin's flak jacket was red to his waist. Debro tied the knot below the jaw, on the opposite side of the wound. "Best you stop bleedin," he said, and didn't add: *How the hell anyone take a piece of steel in the head and still be alive?* He picked up Tomlin's helmet and tried setting it carefully back on his head. Thought better of it and laid it beside him.

When the world stopped spinning Tomlin was in a desert, plagued by thirst. He slapped his cargo pockets. No canteen in either one. Without a word between them Debro passed him his own. Tomlin intended to take just a swallow. The canteen hit his lips and he felt like a sponge. He had to tear it away.

"Drink it all, white boy," Debro said.

Tomlin refrained and handed the canteen back.

"Thanks. By God, now that's a damn fine brew. Love that smoked halozone flavor. I get home, make my own fine brew, it'll taste just like that." He settled back. His toes tingled. Something Debro had said broke through the mist settling behind his eyes, then he forgot it just as quickly.

"I'm not thinkin right," he said.

"Head wound, man."

After another moment's silence he remembered.

"Hell's an interval moon?"

Debro was back staring through the gap in the collapsed roof, rifle up as though considering a shot.

"Maybe best I don't tell you. Maybe what you don't know don't hurt you."

"Go on. I believe in higher education, forget I dropped outta school. What kinda moon's an interval moon?"

Debro laughed bitterly. "Higher education." Shook his head. "Interval, man. College boy like you know what a interval is."

Tomlin had to think hard again. Answers were slow in coming. Definitions were elusive.

"Interval comes between one thing and some other thing," he said finally.

Debro made a noise thick with scorn.

"That's a damn B-minus, college boy. It's a hell of a lot more'n *that*. It's somethin between somethin *good* and somethin *bad*. Let ol D-brother draw you a picture. Take any damn grunt his first day in-country. Lands at Da Nang airport, steps off the plane from Okinawa. Don't matter a damn what color skin he wrapped inside, he white as milk, black as night, brown as Santa Ana or red as Geronimo. Steps down from that big old civilian jumbo jet, stewardess there at the door smilin and sayin goodbye. That man don't know it yet but he damn sure gonna find out quick. The *good* is *over*. That sweet curvy lady noddin and smilin as he passes by hopin to brush up against her before he heads down that ramp, them curves somethin he gonna dream about but aint never gonna touch, that's the end of the good. Now he in the *interval*, man, right there steppin off that bird, and until that man get back on that big bird home he gonna *stay* in the interval. In the interval all you doin is dodgin that somethin *bad* that's lookin to find you. It's lookin to find you day and night. Like the moon the interval don't sleep. You might think you know what I'm talkin bout but here's what you don't know, college boy. Interval gets closer, it changes, man. It says to you, 'Here I am, and what the hell you think you gonna do about it?' That's when you see the moon. That's why short-timers act crazy way they do, they know the Interval lookin for em. That moon gets into their head. That moon right up there starin back at us. Lookin down on us. Lookin to *find* us. Yeah, we sinkin down, alright, hittin the next level, if we seein that moon. This current damn situation, we a interval *down*. Between somethin *bad* and somethin *worse*."

Tomlin said, "Like circles of hell."

"What?"

"I don't remember what I just said."

Debro found another slot in the timbers to peer through. "Like we sinkin down, man. On our way down."

Tomlin didn't reply.

"Well?"

"Maybe, D-brother. It aint rainin, man. It's just a moon."

"Aint rainin? What, it aint rainin mortars now? AK rounds all mornin? You might be wantin a month of real rain fore this day's through." Debro took his helmet off. " 'Just a moon', says college boy." He tugged at the battered camouflage cover. Debro got nervous, Tomlin knew, he fiddled with his helmet. Debro added, "And why so damn quiet round here all a sudden?"

Tomlin shrugged. The movement drove a knife blade inside his skull. "Every big war movie got to have intermission, D-brother."

"This damn movie lookin to be *The Alamo*."

Debro ran his hand over his head, wiped his hand on his trousers and put the helmet back on and buckled it. Stared through a hole at the world outside. "Hell, I oughta be worryin about those little yellow men all over the front of that temple. I oughta be worried about them damn mike 60s and where the hell *they* comin from. But it's all I can do not to shoot that fat white moon right off the horizon while I can. Maybe I damn will. Just let fly one round right inside the devil's house."

Debro picked up a piece of broken tile beside him and examined it critically.

"My grandfather used to come to the city and visit from some little country town. Old ramblin alcoholic didn't weigh a hundred pounds. Teeth just fallin out. He smelled *bad,* man, and when I complained, my daddy said I spent a life cleanin up after crooks in white man's banks I'd stink too. A whole life, man, moppin them floors, cleanin them fingerprints off glass doors, aint got permission to use the bank's toilet." He tossed the shard of tile through a gap in the wall into the street. "One day that old man comes up behind me when I'm sittin on the porch stoop mindin my own business and takes my ten-year old skinny ass between his knees and don't let me go. Holds me *tight,* man, it's like gettin caught in the gates of hell closin. For all I know this scurvy old bag of bones *is* the Devil. I panic and start cryin. He slaps back of my head, tells me to shut up. 'I'm savin you, boy', he says. 'You see that white ball up there? Full moon in broad damn daylight? Aint jus no ordinary fat moon. See how it *shine*? See how it *smilin*? That a *interval moon,* boy. Interval between good and bad, the Lord and Satan, livin and dyin, heaven and *hell*fire.' He keeps on, sayin, 'Last night I'm lyin in my room and I hear them angels, boy, fluttin them *gos*mer wings and talkin that heaven talk you hear but don't understand, shepherdin what loose souls they can away from here while they's still time. The light from that moon hits your head long enough, you gonna get the Mark of the Beast. Don't matter you a chile in a crib or a bush-haired old cotton picker, tonight the Devil in a red carriage gonna be ridin up and down the street harvestin these houses clean of all them lingerin souls got that Mark on their heads. Them souls won't never hear the word of God no more and God gonna cut em right out of his Book. You understand me, boy? You understand you in the *interval* long as you see that moon?' I didn't, but I said I did, scared to death locked between those bony knees, that wino breath stinkin all down my neck. Old man gets to coughin and I tear myself loose and run up the steps, him callin behind me, laughin and coughin like a crazy man sayin, 'You run, boy! You run from the Devil! You git inside the house and stay inside the house or tonight the Devil comes to your room and gits you and everbody else walks under that moon today!' I slammed the door shut at the top of the steps, that old drunken fool still laughin and coughin goin on and on."

Debro had his helmet off again, his fist inside it, the helmet spinning.

"Let me tell you, the devil didn't get *me*. I run up to my room, pulled the curtains tight and got under the bed and didn't come down for dinner. Family comin in there all night lookin for me. I didn't say a word, huggin a blanket over my head, my mother throwin a fit downstairs at my father to go back out and don't come back till he finds me. He found me all right, past midnight, still under that bed. Beat me good for makin my mother crazy, never mind the devil. I never seen no such full moon in daylight again till just now. Seen half-moons, quarter moons, little pieces of moons, *slivers* of moons look like knife blades, moons got fuckin cows jumpin over em. But not no fat silver dollar moon like what's sittin out there right now. You see it?"

Tomlin sized up the journey to the front of their cavern.

"Take your word for it. That's a long way to be movin right now."

"Get up here, take a look at it yourself."

"I'll pass, D-brother. But that's a damn fine ghost story."

"Aint no ghost story. I remember it damn *verbatim*."

"I believe you."

"Come look at it."

"That's all right."

"You think I'm bullshittin."

Tomlin picked up his discarded helmet and set it gingerly on his head.

"I got no reason to believe you aint speakin the gospel. You mighta brought all this up with LT this mornin when he was handin us this little canteen run."

"Hey, I only just *seen* the damn thing. And I'da wasted my breath sayin anythin to LT."

"Too late anyway. Not a bed nowhere to dive under. Besides, I got the Mark of the Beast now, don't I?"

Debro looked over at him, annoyed. "Hey, you got a damn head wound from a sixty millimeter mortar round. Friendly fire is what you got."

"It don't feel all that friendly, D-brother."

"That's a *head wound,* man. What you expectin?"

Tomlin said, "Maybe you ought to go on and put a round into it."

"What, into your head?"

"The moon. Like you said."

Debro looked him over again. Tomlin felt probed for irony. He eased his helmet back against the wall. A stabbing pain and the hell with it. He took the helmet off and tossed it into the broken street to follow Debro's piece of broken tile.

"You might be needin that steel pot," Debro said.

"Not today I aint. Go on and put a round into the moon."

"Into the moon," Debro repeated, like it was a new thought.

"Hell, yeah."

"I just told you I *considered* it, but I aint doin it. Hell good would it do?"

"Make a statement," Tomlin said. "Go on, shoot the damn moon. Put a hole in it for me, too. Make that moon look like the back of my head. Do it for every grunt in every war ever had to put protoplasm up against metal."

Debro worked the magazine release of his M16, dropping the magazine and re-inserting it methodically, a sure sign of reflection.

"What if old devil don't know we're here? I squeeze one off at him, what then? And hell's wrong with you anyway? Aint no bullet gonna make it to the city limits, much less to the moon."

"That aint the point. Forget physics. It'll wake Beelzebub up. Put him on some kinda notice."

"Notice of what? That we're *here,* that's what. Get him started hitchin up them horses to that red carriage."

"You're the one wanted to shoot the moon," Tomlin pointed out.

"I didn't, though, did I? I was thinkin it through."

Debro put his helmet back on, buckled the chin strap and said, "Maybe it aint that damn smart to piss old Mephistopheles off."

"Well, if my head aint got teeth marks by the Beast like you say it aint, I say let a sleeping dog lie, especially if he buries his bones in Hell."

Debro fell quiet again. Somewhere in the preternatural silence a jet's engine rumbled at the edge of hearing and then receded.

Finally Debro said, "Hell does an old smelly skinny-ass wino know anyway?"

Tomlin knew consensus when he heard it. He was glad to change the subject. The firefight at the front was still catching its breath, and he almost felt relaxed. It seemed like a good time for small talk.

7

THERE WERE ALWAYS RUMORS. Passing them along seemed to help the back of his head. Tomlin said, "Heard from Timmy Taylor a while back. Medevaced down to Cam Ranh with jungle rot, aint he the skater. Says Phineas quit drivin big rigs back in the world, re-upped for six more months. Says he's in Okinawa now, waitin on orders. Danny Hardin's been back in-country a month. You believe it? Them two got a basket of AK rounds and shrapnel between em and home still aint better than more of this. Timmy said with three wounds Danny had to sign somethin to get back in-country."

"Interval gonna throw em a big welcome party," said Debro. "And you told me all this yesterday. You sound like a old woman gossip. Keep your eyes outboard and watchin behind us."

"You believe how guys keep comin back? What's wrong with runnin water and feather beds?"

Debro spun an index finger near his temple in the timeless sign of insanity.

"All three white boys you just named are crazy. They *dinky-dau* from that Texas tumbleweed juice. You from Texas too, probably do the same first time you rotate, what, less than a month now?"

"There it is," said Tomlin. "Twenty-six days and a wake-up and this bad dream's over. And I'm a one-story house, D-brother, I aint made of multiple tour like some of these boys."

With each city's name Tomlin grabbed successive fingers, starting with his pinky.

"Da Nang. Honolulu. San Francisco. Houston, maybe Dallas. Hump my seabag to the bus station, leave the drivin to some good ol boy bus driver and hello, San Antone." He wagged his fist in Debro's face, then flicked two fingers and flashed him a peace sign. "Let my hair grow and march on the Capitol."

Debro laughed. "You won't make the grade as a hippy, white boy. You be back after thirty days. Aint San Antonio got the Alamo? Aint every cowboy believes he gotta die like Davy Crockett to be a man? Texas boys think they a bunch of Lone Rangers in a cowboy movie. Rest of your lone rangers gonna still be here in-country callin you back. You'll be hearin em across the ocean. They gonna pied-piper your ass right back. You wait and see. And somethin else too."

Debro spat and was silent a moment. Tomlin recognized the prelude.

Debro said, "What *I'm* doin here, place where my half-ass country bombin and burnin a bunch of yellow folks wouldn't know *Krooz-chev* from George Washington? What I'm doin here? Had a job paid the bills, a beautiful baby girl don't matter her mother good for nothin, a fifty-six Chevy I just puttin the finishin touches on, that car ready to *dominate*, mister, make me some serious after-hour money and what? A goddamn letter from the draft board, that's what. My name on that letter, yes, sir. Why my name on that letter? Because you don't get no college deferment you workin since you thirteen. And I aint got no con*gent*al heart defect or no *sis-tal* fibrosis to 4-F me out. And my old man aint on no city council. *That's* why. I got all the qualifications make me *prime* for the takin. Yessir, I am Grade A *prime cut* USDA war steak. Look here," Debro said, now grabbing his own fingers: "I'm stupid, I must be I aint in college am I? I'm healthy, I must be I aint on crutches, right? Forget I aint ever *had* a doctor. And dig this, man, don't no one in selective service got to worry about phone calls from the mayor tryin to deal *my* privileged white ass out."

Tomlin got another shot of memory: A night a long time ago, him and Debro in a hole in the ground up to their neck in mud and monsoon, just enough daylight you could still be talking. Debro talking low, saying how he'd gotten the draft notice and sold his car, opened an account for his daughter and made his mother the trustee, then stayed drunk most of a week. When he finally sobered up enough to show up at work, he thought his boss had gone crazy, handing him a check and slapping him on the back, bringing out the rest of the shop mechanics to join him in a round of applause. It turned out his boss had a friend who worked at the post office and when Debro came staggering out waving his enlistment papers around to spite the draft board and belching the Marines' Hymn, the friend recognized the shop patch on Debro's mechanic uniform and called his boss. Debro still had three days before he had to report for his trip to Parris Island and the check *by God is payment in advance. God bless the Marine Corps God bless you*, says his boss. The three days were his to use as he pleased. Debro took the check to the bank, added it to the proceeds of the car sale and reported for duty three days early. It messed up their paperwork and the Marines didn't want him yet but Debro said take me now or you'll never see me. They put him on a Greyhound but before it left a white recruiter with a scar running from temple to temple stalked onto the bus and put his face against Debro's and told him he'd just made a long distance phone call and wait till they got his blackmailing black ass in boot camp.

In the Now, inside their remains of pagoda roof, Debro went on, "And somethin else. I told you when he left, didn't I? I told you a few months back in the world and Phineas be back. Him and Danny Hardin both. Aint none of em gonna go home again, neither, not Phineas not Hardin not Timmy Taylor not any other them cowboys from that damn all-Texas-boy squad back on a second tour. Keep askin for it long enough, you get it. You remember that, short-timer, you lucky and smart enough to make it outta here and get back in the world and find it rough goin. You from Texas too. You gonna start missin your cowboys back in the *good ol Nam*." The derision thick as the fog pulsating in and out of Tomlin's head. "You be on your guard, white boy. You remember it. You remember what your D-brother told you you start walkin down memory lane. You get out this interval, you don't even *think* about comin back."

But what Tomlin remembered just then, bright as a lightning flash through the mist in his head, he didn't say: Yet another night two months ago, the squad back in the rear a week, Phineas gone, Danny gone, Red Man dead and Debro long since rotated. Tomlin lonely as an orphan, monsoons raging and rain pounding the canvas of their hootch, wind blowing it sideways and nearly off its plywood foundation. Even over the storm's barrage he had awakened to the sound of Debro's seabag hitting the deck. In the flicker of a lone incandescent bulb Debro hadn't looked happy, a perfect contrast to the last time Tomlin had seen him and the last time he thought he'd *ever* see him: hanging from a strap at the back ramp of a CH-46, wind from its twin rotors rippling the elephant grass in a wide circle, Debro grinning and pumping his fist, homeward bound, his thirteen months up the next day. Tomlin knelt at the edge of the beat-down grass, purple smoke streaming away in the windstorm, his rifle outboard but his eyes fixed on Debro as the chopper floated away, feeling himself saturated with the envy known only to a grunt with half a year left on his tour of green hell and the monsoons coming on to make it a greener hell still. Now there in a rain-hammered hootch two months and ten thousand miles from Detroit later, was Debro again, where he wasn't supposed to be ever again, water pouring from him like his whole body was crying. Debro hardly said a word for days, back on his second tour.

Inside the pagoda cavern Debro read his mind.

"I needed that damn re-up money, man. My baby girl's got a bad heart."

He picked up another piece of ancient tile and flicked it away from him.

"Oh yeah they *proud* of me back at the garage but *no openings*, man. *Sorry* bout that, Maurice. Wasn't no job nowhere in that whole damn city, nothin would pay the bills. Not for some baby-killin grunt fresh out the boonies. People lookin at me like I eat children or got the rabies. Place damn unfriendly they find out where you been. And you know what? Comin home I get to Frisco, walkin through the airport, man, feet not *even* touchin the ground, wearin my Class As and lookin around like a sinner got took back into heaven. Some woman in Indian beads and hair down to her crotch comes up, not sayin nothin at first, just starin me down like I'm public enemy number one, then tells me how I oughta be dead and everone like me too. She spits in her hand and wipes it on my uniform. My *uniform*, man. It aint nothin like perfect but that's my *country*, man. She don't say nothin else, just stands there starin at me, the hate drippin off her like the spit runnin down the buttons my coat, like she darin me to knock her ass down."

Debro tossed a piece of tile, hard enough to splinter it against a roof timber. "I aint never touched a woman and never will but it was all I could do not to put that hippy bitch in the ground."

Tomlin changed the subject again. With Debro small talk didn't always work.

"Hell's gone quiet," Tomlin said. His eyelids suddenly wanted to join. He could have slept, lulled by the colored wheels that kept traversing his field of vision, eyes open or closed. "The whole world must be reloading."

"Aint gonna last," Debro predicted correctly, and the temple walls across from their shelter suddenly rocked. An explosion rent the

front of the temple in a dragon's breath of fire, dust and splinters and a massive red-lacquered door flew end over end across the cobbled street and vaulted skyward. Before it landed and disintegrated on impact a firefight broke out inside the temple. The familiar dueling of AK-47s and M16s, each with its own distinctive voice.

"We got company," Debro said.

Tomlin bent down to look through gaps at the base of their shelter. He could see the pith-helmets bobbing forward along all fronts of the temple plaza, moving in quick darts from low walls or piles of rubble to overturned vehicles or more piles of rubble. Lots of pith helmets. Debro was already firing away. Tomlin forced himself forward and found a hole in their cave to shoot through. Thought, *Keep this up we'll both be deaf for life,* and instantly added, *Then again, exactly how long is that gonna be anyway?*

Tomlin had an easy shot at an NVA soldier crouched at the corner of a wall, the man's attention riveted on the front of the temple. One round and the soldier slumped forward on his knees as though in prayer. Debro was firing in bursts of full auto, Tomlin couldn't see at what. The rattling of the M16 reverberated in the back of his head. The colored wheels were pegged against the periphery of his vision, rotating along the domes of his eyelids.

"They don't know we're here!" Tomlin yelled. "Slow down and aim, damn it!"

Instantly the top of their broken roof began to vibrate under bullet strikes. Thirty-caliber rounds sank into centuries-old timbers and smashed roof tiles made before Paul Revere's ride. Ingots of light appeared where tiles imploded overhead. Shards bounced from Tomlin's bare head and Debro's helmet.

"Hell they don't know, college boy!" Debro yelled back and fired again, cursing as his bolt locked back on an empty magazine. He dumped the magazine and tore the bandoleer of loaded magazines from around his neck, fumbled a new magazine out of its pocket and inserted it in the magazine well. Slapped the bolt release and paused after the bolt slammed home. Looked over at Tomlin and flashed him a grin.

"Well, start shootin, white boy," he said.

College boy, white boy. Debro seemed to think of him as a pair of identical twins.

8

TOMLIN DID START SHOOTING, but left his rifle on semi-auto. A hundred yards away, an NVA with a pistol leaned out from behind the burnt husk of a small car and motioned angrily at a column of soldiers stretched along a broken wall. Tomlin could just see their pith helmets above the general wreckage. He had the officer lined up in his sights when the gate of the temple courtyard exploded and came off its hinges, slammed into their shelter and sent Tomlin's round skyward as the wave of the detonation rocked the street. When he looked back, Debro had his rifle swung *right past my brain housing group on full auto* to cover a gaping hole in the courtyard wall through a new aperture blown in their cavern. A piece of smoldering iron gate still vibrated blade-deep above the opening a foot from Tomlin's head. What with mortars, flying doors and bludgeons and Debro's gun handling, his noggin felt exceedingly overmatched.

"Doors round here takin a *beatin*!" Debro had a flair for running commentary, like they were a pair of sports announcers.

With Debro's attention elsewhere Tomlin kept watch on the front of the temple. He had another view of the NVA officer, who yelled something and rose waist high to fire a pistol round in the direction of his own soldiers. Tomlin's shot doubled him over. The line of pith helmets, freed of external inspiration, stopped its grudging motion and dropped from view.

Tomlin looked across the cobblestone road at the temple. Two Americans in army fatigues appeared in the abscess of the former gate. They all saw each other at the same time.

"U.S. Marines!" Debro yelled as the two men snapped their carbines up reflexively. "Friendlies!"

Satisfied, one of the men made hand motions behind him, to someone out of their sight, and then disappeared himself. The remaining man crouched down, reached in a fatigue pocket, removed and lit a cigarette. He paid them no further attention.

"Who you with?" Debro yelled again over the rattle of the firefight in the temple plaza.

The man spat a filament of tobacco, punching it out with his tongue and upper lip, watching it fall. He smiled up brightly at Debro and said something.

"Shee-it," Tomlin heard Debro say. Debro moved back to cover the front of the temple.

"What'd he say?" Tomlin asked, nervous even when Debro said *shee-it* without much intensity.

"Oh, somethin like, I tell you I got to kill you."

"Well, don't ask him again. Things round here lookin bad enough." He added: "Monsoons are here, be happy it aint rainin." Didn't everybody hate the monsoons worse than death? Didn't the rain soak you, wither you, rot your flesh, raise the bones of your feet through the skin, fill your pitiful sleeping hole, drive you down a mudslick mountain trail a hundred yards for every fifty that exhaustion gained you, keep the resupply choppers from reaching you, blind you to booby traps, bring you to blows with comrades, break your spirit and crush every hope of redemption? And all before the sun came up, if it ever came up?

"Yeah, white boy, it aint rainin." Debro participated in the ritual, but without conviction.

"Good to look on the bright side, D-brother. No money in bein negative. Boys inside that temple probably feel the same way. Whoever they are."

"Fuckin spooks, that's who they are. They aint soldiers and they damn sure aint marines. And they aint fightin the same war we are, I tell you that."

A round whistled through the space between them, followed by more bullet strikes and cascading splinters and pieces of tile.

"Them little yellow people whittlin this place apart," Debro said. "We gonna have to move soon."

"What I been sayin," Tomlin replied. "Hope it's dark by then. Cause it's sure gettin dark in here."

Meaning the curtains rising, then falling inside his head.

He thought it was a clever segue: the dark of the outer world yet to come, the dark inside his head right Now. Debro ignored him as usual.

They were going to have to displace, but with a firefight in progress Tomlin didn't fancy a dash in broad daylight. The mist was moving in again. His head felt weightless; a few seconds later he could barely hold it up. Never a dull moment with a head wound.

In front of the temple there were suddenly a lot more brown-clad soldiers, crouched and then dashing from cover to cover. Sound merged and lost direction in the general cacophony. Most of the NVA seemed still unaware of the intermittent rifle fire coming from their ragged little hut or had their attention more forcibly engaged by whatever marines faced them across the temple plaza. Tomlin held his fire; Debro had only grudgingly gone to semi-auto.

"Who them yellow people fightin up there, anyway?" Now it was Debro doing the asking.

Tomlin said, "We came up the other side, running northeast on LT's map. But I kinda lost track of city streets, what with all the remodelin goin on and the compass takin that AK round. Who's west of us, First Marines, maybe the Fifth?"

"First, Fifth, don't nobody know nothin, you included."

"Hey, same windows, same train."

Debro aimed for a change and fired.

"Good night, *I-rene*. Now you sleepin in the arms of your Maker."

Loud as it was outside the temple, a sudden flaring of small arms from high in the temple drowned out all sound momentarily. The varying tones of M16s and AK-47s merged and crescendoed. The AKs dropped an octave and diminished, then resumed from a new location. Tomlin could read the signature of the firefight: the Americans and NVA engaged upstairs, the enemy beaten back a flight lower. More bursts from a trio of M16s on the ground floor and the last AK went silent. Debro kept the commentary alive.

"Irene's sister in the temple gone lullaby too," he said.

An assault of bright color startled them and something wrapped in orange landed in front of them. The something was a body inside a robe. Bones cracked against stone, bounced and lay rigid as stone. Instantly a stream of red flooded the canals in the cobblestones and flowed back toward the temple.

As though on cue the American across from them dropped his cigarette and stood up, scanning alertly to his front. Tomlin watched as he signaled and another man joined him in the courtyard wall opening. A word passed between them and the second man leaned out and began firing. His comrade darted into the street, headed toward the back of the temple and fell flat on his face and didn't move. A distant memory came to Tomlin, distant as a few minutes ago.

Surprised at the amount of effort it took, he crawled to the back of their shelter and looked through new gaps at the jagged skyline. Earlier, he had seen motion.

The American in the street was dead, he was sure of that. He could have been shot from any direction, despite his buddy's covering fire. But Tomlin saw what he thought he'd see. Movement behind the remains of a window.

He turned to yell at the other American at the courtyard opening. But he was too late. The American stepped out and was firing toward the front of the temple as he moved decisively toward his fallen friend. At the man's side, he put the carbine down and rolled the body over, slipped his arms beneath its armpits, leaned over and recovered his weapon. He began dragging his burden toward Tomlin and Debro.

There was no other cover. Just Tomlin's and Debro's slowly condensing bit of pagoda roof. Tomlin had no clear target and no choice; he started firing into the black hole of the window. His bolt locked back and he swore and dropped the magazine. You never ran out of ammo at a good time.

"Hell you shootin at back there?" Debro yelled.

Tomlin fumbled in his fatigue pocket, cursed again as the fresh magazine hung up somehow, finally pulled it out and slapped it in and hit the bolt release. When he looked back there were two dead Americans, the second one shot in the head. A dollop of gray matter lay in the street behind him. It was easily a hundred and fifty yards to the window, and the American hadn't been standing still. Someone could shoot.

"What's goin on?" Debro yelled again.

"Don't nobody know nothin!"

Tomlin felt himself fighting another strange exhaustion. He felt alert and vital in his mind; just really tired everywhere else. With great effort he dragged himself next to Debro.

"Got a good shooter behind us, up in a window. Killed two of those guys in the temple trying to get out the back way. We better remember that."

Debro looked over at the two Americans in the street. The motionless figure shrouded in orange.

"Bodies was firewood, we set for the winter," he said.

Turned away and stared through saw-toothed gaps toward the front again.

"Look what they done," Debro said.

Their cavern had been a dark hole; now ribbons of grey light from bullet damage to the roof crossed in crazy lines everywhere and cascaded along Debro's face.

Tomlin put his head beside Debro's and looked out at the blood-soaked orange robes. Only the body's legs were visible, as though two stems ran to a single flower.

"Killed a man of God," said Debro. "Why them bastards do that?"

"We don't know what happened," Tomlin said.

"*I* know what happened. I know that shit aint right. I know you don't live long, pullin that shit. Ask them two dead motherfuckers in the street."

When Tomlin glanced at Debro he was surprised to see tears in Debro's eyes. Nearly a year in the bush together and a world of hurt and sorrow behind them, he'd never seen Debro cry. Not when he got the letter from his wife. Not when they'd pulled his best friend, Red Man, the big Navajo, off shit-covered bamboo stakes. Out of nowhere he heard Phineas saying: *And not when it was me got the last seat on that R and R bird to Bangkok.* Even in imagination Phineas lived in some other world, a place where Death was only a joke on the living.

Tomlin looked away from the dead monk and saw a third American kneeling in the gateway. This one wore a radio in a chest harness, a smaller rig than the Prick 25s the marines carried, or any field radio Tomlin had ever seen. Tomlin could see him staring at the bodies of his two comrades. More rounds struck their shelter and another angry bee sang past, spitting in Tomlin's ear on its journey. Debro resumed shooting. The noise was deafening, but what the hell, he could hardly hear anyway. Over the hammering of Debro's M16 Tomlin yelled at the man with the radio, who was talking calmly into the handset. Tomlin heard the rotors of a chopper in the bright lulls of small arms fire.

The radioman glanced at Tomlin, looked away and kept talking.

"Behind the temple! The roof, damnit, the window on the roof!"

Tomlin thought he was doing a fair job of shouting, but the truth was he barely heard himself. Was his mouth connected? He picked up a piece of roof tile and threw it through the opening in their shelter at the American. It disintegrated close to the man's head against the wall, but the man never noticed it or looked over to see Tomlin jabbing and pointing at the high window behind the temple. Tomlin tried it again, with no result. The effort seemed to condense the edges of his vision. Exhausted him. He leaned back against a curved roof rafter to catch his breath. Watched the front of the temple through a hole in Debro's wall, reduced to sightseeing like any tourist.

A Huey roared in above their heads and swept across the temple to the other side. The chopper pulled up above the plaza like a cowboy braking his horse at speed and spun itself around to face them rocking side to side. One of the door gunners opened up on the NVA in the street at the front. A pith helmet in sandals and brown fatigues rose suicidally from a low wall surrounding the plaza and fired up at the chopper, not even emptying a single magazine before he danced crazily sideways in the hail of returning .30 caliber bullets from the chopper's M60s and fell face down straddling the wall.

"You see that?" Tomlin shouted to Debro.

"Sometimes a man just wanna get it over with," Debro said.

The chopper was drawing all the attention of the NVA, apparently to the satisfaction of the American with the radio. He signaled behind him and took one step into the street, and before Tomlin could at least put some covering fire into the window behind them, was hit immediately. He stayed on his feet but changed direction, toward Tomlin, who could see the dark stain spreading across his chest above the radio. The American went to his knees and fell forward, his head cracking against the street only a yard from the hole blown in their piece of pagoda roof. He lay still. Dust and splinters rose and scattered from the cobblestone near his nostrils.

Tomlin wanted to say something to Debro, to ask him to cover him, or just to say goodbye, but there was no time, and he wasn't sure his mouth was working anyway. With difficulty he wrenched aside the piece of iron gate embedded above the hole in their cavern and threw himself out. He fell forward and grabbed the man by the harness straps on his back and tugged him backward. At the shelter he backed in with all he had left and yanked the man in on top of him.

By now Debro was hauling both of them the rest of the way inside. It was cramped with three bodies.

Tomlin worked his way out from underneath the radioman, who wasn't resisting, but wasn't helping either. Debro turned back to his position near the front.

"Well?" Tomlin asked, struggling to breathe.

"You a hero for nothin," Debro said. "A half-ass hero for nothin. Man's gone."

Tomlin sat up. He was so thirsty. He couldn't help himself. He felt around on the back of the dead radio operator's web belt and found the canteen. He unsnapped the cover clasps and had the canteen out and cap unscrewed in the same motion. He was startled how cool the water was, how good it tasted, no halozone bite. He finished half of it, leaned forward and dangled the canteen in front of Debro, who took it and drained it.

"Pause that refreshes," Debro said. "Spooks carryin better water than you and me."

The chopper maneuvered in fitful little jumps above the temple plaza, firing in continuous bursts as it rocked and slid. They could hear the intermittent AK fire in return, but it seemed like the Huey had been firing full auto forever. Tomlin imagined the NVA lying on their backs behind cover, rifles held away from their bodies, firing without aiming. He knew the technique himself.

Tomlin said, "How much ammo can that bird be *carryin?*"

"He got Hollywood ammo," Debro replied. "He aint never gotta reload."

Their shelter was taking more impacts from enemy fire, splattering more bits of clay. Wood beams absorbed most of the rounds, but some were finding the empty spaces behind the tiles.

"Man, no shit, we got to move," Debro said. "This place fallin in."

Tomlin knew he was right. Knew also that high window meant one or both of them were dead the moment they stepped out. It would be nice to have some air support of their own.

Right there in front of him.

His mind really must not be working right.

All this time, staring at a radio.

9

QUICK RELEASE STRAPS HELD the radio inside the bloody harness on the dead man's chest. Tomlin popped the buckles open and the radio slipped out easily. Half the weight and size of a Prick 25, narrower, more sleek and slender. Less than a foot of whip antenna, nothing to mark you as a primary target. Their last radioman had been shot off a rice paddy bank neat as you please, chosen by a sniper among a dozen nearby marine candidates. *E Pluribus Unum*, Phineas said to Garrison, who inherited the job on the spot. Garrison lasted three months. Now it was Bender, who would kill for the radio Tomlin had in his hands. That is, if Bender were still alive himself somewhere.

Of course he was.

Tomlin pressed the handset. "U.S. Marines calling chopper, over."

A flare of static immediately, then a voice. "This is Icon One-Niner, Six speaking. Who's this? Over."

Tomlin pressed the handset again and spoke slowly and loudly, forcing himself to *stay present* as he spoke and to *concentrate*.

"Six, there are two of us U. S. Marine Corps in some cover down here, I guess northeast your position, middle of the street other side this big temple, maybe nine o'clock from where you dropped your team in. Request you advise your gunners our location, they aint askin permission where they open up. You got a problem down here. You have three of your men KIA, repeat, three KIA including your radio operator. Make a one-eighty look south and down and you can see em in the street. You have maybe two remainin in the temple dead or alive I don't know."

Tomlin felt his heartbeat racing and the fog rolling. *Concentrate*. "Six, listen up. There is a shooter in a building behind the temple, up high, on the skyline, only window still standin that high in a broke-up building. From your position, I say about twelve o'clock. Repeat, sniper in a high window behind the temple, this is the shooter killed your men, window at high noon. You got part of the temple between you and the shooter, suggest you keep it that way. Some shootin still going on inside the temple. Do you copy? Because my head aint cooperatin and I'm forgettin things fast includin everythin I just said. Over."

"That's a roger, marine. I copy that. Can see my KIA and your position. How do you come to have this frequency? Over."

Tomlin told him.

"Roger, copy that. Can you enter building and alert or be of assistance to men inside? Over."

Tomlin looked at Debro, interested enough to be watching him. The AK fire up the street was starting to pick up, still directed mainly at the chopper. The helicopter backed away from the temple, rocking as evasively as it could side to side, returning fire but careful to move laterally, heeding Tomlin's advice, keeping the remains of the temple roof between his ship and whoever it was behind that tall window. Now only a few rounds were coming their way from the plaza. But Tomlin's worry was the shooter behind them. Three steps and anyone in that street was good as dead.

"Negative," Tomlin said finally. "We can't get inside the temple and we need to move our own position. There's better cover across the street and we can at least provide some fire support to your men they come out this way. Six, we could use some assistance."

Nausea again. He fought back the urge to puke. "Wait one," he said. Brought the handset away from his ear.

The nausea passed. Now he was fighting off sheets of mist that were rolling in; so much for his mind being alert. It was an effort just to keep the handset keyed and not run all his words together in a big train wreck. He shook his head to restore his vision. Didn't work. Did it again, harder. The pain at the base of his skull cleared an opening in the fog. He rekeyed the handset.

"Six, can you lay some fire into that window, keep that sniper down? We need to change location if we gonna help your men. Over."

"Roger, marine. Wait one."

A pause. Tomlin thought, *him talking to his gunners*.

Over the radio: "Coming about to lay down some fire."

Tomlin knew the pilot was taking a chance himself, giving up his own cover behind the temple, making his ship and crew more vulnerable to small arms fire from the plaza. He motioned to Debro and pushed himself forward. Debro leaned in.

"We gotta go when that chopper unloads behind us. He's gonna keep that shooter down. There's what's left of that wall yonder, that's where we're gonna displace."

Tomlin pointed across the street. Between drifts of inner fog he had identified the remains of a building, somewhere to go. What may have once been a café had collapsed backward, leaving a low crenellated section of wall they could crawl behind, below a heavily leaning second story. *Be it ever so humble*. It was his grandmother's voice. Behind her voice the Texas night was suddenly alive with cicadas, and the dry heat of a west Texas drought was in his nostrils.

Tomlin was fading. An image of a ramshackle home on a dirt road commingled with the ruins across the street. He heard himself say: "We run when that bird opens up," but what bird? Where to?

Debro nodded and removed the magazine from his M16 and slapped in a new one. He pointed at Tomlin's rifle. Tomlin looked puzzled.

"Change it out, man. Get some rounds in there." Debro put a hand on Tomlin's shoulder and shook him. "Get it together, white boy. Change that magazine."

Tomlin swallowed something warm and sweet, nearly choked. Another tide of nausea flowed in, then ebbed out. He punched out his old magazine and somehow got a fresh one inserted. The sensations of his own motion came slowly, in waves, as though sound, sight and touch had come unsynchronized. Malarial. Only something else.

Debro picked up Tomlin's ejected magazine and stuffed it in a pouch in Tomlin's flak jacket. He shook him again, then spread two fingers and pointed at his own eyes.

"I need you to *focus*, man. You from Texas, you gotta cowboy that shit up. We cross this street we goin be all right. Lay up inside, send to cemetery any of these little yellow men come callin, wait on the cavalry help us take care of the rest. You copy that, college boy?"

"Copy," Tomlin said, hearing his own voice after his lips stopped moving. "Wait on Calvary."

*...calvarycalvarycalvary...*His head was an echo chamber.

Debro said, "That bird starts shootin, that takes care of our six. I count three, I gonna lay fire down to the front and you head straight to that wall, you get there, do the same for me. I be right behind you and I mean *right* behind you."

"Copy." Tomlin managed to focus. There was Debro. There was a helicopter somewhere in the grey sky. Across the street, that's where they were going. "I'm bringin this little girl scout radio."

...radioradioradio...

"Damn fine idea. We might wanna order us up some takeout."

Tomlin's voice kept catching up to him, then doubling up and reverberating, like one of those gimmicks attached to his brother's stereo system. Brother so proud of that stereo, worth more than the damn trailer. Melted steel in some junkyard now.

Debro set himself at the side entrance to the shelter. They heard the chopper approaching on the other side of the temple. Its shadow crossed the courtyard, and then it was hovering above them not fifty yards away, the pilot now keeping the temple between the chopper and the enemy soldiers at the front of the street.

"You with the program, jarhead?" Debro shouted over the turbines. "You ready to kick some *ass*?"

Tomlin clutched the radio against his flak jacket and took his rifle between carrying handle and gas guards. His instinct was to shoot as he ran, but it was either leave the radio to have his hands free for shooting, or take it and leave the shooting up to Debro and the chopper. And they might need to talk to that bird again.

"I am one *four*-star, *white*-boy, *flunked* outta college, ready-to-kick-some-ass mother*fucker*," Tomlin said. Words pinballing against the walls of his head...mother*fuckerfuckerfucker*...

"We a damn cowboy movie!" Debro yelled, but before Tomlin could reply both door gunners in the chopper opened up. Tomlin fought the urge to look behind him and listened to Debro count. He could only pray the chopper gunners had the right window. Then again, if they didn't, he was never going to know it.

"...three!" Debro shouted, leaned out and began firing.

Tomlin bolted out, eyes fixed on the broken mouth of the building fifteen yards away. He felt surprisingly strong. Halfway across he recognized the air vibration of bullets passing overhead, felt a strange sense of gratitude that it was coming from the front not the rear, and heard Debro's M16, still on semi-auto—so uncharacteristic of him—popping away with return fire. At the stubby wall he stepped up, ran over the edge and dropped into the space behind. What remained of the rest of the wall lay crumpled backwards, leaving a kind of crevasse at its base two feet wide to shelter in. The cracked and bulging second story floor above failed to inspire Tomlin with confidence. *Be it ever so humble.* But at least now there would be something solid between them and that shooter at the back—though Tomlin doubted anything in the vicinity of that window could survive the pounding the Huey's two machine guns were delivering.

Tomlin dropped the radio and knelt behind one end of the half-wall to cover Debro, his vision suddenly clear, his strength returned, feeling so right he wondered what the problem had been earlier. Motion, any motion, was good.

It was Debro's turn. Tomlin had no targets but began firing over the broken wall toward the front of the temple. Debro darted from cover and charged towards him just as two North Vietnamese soldiers ran full speed from the temple courtyard through the gateway entrance, past the two dead Americans and the collapsing heap of pagoda roof timbers, also straight at Tomlin's position.

For a moment the enemy soldiers and Debro were abreast and oblivious, the way runners in a race ignore each other and fix on the finish line. Tomlin saw his own surprise mirrored in the first NVA soldier's eyes and realized everybody shared the same destination, no one expecting any company.

Tomlin had to pivot to bring his M16 to bear and the closest NVA soldier got off a burst of rifle fire first. The AK rounds were to his right and Tomlin's own volley sent the second soldier lifeless into the cobblestones. Before Tomlin could fire again the remaining soldier got off another short burst but then slammed face first into the street and lay motionless. From the corner of his eye Tomlin saw Debro stumble and fall, but he was focused on the space behind him, on another American in the temple gateway still pointing his rifle in Tomlin's direction.

Tomlin was fading again, and angry about it. He needed all his senses and here he was struggling with simple math. One, there were the two NVA; two, he shot one NVA leaving one NVA. Three, he shot the second NVA. Negative, he hadn't. Three—three, who shot the second NVA? Four, who had shot Debro, leaving Zero motion in the street? A bright yellow rubber duck fell down from the sky and bobbed above the carnage. Tomlin couldn't read the script on the white placard hanging below it, but somehow he knew exactly what it said:

> *The American you're looking at shot NVA #2, who shot Lance Corporal Maurice Debro, adding up to a sum of Zero motion in the street. Th-th-th-that's all, folks!*

The duck jerked upwards as though on a string and disappeared. Thick black eyebrows vibrated above cigar smoke. Winked and were gone.

Somewhere an audience laughed. At what? All Tomlin could see was a street full of bodies. He thought remotely about counting them, but that was just more math. He closed his eyes and willed the fog away. When he opened them again the American across the street had lowered his carbine. A second man had joined him, a metal container strapped across his chest in some kind of harness. They conferred for an instant, the first man pointing across the street at Tomlin. In the tiniest interlude between rifle and machine gun fire, all three of them heard a round, then a pause, and then another round, leaving a mortar tube.

Debro was face down in the street, five yards away. Tomlin didn't wait on the mortars and left cover just as the first mortar landed ten yards in front of their former haven. Tomlin flung himself down, stone and metal fragments peppering the broken building behind him, chunks of cobblestone slapping into him and scattering by him in the street. Pieces of wood flew past his face. Something stung a leg. As he crawled toward Debro, Tomlin looked up and saw the Huey clearly through a grove of courtyard trees. It slid backward, machine guns still working away. The second mortar round landed inside the courtyard, lopping off a half-dozen tree branches. Once beside Debro, Tomlin recovered Debro's rifle and bandoleer and slung both of them, took hold under his armpits and began dragging him. Debro wasn't a big man, but dead weight was dead weight.

"Let's *go!*" he ordered, and as he pulled, Debro lurched forward. On hands and knees they reached a low spot near the center of the wall. Tomlin unslung and tossed Debro's rifle and bandoleer, turned his back to the wall, pushed off and pulled Debro over and on top of him. Debro lay still and looked off somewhere past Tomlin's shoulder. Tomlin caught his breath and extricated himself from below Debro, who hadn't moved. A jagged edge of synthetic armor plate poked through the fabric of Debro's flak jacket. Tomlin ran his hand inside the flak jacket and around Debro's back.

Tomlin said, "Talk to me, man," and then a mortar round exploded in the street, the explosion louder and more violent than earlier ones, and another, and another, filling the cavernous space behind them with shrapnel and debris. Tomlin ducked so hard he thought his head was coming off his shoulders. The pain lodged somewhere in his boots.

Bits of wood and plaster fell from the ceiling. The building shook, threatened to collapse. Dust blanketed them. Then silence. Just the sound of the turbines and the chopper rotors, guns quiet now, still hovering somewhere, maybe waiting and watching the window, a cat outside a mouse hole. Recovering and looking over the wall Tomlin saw their former rooftop sanctuary was gone, coils of smoke rising from what had been its center. The body of the dead American inside was missing too, as though vaporized. Well, these were bigger rounds, 81s or 82s, depending on what side was doing the shooting. And just which side was that?

Nobody knew nothing.

10

TOMLIN FOUND THE WOUND on Debro's left side. In and out, back through lung. In another sudden quiet he could hear the frothing of air and blood. The hole in Debro's back was barely wet, but he was hemorrhaging from his chest. Without something to seal the exit wound, he'd be breathing through that hole.

Tomlin needed plastic. He looked around helplessly. Smashed furniture, broken glass, bulged and leaning walls. An absurdly unbroken dinner plate on edge in a pile of rubble. Charred newspaper. Nothing useful.

Mortars again. Up and down the street, in the courtyard, on the temple roof. Shrapnel stung the air and pieces of clay rained down everywhere. Plaster flew from the walls and pulverized cobblestone browned out the world. When the dust cleared enough to see again, the two remaining Americans across the street had disappeared, whether gone to cover or dead, who could tell.

Plastic. Tomlin spat a mouthful of minerals and shook his head in self-disgust, hard enough to make it hurt. *All this noise makin me stupid.*

From his back pocket he unfolded a bundle and shook it. Wallet, photographs, packets of sugar and coffee, toilet paper and a chocolate bar, all the paraphernalia of the bush, tumbled from the plastic binder that guarded precious contents from rain, sweat and blood. He shook it again and an envelope and a playing card fell into the pile, the Queen of Hearts, a farewell gift from his girlfriend eleven months, three weeks and six days ago. The morning of their last day together he awoke late. She was up and making breakfast. He found the card under his pillow beside her note: *I've got the king. When you come home, we'll make a little prince.*

Instinctively Tomlin picked the card up and stuffed it in a cargo pocket containing a pair of hand grenades.

A wave of exhaustion coursed through him. The receiver on the radio handset was squawking. He focused. It wasn't good when things slowed down. He planted the plastic binder on the dark hole in Debro's chest and noted how the plastic was instantly sucked inward as Debro inhaled, sealing it against his bloody skin.

Tomlin wrestled Debro around and managed to set his back against the wall. He pulled off Debro's flak jacket, wet with blood, but not as much as he expected to see. Over the crash of mortars the Huey's turbines whined higher as it maneuvered backwards, M60s raging again, at what Tomlin couldn't tell. He didn't watch it pivot, bank and fly off to the west, into the sun. Up the street the AKs paused in relief.

Tomlin fumbled with the ends of the battle dressing around his own head, frustrated almost to rage with his clumsiness. He finally loosened the knot, untwisted Debro's careful windings and lifted the dressing gingerly from behind his ear. He couldn't feel anything there anyway, just a sensation of wetness, and a kind of spreading warmth.

"Talk to me, D-brother," Tomlin said again. "Don't go faraway on me, man. Got something for you right here."

Debro had a slight smile on his face. He worked his lips without opening his eyes. Tomlin bent closer but the lips moved without sound.

"What? What's that? Say again, damn it!"

Debro didn't. The plastic binder had slipped downward and hung like a wet red flag. Tomlin adjusted it back into place and set the battle dressing over the plastic and held it there with a bloody forearm as he worked the ends of the bindings around Debro's body and snugged it all up with a knot along his ribcage. He twisted him to raise the undamaged lung slightly. When Debro cried out Tomlin said, "Sorry, man. Got to keep that good side above the water line." He propped up Debro's head with his helmet.

"Cowboy movie," Debro blurted out and spat blood. He coughed spastically, opened and closed his eyes, spat more blood. Left a smile in place when he quieted down. The world shook as another volley of mortar rounds descended, marching up, then down the street. Just as abruptly, silence again.

"Water," Debro demanded.

"Not good for you, man. Go down the wrong pipe you'll be plenty pissed at me."

Debro opened his eyes and rolled his head on his helmet. "Been pissed at you since I know you. Gimme some fuckin water."

"Can't do it, D-brother. We get movin, I'll buy you a beer."

Debro looked away, closed his eyes again. "Then I'll watch this fuckin cowboy movie."

"Sure thing," Tomlin said. "You hang in there with John Wayne. I'm gonna get us a bird outta here."

Debro's legs lay elevated on a mound of broken concrete. Not good for a chest wound. Tomlin paused to lower them, then low-sprinted the few yards to the radio. He huddled behind the wall and keyed the handset. Tomlin wasn't good at names even without a piece of shrapnel in his head. He couldn't remember the chopper's call sign.

"Chopper, US Marines, over," he said.

Looking over the wall he surveyed the street between the back of the temple courtyard and the buildings behind. There looked to be room enough for a Huey to land, or at least hover over the rubble. Close damn enough for a Huey that didn't seem to mind hovering over a nest of AK-47s.

"Chopper, US Marines, over," he repeated. "Us on the ground, you in the sky. Over."

Static, dead space, more static, and then the pilot's voice. "Marine, this is Icon-Nine. Give me a sit-rep, over."

Tomlin was having to focus for all he was worth. Half his body felt detached, not from waist down or waist up, but kind of in roving sections, as if body parts were taking turns deserting a sinking ship. He composed himself enough to speak.

"Sir, situation is I need a medevac *now*. No sight of your men yet. I am in position to cover them at the temple when they move, but right now I got a buddy hurt bad, really bad, and I need to get him out. There's some kinda LZ behind the temple, sir, it aint exactly groomed, but it'll fit your bird. And that shooter at the window's gotta be history now. Need to get this man out, sir, *right now.* I will get him to that LZ and I need you to come on down outta heaven and pick him up and I'll stay right here in hell and cover your men when they make their move. Over."

He got the answer he expected but that didn't make it right.

"This is Icon-Nine." Static and a pause, and then something like a sigh: "Son, in five minutes over your location I got more daylight in this magnesium crate than I had my whole tour. Mortar rounds dropping fore and aft and I got a crew member shot too and top of that I got mission orders, son, and that's the only reason I'm in this airspace in the first place. I'm sorry, marine, that's a negative. No medevac anywhere is going near that position until it's secured. Over."

Tomlin had the impression he might not have been very clear. Or was the fog in his head the problem? He needed to think.

"Six, wait one."

He unkeyed the handset. The kind of mist that could hide the Golden Gate Bridge threatened to move in. Tomlin fought it off, took refuge in the grip of a cold fury. He felt himself unraveling but didn't care. He must have closed his eyes because an image of Phineas arose.

Phineas in a bar, Danny Hardin beside him. Phineas laughing. Tomlin remembered the occasion. It was the first time he ever heard the cliché, the night half the squad broke curfew and dragged him bar-hopping in Da Nang, Tomlin just off the boat from Okinawa, seeing Viet Cong behind every door and window, Phineas the old salt, a man without a care in the midst of hard, shadowed faces huddled around small tables, speaking quietly among themselves and casting dark looks their way.

Phineas saying, *Relax, Private Tomlin. Tell him about VC, Johnny-One.*

The Vietnamese bartender slid a beer into the depths of the counter and leaned forward, light from yellow lanterns dancing in black eyes above a disfigured nose and scarred lips. He wagged a finger in Tomlin's face and recited proudly: *No VC! no VD! no MP!*

Phineas handed Johnny-One five dollars in MPC and said, *Take a look down your sleeve, Private Tomlin. See any chevron—even a single chevron—attached thereto? What you got to lose? Now cast those baby blues around these four walls. Well, bless my soul and oh my goodness, we aren't in Kansas anymore, are we? This aint exactly the hallowed halls, is it? Bullshit college days are over, jarhead. Now it's time for school. Real school. Welcome to the University of Da Nang. North campus, College of Nam. School of the people, by the people and for the people. Curriculum aint nothin but a long ass field trip. Classes held in the bush, professors all carryin AK-47s.* Phineas clapped an arm around Tomlin, squeezed his shoulder and tipped his cap from behind so the bill came down over his eyes. Johnny-One grinned, popped a bottle cap and slid a beer toward him. Phineas intercepted it and took a swig before handing it to Tomlin. *You are bottom rung, newbie. Now hear this. You broke curfew?*—placing his hands over his mouth and opening his eyes in mock terror, then delivering Tomlin's introduction to the cliché—*Hell they gonna do, bust you and send you to Nam? On behalf of the Marine Corps from John Wayne back to Smedley Butler and by authority vested in me by the poor bastard wasted before me resulting in my humble elevation to squad leader: Have a damn beer, for chrissakes. For tomorrow we die and if we don't, then there's the tomorrow after that and if that fickle bitch lady luck is still with us and we don't die then either, one thing's for damn sure: tomorrow and many tomorrows may pass before ever you see another beer cold as this served up inside any establishment fine as Johnny-One's Home for Wayward Round Eyes. Carpe. Fuckin. Diem! Or Nochem, as the case may be.* Danny Hardin on the other side of Phineas, smiling and raising his bottle in a toast to wisdom. *At least tonight,* Danny said, in the half-amused, half-resigned tone reserved for times when it was useless to argue with Phineas. *There it is,* chimed in Timmy Taylor from a seat at a corner table, his silhouette leaned in against the silhouette of a Vietnamese woman, the black pearls of her eyes watching Tomlin accusingly, as if he remained unconvinced.

Back in the Now, Tomlin shook his head to clear it of memory and pressed it against the stub of wall as two more mortar rounds exploded in the street. There was only one wisdom left, and that was to cast wisdom aside and get that chopper out of the sky and onto the earth. Only way to do that was Phineas style: damn the torpedoes.

He held the handset to his undamaged ear and ordered himself to speak slowly. He couldn't hear from the other side and he felt like he had half a face. Hard to keep the words from running into each other. Tomlin keyed the handset, held it in a death grip and heard Phineas again: *Hell they gonna do, bust you and send you to Nam?*

"Six, Marine on the ground here, sir. Meanin no disrespect, sir, but that's one sorry-ass reply to my situation, *I shit you not.* This is a damn good man with a sick baby that needs him back and he didn't ask to be here in the middle of your mission orders and I need you to look down, locate and *grab your balls* and bring your bird back and join this party on the ground and help me get this good man outta here and I don't want to hear any more of your chickenshit problems cause the whole fuckin world is full of em and I don't give a damn inside the hottest fire in hell if you, your bird and every swingin dick aboard goes down inside this shitstorm for tryin, sir, because this man dyin here is a good man and aint none of us exempt from any of this bullshit just cause some of us can fly away from it at any fuckin time, sir, so I need you to accomplish that aforementioned testicle-finding and come down and help me get this good man out, sir, and I need it *RIGHT FUCKIN NOW cause the fuckin time I got left to beg you to do this is FUCKIN RUNNIN OUT!*"

Tomlin rekeyed the handset. "Sir," he added.

Unkeyed and then keyed it again.

"Over."

In case protocol still mattered. Or might appease his mother. *You aren't swearing now, are you, son?*

"Marine, now you need to listen to me—"

But Tomlin was done listening. The radio had two knobs. One of them was clearly for volume. He saw FREQ in caps on another and began dialing, grateful for the clear white lettering that broke through the fog. The only numbers he still knew by heart were his service number, his girlfriend's figure and India's frequency. He dialed the frequency in, waited for the third platoon commander to shut up, and then barged in.

"India Two, this is Two-Charlie, over."

Tomlin looked up and saw an NVA soldier moving stealthily forward along the courtyard wall across the street, thirty yards away, his AK up and leveled at the temple door. Without dropping the handset he picked up his rifle and laid it across the broken wall, steadied it and lined the soldier's chest up in the ghost sights. Pressed. Fired a single round. His rifle skidded sideways. The soldier fell forward, curled his legs up and lay still.

"India Two, India Two, this is Two-Charlie, over," Tomlin repeated.

The static broke and the voice on the other end startled him with volume and clarity. Tomlin almost looked around for whoever must be *right there* talking to him. It was a damn good radio.

"Two-Charlie, this is India Two. Who's this, where the hell are you and who's with you, alive or dead?"

It was LT, pissed as usual. Even with half the command bunkers in I Corps monitoring the frequency, LT spoke his mind. Like all southerners, Kestermont dropped the hard "g" at the end of his present participles; on the radio, everything dropped harder and the southern drawl thickened. Phineas had noticed it first and told Kestermont he was proud to have a redneck for a platoon commander.

Now Kestermont said, "We got your whole squad MIA and nobody knows a *steamin* pile from shinola. What's your location? Over."

"India Two, this is Tomlin. Hell, sir, there's just me and Debro up at that big temple you sent us to recon, everybody else scattered and gone I couldn't tell you where and I aint proud to say it. Temple under heavy attack but couldn't tell you who's doin the attackin or counterattackin."

A mortar round landed directly across from his position, near the blown gateway of the courtyard. Tomlin ducked but kept talking.

"Got AKs up front, mortars everywhere, snipers and spooks, sir, and it's the end of the fuckin world. We are toward the back on the east side in some broke-down cover and Debro needs a medevac, he's shot bad, say again, need a medevac right now. There's a clearing behind the temple for a bird to set down. Situation critical, sir, this is gotta happen now. I got purple smoke, I can bring a bird in. There aint no time for waitin on a gunship, LT. That medevac's gotta get here now. Over."

"Wait one," Kestermont came back. "Got to change freq. Over."

Tomlin glanced over at the gateway. The last few mortar rounds had done some remodeling. A portion of the courtyard wall lay in the street. Rubble half-covered the bodies of the sniper-shot Americans and the orange robes had turned grey. There was no sign, living or dead, of the Americans he'd last seen in the opening.

Kestermont again. "Two-Charlie, this is India Two. Tomlin, listen up. That's a negative on the bird, they will not fly to your position.

It's too hot, repeat, too hot for a medevac. Better part of an NVA regiment on the move in broad daylight, units all cut up and cut off and nobody knows nothin. Hell's breakin loose all over Dodge. I am comin up with what's left of Two-Alpha to reinforce and get you out. I run into the rest of your squad I'll bring em along. We have Doc Baker and a stretcher and a team of 0331s. We *will* get you and Debro out. You keep your head down and do what you need to do. We are movin now, repeat, movin now. On my map estimate we are ten, maybe twelve blocks away. We got some shootin to do to get where you are but we are en route now. ETA twenty, thirty minutes. Do you copy?"

Tomlin fought back his disappointment. In place of anger he just felt tired. He closed his eyes.

So people died. That's what they did. Everyone and everything.

The enemy died, friends died, your pets died, your baby sister died face down in her crib, your brother burnt to death in his own fucking trailer too stoned to know it, the old man went through a windshield into a tree on a stretch of two-lane blacktop, cancer cut down every second relative. Everybody Fucking Died. Suffocated dreaming of puppies, cremated sleeping in bed, shot through the lungs. Broken in half and bleeding out alone on a Texas night in a ditch, coughing up their guts in a sterile room. Death the compassionate, Death the truest democracy. The United States of Death. The Republic of South Death. The People's Death of North Death. A United Nations of Death. Turned no one away. You were citizen by birth, didn't matter a damn where you were born. Same black flag, different capitols. Everywhere like God was everywhere but at least Death left you bodies you could touch, weep over, put in a hole in the ground and sing hymns for.

All God left was a book full of rumors.

He was staring at gray sky and broken clouds. From behind the clouds he heard: *Hell I can hear you Hell I can hear you.*

"Hell you can!" Tomlin shouted. "Hell you can!"

No reply. Just the clouds. Broken clouds and gray sky. From somewhere, a sound like a stone rolling, crushing earth, shutting out the light.

"Hell you can," Tomlin said again. His voice hung in a millisecond's tomblike silence. A brilliance like lightning, and then darkness. He heard Kestermont's voice, sounds without meaning. The world paused. In that instant he could hear the trickle of concrete dust seeping from wounds in the ceiling, intermingled with Debro's labored breathing. The dust fell across his shoulders and ran down his back and the instant was over. Mortars crashed again and he sat in the cement rain and waited for LT.

11

MORE FOG WAS ROLLING. Tomlin's vision blurred and pulsed, nauseating him. He wasn't sure, but thought he was vomiting at last. Crud along his arm, on the handset, down the side of the receiver. A sound of distant retching, as if heard on a sidewalk through an open window. But unmistakably him.

Could use a taxi. Not a taxi around. Remembered a friend in Texas, his father owned the cab company. Did his own dispatching in the day, all the driving evenings and Sundays. Hardly known to sleep. Was today Sunday? Drunk half the time, but the old bastard always came when you called.

A voice, not a cabdriver's. Kestermont, calling him back.

"Two-Charlie, this is India Two. Tomlin, I say again, do you copy? Over."

Somehow he *focused*. Wiped the slime from his chin and the receiver. *Clean that shit up, maggot!* Sweet words from boot camp. Stay presentable.

Presentable. Now his mother's voice. *All my little darlins got to be presentable*. Him not five years old, his brothers three and six, his baby sister dead not three days, lying on her bier of dirt under its blanket of artificial grass, the flowers already wilting in the heat, her miniature body in its miniature box waiting for them to come and stand beside her, to say their goodbyes spoken or silent and stare at the box encasing the little body over the hungry little hole in the earth, the women in veils in their best black dresses, the men in buttoned shirts red-faced and streaming sweat in the Texas summer, ties narrow and black like a hangman's rope, their communal presence a whistling of the gathered living past the day of their own graveyard, their rainbow-hued flowers a feeble design to underwrite the beauty of life against the napalm of its passing as though these selfsame multicolored petals would not themselves turn brown and decay and hang lifeless above her after they lowered her into her miniature hole her miniature life already an echo in his four year old head her cooing and gurgling reverberating there denying it could be erased forever and pleading to never be so forgotten his mother with no answer but a creak of vocal cords from a ship lost at sea when he asked *But how will she find Heaven if they put her in that hole?* her grieving obsessive fingers fiddling with his bowtie nearly choking him her mascara riven beneath wild and bloodsoaked eyes saying only *All three my little darlins got to be presentable* and then choking so hard tall men beside her lift her away and the sun she blocked with her ministration now in his eyes and then above them all and above even the sky even to the clouds and beyond he thought the world full of the wail of her sudden loosed agony putting animals in flight through forests as though fire chased them as though they would be consumed if they dared stop as if whatever devils animals fear were upon them as if all was lost if they did not run for their lives even if their hearts burst as he felt his own split open looking at that miniature box poised over the only home it would ever know again and lost forever and Death and Silence and only the weight of the earth now hidden under flowers but later upon her forever and waiting out there for him in his day and he knew only then would he ever see her again whenever that was, wherever that would be, on that day, on *his* day, on the day of the earth waiting for him *was this his day?*

"Two-Charlie, this is India-Two. *Repeat,* do you copy? Over." Pause. *"Tomlin, pick up the goddamn handset. Do you copy?"*

Tomlin had, in fact, dropped the handset. How did LT know? Was he watching the same movie? *Dreams of my Sister. The Early Harvest. Hole in the Ground Hole in the Head.* Well, titles were flexible things. Sort of like the walls around him. Sort of like his head.

Limp from the battle of memory surfacing, Tomlin found the handset and pressed the key.

"Roger, copy, LT. Over."

No fight left in him. There were pieces of him all over inside of him. He collected enough to form a quorum.

"India Two, are these our mortars? They're beatin hell out of us. Can you turn em off? Over."

"Negative, not India mortars. Not Lima or Mike either. This is not friendly fire, repeat not friendly fire. Same tubes been poundin us all afternoon. Got some fast movers upstairs lookin for them but Phantoms been useless all morning, now they say too many our own people mixed in with NVA to drop ordnance. You hold on right where you are. Stay by the radio. Over."

"India Two, those fast movers—" Tomlin dropped the handset again. Scrabbled for it but it mocked and dodged his clumsy fingers. Finally captured it and Kestermont was already telling him what he needed to know.

"—have alerted all FOs to your presence there. Phantoms will hold off *no matter what* until my further notice and we have you out. Repeat, your coordinates are known and the fast movers will not move in until you and Debro are clear. Do you copy? Over."

Of course, thought Tomlin. *Copy is what we do. What the world does. What it has always done. A-copying we will go. Copy until we copy no more.* He felt an epiphany pass him by, unrevealed.

"Copy that, LT. Over."

Nothing left to say but goodbye. What, *thanks anyway? We who are about to die salute you? Dulce et fuckin decorum est?*

"Two-Charlie out."

"India out."

Tomlin flipped the handset away. It shot to the end of its coil, then skipped backward just as quickly, as though reconsidering freedom. Tomlin could hear Debro singing, a whisper wet with blood, the same white girl tune. He crawled over closer, keeping his rifle leveled at the street.

"When you're singin, the whole world sings with you," he said.

"*Cry if I want to, cry if I want to,*" Debro went on, his eyes closed, half-smiling.

"Aint gonna be no cryin for you, man. You hear Kestermont? Comin for us his own damn self, that's how vital we are to this war effort."

Debro seemed oblivious, then rolled his head slightly on his helmet and finally spoke.

"You the most optimistic white boy I ever know, man." Pink froth ran along his chin down his neck. "Got a bit inflated idea how important you are, though."

"Considerin you're all shot to hell, you're lookin fine," Tomlin said. "Tomorrow a bed at Cam Ranh, Red Cross girls bringin you breakfast in bed, back to the ghetto in a week. Leavin your white boy on his lonesome in the bush. Your ass home before mine, when I'm the damn short-timer. Don't think I won't be pickin that bone with you when I rotate out."

Debro raised his head and spat up more blood.

"Fuckin drownin," he said, closed his eyes and was quiet a moment, almost peaceful. But for distant gunfire the world fell silent again. Not a sound from in front of the temple. The world licking its wounds. So silent it startled Tomlin when Debro said, "Read your damn letters."

"What?"

"Your letters. Read em."

"What letters?

"Hell what letters. The letters people send you. The people who give a shit about you. The ones you don't read. Don't say you don't know what letters."

Tomlin didn't answer.

"Well?"

"We left our gear behind. They're in my ruck."

"Not all em."

"Just one with me."

"More than one, don't bullshit."

"Hell's it to you?"

"Read em. Read em now."

"What for?"

"Because—" Debro raised his head as if to vomit. His stomach heaved and another jet of blood pulsed from his mouth.

Tomlin scrabbled inside a cargo pocket, found an olive drab handkerchief, part of it unstained and not hard as rock. He leaned forward and wiped Debro's mouth and chin. Felt around his back. The entrance hole not bleeding. The exit hole not bleeding. Debro was hemorrhaging internally. "Quit talkin, damn it." No swelling that he could see in Debro's chest. Where was the blood going?

"Aint it enough I ask you to read em?" Debro said.

"Well, *shit*."

Tomlin dug around in his pockets again. Nothing there. His wallet missing. He felt the Queen of Hearts, felt his heart shift in the same instant. He would not think about her. Looked behind him, saw his wallet in the rubble, packets of coffee and creamer. Two letters beside them, envelopes mangled and yellowed from dirt and travel. He crawled the few yards and picked up both, examined them and sorted one back into a trouser pocket. Leaned back against a smashed and overturned table and tore the other open.

"From my brother. Little fucker."

"Don't read it to me. Read it to you."

It was a single sheet, the writing on both sides in his brother's style. They all wrote long letters. His mother, his brother, his girlfriend. It was curious to him, lying bone-tired in muddy earth at the end of a day, the distance he tried to put between himself and the world they inhabited. It had nothing to do with love. Yes, he loved them. He missed them. But the letters had become descriptions and trivia from lives being lived on another planet. The tenth planet, a planet named Back in the World. A planet discovered newly by every grunt on the occasion of his first night below that limitless wash of stars. It was a thirteen month journey back to that planet. A year of thirteen months. You could hump forever and a day and never budge an inch under that sky, and before the first month was out you knew your boots would never bring you home. Thirteen months! Unfathomable. Forget the calendar. Forget those things that nailed you to that calendar. Think instead about where you put those boots. One wrong step and the earth took your boots from your legs, your feet still inside. Now there was incentive! Where to walk? What patch of ground was safe, which might change your world forever? That was the right obsession. Walk where the man in front of you walked. Let the enchantment of where to place your boots on the suspect earth blot the tenth planet from the night sky. Good, practical advice. Phineas advice. Forget the calendar. Forget that planet. Forget them well enough, pay attention to where you walked, and one unimaginably distant day wake up at the end of those thirteen months, both feet attached, boarding a flight destined for Back in the World.

Tomlin had to squint to read his brother's cramped and tiny script. Amazing his eyes would focus now. Amazing he could read, fantastic that words made sense. His brother liked to talk and he liked to write. In all other ways he was thrifty. The only one in the family who was. Bought his first car with a childhood's saved allowances. His first violin by mowing lawns. His playing style economical too, focused and taut, not a single note lacking purpose, no one better at stating melody. When his brother got to college in California his handwriting shrank, the better to splurge on verbiage and economize on paper. Billy didn't waste time with openings. Or add dates to his letters. You were meant to picture him right there in front of you, right Now.

Tommy, big brother, never hearing from you is such a downer I think I ought to hardly give you the time of day, but like Hemingway I don't have time to write a short letter. Okay you don't write me but it drives Mother crazy. Between us, she's crazy enough. I can hardly say two words without spending the rest of the conversation in a total defense of my life. I think it's because she never hears from you that she has so little patience with me. You drop out of school and get sent to a war zone, she hardly says anything, not a word, nothing, just the woe-is-me routine. I change my major from classical to modern and the sky falls in. What's the difference, man, music's not music? How about that one letter sometimes, brother, that's all. Just ten words: "I'm doing fine, it's cool my little brother is playing rock and roll." Okay, my math stinks, that's more than ten. Seriously, brother, one letter a week. Hell, to someone. Even one a month. You never wrote when you went away to school but everyone knew where you were. No one was trying to kill you. I know where you are, it's on the news every night. Like this war is just another course to dinner, served just before dessert. I can't look and I can't not look. Grandma says Mother leaves the room when the news comes on. I tell her last I heard you were in Okinawa on your way to Japan. I lie for love, brother. If you told her you were in Tokyo it would make me a hero, forget what it would do for her. I love you, brother, and I think of where you are and my head spins a little. There were four of us, there's two now. You only got three months left, right? You got to keep your head down. For the cause, man. The one you left behind. The one only you know you left behind. Too damn bad you didn't meet your lady before you signed those damn papers. You might have listened to her, that is if she didn't get her long-awaited letter coming from boot camp day before Christmas like the rest of us.

Something you should know. It annoys hell out of me and makes me laugh too. Remember that last visit up in the City, maybe a week before you left, we played that dumpy little bar near the Wharf, the one that had the stupid lava lamps in the windows and black lights and strobes everywhere? Half the room on acid, the other half drunk? You didn't know it (but I did) some pretty decent producer was there secretly recording acts (but everyone knows he does it), looking for raw meat to grind up inside some slave-making contract. I called you up on stage to hammer that beat up old house upright and we played around that ragtime blues thing you like to do. I know you remember it, you actually had fun that night. We weren't just cooking, we burned the joint down. I know we did, so last winter I was up in the City (not to buy dope, I quit like I said I quit, so just forget about it) and I stopped in and made an appointment with the big-time record producer for five minutes of his precious time. He remembered us and when I asked him what he thought of my band all he said was, "Send me that fucking piano player I can put him in the studio tomorrow." I was proud and pissed off at the same time. What the hell. We're doing okay. We open for a bunch of drugged up Englishmen at the Cow Palace next month. I'm writing, Jessie's writing, we hardly do any more covers. Covers get you nowhere. That's why the swelled head producer remembered you. He never heard that Texas honky tonk before. So here's the plan. You get back, join us. Add that acoustic keyboard to go with all this electric wahwah we do. The band thinks it's a great idea. So what you're not going to be a doctor. You've got surgeon hands. Ask any piano you ever operated on. Maybe we'll never get rich but maybe we will and it beats hell out of running in the streets and throwing rocks at police. And the girls, man, it's crazy. It's far out crazy. But I know you're set for life on that one, Mr. Family Man.

All I got, man. Take mercy on your mother and write her. Take care of yourself. Take care of those hands. Bring yourself home. You're what I've got. Like I said I've got all the girls. They can't resist the music. Never thought I'd meet girls crazier than west Texas cowgirls. I take advantage of it but man I'd give it all up today and this electric fiddle forever if it would bring you home right now. It comes down to it you're what I've got, big brother. The fact is you're all I've got. Sentimental shit, I know, man, but that's the truth. I can't lose you. You didn't have any right to put yourself where you are and leave us the way you did. You didn't. So you have to make it right, brother. You have to come home. I don't care what you have to do to come home. I'm asking you from the bottom of my heart to come home.

I'm asking you not to make me an orphan. I can only take so much.

I love you. B.

Tomlin folded the letter and put it back in the envelope and into his pocket. His fingers brushed the Queen of Hearts again and his heart raced. Involuntarily his fingers felt the small of her back. Not the time for memories. Not the time for letters.

Debro said, "Well?"

"Brother's a baby. Little fucker still in diapers."

"You read em from now on."

Eyes open and coughing up blood Debro pushed himself upright and settled back against the wall. Tomlin started to say something but Debro raised a hand to cut him off. He stretched his legs out across the rubble.

"Can't breathe like that, man. I go, I don't want to go twisted all to hell and suffocatin. Just leave me be, white boy. You aint in med school and I aint no damn schoolboy with the clap. And you my squad leader don't mean shit right now."

Tomlin couldn't argue with that. He checked the battle dressing. The plastic seemed to be doing its job. Still no swelling in his chest, no sign of air trapped inside the body but outside the lung. Just had to get him out of there soon. Twenty minutes a long time, even for an optimist.

"*You would cry too if it happened to-ooo you,*" Debro managed.

"You keep singin, I'm gonna watch the street," Tomlin said.

Plus it was better than watching Debro die.

12

STARING OVER THE WALL, Tomlin felt a wave of heat travel down his right side followed by a wave of panic. A jolt of electricity played ping pong with the left and right side of his brain. He couldn't move his arm; then he could again. Street, sky and crumbling Buddhist temple solarized and went psychedelic. *No tab of acid like a head wound. Wait'll I tell the hippies.* His hand cramped, went spastic; one arm went rigid again. He worked his fingers, rolled his arm in its shoulder socket. The world pulsed, went black and white, resumed a kodachrome fidelity. His arm returned to normal. His hand unseized. Panic receded but hovered nearby, there to remain, on call for active duty. Panic, the good soldier.

Not good to slow down like this. But not like he could step outside for a round of calisthenics either.

Across the street the two remaining Americans suddenly appeared again, on either side of the broken gateway. One of them tossed something inside the temple and they both plunged into the street, headed for Tomlin's position. There was an explosion, and smoke and dust rolled above the courtyard wall and out of a ground floor window. The two Americans arrived, leaping over the wall. One of them low-crawled over to Tomlin and grabbed his arm. Florid face with bright blue eyes inches away, breath foul with stale tobacco.

"Saw you take the radio. Where is it?"

Tomlin shook his arm free. The other American had already found it.

"Icon Niner, Ground One. Over."

The radio operator waited, scanning up and down the street.

Static and then *Say again, over*.

Tomlin recognized Kestermont's voice. The radio operator frowned at the dials and said to no one, "Freq's all screwed up." He spun the knob.

"Icon Niner, Ground One."

This time Tomlin couldn't hear the reply in the handset, held to the man's ear. He twisted so he could watch the street better. Looked for a moment at the NVA he'd shot earlier, dead in a fetal position. Curled up like a sleeping infant. Looked away.

The mortars had stopped, but small arms fire at the front was raging again. Fewer rifles now. To clear his head Tomlin tried to make sense of it. By variance in the sound of their firing, he thought he could pick out four or five different M16 positions. Everyone on semi-auto, conserving ammunition.

The NVA, too. Maybe a half dozen AKs seemed to be active following the Huey's aerial assault. A squad of marines, maybe, what was left of them. The remains of a platoon of NVA. Maybe everyone on both sides just as lost as he and Debro.

Bad luck to be heading somewhere else, turn a corner and run into each other. Bad luck for the Huey to drop into the middle of a firefight. Bad luck for the NVA to have a chopper full of cold-blooded, hard corps spooks roping in. Bad luck in turn for the three dead spooks from the chopper. Bad luck for him and Debro. For the shooter in the window. For the monk in the saffron robes.

Bad luck all around. How much bad luck left under Debro's moon? And where was the air support? That could change luck in a hurry.

"Icon-Niner, this is Ground One," the American was saying. "Target secure. Repeat, have mission target in hand. All of Ground Two KIA. Moving to mark Yellow Seven, repeat, Yellow Seven, ETA five minutes. Advise on inbound direction. Get that net ready, Chief. Over."

Tomlin kept his focus outboard. Focus was important. His toes and fingers were tingling. He was developing a headache. The headache vanished. Fog rolled in and out. Colors vibrated at the edge of vision, enclosing the world inside an electronic picture frame. Then the world went black and white and lost substance, turned into line etchings in a fishbowl. Back to Kodachrome. One instant he was deadly thirsty, the next not.

Your switchboard just gone all to hell, he heard Phineas say. *Aint life grand?*

"O happy morning," Tomlin replied out loud. Debro opened an eye but didn't say anything.

The radio operator had the handset jammed to one ear and his free hand over the other ear. He was listening intently. Looked over at Tomlin and Debro.

"Roger, two guys here, Chief. Look like marines, what's left of them. Over."

Another mortar round, then another, then nothing.

"Say again, Chief. Over."

More mortars.

"Chief, you sure?"

The radio operator was shaking his head. At the front of the temple fragmentation grenades exploded, followed by renewed firing, now everyone on full auto.

"Copy, Chief. Wait one. Over."

Leaning out Tomlin could see a blur of bodies shifting and darting. One side preparing to attack, or maybe both. Probably both. The NVA officer running the show up front would know he couldn't just sit fat, dumb and happy behind broken walls with Phantoms and Cobras on call around the city and marines swarming everywhere. The marines couldn't just hunker behind broken concrete and hope another beehive of NVA wasn't about to turn the corner. And everybody wishing they'd never met in the first place.

Tomlin realized someone was talking to him. His thoughts were coming in slow motion. He looked up to see the radio operator moving away from him.

"Christ on crutches," he heard the second man say. "We got to move. Hell is going on?"

The radio operator ignored the man and spoke into the handset. "Chief, Ground One. These guys are all shot up. Got one near dead, other one's on his way, deaf with a head wound bleeding bad. They can't travel, Chief. Over."

The radio operator listened, gaze fixed on the ground.

"What? Say again. Over."

The reply came back.

"Wait one. Over."

He turned to Tomlin. "Marine, what's your name and outfit?"

That much Tomlin knew. He told him and the radio operator relayed the information. Pause as the radio operator listened. He leaned forward and looked in the direction of the street behind the temple.

"Roger that, Icon Nine. There is a clearing there but this area is too hot, repeat, *too hot*, got more ground fire up front again, mortars raining and boatloads of NVA moving to join up. Six, advise a net extraction at mark Yellow-Seven as planned. Sir, we got *mission orders*. All respect, Chief, two tours I have not seen a good deed go unpunished. Over."

Another pause. Tomlin was focused now, listening.

"Roger that, Six. Wait one. Over."

"Fuck's goin on?" the second American asked again. "He comin or not?"

The radio operator moved closer to Tomlin.

"Marine, can you travel?" He was nearly shouting.

"Hell, I can hear you, you aint gotta scream."

"Can you travel or not?"

"Depends on where." Tomlin was just being honest.

"Maybe a hundred yards down the street, behind the temple. Chief has this crazy notion he wants to medevac you and your buddy. Can you move yes or no?"

Tomlin looked at Debro, head to one side, chest rising and falling in quick little beats. The half-smile still there, blood trickling at one corner, enjoying that cowboy movie.

LT said twenty minutes. In five city blocks he could get held up for hours. And then there was getting Debro to a doctor. Not much more a corpsman in the field could do for him. That was more time. Moving him might kill him, but Debro didn't have the twenty minutes, from the looks of it. Sunday or not, no taxi was coming.

"I can carry this guy back to Texas if I need to," Tomlin said. "Let's go."

"Shit," the second man said. "War's *fuckin* with the business." Took a last drag on a cigarette. Flicked it behind him.

The radio operator said, "All right then. Listen up. We get a pause in these mortars we move out separate. Me and my man first, get up there and set up some security for the chief, you and your man behind us. We get set and I see you coming I'll bring the bird in. You stop moving, get shot, go to cover or hell breaks loose any other way, I'm aborting this whole circus and you're on your own. Nothing personal, marine, but you are no part of my mission orders. If you're coming, those are the terms."

"Fair enough," Tomlin said. "You get out there, watch those rooftops. You got a sniper up there killed them others. Least you had a sniper before the chopper unloaded."

"Chief told me."

Tomlin didn't think he looked worried enough. Tomlin was damn worried, chopper or no chopper.

Without a word between them the two Americans moved to the abrupt end of the low wall, where in all likelihood there had been a doorway at one time. The radio operator surveyed the street and after a moment spoke to his team member, pointing, Tomlin knew, in the direction of any likely sniper positions on what was left of the building roofs. They checked their weapons and changed out magazines.

"Debro."

Tomlin shook Debro gently.

"Debro." He lifted Debro's head.

"Debro, listen up, you hear me?"

Debro's eyes came open, glassed over. "What?"

"We're movin. A hundred yards and a medevac."

Debro closed his eyes again.

"Hundred yards, hundred miles. Don't make no difference."

His face was graying and he breathed in little fits, pools of blood still bubbling at the corners of his mouth.

"Then you best keep your hush puppies on," Tomlin said.

When he looked up the two Americans were gone. He picked up Debro's rifle. Realized he couldn't carry two rifles and Debro too. Tomlin dropped the magazine from Debro's rifle, picked it up and stored it in his own flak jacket. Ejected the round from the chamber and left it where it lay. Broke the rifle into receivers, tore the bolt and charging handle out and flung everything in different directions.

Now that he was moving, Tomlin felt better. Something going on with his vision out at distance. Not important. World flicking from Technicolor to black and white and back again, waves of electricity surging over him. Not important. A hundred yards and airborne. Important.

Tomlin laid his rifle on the low wall, took Debro's arm and raised it over his own shoulder and settled his body beside Debro's. He leaned forward, pulled and fought his way to his feet.

"*Shee-it!*" Debro cried out. He half-rose onto Tomlin's back.

"Way I feel," Tomlin replied, struggling to keep his balance. "And you gotta use them boots, help keep this caravan movin."

Too late, Tomlin looked at Debro's bandoleer of ammo a thousand miles away on the ground. No recovering it now. *Not thinking again. What gets you killed.* Tomlin stumbled forward and nearly fell picking up his rifle from the wall. He shuffled into the open, side-stepping the bodies of the two dead NVA. Incredible that all the rifle fire remained concentrated up front, the two of them easy targets in the open.

Debro hummed his tune. Tomlin could feel the vibrations. Then he was saying something. Tomlin kept moving, trying to ignore Debro so he could concentrate on staying upright, but Debro kept talking. Wouldn't shut up. Exasperated, Tomlin finally stopped. Absurd he couldn't listen and walk at the same time, but there it was. And both of them in the middle of the street, begging for an AK round.

Debro raised and twisted his head, spoke in ragged little fits with his mouth next to Tomlin's ear.

"You…the *damndest* driver…I ever hitch a ride with."

He coughed and spat. Blood and spittle landed along Tomlin's neck. Inside the monosyllabic cough Tomlin sensed a peal of laughter and Debro managed an unbroken sentence.

"Aint we two half-ass grunts there ever was any?"

"Two halves make a fuckin whole," Tomlin said. "And I'm too busy to listen to any more bitchin. Keep them boots movin." He stumbled forward again.

Thirty yards along, Tomlin heard the mortar tubes. A deep bass, deep and distant. 82s. Big boys. Fly higher, fall longer. Kill faster.

He couldn't spare the strength it took to care. Forced himself not to count the rounds, what was the point? Thought about turning back, but where to? Mortars and snipers, two little flies in the ointment, *cry if I want to*. He kept moving.

Bad luck about the mortar tubes.

Bad luck all around.

What the hell, it wasn't raining. Unless you counted mortar rounds.

It occurred to him, shuffling on and waiting for the first round to fall, that maybe he had seriously erred in decoding the firefight at the front of the temple.

Maybe not just a squad or platoon of NVA up there. Maybe more like a company. Maybe something bigger, temporarily stalled by a chance encounter with a handful of marines. Maybe what LT said. A last offensive of some kind, some desperate surge in the full light of day, a strategy built around its own annihilation.

Maybe the temple just a set of coordinates on a general route of advance.

And maybe that stray mortar round early on not so stray. Maybe NVA gunners pre-plotting the back of the temple, just walking the NVA along a predetermined route of attack. Along pencil marks on a map in some plan cooked up in some below-ground enemy bunker back Then. Pencil marks on an NVA map riding parallel to pencil marks on LT's map. Pencil marks on separate maps that converged, merged and became a single corridor on both maps. Unfortunately the same corridor he and Debro happened to be stumbling along in Now. *Two roads*, thought Tomlin. *Two roads converged in a yellow Asian wood. I took the one more or less traveled by and what difference does it make?*

Immediately there was Phineas in some eighteen-wheeler, rolling across the Midwest, sun-burned arm half out a lowered window, Phineas saying, *Maybe a division of General Giap's finest on their way up your backside right now. How's that for a difference?*

Nobody knew nothing. Between nobody and nothing, though, Life. Lots of Maybes. Maybe you do, maybe you don't. Maybe you'll make it, maybe you won't. Life. Another epiphany passed him by.

And where were the Phantoms? Tomlin went for a dip in a pool of sweet bitterness. All the forward observers in the city, not a *damn one* calls in some hotshot rocket jockey to take a chance on a column of NVA? Sure, maybe some friendlies *a tiny bit* in harm's way, but not like any of *their* neighbors' kids would get accidentally wasted in a good cause. No memories of bright, red-cheeked faces to disturb *their* sleep with, especially since a Phantom driver never knew who the hell was down there anyway, and besides, even if the evening news did scandalize the officers' club momentarily, right there handy to conscience was mankind's forever excuse for its killing ways, beautifully encased in the golden, the exculpatory phrase *fortunes of war* spoken so solemnly beneath such furrowed brows years and years later, the beautiful hackneyed years later, all the years of their lives later, over cocktails and putting greens, funeral services and the aging bodies of bored mistresses, three words *fortunes of war*, falling from creviced faces like shovels for a soldier's grave. In light of all this, how come some dead-eye airborne surgeon just a bit south of cynicism couldn't slip on down out of the ether and plant a few five hundred pounders *surgically* inside a parade of pith helmets? Surgically enough for government work, anyway?

Tomlin kept stumbling along, conjuring up rationale for a nice, neat, precision air strike when it counted most. It seemed like a weakness, and maybe he'd been wandering in the wilderness too long, but was it so wrong to petition a little help from above? Then of course Phineas weighed in: *What, a little whining to occupy the mind? Easy to pray for air support when you aint the poor bastard dodging five hundred pound bombs from your own jets.*

Okay, Tomlin replied, ready to change yet another subject. *Sorry I brought it up.*

Phineas laughing as he soared away: *Shoe fits, wear it, cowboy. Cross fits, bear it.*

Talking to Phineas like he was talking to God. For all he knew neither of them existed.

And still the mortars hadn't landed. Even bigger mortar rounds, launched from further away, expelled from fatter tubes dragged along by larger units, battalion- and regiment-sized units, ought to have been on the ground by then. Like his thoughts, Time seemed to have gone elastic.

Tomlin let the voices in his head go and concentrated on the sure thing of his simple plan. One, less than a hundred yards of open ground. Two, put Debro on a bird. That was it. One, Two. Three, well, Three was later: Hot chow in a mess hall, a dozen squad members all talking at once. The head of the table empty, where Phineas used to sit.

Well, *once* there'd been a dozen, a long time ago.

How long *did* it take a mortar round to fall? Had he really heard the tubes? Had Time lost connection to Now? And he to Time?

Debro's weight had grown surprisingly light, but his own feet responded erratically, as though free to wander in genetic anarchy. He heard more humming, the same tune, and again thought it was Debro, but damn if it wasn't him doing the humming now. Then the words of the song infiltrated the screen of his mind, riding just above the tune, which seemed to be coming from an orchestra at the foot of a stage. A bouncing red ball and he was singing along with Mitch: *It's my party and I'll cry if I wa-ant to...*

The first mortar round landed far ahead of them, in the intersection formed by another two streets converging at the end of the courtyard. Right where the Huey would be looking to set down. Hornets of white-hot, invisible metal sang by his ear, one of them whispering his name as it too sought union with his skull. The closest cover was too far way, and if he went to ground now as he almost reflexively did at the explosion, he doubted he could ever get himself and Debro up again and moving, and the two spooks would leave them where they lay.

What was going on with his legs?

But Tomlin kept moving, and humming. Couldn't get the tune out of his head, which annoyed him: *...cry if I want to, cry if I want to...* He gave up trying. If he had to listen to voices…he changed the channel and switched to Debro's, a quantum improvement.

In front of him, at the first explosion, the two Americans had gone on their faces instinctively, long enough to look around and decide against changing course. They rose almost as instinctively and as far as Tomlin could tell, seemed to be headed for a section of wrecked courtyard wall, maybe just for cover, maybe to set up security for the chopper. He wasn't ever going to know for sure, because the Americans disappeared from view in a thunderclap of two, three, then four mortar strikes. He watched numbly as one of them pirouetted into the air inside a geyser of shrapnel and smoke, body separated at the waist, one arm detached and spinning free, traced in red as it cartwheeled across the sky.

But what fixed Tomlin's attention was a flickering wheel of light, something squat and metallic, flung from the funnel of high explosive and pegged by centrifugal force inside a container he recognized as the one attached to the chest of one of the Americans. The container hit the ground and the bright object flew from inside it. As it turned and bounced, an exquisite streak of molten red pulsed once and vanished. The object came to a halt in a pile of rubble and sparkled in a shaft of rays from low westering sunlight.

Tomlin couldn't tear his eyes from it, or keep his legs from changing course in its direction as he kept dragging Debro onward.

Little wonder it beckoned to him.

The world on its easel was a dreary palette of muted death. In savage strokes butchered from Van Gogh's tortured soul, the reaper had mingled the grays of shattered walls and stalking skies with the blacks of high explosives, then smeared the image with blood clot reds and gangrenous browns from shredded brick and wood. Using his scythe for a brush he had paused only long enough to daub in the rotted yellow of week old corpses before crowding it all onto the shrinking canvas of Tomlin's life. And into this bleak vista tumbled the richest, brightest vortex of purest color he had ever seen, drawing him to it as if he were falling, as if anything that glittered so brightly in so much gloom must be the source of gravity, or at the very least pointed the way to salvation.

With nowhere else to go, mortars in the air and some semblance of cover in the mound of rubble where it lay, Tomlin headed for the still, tiny color at the heart of the chaos, bearing Debro along, grateful for anything like a beacon.

13

WE THERE YET, WHITE BOY? Debro's voice could have come from the void.

Tomlin only heard it because Debro's mouth was right there by Tomlin's ear. He would have told Debro about his fascination with the bright object, but recent events had erased that obsession. Moments earlier he had stumbled, lost his balance and slammed into the street hard, Debro's weight grinding his face into the cobblestones. His rage got the better of helplessness, and somehow he had fought his way to the surface of a black sea and gotten both of them up and moving again, Debro crying out in agony. He knew he couldn't do it a second time, and Debro wouldn't survive it anyway.

Tomlin also knew they were both dead men walking, though to be accurate Tomlin was doing all the walking, Debro contributing only the occasional shuffle. There would be no bird now, no god lowered in on some cushion of air from some off-stage bellows. They had no radio and if they did, no way to provide even the pitiful fire support of two rifles to bring the chopper in. Tomlin remembered his conversation with the Huey pilot, felt sorry he couldn't issue an apology. The pilot deserved one, whoever he was, spook or mercenary or like him and Debro just more cannon fodder following orders.

He scolded his legs along; he couldn't tell if they responded. He seemed to have one basic forward speed. His lungs burned. Air everywhere but not a drop to drink.

Here it was Debro with the sucking chest wound, and his own lungs about to collapse.

"We there yet, white boy?"

Tomlin found enough wind to speak. "We gonna find us some cover. Wait on the cavalry in case that bird's runnin behind schedule."

Debro answered in that voice a thousand miles away. "Be good to lay still a while. Shock absorbers in this rig aint for damn."

The humming again, the words unspoken but traveling alongside. Tomlin couldn't tell anymore who was doing it, him or Debro. Didn't matter, though he would have preferred hearing the sweet music of cavalry bugles approaching.

...it's my party and I'll cry if I want to...

A symphony of AK fire rose up at the front of the temple and drowned out the last players in the ensemble of M16s. The AKs were soloing. Figuring that one out brought Tomlin out of a tunnel. Some of the fog lifted. Hell was the matter with him?

He *focused.* And where the hell was he going? Radio or no radio, hope or no hope, they needed to make that LZ if only on the theory it represented a last known destination. It was a Plan.

Always good to arrive. Always good to have a Plan.

He looked up, surprised to see how far along they had gotten. They were at the back of the temple, ten yards from the intersection of what high explosive had rendered barely recognizable as a street, but where conceivably, in this best of all possible worlds, a Huey could make a landing. They were exactly where they needed to be, only there was no radio, no one alive to provide security and no chopper besides.

Behind him he heard a sudden gaggle of angry voices, summoning him fully to Now, banishing any lingering memory of brightly colored objects. What he had known would be coming as soon as the mortars got turned off. Whose absence since then was a complete mystery. With as much urgency as he could bring to bear on the situation, he looked around for cover. He calculated through his mist that he and Debro had about ten seconds to live unless he found that cover.

Not far from where he trudged along, artillery, or mortars, or air strikes, or each in turn or altogether, had blown trenches in the cobblestone street, leaving mounds of debris along their sides. The holes not deep enough and the mounds not high enough but the beggars and choosers thing applied. If you were generous in your definition, it was cover.

He dragged himself forward the last few yards and as he twisted to ease Debro to the ground, the shouting in Vietnamese grew strident. After the mortars went quiet and the contest for the front of the temple was decided, heads were going to swivel in other directions. And *someone* with an AK-47 in his hands was bound to notice the spectacle of two Americans strolling up the street.

Within that ten seconds a first burst of rifle fire sent .30 caliber rounds overhead and into the hulk of the building behind. Tomlin was surprised to hear glass breaking. A window in the city with unbroken glass? More surprised to find himself in no worse condition. Well, sometimes people saw you, fired, *then* aimed. Praise the Lord. All part of the Plan.

Tomlin did his best, but it was a rough landing for Debro inside the narrow crater. Debro's stream of cursing was delivered half-unconsciously. Tomlin was impressed nevertheless. This was hopeful.

"Change doin you good," he said.

He tugged Debro forward as gently as he could, trying to convince himself he was making him more comfortable. But a bed of rocks was a bed of rocks.

"Hell kinda place this is?" Debro complaining, another good sign.

"Accommodations aint all they could be," Tomlin admitted.

A retinal flash of light distracted him and he looked up. Above Debro, three yards away in the rubble and half buried in cobblestone, something stared at him. Something alien, something shiny. But something he vaguely recognized. *I know you,* he thought. An alien, yes, but one he'd seen before. An alien that had a name. But what? His slow-motion memory embarked on its sluggish search. The bright object had its own face, and it wasn't staring at him so much as watching impassively, poised at a slight angle in the mound of debris. It was a face capable of boundless serenity, above sorrow or pathos, beyond the travail of the final human experience, to which, Tomlin knew, his own life was drawing near. But it was not the face of a mere idol. The craftsman's art had breathed life into the little statue. It lived, and watched him now. But who was it?

Memory returned from somewhere with the answer. *Gautama. Gautama Sakyamuni. Siddhartha. He Who has Attained His Goal. The Enlightened One.* How had he remembered this? Some college class long since forgotten? Billy had desperately wanted to introduce him to the new ways of thinking, what he called the *counterculture*. Had his brother dragged him to some hippy commune in the days after boot camp?

No more answers arrived.

But it was undeniably Buddha. Infinitely Buddha. Fancy that.

Fresh out of boot camp, Tomlin had turned a street corner in San Diego and nearly bumped into a television star from his youth, a black-and-white cowboy who rode a golden horse. Even without his hat, Fortune's glow emanated from the cowboy's perfect white smile and washed over him ever so briefly. Now here, ten thousand miles away on a different street entirely, Tomlin felt that same emanation in the presence of another celebrity.

It was in the nature of a Buddha to be serene; Tomlin wasn't surprised about that. But such a Buddha as this one he had never seen. Neither had he ever owned gold, but he knew gold when he saw it. A fiery light shimmered and moved behind the facets of a ruby set in the Buddha's forehead, as though a magical creature inside strove restlessly to find its way out. As if Buddha had worked himself free of a dead man's container and the designs of wicked men. As if Buddha called on Tomlin to be free as well. To awaken. To listen. And to *look*.

Tomlin *looked*. Maybe he looked for the first time in his life. In his existence.

Was this why he had come to this strange land, in this strange role? Why he had left her, when his whole being tugged in her direction?

To *look*? To be *made* to look?

He looked again.

Precious metal, precious stones.

Yes, he saw it now. Could it be? That? Yes, clearly it could. *Elementary*.

If he'd had the strength, he would have slapped his forehead. Hard.

Why else had there been a Huey, willing to violate every known tactical protocol and hover over a firefight?

Why else had there been mission orders?

Mission orders for him and Debro.

For the five spooks from the chopper.

For the forward observers that ensured the Phantoms kept boycotting the temple.

For the chopper pilot.

For LT.

Who's they?

Who the hell really knows?

Hell we do when we get there?

Someone tells me I tell you.

Mission orders that left too many dead men to count. And him and Debro in the middle of it.

All for what?

For the same thing as always.

For the same carrion call that launched armies from Attila to Armageddon, from Marathon to the Blitzkrieg.

For money.

For gold.

For a blood-red stone.

For rich linen, chrome-gilt cars, columns on the portico, the spark of diamonds on every wife and mistress. Beds on seven continents, thrones in every corner of earth, entrance to every chamber of base sensation.

For the gluttony of power.

For domination.

For the favors of warm and wet flesh stolen from youth and virtue and corrupted inside the pasty folds of ghouls paid to stand on podiums and preach the gospel of the undead.

For wealth like a river sprung from captive nations. Nations full of souls chained in bondage by the great pretenders in universities and their babble about brains and synapses and *the beast within*. Preached from their classrooms and auditoriums, years on end, high school to med school. *The beast within,* always the message. *Man the animal and his beast within.*

When all the beasts there were, were themselves. *Out there.* Stalking.

Stalking a world of crafted darkness, full of illusions forged over eons to reduce the soul, to harness its own labor to its own doom, to set it wandering inside a mist greater than the mist in Tomlin's head, lost and battered by a reek and gas emanating across the centuries from the sulfurous dens of moneylenders and orators, priests in bloody robes, bureaucracies high and low, craven creatures tending their rats and mazes. A cavalcade of con men, flaunting their wax tablets and Gothic rumblings, their newsprint and air waves, the messenger shape-shifting over the years, the message always the same: *The Beast Within.*

The scroll above this world reading *All hope abandon, ye who enter here.*

And once entered, leading where?

To hands eternally on the purses and rifles to the heads of working cattle, sheep to be sheared, children to be torn from their mothers. To be groomed for killing. To be taught to hate.

And to be prepared.

For War.

And more War.

And more War.

War without end Amen.

Until the Domination was complete.

Tomlin stared at Buddha. Buddha stared back. For all its beguiling presence, wasn't it just a foot-high Buddha made of gold and colored rock? A centuries-old idol stolen from its own safe house?

Or had Buddha alive in his golden flesh and shimmering eye come to test him? To ask *And what say ye now? Is there any war left to wage but on ignorance? Will ye enter this maze too, or will ye find your way back?*

But which way led inside, which way back?

Tomlin could revise his opinions downward about his fellow man, but what was the point? To enshrine *their* victory inside him? To agree that every man's reflection in a mirror matched their own pocked bestiality and that all should be happy in their hatreds and lusts? That all men were animals and some had longer teeth and the rest were meat for the table, that like themselves he should shut down even to the last spark his own soul, his own hand extinguishing the flame?

No.

That way led inside.

For every spook, a Mother Teresa. For every killing moon under every starless night, candlelight spilling from an opened door. For every half-ass war, a Lance Corporal Maurice Debro walking a sick child in the night.

For every faithless politician, a day of reckoning.

For every enemy of Man, a hanging judge.

He would find his way back. Fight his way back. Wherever that road took him, whatever he had to do, this last time.

And Debro was coming with him.

"Where my rifle," Debro said.

Tomlin wondered if Debro spoke for the masses. But Debro said no more and lay still in his narrow trench.

Work to do. Buddha was on his own.

Tomlin leaned over and tested Debro's battle dressing one more time. It was loose, but the plastic underneath seemed to be doing the job, keeping Debro's air in and the world's air out. Not satisfied, Tomlin undid the knot and as quickly as he could guide his clumsy fingers in such intricate work, snugged the battle dressing. Debro winced.

"Sorry, man," he said. "Hell was I thinkin, I'd make a lousy doctor anyway."

There was more excitement up the street. Tomlin picked up his rifle and looked through a small valley in the low wall of debris above him. A dozen NVA soldiers were making their way forward, running in diagonal spurts. Behind these Tomlin could see pith helmets bobbing like corks in an ocean. He saw the closest soldier, maybe fifty yards away, raise his rifle. Tomlin fired instinctively, without aiming, then dropped back down as a volley of return fire erupted, the rounds hitting low and skipping overhead.

Tomlin rolled onto his back. Took a deep breath. Despite himself and knowing better, considered his mortality. Saw that leading nowhere fast.

Exhaled.

Well all right.

14

HE ROLLED BACK OVER with the M16 on full auto, thrust it overhead and emptied a full magazine blind into the street. Flopped back down, dumped the empty magazine without bothering to recover it and replaced it with another one from his bandoleer. Went to semi-auto, looked out again and shot the closest soldier, twenty-five yards away. The rest of the NVA scattered to cover. Tomlin pulled the remaining magazines from the bandoleer and stacked the six of them in two piles, making a third stack with the partially empty ones from his flak jacket pouch. He wasn't impressed with what he saw, or the thoughtlessness that had left Debro's ammo behind and hadn't put Debro back in his flak jacket when there'd been the chance.

Not thinking, that's what gets you killed.

Others, too.

He slipped out of his empty bandoleer and wriggled out of his own flak jacket, dumping his two remaining hand grenades into the rubble, a grenade from each of the jacket's pouches. Somehow in the general confusion he had lost the grenades he carried in his trouser pockets. The Queen of Hearts gone too. He would not think of her. Of having lost the card. Having lost her. *When you come home we'll make a little Prince.* He would not think of her. Best to sever Now from memory. He fumbled Debro's .45 out of its holster along with a spare magazine, then spread the flak jacket lengthwise over Debro's chest and legs. Debro stared past him into the sky and didn't speak.

When it started back up the AK fire went mad. Rounds beat against the flimsy wall of their formless protective mound. It rained fragments of brick and mortar. Tomlin watched the fog roll in again, helpless to repel it. *Your switchboard just gone all to hell.* A crippling tiredness suddenly riddled him. Debro was motioning to him. When Tomlin found the reserves to lean over, Debro reached up and grabbed him and with surprising strength pulled Tomlin's face close to his own. Tomlin dropped his head onto a bank of cobblestone gravel and fought off the misting. Debro spoke into his ear to be heard over the gunfire.

"You wanna know why I been pissed at you since day one?"

Through the fog Tomlin recognized the mood. Debro was Debro, in the back of a chopper headed home, ignoring a war to remark on the flight of a bird or stretched out in a shallow grave dying from a chest wound and a regiment of pissed-off NVA coming to bury him.

"Got it figured out yet?" Debro spat the words and more blood too, wracked by a spasm of coughing. When he could breathe again he said, "Fuckin drownin."

"Maybe you should shut up."

"Fuck shut up, white boy."

Tomlin felt Debro's blood running hot along his own neck. The AK fire had turned intermittent, like last popcorn kernels over flame. He was too tired to move or say anything else, too tired to argue that Debro should save his strength, too tired to think, too tired to do anything except let Debro do what Debro was going to do. Which was what Debro always did anyway. And what he was going to do now was talk.

"You coulda been back in the world suckin on that silver spoon you born with. Now aint that right. Nice tight college deferment. *Poundin* them sweet coeds till your male member black and blue or almighty God don't love a sinner. Aint that right. Coulda skated all the days of your natural life, bouncin them grandchildren on country club knees, life of Riley spreadin out front of you like you Moses crossin the Red Sea. Ain't that right. But nossir, you *asked* for this shit. You walked into the showroom sellin this half-ass war and put hard money down on a bill a goods worse'n a broke-down Ford got water in the gas. Sold your half-ass soul for *what*? A ditch in a road, that's what. A ditch that aint gonna be deep enough to keep the crows from pickin your bones clean."

Debro rolled his head and spat again, still holding onto Tomlin's bloody fatigue shirt.

"But that aint it, man. That aint it at all. Aint even *close*. Anyone got sent to this hellhole fucked it up his own way and it don't matter a *damn* how. What matters is you here. That's all. Aint nothin else mean *nothin*." He tugged Tomlin's shirt and Tomlin felt his head sliding across the rubble, as though it rode a cheap ride in an amusement park. "I knew you a marked man day I saw you. Lamb to the slaughter. Been doin my best, man, what I could do, keep your half-ass alive. I come back on this second tour, find you still breathin, that a shock, man. Somehow you stayed alive without your D-brother watchin over you. I know right then I musta taught you somethin. I figure I been doin okay, been makin the grade. Till this mornin. And that moon. That *goddamn* moon." He pulled harder on Tomlin's shirt, the desperation more in the tug than in the words. "Look at me." Tomlin couldn't. "Look at me." Debro tugged harder.

Tomlin found the strength to lift his head, in time to see a tear darken the dust under Debro's eyelash. The effect was startling, like watching life being fitted for a death mask.

Debro said, "*White boy, how I'm gonna save you now?*"

Tomlin dropped his face back into dirt and gravel. Of course. Debro's cross was Tomlin's. It was anyone's. The world's. The same cross any poor bastard anywhere picked up the day he was born, whether he ever found out about it or not. Most didn't, and crucified the ones who did.

Debro fell quiet. For a moment in the middle of war there was just the sound of the two of them breathing.

Tomlin said, to be saying something, "That's some weak sentimental shit, man. That shit get you sent back to boot camp."

The grip on his shirt went slack. When Debro spoke again the voice was small and the anger gone.

"No gas left to stay pissed at you, white boy. Runnin on empty. I be seein you the other side."

Tomlin pushed his face out of the debris. He shook his head until the pain cleared the mist. No one like Debro to put things in perspective.

"If that's where we're headed, damn straight you will."

"Oh, we headed there all right."

"Maybe," Tomlin said. "But it aint rainin."

"Aint rainin." Debro let go of him entirely. Repeated in disbelief, "White boy says it aint rainin."

Tomlin pushed his upper body along the mound until he could see the world around him again. No sign of anyone. No pith helmets. Where the hell were they? He realized they couldn't know it was just him and Debro. Just two half-ass grunts. Always cautious, the infantry, whether green troops or seasoned veterans. Especially the veterans. Seeing enemy behind every window, every broken wall, every shadow. Never in any hurry to die, the infantry. The scourge of officers.

Quiet again. The sound of other battle blocks, miles, oceans away. From the corner of his eye Tomlin saw colors. Familiar colors. Orange, red, black. Colors of his heart.

She was less than a few yards away, just outside the other end of the crater. Lying there looking at him. Beside one of the grenades that must have fallen out of his pocket at the same time. Just out of reach. Out where he knew they were watching, waiting, getting ready.

But only a yard or so, really.

If he left her there, she'd understand.

But he didn't need understanding. He needed her.

"Be right back," he said.

Tomlin had to manage turning himself around without bobbing up like a cork. He crawled to the edge of the trench and looked over again. The place was empty as a tomb. The firing and explosions in the background, in some other world entirely. Maybe everyone went home. Retreated. Or just got tired of it. Changed their minds. *What if they gave a war and no one came?*

He could reach her, return to cover in seconds. Quick like a bunny, lucky like a rabbit's foot.

He threw himself over the edge and pulled his way forward. Only everything he grabbed was loose rubble and slid toward him. Only he barely moved, but moved enough to be exposed. He kicked himself forward and was only a few hand lengths away when they saw him. *Let me count the AKs* he thought as rounds impacted to the left and right and whispered overhead. The grenade lying beside the card leapt and caromed against thin air, hit multiple times.

Why the image would come to him he didn't know, but as he reached for his Queen he thought of Michelangelo on his scaffold, his weary artist's hands, the assistants below anxiously awaiting the master's needs, vying with each other to anticipate them. He thought of his own hand right there in front of him, stretching for his Queen like Adam's for God and at no greater distance from his Queen than Adam's finger from God the card exploded. In the same instant his arm recoiled from a kick by a mule or had God's own finger reached out and flicked him hard? Just walloped him? Why would God do that? He was slammed back behind cover. From a curled up ball he looked at his left hand, at the thumb hanging by its hinge of skin, the bone separated like a piano key smashed by a hammer. An ivory stub, bald and bewildered above a ragged red hole in wet flesh. He dug the filthy cloth from his pocket and wrapped it around his hand, clutching the ends of the cloth in a fist. The arm was numb from the wrist to the elbow. When the pain blew through the shock he jerked his body straight and shoved his head into the rubble, held his breath and waited it out.

Finally he looked up and looked around. Debro had raised his head and was watching him. The better to read his mind.

"Woman's nothin but trouble in this world," Debro said. Laid his head back down and closed his eyes.

Tomlin could breathe again.

"Only trouble worth havin, D-brother."

Debro didn't answer, or move. The AKs had stopped firing. By now the NVA would be picking their way forward.

Work left to do.

Tomlin twisted himself around, picked up Debro's .45 and made sure Debro's hand wrapped firmly around the stocks. Laid the spare magazine by Debro's head.

"I'll be nearby makin noise," he said.

Tomlin belly-crawled the few feet to his small pile of ammunition, took one of the grenades and rolled onto his back. He removed the cloth from his hand. The remains of the thumb went with the cloth. Not that much bleeding, dirt already at work. Nature's styptic. But what blood there was made his grip slippery. Tomlin pulled the pin and threw the grenade, watched it wobble away in a direction of its own. Clumsy handling wet grenades without a thumb. Followed it with the second grenade, clumsy again, then grabbed his rifle, even worse with no thumb to secure the forend. *Aint I the ballerina,* he thought. When the first grenade exploded he rose to his waist and dropped the rifle barrel inside the little depression in the debris. Kept his head down until the second grenade detonated seconds later. An NVA soldier twenty yards away tried to burrow himself deeper into the ground, then couldn't resist looking around. Tomlin shot him. Another soldier in the open picked himself up and ran toward the courtyard wall. Tomlin's first shot missed; on the second one the man fell as though deflated. The rest of the NVA went back to cover.

In a moment the return fire would be massive and uncontestable. All he could do was keep them snugged behind walls and buildings. As he counted down on his supply of ammo. When he looked down the other letter was in his good hand. Funny how instrumental two thumbs were in opening a letter. He finally used his teeth to rip it open, like some savage regressed to a natural state.

A pith helmet eased from behind the courtyard wall. Still holding the letter now smeared with blood and dirt Tomlin put the post of his M16's front sight a foot below the helmet and centered it in the blurred circle of his rear sight. He took the slack out of the trigger and waited.

The pith helmet revealed a face, then a uniform. Tomlin increased the pressure on the trigger, watched the front sight and somehow managed to be surprised when the shot broke. The soldier stumbled forward, spun and pitched onto the cobblestone, just as another soldier, bayonet fixed on his AK-47, broke from cover twenty yards away and with a war cry charged straight toward Tomlin firing as he ran. For a moment Tomlin felt confused. Then there was Debro's voice in his head, Debro as always bringing the light: *Sometimes a man just wanna get it over with.*

Tomlin resisted the urge to flick over to full auto, ignored the impact of rounds to either side of him and shot the soldier twice at ten yards.

Tomlin recognized the whistles. Three quick blasts, in succession, and there came a small army, rising as if lifted on invisible rope. From behind walls and mounds of rubble, from alleyways and from the temple, they came toward him running and screaming.

O *happy morning.*

"Talk later, babe," he said aloud, and shoved the envelope back into his pocket.

Tomlin concentrated on the lead soldiers, who were doing all the shooting. AK rounds that passed his head on ricochet whined, those passing overhead untouched by the ground made a sucking sound where air and vacuum collided. Tomlin kept firing, missing and hitting, shot the weapon empty. Dumped that magazine and fumbled with a fresh one. The whistling continued. By the time Tomlin sent the bolt home on his third magazine Debro had dragged himself from the trench and was stretched alongside the pile of debris firing the .45 with one hand, holding his battle dressing in place with the other and clutching the spare magazine in his teeth.

That cowboy movie gotta be The Alamo, Tomlin thought, and reached for another magazine to reload and so brought his face close to Debro's.

"It rainin now," Debro said, so weakly Tomlin couldn't be sure he heard it.

On the other hand, maybe he was the one doing the talking.

15

IN A HEARTBEAT, TOMLIN WENT from a stubborn denial of the possibility of his own violent death to a clear and certain understanding of its imminence. Reactions vary in such circumstances. Tomlin's heartbeat of recognition brought the simplest response, rooted firmly in Now.

Not while I have a single round left.

Tomlin emptied a full magazine in under two seconds, dumped the magazine, slapped in another and repeated the process. His hand hurt, in an afterthought kind of way. He couldn't tell if he was hitting anything, but people were paying attention. The wave of soldiers faltered and hesitated but kept coming under the lash of the whistle. Another magazine and two soldiers fell. He reloaded with the last full magazine. There were still a couple of partially loaded magazines, but Tomlin revised his own last manifesto. *Partials excluded*. Might need them on the other side.

Plus he was in a hurry.

The new and correct Plan came to him. A simple plan. The only plan.

The way back.

Debro's only hope was capture. There'd be no quarter if Tomlin kept resisting the obvious.

Elementary.

Tomlin stood, and intended to remain standing.

The simplest plan possible, under the circumstances.

Debro would understand.

Sometimes a man just wanna get it over with.

For a single split instant, before he pressed the M16's trigger to the rear and held it back, in the space between two adjoining notes of the NVA whistle, it seemed to him that the waves of charging North Vietnamese soldiers paused, not in shock or disbelief, but in momentary suspicion of a trick Tomlin was about to play on them.

Or, paused as though by some unseen hand changing the projection speed of the movie Debro kept talking about seeing, images on a mind, images Tomlin had assigned to illusion attendant a mortal wound.

If so, then the whole world was mortally wounded. The whole world was an audience in front of a movie screen. He heard bells. Bells in his head. Phineas, a last time, from on high: *Send not to find, brother. They are a-tolling for thee. Thou art a-toning for them. And how's this for an afternoon matinee?*

The space between whistle notes ended. Just as Tomlin's rifle loosed the final two seconds of his life in eighteen rounds of 5.56 caliber full metal jacket, he realized he had in fact played a trick on the NVA. *Damn clever of me*—only—add another damn—damned if he knew what it was.

His rifle was a hell of a lot louder than it should be.

And how come there were bullet strikes out there, pith helmets flying and bodies falling, when looking down he could damn well see his own bolt locked back uselessly on an empty magazine? Just before you died, or when you were dead but didn't know it yet, did the projector run amok? And make that much noise?

Two stories up, the Huey slid over him, machine guns working, muzzle flash just beginning to be visible in the late afternoon. The chopper had come in at speed low over the rooftops, cleared the buildings behind Tomlin and flared momentarily, then dropped nose low for a clear field of fire. The NVA soldiers, transfixed by Tomlin's farewell performance and deafened by the dueling of fully automatic rifles, were caught fully off guard. It took deadly seconds of reorientation before their predicament came clear.

Both door gunners had targets in the open. On the first pass they dropped a half-dozen enemy soldiers apiece. Dozens more raced for cover and scattered into buildings and behind remnants of walls. In the space of their confusion the Huey threw its nose around and rushed back up the street, flared into a turn and settled toward the ground, guns resuming the instant the turn was completed.

Tomlin was still standing up. He struggled through some reorienting himself. The sting of dust particles on his bare arms from the blast of chopper blades and the sight of the Huey's skids rocking downward brought him around. The chopper slid further sideways and toward the ground, the tips of its rotors flailing in orbit less than a yard from the courtyard wall.

The door gunners fired without pause. Tomlin expected to see M-60 barrels melting in front of his eyes. Behind the gunner, the crew chief was yelling and pointing at him, then at Debro, trying to rouse Tomlin into action. Before the skids hit the ground the crew chief had yanked out his intercom cable, grabbed an M16 and leapt from the chopper.

Tomlin got his legs working, slung his rifle and had Debro in the air before the crew chief arrived. The crew chief took Debro on one side while Tomlin worked Debro's other arm around his own shoulder. Debro still had the .45 in one hand and was saying something Tomlin couldn't hear. As they lurched along Tomlin managed to get the pistol's thumb safety on before firmly removing the .45 from Debro's grip. Debro gave up the pistol reluctantly.

"You grunts look like hell!" the crew chief yelled at him, grinning below dark glasses, ludicrous in his short sleeves and spaceman's helmet.

Tomlin wanted to say, but couldn't find the strength: *Aint we two half-ass grunts there ever was any?* Instead Debro said into his ear, "Where my rifle?"

This time, even over rotors, turbines and machine gun fire, Tomlin heard him. But at that instant he stumbled. In recovering his balance he happened to turn his head toward the ruin of buildings behind him and so ignored Debro in an instantaneous rearrangement of life priorities. In fact, he dropped his shoulder so that Debro's arm slipped away and he freed himself of Debro's weight. Debro cried out but Tomlin paid him no attention.

It was just late enough in the afternoon that he couldn't make out its features, but there was undeniably a silhouette on the rooftop behind them, at the exact location where nothing should be alive.

Fuck.

Said aloud.

Passionately.

As meaningfully as he had ever uttered a single syllable.

Tomlin's dismay was equal parts recognition and admiration. The silhouette stood near the broken remains of that same high window like a defiant flag. It was definitely a woman, its slender form distinguishable despite being inserted inside a man's uniform. Her hair was long and loose, nearly to her waist, tossing a little in the breeze that must have been skipping along the rooftops, or possibly moving in the distant reaches of the chopper's rotor wash. In these respects she may have looked lovely, but Tomlin was filled with the urgent need to kill her. Part of the silhouette included the Chinese B-40 rocket launcher at her shoulder.

Tomlin, the Doubly Cursed.

He had shot the last fresh, fully loaded magazine for his M16 empty, on full auto, expecting to go out in a blaze of glory. When he hadn't, in his bewilderment at the chopper's arrival, he had neglected—it was neglect, pure and simple—to reload the rifle with one of the scorned partially loaded magazines at his feet.

Not thinking, that's what gets you killed.

So, Curse Number One, he was carrying an empty rifle, and therefore his considerable skill with it, at the most critical moment in his career as a rifleman, was academic.

Curse Number two, although he now also carried Debro's loaded pistol, and although the shot was difficult, it wasn't impossible—less than forty yards—Tomlin was an awful pistol shot, a fact which Debro had pointed out when Tomlin was considering adding one to his gear. *You might as well hump a rock around, white boy. You aint hitting nothin with a pistol.* And that was with two good hands and both thumbs.

There was no time for anything but a single shot, from the handiest weapon.

No time to drop Debro, wrestle the crew chief's rifle away from him and bring it to bear on the silhouette on the rooftop.

Or to get the crew chief's attention, point out the woman, somehow deftly signal to him that he, not Tomlin, needed to do the shooting.

Too much complication to compress into the one or two remaining motions that fate, or chance, or the scriptwriter, Almighty or no, had allotted.

All this Tomlin computed in the instant he spotted the silhouette, an instant that bore total dominion over Now. So he had dropped Debro and let his own rifle slip from his shoulder at the same time, the crew chief stumbling under Debro's full weight. The rotor wash sent fragments of broken street scuttling along the cobblestone and a wave of solid dust slamming into Tomlin's body. A chaos of sound from engine, rotors and machine guns engulfed him. Dust threatened to blind him. He blinked his eyes open and leaned against the rotor wash as though against a solid wall while the chopper unloaded to its front, oblivious of its peril from behind, and the NVA responded with the counterpoint of its own frenzied whistling and AK fire.

Tomlin brought the pistol up in both hands. Ignored the vacuums that formed near his head as AK rounds sucked holes in the air. Ignored the throbbing from the hole in his left hand and the confusion in his remaining thumb as it sought its absent mate. Ignored the wind's attack on his eyes. Ignored everything but the front sight of the pistol.

And worked the trigger.

Felt like a surgeon operating with a meat hook in a storm.

And fired.

Saw the round hit low and left at the woman's feet.

All she wrote, was his only thought.

He watched blankly as the trail of the RPG passed overhead and straight into the virtual solid plane of the Huey's rotors, detonating amidships above the chopper's magnesium shell.

Tomlin was half-blinded by the explosion before it deafened him. The crew chief and Debro cried out a cappella and collapsed on one another. In the concussive wave enhanced by the disintegrating rotors, Tomlin windmilled his arms like a caricature and fought to keep his feet but was driven backward, beyond the trench where Debro had lain. Shrapnel from the chopper's rotors vibrated past, pricking his legs, reaching hungrily for his flesh in the same way a sword blade had found and transfixed the crew chief and Debro.

The force of the RPG buckled the ship beneath the point of explosion, dropping the tail assembly and tail rotor of the craft into the street, where the tail blades exploded into shrapnel and twisted the Huey onto its side. The main rotor hub spun in agonized death throes, jack hammering the street and kicking missiles of cobblestone into the air. When the rotor hub froze, the chopper rolled longitudinally with the hub's final thrust, as if to go onto its roof, but the overruling hand of gravity brought it back onto its side, where it rocked, shuddered, groaned and lay still. Air and fluid escaping from hydraulic lines hissed like spirits departing. Smaller bits of metal struck as far away as the temple walls.

The briefest silence and then a celebration of renewed AK fire.

Only part of him worked. He was numb from the waist down. Gray sky returned as Tomlin forced an eye to open. The second eye had gone absent without leave, taking with it the world's third dimension. But Debro was still there, the Debro he carried inside him, singing loud and clear.

...cry if I want to, cry if I want to...

16

SOMEHOW TOMLIN STILL HELD DEBRO'S .45. As he rolled onto one side he heard the jubilant cries of North Vietnamese soldiers approaching, knew they were closer than they sounded. He rose on an elbow and looked past his feet at the chopper. A door gunner in a cocked flight helmet hung backwards from his waist, half outside the wreckage. Blood dripped from his extended arm into a spreading pool beneath him. As Tomlin watched, two NVA soldiers rushed up and began firing into the dead gunner's body and into the pilots' compartment, oblivious of Tomlin leveling the .45. He hit the first one but missed the second one—*just no damn good with a pistol*— and as the soldier whirled in search of his comrade's shooter, he broadened Tomlin's target with a frontal chest view. This time Tomlin didn't miss. The slide on the .45 locked back.

Now he didn't have a single round left. Mission accomplished after all.

...cry if I want to...

Tomlin flipped the .45 away and lay back down, as empty as the pistol. A sparrow flew overhead, one more captive soul fleeing the city.

He couldn't move his legs and had no desire to inspect them. One side of his body was numb, shoulder to waist. Sensation engulfed him and receded in waves. Underlying all was a feeling of being watched. He managed to roll over on his side and look behind him. From the mist he stared again into the impassive gaze of the golden Buddha, the jewel in its forehead still flickering. Again Tomlin thought of a creature inside the stone, desperately seeking a way out.

Like Tomlin, only with better prospects.

He found himself feeling friendly toward the beautiful, intricately featured little statue.

Not Buddha's fault if men craved gold and stones and killed themselves and each other for them.

And the holy men that guarded them.

And anyone else that got in the way.

Beneath his headdress Buddha stared back dispassionately, but not unkindly. Maybe just as surprised, in a Buddha sort of way, to find himself face to face with Tomlin.

"What?" Tomlin said.

Or thought he said.

"What aint the first time?"

Buddha had no reply. Nothing. Just that exquisite face, looking back at him. The pulsing red stone. Pulsing like he could feel his own heart pulsing.

Aint this a dyin swan, Tomlin confided to his new friend, unsure if he were speaking or thinking. Buddha wouldn't need words anyway. *We meet up in eternity, I buy you a beer. Maybe brew our own. Call our brand Nirvana.*

He was malarial after all. Hallucinating. Talking to a statue now. But the statue's lips had moved. Well, maybe they hadn't. But Buddha had spoken. Or maybe he hadn't. Of course he hadn't. It was a statue. Or maybe it wasn't.

Not much question about the light fading, though.

The voices had always been in the background, but as dead as he might look to be, the voices knew dead men didn't make noise, much less talk. The voices marched closer and swelled angrily. He was kicked onto his back. Black eyes beneath pith helmets appeared in the gray mist, sweat running from faces distorted in rage, and from on high came a choir of screaming to keep time with the kicking. A rifle butt smashed the side of his face, crushed a cheekbone, flooded the sky with color. When the gray returned and only half the world with it he recognized the three edges of a Chinese AK-47's grooved bayonet, *the better to stick you with, my dear,* rising and falling in front of his face. The ritual of preparation. *Everyone, on three now…One…Two-oo…*, its proprietor yelling and scolding, restraining the final thrust until the hour's lecture was concluded.

Christ, not through the eye. Tomlin was ready to negotiate.

...you would cry too...

Above the din, a shrill, barked voice. A string of what were clearly orders. Another kick that jarred the pain loose from the ether below his waist, sending him to the brink of unconsciousness. More barking. No more kicks. Tomlin looked again. Only one eye would focus. The bayonet withdrew, hovered, jabbed again in frustration, withdrew fully.

Cavalry?

A woman revealed her promise in the dress she wore. She threw bright colors around her when she moved, rose from the thorns of man's thickets like a flower. She gave him his pleasure, bore his children, softened his killing logic with her kisses and tears. She wore perfumes to mask the open sewers of his world, repaired what she could of the damage he inflicted. A woman healed, nurtured, practiced mercy.

Not this woman.

Not cavalry.

Tomlin raced for sanctuary, couldn't resist any longer. He had not chosen where the end would come, but when it came he chose to be with her.

His Queen of Hearts.

He thought of her now. How they would awaken in each other's arms inside the lost darkness after midnight, bodies already straining together, wordlessly falling into another round of endless lovemaking. How, when the morning sunlight finally opened his eyes, love streamed from the smile that greeted him in the memory of love spent and then widened to receive the five-year-old entering their room and burrowing into the sheets. The child this woman brought with her, this perfect woman's child that filled the perfect hole in him left by a hole in the ground distant years before. The three of them lying in bed like a single naked body.

A woman was a loom, weaving a magic foreign to the coarser sex.

Not this woman.

The face was pretty on one side, the eye dark, bold, accusing; the other side was torn and disfigured, the barren eye socket closed, eyelids seamed together, scars like swollen tributaries running across the purple cheek and down the neck, emptying into the folds of the uniform collar. The dark eye regarded him with the cold hatred he conceived reserved for the bitterest of enemies. Under that gaze he wondered for a moment how he could ever have wronged her, or anyone, so completely, then turned from the thought, recognizing even *in extremis* when he stood yet again at the head of a trail that led nowhere.

...if it happened to-ooo you...

She was a lecturer too, though she seemed to be talking to someone else. He could barely hear her, but he much preferred Debro's lovely falsetto anyway.

Things were receding.

And then for a startling moment, beneath the strident, ebbing soundtrack of the woman's voice, the world was a series of tableaux, edged in crystalline clarity, pulsating in and out of his vision like a slow motion montage in a darkened theater. Was this the final reel in Debro's movie?

Tomlin watched like a member of any audience.

The ruined street behind the woman.

The People's Army behind cover and peering out tentatively or standing ungainly in the open, ignoring the cries of the wounded, AK-47s dangling in paused and nervous confusion.

The temple with gaping holes in its walls from a rain of mortars and machine guns, flames licking the shattered multiple roofs, timbers askew. Grounds once untouched now a shambles.

Debro and the crew chief mingled in death, both impaled by the same fragment of rotor blade, a wreckage of chopper behind them, its lone remaining skid crushed and mangled but still attached to the undercarriage.

The door gunner half in, half out of the chopper in his upside-down pose, mouth open, arm and finger extended, as if seen correctly in a mirror that reversed his image he would be standing and yelling, pointing to the sky where he belonged, and to the moon, where he didn't.

Debro's interval moon.

A moon punctured and torn by the temple's jagged roofline. A moon of two faces, one bright, one dark. One never seen but written in history as the face ascendant. Another to wear garlands and dance beneath. One face to raise the tides, one to send children trembling beneath their beds. One face to break the dominion of night and another to lay soldiers in their graves. A moon for harvest, a moon for massacre. A moon of steel entwined with protoplasm and blood and love and locked therewith in mortal combat the outcome of which alone under the stars might permit children to leave their hiding places or whimper alone where they lay alone until the stars turned dark.

A moon old as time.

A full metal moon.

And as though a featured guest announced during end credits, there sat Buddha.

All these years the calm in his mien mistaken for indifference. Twenty-five Buddhas in the eons of Earth, it was said, and one on his way. Well, maybe not true of every generation, but surely *this* Buddha cared.

Fade to black.

Gravity closed his eyes, pulled and urged him downwards, away from his body, to wherever gravity led. Tomlin held on more from instinct than opposition.

And didn't Buddha die, too? And hadn't Gautama's west coast protégé, his prodigal son Jesus, hadn't even the son of God been shown the door without due regard for pedigree?

Well, there was good company in which to sink.

...cry if I want to, cry if I want to...

Speaking of Jesus, was that himself making all the noise, calling out His name? Hadn't he promised his mother? *...and never in the name of my Heavenly Father...* a fiery pain below the waist, his fingers exploring, wet and red...and still Debro singing the little white girl tune, a pipeline into his head, as though maybe Debro weren't *really* gone...

...you would cry too if it happened to-ooo you...

...yes, Debro again, the part of Debro that was part of him, that *was* him, the other half of his half-ass soul. His half of that combined soul in transit, the other half already on the other side.

He felt himself nudged back into time, lifted by some cold, pointed upstream of solid air. He opened his eyes. Or was it just one eye? Half of him remained in darkness.

The nudging came from the barrel of a rifle. It ran from below his chin, along his cheek and up to his forehead. Turned his head from side to side. A barrel, he noted professionally, all business now, that belonged to a Dragunov, not a Kalashnikov. A sniper's rifle, a rapier for killing coolly from a distance, not the scrappy, dog-fighting bludgeon that was the AK.

Same caliber, heavier round, more power.

All the better to drop kick you into eternity.

At the extremity of the rifle, the woman's ravaged face and savage voice was done barking. Lecture over. *School's out*. Time for recess. Eternal recess.

Tomlin's head lay where the woman had left it, turned to the side. Buddha met his sinking gaze. The little god before him on his throne of rubble commanded him again to look. Tomlin resisted. Buddha insisted. Oh *all right*. He forced himself to lift his head again, the weight almost insurmountable. Looked into the sky, certain now he looked through just one eye. Patches of blue exultant above the grey. Mustered the little focus he had left on the hood of the Dragunov's front sight, its tiny iron rod sheltered queenlike inside, inches away from his eyelids. A Dragunov, a sniper's rifle, but one without a telescopic sight, something he'd never heard of. Like a race car without wheels, a jet without wings. But this was the shooter from the window, he was sure of it.

Damn fine shooting with iron sights.

Truth was Truth, for you or against you.

Better to say the truth.

Better to say that truth was truth though lies would spare you hell.

Better to serve in a narrow trench than reign in hell though hell beckoned behind marble doors.

As Buddha insisted, he *looked*. His eye faded, but his vision sharpened. He could hear nothing near him, yet the morning's soundtrack clamored from the mists. He listened, as though hearing for the first time, as though also so commanded. It was the voice of the measured, surgical instrument above the hyena baying of frenzied AKs. Not a bolt action, though Debro could not be faulted for thinking so. A Dragunov. Like the one above him. Yes, he heard it now. The Dragunov an instrument maybe but less an instrument's voice than a cough from a sickroom. Or a deranged incandescent microsecond howling inside bedlam's riot.

Yes, he saw it now. From the front row for the director's cut. Only change the last scene in the movie, viewed in a single heartbeat, begun in the diastole, done in the systole, because from the heart came all the living and dying the building and tearing down all the caressing all the dismembering and what did not come from the heart good or bad was worthless no matter good or bad that it was and the last scene was the heart itself opened and dissected and contained in that single heartbeat: *His whole squad prostrate, flattened under the heel of this half-mutant, their faces turned, inspected, abandoned*. As she had turned his. Looking for what? Victory beyond mere annihilation? The mark of the Beast? Or did she seek in war's handiwork a time before war, before death and loss and grief, as though all that evil had done more evil could now reverse?

And had his mission orders left her, or her people, any other recourse?

Nobody knows nothin.

But the fog was lifting.

He knew something.

Truth was Truth, for you or against you.

Ask the spooks from the temple. The murdered and vaporized monk. The NVA inside the temple, in the street, at the front of the courtyard. The dead marines sprawled there too. Ask Bender, Swede, Doc, the nameless kid from the Midwest. How many before? How many to follow?

And how many yet to be sent to ground by this same harpy, spared only by the abyss of his own incompetence?

The camera pans across the final scene. It moves past Bender curled up in the rubble as though tired of waiting and so sleeping. Past Doc motionless behind his stub of wall. Swede silent now in the crater where he'd dragged the nameless guy, his journey traced in red across stone and dirt, the one visible hand clenched around a stone's ragged geometry as though a man falling, a man slowing his descent to the inevitable unknown uncertain, a man wily no more. Past Tomlin denying the obvious. Past Debro's ghost saying, *Them's dead I said was dead...*

And always above the fury, as the camera moves, the lone sick-room cough of the Dragunov. An incandescent howling. Above the fury. Under the moon.

Where the camera stops, the temple burns. There are no more credits. The screen goes black, leaving only the moon. Ascendant. The house lights do not come up.

The swell of Tomlin's anger goes unheeded by the smashed machinery of his body. With all his remaining concentration he strains to adjust the vision of his one eye higher but his focus falls far short of heaven and finds instead the finger, the slight, remorseless, blood-stained woman's finger, tightening on the trigger.

Debro sings on.

...it's my party and I'll cry if I want to...

In even a fleeting moment much can be said, but Tomlin chooses honesty and brevity, a path he hopes his new friend the little Buddha will approve.

The path he had come here to find. The path that leads home.

As for the rest of the world, what were they going to do, bust him and send him to Nam?

...cry if I want to, cry if I want to...

"This is *my* party, *bitch,*" he says. *"And I don't want to."*

II

Bich Linh

17

THE HELICOPTER WAS GONE. Furious with herself, Bich Linh unburied her body from the debris, crawled over and pulled the rocket launcher from beneath the rubble. A litany of self-abuse moved with her: Slut, reptile, village cur, traitor, *bitch*.

Would there were food in my body that I might smear shit from my bowels into my face and hair.

She rebuked herself until she ran out of words. Then she dragged herself up, raised the rocket launcher and removed the round from the tube and poured dust, bits of mortar and shredded fragments of roof timbers from the barrel. She sat on the broken remains of the window ledge with her head on the launcher's open end and proceeded to beat her head against its edges. The perpetual scabs from the ruined side of her face opened up and bled a river into the barrel.

She could take the Makarov from its holster and shoot herself, but she didn't deserve to die. Hadn't Fate refused to take her? There must be Americans alive somewhere in the street below. It was not their stupidity that kept them from looking behind them and seeing her sitting there, a duck on a pond. It was *karma*, the wheel of her life spinning along the predetermined course of her soul's sinfulness, the destiny reserved for one so pitiful, so vile, so *detestable* as she. In a final fury she flailed her forehead against the launcher yet again, this time so hard she almost knocked herself out and nearly fell from the window ledge into the street.

After this blow she felt better.

The crime had been losing the gamble she'd taken. She had easily killed the first two Americans from the temple, the second as he foolishly ran to the aid of the first. Then the remaining one with the strange little transmitter strapped to his chest must have radioed the helicopter to return and support his own misguided tactic of rescuing his dead comrades. It amused Linh that Americans in battle scurried to recover dead or dying bodies, as if piecing together broken and empty vessels could restore a life or do more than prolong its agony. When the radioman left shelter, Linh added him to her afternoon tally and then immediately afterwards raced down the ladder to her quarters to exchange her Dragunov for the rocket launcher. Returning to the window, she watched the strange helicopter with no insignia hover behind the highest roof of the temple, sections of it bobbing in and out of sight, keeping the bulk of its carcass and its crew hidden from her view and weapons. The pilot must be insane, trading fire with ground troops from a fixed position. She appealed to any spirits angered by the holy city's destruction: *Blow this metal beast away from the roof and into the open.*

For a moment it appeared her prayers had been answered. The helicopter drifted backward and away from the temple, concentrating its fire into the plaza, exposing itself fully to view. But such a shot it presented was no sure thing. It was within the launcher's range, but at its extremity. *Curse the miserliness of instructors.* Though she had paid keen attention to the exact regimen of aiming and firing the B40, she was given no chance in her training to launch a single round at a target. The crude sights did not inspire her with confidence. She had no experience to draw from, and no certainty in such a long first shot. Training had made her impeccable with only one specific weapon, and the Dragunov was not the RPG.

She had just the one round, the round that sat inside the launcher. The gamble was two-fold. She could fire, and possibly miss, but possibly not. Or, she could wait and gamble instead that when the helicopter flew off, which it had to do at any moment to survive the ground fire it was taking, it would come toward her, into a range where even without experience she knew she could not fail. The gamble was lost if the helicopter flew away from her, to the west, instead of southerly to her position. She placed skill high above the prospect of fortune. Her skill with the B40 was lacking, and her nature inclined her to gamble and wait for a sure hit rather than gamble and fire prematurely.

Of course, with the Dragunov she could kill one or two of the American crew members she could see clearly enough as the helicopter swerved into and out of view. She also knew that if the pilot spotted her after she fired the RPG, and she missed, she would be no match for its weaponry.

Childishly, though, the real reason was *she wanted to use the B40.* She wanted the big-game trophy, the way some men wanted to kill a tiger.

Add the sin of pride to her crime.

She had lost the gamble in an unexpected way. The helicopter turned from the plaza below and indeed had come toward her. Behind the remaining unbroken column supporting her window, she suppressed her elation and calmly reviewed the readiness of the weapon. Round properly engaged in the slender tube, sights positioned and undamaged, safety off. But in the instant before she took her first step into the window opening to shoot her tiger, the tiger clawed back.

Both machine guns came at her. Not fear, but surprise, and anger, overtook her. How had the pilot found her? The gunners were not sweeping the rooftops with cautionary fire. *They were coming after her.*

She was trapped. Streams of 7 mm bullets chiseled and pulverized the mortar, stone and remaining wood timbers of her sanctuary. What was left of the frame above the window disintegrated. Rounds ricocheted and careened against bits of walls and ceiling. Spent bullets fell spinning and bouncing onto the floor, their tips distorted and glowing like fireflies. The building vibrated from the fury of the pounding. Vibrations oscillated wasted bullets into small piles, sending the rounds pulsing and climbing over each other only to separate and regroup as though by alternating poles of magnetism.

Pressed to the wall she could feel the steel rain hammering behind her, harvesting dust from the slight plaster and stone façade, dutifully seeking her flesh. Inside a chaos of crumbling façade, hammering of steel against stone and burning wood splinters ignited by tracer rounds, she slid to the floor and stretched herself out along the base of the wall. It was like being inside a deafening monsoon, only not rain but dust and kernels of rock were drowning her.

Or the dust and stone were the shallows of the ford at her crossing of the river, and a lone machine gun was firing from a river bank no more distant from her than the chopper above, sweeping the river clean of life.

Against the wall where she lay, water rose to her knees and serpents rose from the dust, gorging themselves on her children.

Sorrow wracked her but no tears flow from ruined ducts. The steel rain kept up for an eternity.

When the storm finally moved away the serpents left too, leaving her to drown inside a grave of debris, a childless widow a second time.

18

AND SO SHE HAD RISEN FROM THE GRAVE and into her fit of self-loathing. After this passed, she moved away from the building edge and out of the line of fire from the street below. The taste of her own blood restored her. The pitiful Americans had done their best and failed. The Americans, not her, had gambled and lost. They had sent the symbol of their deviltry, their flying wasps, against her and the people, and she, and hordes of the people, still lived to kill more of them.

And she remained alive to pursue the dream that drove her on: Find the Hated One.

Her rage spent, she stanched the bleeding in her face with a dirty rag and then used it to wipe dust from the rocket launcher. The housing around the firing mechanism was dented, but not critically. The tube looked intact. She removed, cleaned the rocket and snugged it firmly back into place. Neither assault by American helicopter nor her own wrathful head appeared to have ruined the B40.

There was an explosion outside, and she peered around what remained of the window sill's support. Smoke rolled from the ground floor windows near the back of the temple. Two Americans crossed the street at a full run, leaping over the body of a dead monk and disappearing into the hulk of a building. Opportunity eluded her. Her Dragunov remained in the small room below where she had exchanged it for the launcher. Time enough for these two later; she knew where they were. Exhausted, she turned her back to the street and slid lightly against the precarious window framing to the rubble-covered floor. She leaned back against the fragmented remains of the wall and closed the one eye. Sleep beckoned but Linh gave herself up to memory instead...

...She ran lightly again across highland trails, leaping little rain-gorged streams easily, bounding from boulders strewn along her path, youthful in her vengeance. The rare Russian-made SKS rode at her waist and balanced perfectly in the sling she'd fashioned from the belt of a dead GI. Governed by the loose allegiances of a citizen-soldier, she worked rice fields in the days, honed her skills at setting explosives at dusk and dawn, and hunted Americans when the moon rose.

Everything changed when the northerners arrived, reeking of industrialized conceit and self-righteousness. They traveled in unsmiling little groups, brandishing their pamphlets and proselytizing the countryside, so that no farmer could tend his crops without interference. She scorned their speeches and constant harping to enlist her into their army. Had it not been for her fascination with Thanh, who served in a platoon of riflemen accompanying the political officers as security, she would soon have moved away from the valley and its pitiful rice crop and found a home in the mountains, living happily enough on meager resources. Her dallying proved to be a mistake, and by the time she saw her error it was too late. The political officers stopped using words and employed conscription. To break her continued truculence, she was accused of collaboration and taken with a dozen others to a camp further north, there to be re-educated along party lines. Her scarred face spared her the fate of her more nubile companions during the journey, but once at her destination the camp commandant took to arranging beatings for her when she consistently spurned and mocked him during his clumsy advances.

Weighing her options, and to escape the grotesque pawing of her superior officer, Linh volunteered for service in a forming corps of sappers to learn *advanced techniques of national defense*. The recruiters for the new unit promptly pronounced her rehabilitation complete and transferred her to another camp, where she quickly came to feel grateful that the attentions of the lecherous old commandant had motivated her new choice of service. She had found her spiritual home, a church where the religion was war and the catechism was remorseless killing. In the inner sanctum of this new religion many of the instructor-priests were Russian and Chinese, their frocks crisp and starched, heads shaved and boots polished, imparting their mysteries with cold ritual through equally cold interpreters.

No neophyte in the history of Tibet matched Linh for devotion.

She excelled in all parts of the catechism. Driven by dedicated study, the skills came easily. She learned in stages taught at a frenetic pace, eating little and sleeping less, at first gaining aptitude in the common weaponry of both sides, then in silent killing with garrote and blade. Next came infiltration under all circumstances, whether barbed or razor wire, wooden barricade, dug trench, minefield, cleared perimeter or highland rain forest, in the grey of dawn, under full moon or in pitch-black night.

There was the gospel of the fashioning and placement of undetectable explosives, then the art of disguise and evading detection inside rural populations of non-combatant southerners and finally—to the great pleasure of her mind—she was given a course in *The People's Art of Persuasion*. The Russians were the acknowledged high priests of this skill. She protested, but was not allowed to keep any of her instructional materials. These lessons in torture she particularly committed to memory.

On the day of her graduation in Advanced Techniques, receiving honors as Exceptional Student Patriot for her prowess, an officer arrived and stood at the back of the tent, rain falling and cascading along its sides, waiting quietly and impatiently. When the brief ceremonies were over, he approached and introduced himself brusquely before congratulating her on being chosen to learn *The Way of the Long Rifle*—stiffly handing her the pamphlet—under the tutelage of the army's finest instructor, whom he had no qualms revealing as himself.

"Colonel Trung, why me?" Linh asked unhappily, since such a further assignment would serve only to extend her unwelcome stay in the north.

"You were honored as Exceptional Student. I have no choice but to select you," the Colonel said and turned on his heel, leaving behind him a scowling soldier, who motioned for her to follow. She was led to the back of a military truck without windows and transported for hours on rough roads, the first time she had ever ridden in an automobile. The sensation of forward motion while she remained seated reinforced her impression of the future being stolen from her.

The truck stopped at dusk in hard rain and she was shown to a roadside shelter also without windows, where she lay in a sagging cot between two soldiers who coughed fitfully through the night, in turns, as if her presence interrupted a single illness shared between them. At some hour before daybreak she was awakened and put into another vehicle and driven away. It was still raining, but by the time they came to a stop the sun was out and the skies were clearing. The driver got out and splashed through mud-red streams in the road to lower the tailgate. He motioned her forward and at the driver's door she could see another soldier inside. The driver handed her a small package, pointed to a trail and told her she would find a small camp at the trail's end, to remain there and wait for instructions. He climbed back inside the vehicle.

"A woman," the driver said to his companion. "A whole army and they choose a woman."

"Who shot her face off?" she heard the second soldier say as they drove away.

At the end of the trail she found a one-room hut at the edge of what was clearly a firing range. There was a small stove with pot and pan and bundles of sticks for cooking. A cot with straw rick. Windows open to the air. Inside the package from the driver were separate containers of rice and dried fish, matches and propaganda. She started a fire with the propaganda leaflets and prepared her evening meal with water from a tiny ribbon of nearby brook.

No one came that day. Her first night in the hut it rained again, so hard the wooden steps at the front door washed away. One corner of the roof leaked furiously. In the morning Colonel Trung appeared in a strange contraption he used a strange word for, *Geep*, a vehicle captured from the Americans. He stood in the mud where the steps had been and handed her a brand new Russian Dragunov still wrapped in grease paper, along with a kit of tools bundled inside oilcloth. He gave her a well-worn manual of care and operation and told her he expected her to be able to field strip and reassemble her rifle in the dark by nightfall or her education would be summarily ended. The manual was in Cyrillic, with no translation. Inside the manual was a crudely drawn map with directions to his quarters.

Hours before dusk, while the sun still hovered high enough to draw steam from the soggy earth, Bich Linh presented herself at his small wooden office two kilometers distant, in a larger training compound, Dragunov in hand. She knocked on his door and stepped back down the steps. When he appeared in the doorway, she knelt and spread the grease cloth on the ground, placed the Dragunov on top of it and stood up. From a uniform pocket she pulled out a black cloth and blindfolded herself, then knelt again behind the rifle and proceeded to take it apart. As she disassembled it she barked out the name of each part in a voice thick with insolence, until the rifle lay in pieces neatly arrayed on the cloth. Just as perfunctorily, she picked up each part and again called out its name while assembling the rifle without fumble or wasted motion. Snapping the bolt once to the rear to show its mechanical readiness, she laid the rifle down, stood and removed the blindfold. Colonel Trung looked up from his watch, having apparently timed her actions.

"Acceptable," he said. "We start at sunrise." He went inside and closed the door behind him.

19

FOR A FURTHER NINE DAYS LINH TRAINED as the single pupil of the unsmiling crew-cut officer, who spoke not one word of disparagement or encouragement during its entirety. If he resented concentrating his skills on a woman he did not show it. If he admired anything about her progress he was silent.

Throughout the first days the Colonel would not speak of telescopic devices. He trained her exclusively in the use of the Dragunov's iron sights. Making her notations in a crude pulp-paper shooting log, she learned how to translate the distance her shots impacted from the target's center into adjustments to the windage and elevation controls of her rifle's sights. She improved rapidly. By the third day she was shooting consistently into the center circle out to five hundred meters. The Colonel himself never fired a shot, but instructed by weaving himself into and out of traditional shooting positions with a grace that belied his graying temples: standing, kneeling, squatting, three variants of sitting and two of prone. Bich Linh matched her instructor in showing no emotion but had to suppress her own admiration and wonderment at his agility.

In even and noncommittal tones the Colonel corrected, coaxed and cajoled Bich Linh's fully matured but undisciplined suppleness into contortions that yet seemed natural to her. These, combined with her constant sight adjustments, produced steady, incremental increases in accuracy. At the end of each day she stood before him and opened the bolt of the Dragunov to display its empty chamber. The Colonel nodded, returned to his vehicle and clacked away, trailing wisps of blue smoke, releasing her to the solitude of falling dusk.

Linh might as well have been in a dream. Delivered to the range in the back of a covered truck, she had no idea what part of the North she was in. The distant mountain range was unfamiliar. There were odors of plant life she didn't recognize, two or three bird calls she couldn't identify. It occurred to her that disorientation might have been part of the Colonel's plan. Possibly they thought she might try to escape if she knew where she was. Escape where? She knew where, and put Thanh out of her mind.

On the first night of her training, in the small oilcloth kit of tools, Linh found cleaning rods and bristles, a bottle of powder solvent, rough cotton rags for cutting bore swaths and a tube of lubricating oil. Included were a crude adjusting tool for front and rear sights, a slender metal file, and a short but sturdy steel rod, four-sided and bent at one end ninety degrees. The operator's manual did not discuss the file or the rod. When she asked the Colonel their purpose he said irritably, "If you need them, you will discover such things for yourself."

The Colonel grew voluble only when discussing technique. Under his tutelage she grew fond of the heavy and ungainly Dragunov and marveled at its great advantage in accuracy over her SKS. When she mentioned this to Colonel Trung, he made a dismissive noise and told her the Simonov was a rifle for peasants to serve their masters and the Dragunov a weapon with which to overthrow them.

Linh quickly found the Dragunov's weakness. It was by design a sniper's rifle, intended for use with telescopic sights. The rifle's front sight seemed to be an afterthought in concept and manufacture, consisting of a simple upright post inside a protective hood. At six hundred meters the post was so much larger than the bullseye of her target that she had difficulty judging when the base of the bullseye was precisely aligned above the tip of the post. Also, examining the post under her oil lamp at night, she realized its tip had been indifferently flattened in the manufacturing process and left pitted with tiny gouges and irregularities. These defects played further tricks on her eye as it searched intently for a precise point of focus on the front sight. By the second day she was complaining about this to the Colonel.

"If you are meant to overthrow masters, you will solve these petty problems," the Colonel said, as always never concealing his irritation.

That night Linh put aside her ballistic charts and moved closer to the stove for warmth. She opened the cleaning kit in its oilcloth binder, removed the metal file from inside and held it beneath the oil lamp. It was about the length of a common nail file, but heavier in gauge and narrower. It was fine-toothed, clearly for finish work. She brought her Dragunov from the corner of the room and into the light. Outside her hut, a symphony of crickets and frogs played for her as she slipped the narrow file through the protective hood over the front sight and ran it successively and evenly along the sides of the post, stopping frequently to raise and sight the rifle in the flames of the open stove, adjudicating her progress, ensuring the post remained plumb against its base and of even width along its length. When she was done the post was little more than half of its original thickness, and her eye no longer detected burrs, gouges or other imperfections in its surfaces. Still not satisfied, but afraid she would whittle the post into oblivion seeking perfection, she laid the file and rifle aside.

She had forgotten to eat. Linh added water from the stream to her pan and warmed her meager evening meal indifferently, directly on the coals of the stove, unaccustomed to the peace that had settled over her. She ate the moistened rice with its bits of slightly rank fishhead and listened to the frogs and insects, contemplating without specifics, feeling the journey of her life from its birth through its current state, knowing its end likely to be at the hands of her enemies or the random whim of fortune, or both, whether tomorrow or in many years of tomorrows. A life disfigured, as her face was, as the front sight of her Dragunov had been. She opened her rude notebook and wrote on the possibility that she might one day show it to Thanh: *Any life is sorrow and imperfection, coarse and unpolished. The spark that burns inside it either discovers its own file or fails to, and if found uses it or not, and so determines its own fate.*

I will overthrow all masters, beginning with myself.

Still sitting, she took her rifle again and held it between her knees, pointed at her heart, the post of the front sight a hard silhouette against the fire in the stove. With three quick strikes she attacked the post's top edge, turned the rifle around and sighted into the flames. Better. She repeated the process. The final touch was a series of single strokes, angled downward with the rifle now pointing away from her, her fingers restrained to keep from removing too much material. This gave the post a ramp away from her eye and the semblance of a blade's edge, a clean, crisp plane that, as she tested it, presented no argument to the fanatical insistence of her lone focusing eye.

Bich Linh owned no watch and had no idea of the time. The crickets and frogs had left the night's stage, taking the moon with them but leaving the stars. She moved from the stove's embers and sat timeless minutes longer in the open doorway, staring into the life in the heavens, where distant pinpoints glowed and winked and clustered in families and laughed and disputed among themselves in regions where serpents could not go. She traced a pattern of stars and saw a dragon, the magical beast of the gods and her country's guardian through ages lost in antiquity. When fatigue finally overtook her and she could watch no more, she turned from the sky and slept as she always did, with her thin mattress moved from its bamboo frame and placed in the door that opened to the east, so that the first rays of dawn would awaken her well before the arrival of Colonel Trung.

In the morning her first shots were completely off the target, to the consternation of the Colonel. Bich Linh said nothing and fired steadily through the mist burning from the carpet of low wild foliage between her and her target stand. By noon she had refigured the settings for all her distances, as required by the change of shape of the front sight. Before dusk of that evening, with Colonel Trung watching, she fired four rounds in succession at each of six targets, from one hundred to six hundred meters, one shot from each of four positions, standing, sitting (folded so far forward over her lower body she looked broken in half), kneeling and prone. The rifle was so heavy, and Linh so slight of build, that to shoot standing she leaned backwards and found balance in a position so contorted that the Colonel named it the "The Falling Tree". He frowned unnaturally when he said it and Linh thought he might be disguising a smile.

Leaving her at the firing line, the Colonel drove the American *geep* into the range to recover the five targets. Linh watched as he arrived at each target. At one hundred and two hundred meters, he tore them from the target frames without pause. At three hundred meters he took hold of the target and hesitated for a moment before removing it. At four hundred meters, he sat quietly in the jeep noticeably longer before reaching out and pulling the target down. At five hundred meters he parked at a distance too removed to be able to discern the bullet strikes and walked slowly to the target stand. He stood and stared at it without moving. He removed his cap and ran a hand over his head before replacing the cap and pulling the paper target from the stand to inspect it further. She saw his hand move over the target. At that distance she could not be sure, but it seemed to her he was counting the bullet holes, as if his fingers might discover some error in his eyes. At six hundred meters she observed the same ritual.

On returning he handed the targets to Bich Linh and before leaving said over the wheezing of his vehicle, "The groups could be tighter but we will move on. Chamber." Linh opened the bolt of her rifle. The Colonel glanced in its direction and drove away, leaving her to fan the blue smoke from her face.

Linh examined her targets. Each shot she had fired, four shots on each of the six targets, were dead center hits, including the standing shots at five and six hundred meters. She could have covered the holes on any target with her small clenched fist. Without any thought of her own prowess but neither with any regard for humility, her lone and novice eye knew it stared at something exceptional.

The Colonel, she had already noted, did not impress easily.

20

BY THE TIME THE SUN ROSE the next morning, Bich Linh had bathed herself in the stream at the back of her quarters and sat watching dawn swallow the last stars in the western sky. Colonel Trung clattered up in his *geep*, drowning out the stream's awakening orchestra of frogs and chorus of insects. He called for her to bring him the Dragunov. When she handed it to him he told her to study her charts and manual and wait for him, then lurched the vehicle forward in a wide circle and drove from the shooting range. He did not return until noon of the following day. Leaving her bowl of rice and fish unfinished, Linh met him where he had parked, on the firing line. The Colonel got out of the jeep, reached in the back and handed Linh the Dragunov. A slender telescopic sight rested above the receiver.

"This is the hammer of gods," the Colonel said. "Forged by a master working through the night, and the only one of its kind, entrusted to me—and you—alone. In all the world, comrade, and among our enemies, for all their wealth, there is none to equal it."

Linh briefly examined the rifle. It looked different, not just by the addition of the telescope. It was shorter. The barrel seemed new, its deep blue finish in contrast to the dull grey she remembered. Anxiously, she examined the front sight and noted the gunsmith had retained the same metal post she had laboriously sculpted. More likely, then, he had reworked the same barrel, leaving the sight intact. But would the iron sights still shoot true after so much alteration? The rifle felt lighter. Instinctively she ran the bolt and tested the trigger. The bolt moved as if gliding on a cushion of air, and the trigger broke quickly and cleanly, surprising her in the minimal effort it required.

"Forget the vaunted reputation of the factory Dragunov," the Colonel said. "Propaganda. At battlefield ranges, it suffices. The truth is most will not group satisfactorily beyond 800 meters. But its inner nature can be reached and brought to life. As has been done with the one you hold. It is no longer an ordinary rifle. It has no limits. Only the shooter has limits."

The Colonel took the rifle and impulsively shouldered it, aiming into the sky. As though rebuking himself, he quickly lowered it.

"This rifle was made for you, not me. The master lightened it, contoured it, reduced the length of the stock. Made it to fit you. At my request he made sure to respect the iron sights. Working all day and through the night, he did not spare his labors. Mother Russia would pay dearly to have this child of its factories back. But it is Russian no more. It is *dragon* now, and it is yours. With it you can shoot across oceans and bring America to its knees." He handed the rifle to Bich Linh. "Take the hammer. Let's begin."

Linh had seen the ocean only from the mountains, but over the following days, now training only with the telescope, her hammering quickly proved adequate out to one thousand meters.

In the evenings beneath a smoking oil lamp she kept her single eye focused on the new instruction manuals the Colonel had also given her: ballistic charts, bullet drop at succeeding distances, the effect of any day's wind or humidity, elevation of the shooter above or below the target. Tract after tract on marksmanship, especially the need for the motion of a trigger finger so imperceptible as to result in complete wonder at the instant of a rifle's firing. There were too many pamphlets, too much information: all the esoterics of precision shooting, most of the manuals advanced in minutiae and theory beyond her comprehension. Learning to use the iron sights she had felt relaxed and natural. With the addition of the telescopic sight came a vague uneasiness she could not identify, but under the Colonel's insistence she bent herself to the task of learning its fundamentals.

During the days of training with the telescopic sight, the Colonel often left his jeep parked and there were long, quiet walks to mark her targets at eight hundred, nine hundred and one thousand meters, walks made longer because the Colonel had a noticeable limp. He obviously took pains to disguise the fact, but the farther they walked the more apparent it became. He informed her coolly early on that the pace was his, not hers. Sometimes he lectured briefly, but mostly they walked in silence, the only sounds the stubble of foliage disturbed by their passing.

The vehicle he seemed to employ grudgingly, and usually only when his discomfort at walking grew more noticeable, or toward the end of the day, when darkness threatened. And possibly, she thought, because he was simply resentful of its mobility. It occurred to her as well, though she could not imagine why, that he was in no hurry to have her training end. He made it clear he did not believe in the spotting scope to determine a distance's final shots, refusing also to examine bullet strikes through her rifle's telescope. "A shooter must invest his entire being," the Colonel told her. "Including his legs."

Bich Linh used the silence in these walks to refresh her purpose. That purpose was not to master the skill of shooting from a distance, or even to grow yet more learned in the art of mayhem. It was certainly not to impress this cold slate of a man. Her purpose remained a simple one: to kill the enemy where she found them and the Hated One *when* she found him. The former, at least, she had done adequately enough as a simple rice worker in her southern valley, and she missed her freedom. She resolved to disentangle herself from the grip of the northern army, with its pompous airs and self-regard, as soon as she could.

She was not given to self-deceit, and did not pretend that her thoughts did not also center around the young northern conscript.

Thanh, with his quiet smile and bright eyes, who might no longer be there if she did not return soon to insist on his remaining at any cost. The prospect of returning to find him gone caused a small panic to rise inside her.

One afternoon Colonel Trung put her through her paces out to seven hundred meters. It was not late in the day and there was a noticeable change in the wind. The air had grown moist. Though she needed to verify her telescope's settings in these new conditions at all ranges, the Colonel turned abruptly away from her and limped to his jeep parked near the little hut. He got in and drove to where she stood beside her shooting mat.

"Your formal training is concluded," he said, the ungainly vehicle shuddering as it idled. "I have arranged your test in the morning, elsewhere, to begin the moment shadows have cleared the firing range, in a field lying east-west, so that you may have the considerable advantage of the sun directly behind you. We leave before dawn. Be ready when I arrive, with all your gear. Leave nothing behind. You will not be returning."

"I would like to shoot out to distance," Linh said. "The wind has changed today, both in direction and speed. The air is heavier. My elevation and windage needed adjustment at seven hundred meters. What correction will they need at distance, if this wind holds tomorrow?"

"Training is concluded," the Colonel repeated, and drove away without bothering to inspect the chamber of her rifle.

21

THE NEXT MORNING, with just the faintest glow in the eastern horizon, Colonel Trung pulled up beside her hut and sat quietly behind the wheel while she loaded her rifle, shooting blanket and small pack of personal belongings into the jeep. As they drove away Bich Linh was amazed again by the sensation of motion not arising from her own expended energies but from those of the strange little vehicle. The early morning journey passed without a word between them. The jeep stopped at the end of an unpaved road, the sun now fully above the horizon, the day already hot but menaced by patchy clouds, the countryside wild and uncultivated.

"Bring rifle, mat and shooting log," the Colonel said. "Your pack you may bring if so inclined. Although I think it highly unlikely you will be using your tool kit at this final hour."

The evening before, having fired so few rounds during the day, Linh had decided not to clean her rifle, certain from the beginning of training that excessive cleaning would not mirror her practice in the field—on the battlefield. She would shoot it dirty that morning and live or die with any variance in the impact of first rounds. The tool kit with its cleaning gear did seem unnecessary, but at the last minute she threw it inside her pack, struck by some vague notion it would be unwise to leave anything familiar behind.

She and the Colonel walked a hundred meters, passed through a small treeline and then turned alongside a reviewing stand built from rusting metal and wood planks. A half-dozen officers sat in the stand, guarded by a pair of soldiers on either end standing rigidly at attention, bayonets fixed, as if they expected attack at any minute. There were two men in white civilian suits with narrow ties and narrow-brimmed hats, the uniform of politicians. Officers and government officials ate cakes from a wooden platter and drank from wooden mugs and spoke in hushed tones. Mostly, from what she could tell as she passed, about their wives. There was laughing, and one of the white suits spat.

They were in a clearing, and as she followed the Colonel she realized the expanse of land extended well into the distance, further than any length of cleared open ground she had ever seen. The clearing pulled up short at a small wooden structure. From its flat roof the national flag flew against a wall of untouched foliage that formed all the horizon she could see.

Across such a distance the building seemed little more than a shed. Shocks of wild grass grew low to the ground everywhere and curled in and out of the small shrubbery dotting the length of the field. Brightly colored little birds darted and twisted after insects in all directions, chasing breakfast in a blur of instinct. Flowers she didn't recognize grew in clumps around the largest shade trees at the edges of the fields.

On the building downrange the patriotic flag moved fitfully, east to west. She mentally sought adjustments to her windage, refusing to feel yesterday's anger at the Colonel's blunt denial of the opportunity to test her settings at the farthest ranges.

To the side of the small building, standing farther away than any target she had trained on in the preceding week, stood a wooden frame above a single target pit, the excavated wall of clay earth behind it red in the morning sun. The target stand was half raised, its single, solid black circle hardly visible. She was momentarily incredulous. The distance seemed well past a thousand meters. Was she expected to shoot out to such an untried range, with no prior opportunity to determine her telescope settings?

Between her and the building, at regular intervals which she recognized as one hundred meters, stood additional, above-ground target stands. In the center of each was the same single black dot against a white field, at the most fifty centimeters in diameter, with no outer rings. She had not seen such a target in the earlier days of training. This she understood quickly to mean that her test was to be Pass/Fail, not the average of all shots taken, with no second chances provided by later targets for errant rounds on earlier ones.

Beside every target stand barely a meter away stood an unarmed soldier. In their brown uniforms and cloth helmets the effect of distance made them duplicates, impressions from a single mold. The soldiers held a small disc in each hand, one white, one black. Their motionless figures grew successively smaller as their positions receded toward more distant targets, as if they represented the foreshortening of life itself.

The Colonel led Linh to the back of the clearing, where four small yellow flags formed a rectangle in the bare earth of the shooter's position. A metal clipboard with a sheet of yellowed paper and a pencil lay in one corner. He instructed her to ground her shooting mat and notebook within the rectangle, but to keep her rifle slung and stand to attention, facing the reviewing stand. She did, and for a moment felt the attention of the officers and the two politicians mauling her, and in particular the ruined side of her face.

Colonel Trung reached in his pocket and brought out two packets of ammunition for the Dragunov, the tips of the rounds visible in each container.

"Soldier, prepare yourself," he said. "Empty your mind of limitation."

The Colonel dropped the two packets of ammunition from one hand into another absently and rhythmically as he spoke. For a moment he was silent, shuffling the cartridges from hand to hand, as if emptying his own mind. Linh found the noise irritating and wished he would hurry up. When he did speak she could discern a note of irony she was sure he intended.

He said, "I have invited very senior patriot officers and comrades to witness the first perfect score ever fired at first attempt on this precision course. *By anyone*."

The Colonel bowed briefly in the direction of the reviewing stand, where consumption of the morning's refreshments had resumed as the object of the officers' interest.

"Of course, I issue the same invitation to the same patriots following each pupil's training period, and make the same claim for the student's skill. I have been proven a liar every time. I do not expect it will be you who will end the institutional hyperbole of this custom and succeed in clearing my good name. But who knows?" He waved a hand downrange. "Maybe only the ancestral gods of this little known patch of earth."

The Colonel paused, possibly expecting commentary, or rebuttal. Bich Linh said nothing. He turned to face her, and she noted what seemed to be a bitter look, quickly replaced by the Colonel's usual composure. He said, "Fortunately for my dismal efforts, the senior patriots find other entertainment during the exercise and continue to support my goal to produce the finest long distance shooters in the world."

"Then you have no reason to complain about anything," Bich Linh said.

"Perhaps." The Colonel nodded. "And irrelevant anyway. You will shoot as follows. On the closest target, at four hundred meters, one round to center. The targets, you will have noticed, increase in increments of one hundred meters one to the next. On the second target, at five hundred meters, fire one round to center. On the third target also one round to center and so out to the fifth and final target for this preliminary course of fire, which is ended at eight hundred meters.

Only a fool or a god would shoot from any position other than prone, but the course allows you full discretion in the matter. You may lie down, squat, sit, kneel or stand, according to your wishes. Stand on your head, if it suits you. Do you understand my directions so far?"

"Perfectly," Bich Linh said.

"Additionally, and importantly, the course permits that you may adjust your telescope for the shot on any target, excluding only the *second target*, at five hundred meters. For this target, you must vary *only* the location of your point of aim. You may not even touch the adjustment knobs of your telescope on pain of instant disqualification. The shot at five hundred meters displays your understanding, or lack of it, of your weapon's own mind. On the preceding and further targets, you may, on your own decision, adjust your telescope as you choose. Is this understood?"

"Your instructions are clear."

"Yes? Then tell me. How many shots comprise this first stage of the test?"

"Five."

"From what distance to what distance?"

"From four hundred to eight hundred meters."

"On which shot may you not make any sight adjustment on pain of disqualification?"

"On the shot at five hundred meters."

"Which is what shot in order?"

"The second."

"Then we are clear. Twice I have had students confirm their understanding of these same instructions and twice proceed to make forbidden sight adjustments on the second shot."

"You will not have another such student today."

"Very well. After this initial stage of fire out to eight hundred meters, and for the honor of proceeding to the final stage, you may not miss even one of these first five shots. The privilege of this honor carries penalty. Miss one target, at any stage, and your test is over and you return to the infantry. Failure to fire exactly as prescribed is considered a shot off the target, regardless of actual impact. Is this clear?"

"Perfectly."

Bich Linh had ceased looking at Colonel Trung as she listened to him. She was again watching the little flag on the distant building. It flicked raggedly, but consistently. If it did not change as she fired, she would add three clicks of left windage to compensate. The elevation she could test on the nearer targets, but she was not overly concerned about elevation. Unless these winds grew more extreme than the national flag currently indicated, their variations posed primarily a horizontal concern and should not greatly affect how a bullet rose or fell. By noting any elevation changes at earlier targets, and consulting the bullet drop tables she had studied and copied into her notes, she felt she could arrive at further distance settings for elevation with some confidence.

It was windage that could undo her well before the final shots. She had fired at no greater distance yesterday than seven hundred meters, and how the settings would change, under the morning's varying wind, from seven hundred meters out to the most distant target presented a variable unknown enough to undo her. The experience, and adjustments, from shooting the long distances yesterday, under at least similar wind conditions, would have been invaluable.

The Colonel had denied her the opportunity to better prepare herself. She felt she understood why. No man had yet passed his course of fire on first attempt. This the Colonel had made clear. And equally clear was that the Colonel was duty bound to test her, but not to allow a woman to best a man. *You were honored as Exceptional Student. I have no choice but to select you.*

"On successfully passing the first stage," the Colonel went on, "you will then proceed to fire on the three final and most distant targets at nine hundred, one thousand, and one thousand one hundred meters.

Again on each target you will fire one round. You have never fired past one thousand meters, thus you have no predetermined formula for adjusting your telescope crosshairs at the final target. Bullet drop over a hundred meters of ground is geometrically increased at increasing ranges. Thus how to adjust by changing point of aim is no small undertaking. Thus adjusting your telescope crosshairs to compensate is the same critical problem in mechanical form. Thus your skill is truly tested. And thus no one has ever completed this course of fire on first attempt, excluding, of course, myself. And this morning there is the wind. You may set your weapon down."

Linh did so, then stood again in front of Colonel Trung.

The Colonel said, "Soldier, do you wish to proceed, or to withdraw? Withdraw or fail, either one, the infantry awaits you."

"I withdraw from nothing," Linh said, locking the Colonel's eyes with her own. "I could commence this course of fire from six hundred meters. The earlier two distances prove nothing."

The Colonel met Bich Linh's gaze and said, "Each element in a course of fire has its purpose." He handed her the packets of ammunition, five rounds in each, two rounds more than she would need. He then turned and faced downrange, raised his arms over his head, and then slowly lowered them until they were held straight out from his body. Immediately all soldiers but one—the soldier at the closest distance—responded. They turned to their respective targets and all but the soldier tending the farthest target took hold of them and laid them down, then resumed their stance, again holding their black and white markers, one in each hand. The soldier at the most distant target altered this routine by lowering his target out of sight into the target pit before recovering his markers and resuming his place.

The Colonel lowered one arm and snapped the other in a pointing motion. 7 of the 8 target tenders spun to face in the direction indicated by the Colonel, marched 10 meters away and stopped. In unison again they performed an about face and stood aligned neatly along the edge of the clearing at rigid attention. Bich Linh was impressed with their precision, as would be the spectators in the reviewing stand, for whom their drill was clearly intended. The Colonel was part commissar after all.

Only the target tender at the nearest target had not moved. He stood as stiff as before beside the lone upright target. The Colonel turned back to Bich Linh.

"I have given you ten rounds of ammunition. You will be firing only 8 shots. The People will require the remaining cartridges back. In the infantry you will carry the Kalashnikov, not the Dragunov, so they will be of no service to you there anyway. Are you ready?"

"Completely."

"The soldier at each target will spot where your bullet strikes. Once you have fired, the soldier will mark your target. Only a center strike into the black circle matters. A center strike is considered to have occurred anywhere within the black circle. This we will know you have accomplished if the soldier uses a white disc to mark your bullet's impact. If a black disc appears, your round has landed outside the circle and inside the white field and the test is over. If no disc is used, you have missed the entire target. Again, the test is over. As should be obvious, the test is also over if a soldier falls to the ground."

Said without the trace of a smile.

"That target will be laid on the ground and the next target will be placed in its frame by its tender. You will continue firing until you have completed the course or until the first black disc is presented. You are allowed to use the pencil and pad to perform calculations as you wish. There are no time constraints, but remember the senior patriots assembled here have a war to win."

As the Colonel spoke, Linh noted that the distant flag fell straight down, lingered, then rebounded eastward again, its raggedness more frantic. She could add gusting winds to the simple increase of the prevailing wind. And more unknowns to a bullet's flight.

Linh said, "If the senior patriots assembled truly wished to win the war, they would be out fighting it, not sitting on warm benches protected by bayonets while they sip hot wine and eat cakes and ridicule their women, far from the bleeding. Perhaps when my test is over, they would like to join me in the infantry, where their boundless passion for victory might find suitable expression."

The Colonel smiled and then composed himself.

"Spoken like a true daughter of the South," he said. "And now I go to see if the patriots have left any wine in the jug." He turned toward the reviewing stand, stopped and turned back to Linh. Astonishingly to Linh, he was beaming. "If I have had any pupil who could produce eight white discs in a row, I believe it to be you. On behalf of the People, I wish you good fortune."

"But you would not allow me to shoot to distance yesterday," Linh said, and though she had fought to remain emotionless, she could not keep her bitterness from showing. "Today the wind is changing and gusting and you present me with a target farther than any I have shot before. In the matter of fortune, I had better rely on myself."

This time the Colonel made no attempt to disguise his smile. For a moment he looked around with the face of a man enjoying a pleasant afternoon in the folds of nature.

"*Exactly*," he said, and with a final gaze around him, and then at her, turned and limped to the reviewing stand. He took a seat above his spectators and was still smiling as he poured himself a cup of rice wine.

22

TO BICH LINH'S EYE, the national flag on the end of its pole danced in the morning breeze maybe ten meters from the rooftop of the building. The flag must have been three meters in length, but at greater than eleven hundred meters distance it had little more substance than a small insect's wing.

Still, it was enough to tell her she was no god's favorite. The ragged little fillip in the flag, she still deemed to be a three click adjustment out to six hundred meters. After these early shots she would have bullet strikes on targets to adjudicate whether further change was needed. The *prevailing* wind seemed to be constant. What worried her was the occasional flick of gusting that increased the length of the insect's wing. It stabbed toward the westerly treeline at intervals that had no discernible pattern she could discover in studying them. Past six hundred meters such a gust could easily throw her round completely off the target.

Without the wind, she would not have felt challenged at striking center of the black circles out to one thousand meters. She had already proven herself in earlier days. But new wind conditions changed everything. Was this why the Colonel had chosen this morning for the test? Why he had been so adamant at refusing her request to shoot to full distance the day before? To ensure her failure?

Gusting, then, was not her only challenge. She had developed no settings for eleven hundred meters. She decided to resolve the settings for that unknown distance now, insofar as she was able, rather than have it weigh on her throughout the earlier stages of the test.

While still a young girl, after the death of her parents, Linh had been sent into the care of aged and doddering grandparents. In an affront to Buddha the southern government gave them money to send her to one of the province's Catholic schools, where she learned such things as how to read and write, chase numbers into and out of their columns, sing in Latin, and the difference between girls and boys. She learned that the teacher nuns were married to a god and were not allowed kinship with mortals. The priests were married to no one, and were forbidden to lie with either gods or mortals. The half-immortal at the center of their preoccupation once loved a mortal but had forsaken her and all things, even his body, at the command of the Lord of all Gods. The more Linh inquired for clarification, the more the nuns smiled and wove denser webs of mystery around this Lord. If Linh forsook evil, they said, the half-immortal would save her. But who had saved the half-immortal from the Lord of Gods? Linh asked in turn. They frowned at her but Linh soon lost interest in such complicated affairs and met with young boys in the shadows of the convent walls, where all mystery was simple, bright and sweet. She took delight in the studies that made sense, particularly arithmetic, a skill which had remained useful to her over the years, long after the Viet Minh had chased the Catholic nuns and priests from the countryside, and the Buddhists too.

Her nuns had a confusing religion, difficult to grasp, and Linh remembered only snatches of her catechism; but the arithmetic lessons had taken root. Linh lowered herself to her cloth shooting mat. Using the pad and pencil provided for her use, she reviewed her notes on the bullet drops for the Dragunov's ten gram round, for distances from five hundred to one thousand meters. Working quickly, she calculated the differences in bullet drop from seven hundred to one thousand meters in one hundred meter intervals. She used the three figures to project the additional, geometrically increasing drop for her final shot at a further hundred meters. Without suppressing her own disbelief in it, the figure she arrived at was one hundred and twenty-three centimeters. Hastily retracing her own mathematics, she again came to the same conclusion and dropped the pencil in disgust.

There was no other choice. None of her charts gave bullet drop for any round past one thousand meters. She would have to use this figure for sight adjustment at eleven hundred meters in full awareness of its near impossibility of being correct.

A near impossibility, in that a bullet's loss in ballistic power, and thus its drop over distance, was a problem in an advanced mathematics unknown to Bich Linh, or she believed, any mortal. The best shooters made corrections to their settings only after careful live firing. None of them would ever consider such folly as to calculate shooting adjustments with pencil and paper alone. The figures she noted from simple subtraction in her primitive math showed only one thing conclusively: that as distance increased, so did the rate of bullet drop. Her arithmetic was a starting point, at best a crude estimate, nothing more than a basis for further testing. To calculate her telescope's setting with the accuracy necessary to send a *first, untested* round into a target eleven hundred meters away and smaller than the distance between a water buffalo's eyes—

She smiled at the pretense of even scribbling on the Colonel's pad, as though to a goddess disdainfully looking over her shoulder, Linh would be so foolish to argue that numbers were a match for life, or that heaven could be found with a compass.

And then from the goddess hear: *Better you should stand as a falling-over tree and trust in your eye than in your scribblings. And possibly you already have the answers you seek.*

What she did know, from studying the Colonel's manuals under the yellow light of her oil lamp, was that the god of mathematics himself would still have to prove his own findings in the field against the temperature and weight of the air, the attack and direction of the wind, the rotation of the earth, the relative elevation between target and shooter, elevation above sea level, consistency of standard held in the loading of powder in the cartridge, and both the repetitive, unvarying seating of the cartridge inside the rifle's chamber and the placement of the shooter's own eye behind the telescope. To say nothing of variables that expanded under the influence of gravity as distance increased. And a dozen other factors described in the Colonel's manuals, which she had been unable to follow and was just as disinclined to try.

The pursuit of the exact mechanical adjustment to the crosshairs of the telescope, resulting in the shooter's exact, almost infinitesimally small mechanical realignment of the barrel of the rifle in relation to the target, up or down for elevation, right or left for windage, was a complexity that required firing, testing and adjustment, and more firing, testing and adjustment, not the stirring and more stirring of symbols in the cookpot of the mind.

But the Colonel had left her no other choice. Linh picked her pencil up. Knowing the change to bullet strike in centimeters up or down, left or right, at any hundred meter interval for each click of her telescope's knobs, Linh quickly computed the change in elevation produced by each click of her telescope at a distance of eleven hundred meters: Crossing this result with her calculated bullet drop between one thousand and eleven hundred meters—one hundred and twenty-three centimeters—was easy enough. She stirred a final batch of symbols and came up with the number *17*.

She shook her head at the irony. Her age at her marriage. The age her firstborn would have been this year. *17*, the magical, the improbable, the tragic number, the number of times her horizontal crosshairs, inside their metal cavern—*click-click-click*—must be moved downwards in their minute intervals to reciprocally orient her rifle's muzzle upward with the necessary precision to perform the impossible.

The conceit of numbers, to tell her that turning a cylinder not much larger than her thumb seventeen times in the direction of a clock's moving hands would result in a bullet passing exactly one hundred and twenty-three centimeters above the center of a target one thousand meters away on its journey to the center of a target a hundred meters further on.

Arithmetic seemed to be strangling her. For a moment she felt the world spin.

She wrote the number *17* in the lower left hand corner of the pad, circled it, and took one last look out at the flag. After another moment she drew a / mark by *17* and wrote *3* inside the circle, the clicks she gauged would compensate for the increased prevailing wind throughout the course of fire. Beside *17/3* she added *(1100)*. There was nothing she could do about the wind's gusting and no remedy for it beyond dumb luck. She circled the numbers a second time, flipped the pencil away and resolved not to consider the problem again, no matter the outcome. She breathed deeply to clear her head of mathematics.

She had her numbers. They stood ready to open the gate to the rest of her life, and one walked looking forward, not back.

Time enough in eternity to reflect on the thrust of the gods, and how otherwise to have parried them.

As Thanh would have said.

23

LINH LAID HER NOTEBOOK ASIDE and removed the paper covers from the two packets of ammunition. The red symbols in Cyrillic on the wax paper signified nothing to her. She loaded the Dragunov's ten round magazine with the eight cartridges she would need and clicked it into place inside the magazine well. With as much force as she could she freed the bolt and slammed it home, chambering a cartridge into the throat of the barrel.

This first round was set and locked into position inside the chamber by the unfired force of the bolt going home. The second round would be seated inside the chamber by a different energy, by a bolt driven under recoil by the force of the fired cartridge. Such minute changes in bullet orientation inside the rifle were not likely to affect the round at four hundred meters, but still, she wanted to fire a first round blindly, to set all target rounds in the rifle's chamber by the consistency of a single force, the bolt moving under fired recoil.

This the Colonel had taught her, and then created a test that forbade the use of his own teaching. No matter what force she used to run the bolt home on that first cartridge it would not seat inside the chamber exactly as it would under the force generated by the pressure of a detonated round. Like it or not, there would be no first shot into the bushes unless she were ready for the infantry.

For fortune, she would have to rely on herself.

Exactly, she heard the Colonel say.

Linh stretched herself out beside her rifle, referred to her shooting log and dialed in her settings for four hundred meters. The Colonel had prohibited the change of settings for the shot at five hundred meters. She thought briefly about figuring the average of her settings for four hundred and five hundred meters and adjusting her telescope with these, holding low on the first target and then higher on the second one. Decided against it. Better the one devil she would know at five hundred meters than the two that would be created by fiddling with mathematics. There was already the increase in prevailing wind and the unpredictable gusting. Enough devils without inviting more.

Without further hesitation she dialed in the three extra clicks of left wind she had decided upon and laid her thumb on the weapon's selector. Spreading her legs to wake them up, then bringing them together in a line behind the rifle, sling trapped between biceps and forearm, she placed the butt of the stock in the cavity of her shoulder and her cheek on the raised pad of the stock. She moved the selector off safe to the firing position and kept her finger outside the trigger guard as she wriggled into position behind the telescope.

The crosshairs of her telescope determined whether her form was correct. As she settled her body she observed their intersection intently. After some further shifting of elbows and the stock in her shoulder, the crosshairs finally settled easily and naturally, requiring only a single further small twist of her body to find them holding without adjustment or effort at the center of the target, her entire frame completely relaxed. Standing a mere two meters away from the point of her Dragunov's aim four hundred yards distant, the soldier who would mark her target tried not to look concerned, holding himself rigidly at attention, either hand gripping a marking disc.

Praise Buddha, Linh thought, exhaling and imperceptibly increasing the pressure on her trigger finger. When the shot broke it came as the necessary surprise. The crosshairs recoiled as the Dragunov's bolt cycled another round into the chamber.

Linh gently allowed the trigger to move forward until it reset with a *click,* then dropped her finger onto the trigger guard and watched through the telescope as the soldier walked over and stood in front of the target a moment, then inserted the wooden rod of his white disk into the bullet hole.

Linh had held dead center. She had not disturbed the sights when the shot broke. She knew what she should see. But while the white target disc indicated a hit ten centimeters high of center, a variance of some mild surprise but of no consequence to her, it was a full fifteen centimeters to its right, on a target only fifty centimeters in diameter. Unless she had incompetently moved the windage knob of her telescope, or the winds had gusted without her knowledge, the prevailing winds required she add additional compensation of left windage, to bring the bullet back to center. Or had she somehow failed to release the shot properly? Had she mishandled the trigger?

Glancing to her own left at the reviewing stand, she saw the officers peering through binoculars downrange. Colonel Trung, impassive again, sat upright in his seat looking away. His eyes were good; unaided, they had seen what they wanted.

The soldier tending the target removed it from its stand, laid it into the low foliage, and walked solemnly away, disappearing into the treeline at the clearing's edge. A hundred meters downrange, the soldier tending the second target retrieved its frame from the ground, inserted it into its unseen stand buried in the earth, and took up his position two meters from the target's center.

Behind her telescope again, Linh made small movements of her body until the crosshairs relaxed at the center of the five hundred meter target. On this target the Colonel's course design permitted no adjustment of her telescope. Despite the error in windage revealed by the first shot, the thought nagged her that she, not the weapon's settings, had caused the error with poor trigger control. She doubted her prior conviction that the shot had broken cleanly.

With proper aiming and trigger control, the three additional clicks should have resulted in a shot location near the target's center. The flag downrange moved with no more vigor than a 3-click wind, but the fifteen centimeter error made no sense. She decided she must have fired too quickly and resolved to pay adequate attention to the location of her crosshairs on their return after recoil. Properly executed, a precision shot could be critically evaluated by how closely, after the shot broke, the crosshairs returned to their location prior to firing. Reluctantly she compromised her inclination to hold at dead center and instead held five centimeters to the left of center. The shot had struck high at four hundred meters, also a mystery. Why? She had no idea, but for elevation she now did not dare further compensate with a higher hold on the target at five hundred, which otherwise would have been a normal response when shooting longer distances with settings from nearer ones.

Exhaling, she began pressing the trigger when her breath fully released. Before she felt the need to breathe again the shot broke. As it recoiled Linh was certain this time she had not disturbed the crosshairs on firing. Linh watched them intently. After recoil they returned exactly where she had aimed at the moment of discharge. Again she watched through the telescope as the soldier stood in front of the target, blocking her view while his arms moved. When he stepped aside the white disk was nearly dead center elevation-wise but in error of windage even further right of the target's center, dangerously close to the circle's edge. Had Linh not executed perfectly, and not begrudgingly held her point of aim its few meager centimeters left of center, the round would have certainly been off the target. And she would not survive such inaccuracy at six hundred meters.

And then there was the strange matter of shots hitting high.

Through her telescope Linh was still perplexed. How had elevation changed so much? Her four hundred meter settings only the day before produced dead center hits, both for elevation and windage. But today, first at four hundred meters, and now at five hundred, her elevation appeared to be adjusted four to six clicks high. Her four hundred meter settings had produced a high strike at four hundred meters, and then a dead center strike at five hundred, when all her training and recent days of experience informed her those four hundred meter settings should have produced a dead center strike at four hundred and a strike well below center at five hundred.

Elevation should not have been in question.

The only new factor was the increase in wind. Why a wind blowing perpendicularly to the flight path of her bullet, and thus influencing logically and predominantly its course left to right, should also alter its elevation strike upward, she could not pretend to understand. She had read nothing about it in the Colonel's manuals.

It was not logical. It defied logic. If anything, a greater wind sapped a bullet's energy, and should that not result in a lower, not a higher strike on a target?

The Colonel himself had never issued a single admonition regarding such an eventuality. Possibly the Colonel would laugh at her if she mentioned it. But what she saw was what she saw. Instead of accelerating bullet drop, the effect of the left-to-right increased wind was, or seemed to be, somehow retarding normal bullet drop approximately eight to ten centimeters over four hundred meters, resulting in a higher strike. There was no other factor she could observe. It was the same ammunition she had been using all week. The only change seemed to be in the wind. Was the bullet riding up on the cross-axis wind like a passenger on a magic carpet, even as it slid to the right? Was the wind gusting from below the earth, as if some perverse god were toying with her? Only the gods knew. Nothing and no one else.

At five hundred meters, forbidden from adjusting her telescope, and without understanding why the bullet struck high at four hundred meters, she had nevertheless compensated by *not* holding high on the five hundred meter target, thus nullifying in its strike on the target the bullet's strange increased performance—at least *theoretically* increased performance—due (or not) to the wind. The result was the perfect bullet strike with regard to elevation. From all this she concluded it was best to proceed with a cautionary two-click correction downward to her upcoming shot at six hundred meters. If the bullet still struck high, or now went low, it would give her the information needed for further adjustments.

And so, with some luck—and relying on herself for good fortune—she had done the right thing where point of aim for elevation was concerned. But again, this time almost fatally, she had underestimated the strength of the prevailing wind. Ignoring the officers in the reviewing stands and the pendulous movement of their binoculars toward, away from and then back to her again, she stared downrange for a long moment at the flag. It appeared to be moving the same. She waited, but there was no gusting.

In a moment she realized the magnitude of her error.

Thanh would have called it an error in her *Buddha*. *You know not your Buddha*, he was fond of saying. Her mistake was in comparing the visible flag's movement in the wind, that flag in *Now*, to flags that *Were*, flags gone forever, residing now only inside memories of small white pennants fluttering around the range where she had trained with Colonel Trung. The large national flag she looked at was, so obviously now, significantly heavier than that of the pennants. A much *stronger* wind would be required to give such a flag the appearance of a similar movement.

She could almost hear Thanh laughing on the other side of the mountains.

By evidence of her first two shots, bringing the round back to center would require at least another three clicks in windage. A total of six clicks, maybe seven, not three.

Add four more clicks, then, for left windage (further antidote to the prevailing wind), remove three for elevation (whether she understood the bullet's magic-carpet rise on the first two targets or not). Retrieving her pencil, she wrote in the center of her pad *-3H* for elevation, followed by a slash, followed by *+4L*, for windage, then circled them twice. She crossed out the figures *17/3 (1100)* and rewrote these with her adjustments to elevation and windage as *14/7 (1100)*. She circled *14* once to specify the required elevation change at 1100 meters and left 7 uncircled, since she would input the windage correction now and verify its accuracy at each succeeding shot, making changes only if required by the bullet strike. Then she circled both numbers twice in bold, to be prepared for her final shot at a glance. If she survived until the final shot.

She tossed the pencil aside, resentful again at the dominance of numbers and symbols. But she felt foolish at how elementary her error had been, and recognized she had been fortunate not to have her shot thrown completely off the target, as it certainly would have been at six hundred meters. She remembered the bitter pride that led her to suggest just that distance to the Colonel for her first shot. Had he accepted her haughty suggestion, she would have failed the test on the first round.

She heard his voice again: *Each element in a course of fire has its purpose.*

24

BEHIND HER RIFLE ONCE MORE, Linh adjusted her settings for 600 meters, referring to her log book to validate her memory, pausing to add in the additional windage and elevation corrections to her original settings.

One last look through the telescope at the flag revealed no gusting. The flag moved as before. She settled in and adjusted the stock in the bony valley between her shoulder and neck, cheek pressed into its leather pad, solitary eye bent to its task. She squirmed her body around until, on exhaling, the crosshairs of the telescope rested in the center of the now smaller black circle. Tested her hold for consistency a final time, verified it and exhaled again, trigger finger moving like sand through an hourglass. Her lungs empty but not yet in need of oxygen, the shot broke. When the telescope returned from recoil the crosshairs quartered the target once more.

Linh relaxed and waited. The soldier stepped away from the target and the white disc was dead center. Behin her target in the distance the national flag suddenly whipped spasmodically, dipped and straightened. Linh felt the need to outpace the changing wind. While the soldier lowered the target face down to the earth and stepped quickly away, Linh dialed in the settings for 700 meters, added her day's corrections and waited impatiently for the next soldier to insert his target stand and step away. She watched the flag again for any further change of motion, saw none, and placed the crosshairs at the 700 meter target. Lined her body up, exhaled, saw what she wanted and pressed the trigger until the Dragunov fired. She immediately knew she had been too hasty. The rifle came back from recoil with the crosshairs to the left of dead center on the target.

This time the white disc was negligibly high, but only centimeters from the black border of the bullseye, this time far left of center. The edge of the white disc loomed into the white field of the target. In racing against the wind, Linh had fired too quickly and narrowly missed ending her test. The crosshairs had resettled left of the target's center when returning from recoil, reflecting the bullet strike down-range, a sign of a flaw in her shooting, not her settings. She could not fault the wind.

She twisted the telescope knobs again, arriving at her settings for 800 meters, again allowing for the changes to elevation and windage. She stared out at the flag. It moved as it had before, but what did that mean? Did she really think she could observe the distant dance of canvas and detect the equivalent change in a wind's speed subtle enough to move a bullet ten centimeters one way or the other over a near kilometer of the earth?

All she knew was what she knew. Let the wind answer to the gods. She resisted adding another click of left windage and dropped her hand from the adjustment knob.

Through the telescope she watched the attending soldier for the eight hundred meter target step back from the target and return to attention. She noticed the radical diminishment in size of the target at yet another hundred meters away. Her crosshairs were widening as the target shrank, gorging themselves on her predicament. She forgot about the wind and concentrated on technique. Another such shooting error and she would be in the infantry.

The shot at 800 meters broke so perfectly that Linh thought of Thanh, reviewing her image of him standing watch by the political officer's quarters in the village. He was looking at her curiously, with a kind of benign amusement. She stood inside the shadows of moonlight cast by thatched roofs, lost to all eyes but his, opening her shirt and revealing her breasts, whispering where she would be when his watch ended at dawn. Thanh was the first near-perfection she had ever known, the only man in whose presence she could forget the ruin of her face. What little excellence she ever afterwards encountered, of any kind, as the break of her shot just then, always brought this memory of Thanh to mind, without omitting its conclusion: that when dawn came, Thanh did not.

The white disc was back in the center of the target. At that moment Linh hated to alter anything, including her rifle sling, but she had lost feeling in her arm. She loosened the sling and felt the white-hot rush of blood back into its channels. Thanh still watched her inside her shadows, not seduced. She forced him from her thoughts. Now was not the time to consider Thanh's ways, and the ways to overcome them.

Working quickly again, she verified her 900 meter settings with the logbook, adjusted the telescope knobs and slipped back into her sling. At this distance the crosshairs partitioned the black circle into tiny segments barely visible in each quadrant. She fidgeted her body into its aligned position and tested her point of aim, exhaling and watching the crosshairs. Fidgeted again, retested. The traces of equally sized target appeared in the quadrants, dark spots barely distinguishable from the lines of her crosshairs. At the last instant, instead of firing, and without questioning her intuition, she relaxed her trigger finger, removed the rifle from her shoulder and added one additional click of left wind. Settled back in, worked her body into position, concentrated again on the crosshairs, saw what she wanted, and inhaled. The crosshairs rose naturally, then settled as she slowly released her breath. Again she saw what she wanted and began pressing the trigger. A long time later, but before she felt the need for oxygen, the shot broke. Cleanly. If it was off the target, it was her settings or the wind, not her shooting. She dropped her eye from the telescope and looked down, not focusing.

There was a rumble of low conversation from the stands. Looking past her scope downrange, she saw the smudge of white against black.

Through her telescope the white circle appeared perfect left to right, but now low nearly fifteen centimeters, maybe ten centimeters above the outside edge. For another moment she watched the ritual of the target tender. Having survived his duty, he lowered the target onto the earth and strode toward the sanctuary of the treeline. She imagined the stoic relief that flooded his mind, and the opposite feeling entering the soldier a hundred meters further on as he placed his target into its stand.

Telescope settings for 1000 meters were the last entry in her logbook. These were as she had memorized them. She paused before making any adjustments to her telescope. There was a question to be answered.

The shot at 900 meters had struck low. Why? It could have been the slightest imperfection in her execution. It could be an additional ballistic loss of muzzle energy unaccounted for in her settings. The wind could have changed. Possibly a god sneezed. Maybe her round deflected off a butterfly's wing. *Some* action appeared requisite. She placed her fingers on the elevation knob but at the last moment resisted. She had no certainty to guide her.

One thousand meters. Any test should have ended here, whatever the fate of this shot. She felt the resentment rising and waited until it passed, then looked through the telescope past the target and stared at the yellow flag for a full minute. Stared too long and the flag lost any meaning. Looked away and looked back. The flag was doing what it had been doing all day, only this time it seemed to flick once with greater strength. The wind was gusting. So? The wind dancing was the wind dancing. Only her *karma* could adjust for gusting now. But why had the last round struck low? It had been centered at the shot at 800 meters, a shot where she had been sure of her settings and technique. With her corrected adjustments for 900 meters dialed into her telescope, with equal confidence in her execution, this shot should also have been centered. The shot had broken perfectly, she was certain of it. But had she fired at the same moment the wind sneezed? Or while it was still drawing its breath? Why the low strike? On this answer she felt her future rested.

She relaxed behind the rifle and looked into the sky, to match its blankness with her own mind. Reluctantly she considered it all again, forgetting the sneezing of gods and the plight of butterflies.

She might have fired into a gust, but after considering a moment longer, did not think so. There had been no prior erratic movement of the flag to distract her. The shot at 900 meters had been centered for windage. In a gust the significant movement would have certainly been left to right, not down. True, she had added the extra click of left wind, but this she had simply gambled on, not added as a prediction of gusting, such being a task for visionaries. Besides, the minimal change of the single click proving to be adequate argued against an influence by gusting and pointed instead to a minor variation in the prevailing wind only.

She was left with a simplicity. Not a logical, or mathematical simplicity. Nothing from the Colonel's manuals. It was the simplicity of Now. The understanding came from within her and nowhere else.

The chameleon wind that had apparently *lifted* a bullet at 400 meters and continued doing so for the next four shots, requiring an elevation adjustment of three clicks downward, was now affecting it reversely at 900 meters. The bullet was no longer riding the magic carpet, at least without the same vigor, though the wind appeared to blow as steadily as before. *Why*, the gods knew, not she. It was not a phenomenon of past experience, of *Was*, out of manuals or the

Colonel's lecturing. It was a tale being written on her targets in *Now*, using the language of Buddha, in an alphabet of bullet strikes. What influence the wind had at the first five distances the wind no longer had, or had less of, at the sixth.

The bullet had plunged. And between 800 and 900 meters the drop had been drastic, not incremental. The change between the two distances was no longer mathematical, any more than a man climbing downhill progressed at the same pace when he suddenly fell from a cliff.

Maybe the factor was not the wind. It made no sense anyway that an increased wind blowing at right angles to the flight of a bullet raised bullet strike. Maybe some god had tired of toying with her. Or now amused himself by toying differently, all the while laughing at her futile efforts to understand. Maybe some impish spirit tested her. *Why* what was happening did not matter. *Now* was happening. *Now* was alive like the wind was alive, and like the wind would brook no theory. The command of Buddha was to *Look*, not to *Think*. The bullet was plunging. Not enough, at 900 meters, to drop the round out of the black circle. But the next shot, uncorrected, into the same prevailing wind and the same prevailing *Now*, surely would.

Let the devils take theory. Purely *practically* for the shot at 1000 meters, she needed the same left-wind adjustment for her telescope's 1000 meter settings but an *upward* correction to elevation to account for the desertion in *Now* of the wind's prior boost to elevation in *Was*—if the wind was indeed even involved. How much elevation to add?—was the remaining question.

Only a god's mathematics could know for sure. Mere mortals had mere theory.

But her theory required decision, right or wrong. The number came to her: 5. Glancing briefly at her charts, she confirmed her intuition. Her field settings for 900 meters had been gained purely by her live firing. The manuals gave ballistic tables for only 800 and

1000 meters, not 900 meters. The chart showed that two clicks of adjustment at 1000 meters moved a bullet the rough equivalent of fifteen centimeters against a target at that distance. She computed the intermediary movement of a bullet between 800 and 1000 meters for each click of her telescope knob and concluded that 3 clicks would have theoretically adjusted her shot at 900 meters and adding two clicks would do the same at 1000. So add 3, to bring her to center at 900 meters, and 2 more for the 1000 meter shot.

5 clicks. Enough, if correct, to bring the bullet strike back to center a further hundred meters away.

Enough, if incorrect, to send her to the infantry.

Something still bothered her. Some omission in her understanding. Linh looked down at the data she had copied into her shooting log from the bullet drop charts, but her mind was growing numb, rejecting further mathematics. The charts were dead sailors, life was a ship on a stormy sea. She imagined Thanh whispering in her ear: *What does paper know of gods?*

She reached for the windage knob and entered her recorded training period settings for 1000 meters and then added her compensating seven additional clicks of left windage. At the elevation knob she carefully clicked in her last known training settings for elevation at the 1000 meter target. In doing so the omission in understanding presented itself: she was simultaneously restoring the three clicks of elevation she had removed from the prior shots past 500 meters and therefore rather than five clicks of elevation she needed only two.

Karma to live and die by mathematics. Again, she waited until the resentment passed through her. A chance yesterday to fire at this distance would have made such contortions unnecessary.

Something still nagged at her. Some final gap in her understanding. Her idea that a horizontal wind could also serve as an aid to elevation was pure theory, the stirring of her mind's cookpot. She was possibly ludicrously wrong about the cause behind the high strikes of her bullets from 400 to 800 hundred meters. But *whatever actual factor* had surfaced between 800 hundred and 900 hundred meters—witnessed in the low strike of the round compared to the earlier distances—would be even more exaggerated at an additional hundred meters. The bullet's flight, bowing to old age, would likely deteriorate further in trajectory under this unknown influence, whether it was gravity or the gods. The bullet charts knew nothing of this. She did not trust them. They had already failed her once.

She had added back her original three clicks of elevation. She had corrected further with another two clicks. She twisted the knob again. And again. Another? No. She forced her hand from the dial that controlled elevation, found the one for windage. On the same reasoning, she clicked once more to counter the ageless wind's further bullying of the steadily aging bullet. She dropped her hand from the telescope.

Enough. Enough thrusting and parrying with arithmetic. Enough scribbling in the mind or she would think herself into madness. She placed the Dragunov's stock into her shoulder and settled into her shooting mat, forced her cheek into the stock's raised comb and looked through the telescope.

Only the barest hint of the black target showed now against the slender threads of the crosshairs when her telescope quieted, and they disappeared and reappeared with her breathing. She would have to be as motionless as a statue of Buddha at the moment of firing. Linh brought her legs closer together and as directly behind the rifle as she could position them, willed herself deeper into the surface of the earth, and twitched and fidgeted until it was pointless. Traces of the target ghosted in their crosshair quadrants, rose and fell as she breathed. She breathed one more time and exhaled, began pressing the trigger when the crosshairs settled. But there was too much target in the lower quadrants.

She aborted. Lifted her head from the rifle and looked into the coarse shrubbery lining the field behind the reviewing stands. Breathed normally. A sidelong glance and she could see the officers and the two politicians training their binoculars on her. Weak sunlight reflected from the binocular glass and glinted dully on the golden threads of shoulder insignia. Colonel Trung looked steadily out at the target, as though he served in a different army.

How do you like my face? she thought, staring back at them. Do you see a woman or a creature? Am I a proper daughter of the People's will to resist? Will you join me in the infantry?

Despite herself, her resentment was rising. She waited until it faded.

Now her supporting arm was losing feeling again from the nearly tourniquet-tight sling encircling it. She had no choice but to remove the sling and wait while the sting of blood rushed through her upper arm. With normal feeling restored Linh repositioned the sling and once again went through the motions of body adjustments until her crosshairs were back on target. She tested and retested her body position and fidgeted with tiny corrections. Satisfied, she concentrated on her crosshairs. Inhaled and exhaled a number of times. Three times the crosshairs settled correctly. On the fourth she began her trigger press, but now the crosshairs sank, exposing too much of the target in the upper quadrants. She aborted again. Without moving her head from the telescope, she released the pressure on her trigger finger, feeling anger swell its way upward. Linh went inwardly still. Without the walls of her aggravation to climb, the anger would recede into the depths. She waited. The anger passed. Then she flinched her body slightly forward, fidgeted some more and bisected the target again with the crosshairs. Tested it with her breathing. Twice, three times, the target settled properly when she exhaled. On the third emptying of her lungs, in a long seamless increment, she filled her mind with the space above the horizon and began her trigger finger on the journey rearward that led to her future.

The Dragunov recoiled under the breaking shot.

Linh uncoiled the sling from her arm and stood, leaving the Dragunov on the ground, feeling her blood rush to restore normal circulation. A vision of Thanh passed before her. She felt no resistance inside, and the gust of wind that suddenly rose around her, enough to flutter the edge of her shooting pad, seemed to caress her as it passed.

The body of the soldier downrange blocked her view. One of the body's arms moved upward, paused and fell. The body stepped away.

The tiniest star blinked on a field of night under the fitful morning sun.

Laughter and applause from the reviewing stand broke her spell. And one voice wasn't pleased. So the morning's entertainment was disappointing to some, not to others. She heard the bitterness again in the Colonel's voice: *...the senior patriots find other entertainment during the exercise...*

If she looked over, would she see the piasters changing hands? Or did senior patriots make their wagers with American dollars?

The top edge of the shooting pad fluttered more, joined by the lower edge. Then both lay flat again.

Linh thought: *The gods, not gusting winds, are visiting this place.*

At the convent school they had told her about the great European Columbus, how when he set sail, many people feared he would sail right over the edge of the world, where monsters and demons and all that was terrible and unknown lurked beneath boiling seas to tear him apart. There were no settings to guide him, no explorers before him.

Now at eleven hundred meters, where the last soldier stood stoically at attention, his own life now called onto center stage, the edge of the world loomed. Beyond one thousand meters, she had no settings, no bearings and no prior explorer. Were there monsters and demons beyond?

Thanh answered her: *Of course. As there have been behind.*

25

BICH LINH BELIEVED that spirits walked the forests of the highlands.

As a young girl, when her mother was still alive, and years before her longings began, overtook and overcame her, first for the company of boys, then the touch of adolescent males, and finally the pleasure of grown men, the greatest joy of her days had been to leave her village after the tedium and bitter heat of afternoon chores and run into the hills at the base of the mighty mountains.

Linh dared go no higher than these foothills. Just the sight of the immense green walls disappearing into volatile cloud base seized her imagination and left her on the verge of panic. For excitement she dared herself incrementally closer to the wilds of the mountains, yet always she held back. The spirits had their homes in mountain caves, from which they wandered freely into and out of the depths of the earth, and if one of them found her roaming so far from her village surely she would be carried off and never seen again.

In the foothills she felt safe in her natural agility and unmatchable speed. She ran from familiar trails of moss flattened soft as fur onto hard boulder paths inside streams and freshets that gushed from private dens in the hillside, invulnerable in her journey, wide-eyed in a wondrous, a *perfect* world.

Her quest was always the same, to be hidden beside the trail in a perfect warren of leaves and vines and gaze soundlessly upon one of the forest spirits idling along beneath a bower of trees and giant grass. When hours had passed with no sightings but of small deer, fat bristle-haired rodents and chuffing, irritable warthogs—and once a spiny, squinty-eyed, long-snouted animal she had never seen before or since—without a trace of disillusionment she would simply run to one of her favorite streams, step out of her child's dark linens and nestle among the boulders, spending the hour before dusk letting imagination take her mind and the gentle lapping of the stream take her body. She recalled these moments as perfect happiness.

When darkness sank earthward from the clouds and rolled down the mountain, the thrill became the race against nightfall, when darker spirits with bad purpose left their lairs and sought malice among the living. Bare-footed she flew back into the valley, out of the reach of pursuing spirits and demigods, along trails that opened wide to receive her and narrowed in her wake to slow her demons. Dashing inside her hut she would throw herself against her mother's rough clothes and bask in the mock scolding and pretended anxiety over her daughter's fearless journeying. She relaxed under fingers that stroked her hair and love that questioned soothingly about her adventures. Beside the small fire Linh sat with her two sisters and had her dinner, her sisters older and laughing between themselves, ignoring her but without unkindness.

Before long Linh would be nearly asleep in her rice bowl. Her mother would gently shoo her into her corner of the room, onto her mat and blanket smiling and happy, dreaming, still awake, of spirits in shirts made of mist and sandals carved from moonbeams.

Now, these many years later, Linh stared across the eleven hundred meters of open field at the final target, barely able to perceive the tiny dark blemish inside its white sliver of target, the stick figure of a soldier motionless beside it. Enlightenment gripped her. In a motionless fury of awakening she understood why memory had transported her to the days of her childish adventures in the hills.

That she had never seen one of the forest spirits had not diminished her belief in them in the least, to the distress of the convent nuns in later years. But it had matured her to the truth, which now revealed itself fully.

Not for mortal eyes to behold the swift passing shimmer of even the slightest of the gods.

Nor was it for mortal eye to do what it was possible only for a god to do, as now: to raise her rifle barrel to the mosquito's eye of a dot an untested universe away and cause the next round from her Dragunov to find its center.

Without benefit of prior telescopic settings for that additional 100 meters, she might as well set out again to gaze upon another immortal.

Wind fluttered the edges of the topmost sheet in her shooting pad. The bottom of the page leapt upwards, curled and resettled, edges still flicking. Gods spoke through the winds, and she understood nothing. Or did she?

Linh looked at the shooting pad. Her eye took in the frantic scriblings her mind had engaged in as it slavishly sought answers to the riddle of a bullet's flight. Numbers on a page. *-3. 17. 4. + 7.* Written inside circles to transfix her mind. Symbols to command her hands in the turning of knobs.

Masters she had imposed on herself.

I will overcome all masters, beginning with myself.

It had been folly to put any faith in mathematics.

And she knew instinctively that all her computations to this point meant nothing. She suddenly disbelieved utterly in any mathematics she had performed. Wrong. All of it. And in particular, the scribbling that led to this final moment. This she knew. The plan for her entrapment was a buried explosive, now arrived at its final stage. It only remained for her own mind to trip the wire and seal her fate.

She looked downrange at the battle flag. As she watched, it flicked violently, whipped and curled, then subsided.

Heavy gusting, no settings, no prior explorers. The sun, still behind ragged clouds, burned through gaps in the white cover and into her uniform. Did the sun carry meaning in its rays, meant to deliver some message? Some *instruction*? But what? She had the sensation of nature speaking to her, if only she knew how to listen.

Linh turned her whole head to bring her sighted eye to bear on the reviewing stand. The officers and two civilians stared at her through their binoculars, no doubt concentrated on the ruined flesh of her face. Or perhaps trying to gauge her intent, find some clue as to her further capabilities. Certainly the Colonel would have groomed the significance of this final shot to his avid audience, now slavering in its collective mind over the final chance to strike an enriching blow. An impossible shot, yes, but could such a creature do the impossible? Was there further unlikely success in her eye and finger? Or, personally convinced she would fail, did they look at her while scheming to lure some recklessly bold one among them to wager on her next shot finding its mark?

The Colonel watched her also, still without binoculars. He sat rigidly, revealing nothing.

Linh looked at the Dragunov, at the slender tube atop the receiver that extended her sight so far beyond its mechanical limits. To some it might seem the telescopic sight made one like a god, able to reach out from the heavens and strike the unwary dead.

It was clear now to Linh that the sight did just the opposite.

The unwary that fell to the sight was the shooter himself, who placed his hope for godly deeds in a limited vessel. The sight was nothing but a coarse container of steel with dully ground glass at either end, forged on earth and not in the heavens, made by clever but still mortal minds, no more capable of determining the fate of a bullet's strike than they could provide an invariable mathematics of its flight. The telescope was the entrapment, suitable for nothing more than ensnaring the shooter's soul, its purpose not to magnify the enemy, but to convince the soul of its defects, and thereby magnify these.

I can, the telescope said. *You* can't.

For all Linh knew, the telescope served a bad spirit. Perhaps one night while she slept in her crude training hut the spirit had purloined her soul and imprisoned it inside the telescope's body, sealing her inside at either end with gates of glass. The possibility of the only condition she truly feared—her soul's enslavement—gripped her.

Linh knelt, picked up her rifle and examined the telescope closely. At both ends of its long slender tube, the telescope was strangled between steel half-rings mated to small metal bases attached to the rifle's receiver. For the first time she looked at the screw heads that bound the rings and bases. Four-sided slots. She recognized their pattern.

Putting the rifle down, she rummaged inside her pack and removed the rifle's oilcloth tool kit that on impulse she had chosen to bring along. Opening it she found the little four-sided steel post bent in a right angle. On the first day of her training, the Colonel had been unwilling to answer her question regarding its purpose, or of any other tool in her kit.

If you are meant to overcome masters, you will solve these petty problems.

Its purpose was no longer a mystery. Linh didn't hesitate. She inserted the short end of the tool inside one of the screw slots and turned. The screw didn't budge. She held the rifle in one hand and put the heel of the other hand on the long end of the tool and put her body weight behind it.

The screw gave and even with such slight movement the telescope and her settings were now useless. She repeated the motion and the screw turned freely. In another minute she had removed all eight screws and both half-rings and held the telescope in her hand.

She turned to look at the officers, who still watched her steadily. Their binoculars shook under their mutterings.

The Colonel did not move. One of the officers turned to him and said something sharply. The Colonel said nothing.

Linh turned away and struck the large bellows of the telescope on the rifle's stock. Then again. On the second blow the front lens of the telescope came loose. On the third it fell onto her shooting mat. She thought: *Fly away, my soul.*

She tossed the ruined scope to the side, then knelt and returned the small right-angled tool into the oilcloth and the oilcloth into her pack. Still kneeling she looked downrange at the national flag. It fluttered proudly in the anomalous breeze. She felt beckoned.

But she had angered the officers, whose game of wagering she had ruined. Their private strategies must have built relentlessly to this final shot. These were useless now. And what game was left? Who among them would take a wager now? She watched them turn their displeasure on the Colonel, who nodded deferentially but kept looking in her direction. Then he stood and faced them, his hands held wide before him as if in offering. Bich Linh could not make out his words, but it appeared he spoke persuasively.

There were wars within wars. She had given the Colonel such a war, yet she suspected he had fought their like before.

She had sensed a greater kinship with the rifle in its naked days, before the mounting of the telescope. The bond returned. The Colonel had told her the rifle was no longer Russian. It was *dragon,* no longer dragon*uv*. Yes, but not made so by the hand of any master other than herself. It was she who had infused the Dragonuv with the spirit of her people, from whose collective soul had sprung *dragon* itself. It was *her* spirit that had taken the file to the front sight, *her* spirit that had recognized the trap laid for her soul and so removed and tossed the telescope aside. *Her* spirit had done this. And if she were to fail, it would be *her* failure, no one else's. Not the Russians', not the Colonel's, not her people's. Not *dragon's*. Hers alone, in this final test before her, either to prove herself worthy or expose the hollow core of her being.

The iron sights remained unmoved from her last settings at six hundred yards. In her mind's eye she watched again the concluding evening of her training with the iron sights: the Colonel limping from his *geep*, standing before the target and making his fingers verify what his eyes doubted. Four shots with iron sights, six hundred meters. Four center hits, one of them while standing. The shots had clustered in the middle. Two had nearly passed through the same hole, the remaining two landing centimeters to the right, stacked one on top of the other. With iron sights, without the telescope, without the risk to her soul, and with or without the gods, *she* had been doing the shooting. And with or without the gods, she had shot true.

Linh removed her cloth cap and struck the clasp from her hair, which unfurled in long black clusters down her back to hang straight and proud and then immediately to dance in a sudden gust of wind. *Yes, a woman.* She glanced back at the reviewing stand and fought down her rising scorn. She knew the dangers of arrogance, and yet deeply, sometimes nearly fatally, she could not restrain the contempt she felt for such men. Her face was disfigured, but her soul was untouched. With them, just the opposite.

Yet the deed before her, impossible though it was, demanded something like humility simply in the attempt. Not for her to judge in matters of karma, including those she despised.

No one escaped this world, in the end.

All that was evil, evil repaid.

She looked away until she regained herself. Moments passed. She reached down and picked up her rifle, stood and stared out at the flag. Another gusting wind flicked her hair with greater violence. She paid it no attention. Wind no longer mattered. The time was Now.

The jabbering behind her rose in volume as the officers watched Linh reject the logical mathematics of a prone position and raise the rifle, one leg forward, one behind her, bent at the waist as though any moment she might tumble backward to the earth.

The Falling Tree. So named by Colonel Trung, on a day when he hid a smile with a frown.

Was the Colonel hiding another smile now? Or was the frown he had disguised on that day now turned loose to be itself?

She found the impression of an insect's eye eleven hundred meters away and brought the blur of her front sight to rest just under the smidgeon of black. When she switched focus to the whittled front post it burst into sharp relief and the insect's eye disappeared. The rear sight turned to pure mist. She leaned imperceptibly further back, braced against sunlight. The Dragunov's barrel rose the width of an insect's wing.

Another breeze touched her face, this time with the hand of the prevailing wind. She accepted it as before her disfiguring she had accepted the caresses of men.

In her own mind she lay in cool water, waiting to gaze upon an immortal.

Linh marveled at her front sight. It was as still as a portrait hung on a wall of sky, a work of art so perfect she disbelieved that the trigger finger now crawling through a pasture of milk in the direction of her suspended heart was one of the same peasant fingers that had crafted it.

After an eternity the Dragunov fired but the sound barely reached her. The bolt cycled in another eternity. A spent cartridge spun end over end in the morning sunlight as if it would never land. Thanh would say later, beside a campfire in the long years after the Colonel had given up his search for it, *Perhaps it never did.*

By the time she straightened herself and lowered the rifle, the sun had folded back into the clouds and more gusts were harrying the national flag. The same winds sent outlier strands of her hair to anoint the ruined side of her face. She thought she heard voices, as if the gods that spoke through wind were jabbering like the Colonel's guests. When she looked down from the flag the target tender was in front of the target. For a moment, despite the distance and despite his rigid stance, it seemed to Linh that she could perceive an uncertainty in the soldier's tiny form, as though he had forfeited the comfort of his own insignificance in whatever drama was unfolding.

The bickering of the officers abruptly ceased. They watched and waited. The Colonel watched. The bodyguards of the officers watched. The world stood still as a photograph, watching the motionless figure of the soldier. Only Linh looked elsewhere, smiling and unknowing of her smiling, at the piece of lifeless glass lying in submission at her feet, the prison door she had pried loose from the end of the telescope to liberate her soul.

Then the soldier stepped aside and bowed, releasing sunlight. Linh looked up and saw its unmistakable glint on the white disc.

III

Buddha

26

MEMORY HAD BICH LINH IN A TRANCE. Or had she simply fallen asleep? The one eye blinked back to life, into the muted charcoals of broken wall, timbers, concrete, the shards of the world. What day was it? What life? Memory was a minefield, never far below the surface. The past had exploded. *Now* beckoned her back.

Bich Linh rose from beneath the remains of the window. The ladder to her quarters lay in pieces, shattered in the rain of bullets from the helicopter. Stone and splinters cascaded alongside her as she lowered herself from the second floor down broken sections of wall and timber. Inside the triangle of collapsed masonry where she had slept her mat was shredded and her canteen and pack looked like wild animals had torn them apart. The canteen was useless, its neck mangled. Precious contents had bled into the debris, as though rubble could grow if watered.

The Dragunov, tucked away in the back, had escaped damage. She repaired her pack as best she could and threw it onto her back. Her thirst flared and she kicked the broken canteen into the broken wall, picked up her rifle and bandoleer of ammunition and made her way back up to the second floor.

After the helicopter attack the second floor now served as little more than a sagging roof for the remaining building. The sun struggled to break clear of a sullen cloud cover. Where it succeeded, golden patches shone briefly before being swallowed back up. The bass thunder of jets prowled in quarters unseen.

Inside the backdrop of the jets' rumble Bich Linh heard the mortar tubes renewing their attack. People's Army tubes, she was certain, from the east. Larger, battalion-sized mortars. She understood intuitively what must be in progress: Under suicidal orders to retake the city, the army was trying to force its way back inside, in broad daylight, past American marines on the ground, jets and helicopter gunships in the sky, certain death everywhere. And well before reaching anything like a final objective—she imagined some enemy strong point at the city's center—the lead column had already run into a small but stubborn concentration of enemy troops at the front of the temple. Jets patrolling yet not attacking mystified her, but on reflection could only mean that the enemy must be so intermixed with PAVN troops that American airpower could not effectively be used. Yet any delay was simply a finger resting on a trigger. The enemy would wait only so long. When the air strikes resumed, the attacking force would be annihilated. Something she knew only too well.

Thanh had said one evening: *First comes delusion, then come orders. Bodies come last.*

More rafters had collapsed around the remains of her window. The wooden frame above the window opening had severed in the middle and imploded onto the sill in two massive angled splinters, mangling the window posts at the sides, gravity tugging one outward toward the street, one inward toward the building. The whole arrangement looked like a strong wind would blow it into the street below.

A strong wind was coming: Linh recognized the sibilance of descending mortar rounds. She found what cover she could behind the broken walls and waited for the explosions.

A strong wind… Despite herself, memory resurfaced and Now receded. She let her mind wander…

A strong wind took her hair and waved it at the national flag downrange. As though released from all restraint, the breeze built and flailed at the bit of colored cloth. She heard each of the officers take a turn to belittle and then as a group castigate Colonel Trung, alternately pointing at him, at her and at her final target downrange. Loud enough now to be easily heard. The Colonel did not speak.

Unlike the other soldiers tending earlier targets, the soldier posted there still remained, standing statue-like now beside the target rather than in front of it. It was not yet mid-morning. Clouds had appeared from nowhere and the sky seemed unsure how to proceed, whether to swell itself with overcast or inhale its own fine mist and release the sun in full.

The officers' abuse escalated. Linh quit listening. For a moment she was angered on the Colonel's behalf, but one look at him showed her he knew how to deal with fools, his only occasional response a short nod of the head when required for decorum.

And then the officers and two civilians stood and with loud final recriminations, stalked off the reviewing stand and left the field, one guard in front and the other behind, their rifle bayonets fixed in a show of indignation.

Colonel Trung watched them disappear behind the treeline and then limped across the field toward her where she stood expectantly on the shooting mat. To be ready to leave, and accept whatever discipline he would announce, she bent down to recover her rifle and gear, but the Colonel waved her off. As he approached she sensed an animation inside him wholly absent in their earlier days together. Discipline was apparently not on his mind.

"Walk with me, daughter, and forgive my mood," the Colonel said, in a voice so warm it seemed another person speaking. Though recently berated by half the Army Command, he could not have appeared less affected.

As during her training with the telescope, they walked downrange, the Colonel saying nothing, apparently lost in thought, or maybe not thinking at all. Passing each of her targets laid out on the ground and facing the sky, he paused to note the location of the white disc.

He did not speak again until they arrived at the seven hundred meter target. Bich Linh's shot had landed only centimeters from the outside edge of the black circle. The Colonel said, "You shot too quickly. I thought it might be over. But you managed."

A red dot less than the width of a bullet had been imprinted at the center of the target, little more than a stain. Linh noticed it for the first time.

"Such a small bullseye is no help to a shooter," she said. "I could not have seen such a mark at even one hundred meters."

"It is not intended as a bullseye. It is simply a scoring mark. This target was originally designed for other uses, for iron sights only at no greater than 500 meters. In those applications, the scorer notes distance from the red dot in computing results. Your test tonight was simply pass/fail. A round in the black or not."

At eight hundred meters the Colonel stopped and stood pensively, then reached down and pulled the disc from the black circle and pointed at the hole. Her bullet was 8 centimeters below the red dot. Windage was nearly perfect.

"Two clicks up. Maybe one. That shot would have been centered, despite the wind. At eight hundred meters. As I indicated when I delivered this rifle into your care, where most of these Russian rifles fall apart, yours begins to perform. If the shooter is up to it. If the shooter can deal with the wind." He smiled and added apologetically, "You will forgive the hasty manner in which the last day's training concluded, without the opportunity to refigure your telescope at distance. You see, I never intended that the unexceptional would be able to advance.

Better that they fail here than in the field, where lives are at stake." He replaced the white disc and walked on.

The Colonel moved at a much improved pace, surprising her. She hurried to keep up. At the one thousand meter target Colonel Trung once again removed the white disk from the black circle. The shot was centered vertically and five centimeters to the left of dead center.

The Colonel shook his head.

"Technically a better shot than anything earlier. Even with the left windage strike. At this distance, hardly an error. Most shooters in these winds would have killed every soldier spotting targets and not been at fault." He gave Bich Linh a look and then asked, "Tell me, did you notice anything...*peculiar* about the wind?"

Bich Linh thought for a moment. "The wind did not behave like wind. I did not understand the vertical movement of my bullet impact target to target, how it rose when it should not have risen, only to suddenly fall earthward on the final targets, as though it sought to deceive. Luck guided me."

"Not luck, daughter. And not deceit. *Dragon* tested you, and then guided you. As it once guided and instructed me, here in this same place, long years ago. The wind's caprice has brought you more opportunity for understanding than you may realize for many of your own long years." For a moment the Colonel regarded the trees lining the edge of the field. Branches moved gently in the prevailing wind, then flailed briefly under the whip of a sudden gust. "Daughter, the wind has *chosen* you. There are things that are mortal, and those that are not. I have lived to see many of the former, far too many, and had come to despair of ever witnessing the latter." He removed his cap, ran a hand across his close-cropped hair and replaced the cap with care. He smiled at her. "But now I am a witness, and I will say no more, except this, that I am grateful for the day that fate brought you north."

He turned back to the target, re-inserted the spotting disc and looked across the last hundred meters to the final target. The target tender held his post a meter away, still at strict attention. He was so motionless Bich Linh thought he could have been carved from wood.

"Now," the Colonel said, and resumed walking, but more slowly again, as though not to hurry the moment. It appeared to Linh his limp was nearly gone. Fifty meters from the target, Linh dropped back and let the Colonel approach alone. When she stopped behind him he had been observing the white disc wordlessly for some time. Neither Linh nor the Colonel noticed or spoke to the soldier, who peered straight ahead.

Another moment passed and the Colonel said finally, "Soldier."

"Sir!"

"Carefully remove the spotting disc." The Colonel seemed to think the occasion required ceremony.

"Sir!" The soldier stepped smartly to the target and pulled the disc straight backward as though his arm were part of a machine.

"Now step aside." The soldier did. "Bich Linh."

Linh walked forward and stood beside the Colonel.

"Look what you have done."

He nodded at the small single perforation in the black field of the target. The tiny red mark was missing.

It was not possible, but it was what she saw.

"Mathematical," the Colonel said. "I am a witness."

27

BEFORE THE MORTARS LANDED she saw the two soldiers running from their shelter across the street from the temple into the open, toward her position. One carried a radio, the other bore something inside some type of chest pouch. As her rifle went to her shoulder for two easy kills, two more soldiers emerged from the same shelter, one stumbling along half-carrying, half-dragging another, both of them bandaged and bleeding, little more than broken vessels. A single round would do for this pair. But she relaxed her finger on the Dragunov's trigger when she saw the lead American talking into his radio. Possibility gripped her. Were they bringing the tiger back?

And then the first mortar exploded in the street. The first two Americans slowed, conferred in signs, then ran to the side for cover but ran instead into the center of an exploding barrage that disassembled both of them. Blood, flesh and cobblestone flew into overhanging trees inside the temple courtyard.

Something shiny flew from inside the brief flower of the explosions. Kneeling at the ruins of the stone window sill, Linh barely had time to feel cheated of her kills before the People's Army dropped a mortar at the base of her building. The concussion from the explosion was enough to cause the weakened structure below the floor to buckle and send her forward into the path of a dislocated section of window frame. Her head met the jagged timber tumbling on its way into the street.

Too numerous to count, stars appeared on the black cloth of premature night. Linh couldn't help admiring their brilliance before fading with them into the darkness…

When daylight returned Linh was wracked by a spasm of blinking. She looked up into a blur of gray sky and felt a trellis of nerve endings bristling in the cavity of her missing eye. The seizure stopped, replaced by the familiar sensation of blood running along the hideous cheek. The world of rubble, broken wall and gray sky came into focus and with it came the whine of overhead ricochet and the hammering of nearby automatic fire. Mainly Kalashnikov, then the higher-pitched popping of an Armalite. One rifle. Rounds fired singly, a pause, then the stutter of a full magazine. When the Armalite fired, the Kalashnikov abated, as though weighing the merits of another opinion. Then all Kalashnikov and then Armalite and then Kalashnikov again, more persistent now, unconvinced by the opposing argument. In there, too, a third weapon she couldn't identify.

It was a story with missing chapters. To fill them in Linh dragged herself to the edge of the roof. The building leaned like a fighter gone to one knee. The window was gone. A solitary timber slouched backward, defying gravity, dripping barnacles of plaster. In the bombed-out intersection of the three streets below, where two narrow lanes converged on the broader boulevard along the temple, she saw an extraordinary sight.

Five meters below her and ten meters away, two Americans lay in a shallow depression of gutted street along a low wall of broken cobblestone and held up a company of the People's Army, the vanguard of who knew how many more.

Two soldiers.

One of them with nothing more than a pistol. It angered her but amused her too. As she watched, the dark American stopped firing his pistol and lay still along the mound of broken street. Even from her distance she could see the dark one's chest move fitfully. Not dead, but almost. A vessel emptying.

The other one fought on. Enough. Linh looked around for her rifle, couldn't see it anywhere. The rocket launcher had rolled but struck the single remaining upright of the window frame and lodged against it. Her rifle was nowhere in view. Careful to keep her weight back, she peered over the edge.

The building's settlement had twisted the wall into bulging sheets of fractured and wrinkled plaster and wood lath. The Dragunov lay in a crevice between separated planes of wall, just out of arm's reach. To retrieve it she would have to maneuver herself over the edge and turn her back to the street and the American below. She had no other choice. She was useless without the rifle.

Then she paused, listened and came alert. At that instant, his back toward her, one of the Americans rose to his feet and leveled his rifle in front of him. Without taking aim, he opened fire. She paid him no attention. There was no time to marvel at his suicidal action.

Forgetting the Dragunov, she scrambled on hands and knees and threw her body over the rocket launcher, contorting herself into an image of the dead, a skill she had used before.

Her tiger roared from below the roofline behind her and passed three meters overhead, fangs bared and spewing its metal teeth into the body of the People's Army. As it passed up the street tearing life from squads of exposed soldiers, Bich Linh fought the urge to move. It was too soon. One premature action on her part and the tiger would quickly sink its fangs into her. She needed to see the tiger's back.

She knew the Huey would return. As it had howled above her she understood its purpose. It surprised even her in the breadth of its tactical error. The American soldiers below were doomed. Nothing could save them, as nothing had saved the soldiers from the temple. There were four or five other Americans inside the helicopter. Did their lives, and his own, mean nothing to the pilot? And the craft itself, how many American workers, how many American dollars to create such a beast? Throw these all away, why? For cloven vessels, shards of human lives, broken wheels. In any day on earth, uncountable numbers of such.

Americans. Foul-odored and cruel, yet hardy enough as a foe, and many of them brave fighters, as had been the French before them. But sentimental. Devils contradicted by conscience. It would be their downfall, no matter the hordes of their beasts that came to crowd the skies. To conquer the hard resolve of her people it would take an eye that shed blood at death's approach, not tears. An eye like hers.

Above the temple plaza the Huey banked sharply, its guns paused in turning, resuming instantly on completing its spin. Again it charged along the street, finding fewer soldiers exposed on this pass, but with such ferocity of sound and fire that the remainder instinctively burrowed themselves deeper behind their cover in the street or inside the buildings where they scattered.

Bich Linh lay still as a corpse, legs skewed apart, yet watching as the helicopter flew straight toward her, rose at the last instant, rolled and twisted to face the temple again. Again its firing faltered only during the turn. As the *Yu-i* sank toward the earth, the gunners raked the street, the courtyard wall, the temple windows, the buildings lining the boulevard, everything in sight and anything that moved, churning the air into dust as they foolishly, fatally, rode the metal beast onto the broken street.

She had the tiger's back now.

Still lying down, rolling to face the sky, Linh raised the rocket launcher. Round armed, safety off, sights intact.

Not that she would need the sights after all. Not at twenty-five meters.

As Bich Linh rose to her knees, she saw the soldier jump from the helicopter and run toward the American, who stood inexplicably straight up in the shallow trench, his rifle dangling from the end of his arm, shirt billowing in the blast of the helicopter blades. These Americans. Pilots, soldiers. Incomprehensible.

She stood too fast and the blood rushed to her head with the stroke of a hammer. Somewhere sunlight smashed through the grey sky as the world blurred and narrowed. The hammer beat harder, but she held on until her vision cleared. When it did she found herself at the edge of the roof, braced against its slope downward. Standing as though in one world and gazing into another, invisible to all. Below her the dark American was being dragged between two others toward the helicopter. She could hear only the machine guns firing over the fury of the helicopter rotors. Unbelievable. The vanguard of a battalion or larger of the People's Army, no one yet returning fire.

All the fighters are in the mountains.

Then she heard a burst of curt, hoarse Kalashnikov, followed by a handful more of additional rifles. So a few had found testicles to pit against those of this American pilot.

Linh settled the B40 on her shoulder, put the rudimentary sight to her eye but looked past it. The question of the kill was simply whether the launcher would work.

No, there was another question.

Why had the American below dropped his rifle and the broken vessel he was carrying to aim at her with only a pistol? Why would he be more confident with a smaller, less powerful weapon against a danger so clearly identified? She ignored the soldier, and the pistol that sought her form, and concentrated on the trigger of the B40 and her howling target below.

The pistol or the RPG, let Buddha decide which shot broke first.

In his wisdom and mercy the Buddha chose the pistol. Linh felt the bullet strike the top of the wall, near her foot. Bits of plaster stung her legs. In her turn she was not the wise Buddha and there was no mercy in her and the B40 ignited, blinding her in ignition smoke.

The explosion of the helicopter rocked her backward, then almost immediately a secondary blast caused her to stumble. As she fell, shrapnel cut a lock from her hair.

The death throes of the helicopter elated and enthralled her. She picked herself up and watched the beast scream its outrage in a futile spasm of disintegrating metal as it pounded the earth with both rotors until its heart burst from its own fury and the body crashed into the cobblestones, rocked, groaned and went silent. Pieces of rotor blades fell from trees and landed brightly against nearby buildings and in the street as far away as the temple. All in a matter of pulse beats.

Bich Linh dropped the rocket launcher and leaned against the sole upright timber on the roof, all that was left of her window. The People's Army was moving now, coming from buildings, from behind low walls, from inside the temple. As they advanced, their yelling became a chorus, the bitter confusion in their voices turning through anger toward joyful malice. Two soldiers ran to the helicopter. Near it a pair of Americans lay entwined in death, skewered by the same long section of bloody rotor. Inside the belly of the beast a dead American hung from his waist, backward.

She needed her rifle. The two soldiers, heedless of tactics, coming to vent their fury on the helpless dead, had failed to look around them, to the side of the *Yu-i*, where the American with the pistol was waiting. He was half-dead but not helpless, obscured by a wall of debris, his legs glistening like red oil in a shaft of slanted sunlight breaking through the clouds. Linh could see him raise his head, the pistol still in his hand. The two soldiers arrived at the Huey and began firing into its side, into the dead American hanging out of it and into the pilot's cabin.

Reaching over the edge of the roof, pushing herself backward with one hand against the tug of gravity, Linh reached down into the crevice for her rifle. She fumbled with it before finally getting a purchase on the barrel. Pulled it up but too late. The American shot one of the soldiers in the back, and as the second one turned in confusion, shot him in the chest. Both soldiers fell without moving. Linh could see the slide of the pistol locked open, the weapon empty. The American dropped the pistol and lay back, looking up into the sky. He moved his head suddenly as though something had claimed his attention. She could see his chest move, too. Americans died stubbornly.

Bich Linh saw what the American must have seen. A small bird of some kind—a sparrow—flew overhead and out of sight into the battered trees of the temple courtyard. In the battle for the city the birds had not all left during the mortars, during the fury of automatic weapon fire, or later even during the artillery. But after the bombs came there were no more birds. This was the first she'd seen since the jets. The bird knew what some generals didn't. This battle was nearly over.

Linh surveyed the carnage. It was a street of the dead. Bodies everywhere. A trail of shattered vessels, from the temple plaza to the back of the courtyard. Dead countrymen, dead Americans. The smell of explosive hung in the air. It would be thicker on the ground, mingled with the odor of death. All along the street, splashes of red on the grey and brown canvas of afternoon.

The People's Army was moving again, more cautiously after watching the two soldiers fall beside the helicopter carcass. Linh could see soldiers slipping into the plaza at the front of the temple, wending their way through bodies and wreckage. Occasionally one stopped to fire his rifle into a prostrate figure. It wouldn't be long before the bloodletting attracted the jets, the way it was said that in the ocean blood attracted sharks. She sensed the predators in the sky, above the thinning clouds, waiting only for the word to descend. It was time to leave the city. And she knew where she was going, and that she *was* going.

Her eye froze.

A chill coursed through her. It was a vision. It had to be. Or it was hunger, or her thirst. Exhaustion. She looked away and then back, to see if her eye deceived her.

The vision remained.

28 SOMEONE SHOUTED TO HER. She looked down. A half-dozen soldiers advanced on a line, Kalashnikovs at the ready, approaching the helicopter's remains with caution. Dozens more were retrieving themselves from behind buildings and the courtyard walls. The soldier who had called out to her turned from the smoldering helicopter and raised his rifle in a salute.

"You! You did this?" he shouted. Linh could see him clearly. There was something immediately familiar about him.

"Who else?" Linh reached down and hoisted the rocket launcher. "None among you did other than die by its guns!"

"We would have destroyed it," another soldier said in the sudden quiet. "We were attacking."

Bich Linh laughed. The little group of soldiers stopped advancing, stared up at her. She said, "Schoolchildren! I watched your attack, broken by two broken soldiers. Next time, carry a weapon that will kill a tiger!" She threw the launcher at the soldier. He dodged aside as the B-40 cartwheeled into the rubble.

"We moved bravely and we would have destroyed it," the soldier insisted, but Bich Linh had disappeared. When she emerged from the twisted building, the braggart soldier and two of his comrades had discovered the American. They were kicking and cursing him. He was bloodied from the neck down, his face torn and red, but he was alive, one white eye round and large and wandering aimlessly to some new point in the sky with each kick. The soldiers kicked him furiously. Others arrived to watch, some silently, some drawing closer to join in the punishment.

Bich Linh heard the thrashing, but her attention rested on the vision she had seen from the roof. Only not a vision. There the little god sat. And not just any rendition. Almost a living incarnation. This Buddha *lived*. An omen. But meaning what?

Buddha, characteristically, revealed nothing. He sat looking straight ahead, contemplating the soldiers beating the American.

The loud-talking soldier struck the American with the butt of his rifle. Linh watched now as he unfolded his bayonet, spewing nonsense as he apparently prepared to skewer the American. The other soldiers drew back in anticipation.

"Stand back!" Bich Linh approached through the debris. "This is my prisoner, not yours!"

The soldier looked up from the American and stared at her with contempt.

"I will kill the enemy where I find him!" He gave the American another vicious kick.

"I will not tell you again." Linh raised the Dragunov, five meters away. She kept walking. Poised to strike again, the soldier's foot froze. He glared at Bich Linh.

"You are a woman. You fight alongside men as a privilege. A woman takes her orders from a man!"

Bich Linh stopped in front of the man and put the Dragunov barrel a hand's breadth away from the front of his eyes.

"Not this woman," she said.

"You have no rank," the soldier said, seeing no insignia on her sleeves, but in a voice now as pale as his face.

Linh sneered. "I have killed more Americans than all the generals inside all their whorehouses. *That* is my rank. And I would purge you as a coward from this army right now but ammunition is more precious than your worthless life. I will let the Americans waste *their* ammunition. You will be dead by morning and many more of these better men with you. If their karma is good they will die upwind of your stench." She placed the muzzle of the rifle on the man's forehead and shoved him backward hard enough to make him cry out. "Not another word."

The soldier lowered his rifle. He was beaten and he knew it. Linh knew it. The others knew it and lowered their eyes in pity.

A dozen soldiers stood and watched. Behind them a junior officer was approaching. She could see the single gold ornament on the red collar band, the starch in the sweat-soaked uniform, an arrogant set of the mouth.

Before he arrived Linh spoke sharply to the gathered soldiers. "Do you see the *Yu-i*? Do you see this beast of America broken and lifeless on the ground, the white devils dead inside it? Had it escaped, don't you think the jets would be here now? Don't you know they know where you are, only they are unsure if some of their American soldiers here still live? They are weak, and unlike *your* commanders they will not kill one or ten of their own to kill a hundred or thousand of the enemy. Oh, but they are coming. They run for their jets now, they rise and circle behind the clouds, waiting for the word to come and kill *all of you!*" She swept an arm for emphasis. The soldiers tilted their heads backward, as if to avoid inclusion. They looked at each other, or at the ground. The farthest away muttered something but were careful to make themselves unheard

"Look around you. Do you see the destroyed beast? Do you see the American dead? Inside the helicopter, here at your feet, there beside the temple? *I* did this. I alone. One woman. One *soldier*. You are all alive because *I*, a woman, the only woman in her cadre, saved you. And what of the men in my cadre? Where are all these brave soldiers, pride of the people? Gone, dead, deserted. Cowards and fools. I am tired of this army. I am tired of *you*. Have you anything to say?"

No soldier spoke up. The officer had arrived and stood back silently, watching. Linh noticed but paid him no attention. What could he do, demote her and sentence her to go south?

"There has been an omen. Look there." She pointed to the golden statue, its ruby eye gone dark, touched by shadows from the remains of the banyan tree in the courtyard. "Lord Buddha has taken this white devil into his protection. It cannot be known why. If you have touched him, plan on dying. If you touch the Buddha, plan on dying. If not, go your way to battle and maybe you will see tomorrow."

Bich Linh stood above the nearly lifeless American soldier. She saw the open gash at the back of his head, the gray metal inside its ragged clot, flesh already turning green, blood black with dirt. Wondrous that he could still draw breath with such a wound. Yet there were other hurts. His shirt down one side was red to his waist. Fragments of shrapnel protruded from his legs. A mutilated hand. Possibly he had lost his manhood. She lowered the Dragunov and ran the barrel along his forehead and down to his chin. An eye socket mangled. She repudiated the comparison to her own condition. The head moved without resistance as she turned it from side to side with the rifle's barrel.

Not you, she thought.

She brought the barrel to the soldier's remaining eye. Her finger tightened on the Dragunov's trigger. She wanted to tear the eye out, to blind him worse than the serpent had ruined her, and so disavow any similarity between them. She cursed him foully. Spat on him.

"Cry no more," she told the American, but there was no mistaking the stream of blood below his eye for tears. She was prepared to kill him, yet the serpent in her refrained. Lord Buddha watched her. Her heart wanted the kill but the kill would be her own death, and then her killing would be over. It was a bad trade. Buddha knew and forbade it. Why? Why was Buddha there in that instant, among such destruction and death, to protect this broken white devil?

Only the gods knew. Reluctantly she relaxed her trigger finger.

The American said something. It was weak, barely audible, but not broken in spirit. Far from crying, he was defiant, even insolent. Her temper flared. But there sat Lord Buddha the Protector, exuding life and grace, even for the white devil. Including both of them in his gaze.

She stepped away from the soldier and bowed to the statue. Not hers to cross swords with the gods, who alone knew why they did what they did.

To calm herself, for just the space of a moment Bich Linh sent her mind into the mountains, into lush forests, but it would not stay. It returned immediately to prepare her body to leave the wasted city. As she turned abruptly away the junior officer stepped from behind the soldiers and barred her path.

"I listened so I could count your offenses," he said. "They are many, and a court-martial awaits you with extreme due punishment. You are a superstitious, low-bred southern malcontent with a traitor's tongue. Until the People's justice can be arranged, you will fall in with this army, fight beside it and subject yourself to authority. You will do so now without argument!" He brushed his hand contemptuously against the Sapper Battalion marking on her collar. "You are *infantry* now!"

Linh's memory responded with the words of Colonel Trung: *You must never accept such a fate.* And followed these with her own: *In the matter of fortune, I had better rely on myself.*

Exactly. The Colonel again.

Linh looked at the man. Handsome, well shaven. Laundered shirt. In the middle of destruction, this man had managed a pressed uniform. He had the educated northerner's cultivated air about him. Officer's school. Possibly travel to other lands and cities. Even the toenails protruding from his combat sandals looked manicured. She had seen such men in her convent, parents of pampered students. Dandies all.

"What army is this?" Bich Linh asked, genuinely curious.

"No army of *yours*. You will stain no company with a formal assignment. You will take orders from this vanguard of Forward Battalion, Fifth Regiment, Sixty-First Division."

"The Sixty-First? Who commands the Battalion?"

"Your commanding officer, though he would never acknowledge you, is Colonel Dinh Van Trung. Now fall in and prepare to move out." He turned to walk back up the street toward the plaza, where a large body of soldiers were resting, helmets and packs off. Some were smoking. She shook her head. Imagine troops so green they took comfort in the open with a sky full of American jets waiting to fall.

When Linh spoke again the officer stopped in his tracks.

"One question, Lieutenant."

The man turned and glared at her.

"How *is* the Colonel?"

Bich Linh's face contorted in a grin so wide, so hideous that it cracked the forming scabs of her scars into bleeding again.

29

THE COLONEL TOSSED the white spotting disc into the pit beneath the target stand. It hit the crude narrow bench at the pit's bottom, bounced against the earthen wall and came to rest in a corner. The Colonel shook his head and said, "Even such an unimportant object as that, one day will be a relic. Archeologists in the future someday will pock this field with holes until they find it, as all people seek endlessly for signs of miracles. As I myself will go back and recover the cartridge from your last shot."

For a moment more the Colonel contemplated the target on its stand. Then he carefully removed the paper target from the grasp of staples and gingerly scrolled it into a tube. "This I will keep. I would give it to you, but you have no way to safeguard it. If any of us remain alive after this war, find me and I will return it. Meanwhile it will be well preserved."

Linh had nothing to say. The strangest feeling she had ever known overcame her the moment she saw the target. She watched the national flag whipping now in the stiff breeze. A beautiful flag, the lovely yellow star on the red field of heroes' blood, but of what realm, really? What heroes? It flapped noisily, rhythmically, punctuated by silences. Speaking to her. She strained, but what she heard, she couldn't understand, as if spoken in an unearthly language once known but long since forgotten.

"Let us go," the Colonel said.

Linh followed as he led the way back. In ten steps he stopped and addressed the soldier, who had not relaxed from his position of attention beside the target stand. "You, too, soldier," he said.

"Sir?" The private's head moved, but he remained rigid.

"Come with us, private. Your own fate is affected today. And in my experience it is not physically possible to walk while standing to attention."

In fifty paces Linh looked back. The soldier followed tentatively, respectfully keeping his distance, a man journeying toward the unknown. When they arrived at the reviewing stand the Colonel said to Linh, "Recover your rifle and pack and meet us at the vehicle."

When Linh emerged from the treeline, wearing her pack and carrying the Dragunov, the Colonel and the private were beneath shade in a small grove of banyan trees fifty meters away, nowhere near the Colonel's jeep.

The late morning sun, no longer divided in its thinking, had burned away the morning mists and now shone brightly and hotly. The Colonel waved to her. When she arrived he indicated she should take a seat. The private sat next to the Colonel in a pool of confusion, a wooden cup in his hand, at a loss for an appropriate military bearing. The Colonel sat cross-legged, a bottle of rice wine in front of him. Beside him sat a small plastic chest. He had pushed his cap back on his head, for all the world fraternizing with enlisted soldiers.

Linh laid her pack and rifle in front of her and squatted in the way of rice workers everywhere in Southeast Asian lands. The Colonel picked up another wooden cup and poured her a draft from the bottle of wine. Linh took the cup and thought of the small hut in the delta: evenings with her children asleep, her husband stirring her passion as he stroked her beneath the table and they looked at each other and sipped from the same cup.

She took a small drink. A warmth filtered through her immediately. The wine was delicious, better by far than any she had ever tasted.

"Courtesy of our senior patriots," said Colonel Trung. "Fortunately they left in such indignation they forgot their bottle. Alas, they finished the pastries much earlier."

The Colonel indicated the soldier beside him. "This is Banh Tan Nguyen, of northern rice fields beside a village so remote you would not know the name any better than most map makers. Nguyen was a private until this morning, but I have given him the next rank for his excellent service today."

"What service was that?" Linh asked, looking at the soldier, who immediately averted his gaze. "He stood as ordered, did as ordered. He looks like a timid little farm boy soon to be consumed in flame."

The soldier began excavating the earth with his downcast eyes. The Colonel said, "You see, but you don't see all. You judge prematurely. I assure you this young man will be a People's Hero one day. As for his service in the past few hours..."—the Colonel opened his hands in a gesture of humility—"we will let history, and the heavens, be the judge. Now, to share with you the aftermath of this extraordinary morning. Private, must I order you to drink this fine beverage? Do you not drink rice wine in your village?"

The soldier said, "Oh, yes, Colonel. I mean, Yes, Colonel, I have had rice wine, in my village, sir, not, Yes, you must order me to drink." The private's cheeks flushed and he bowed his head and sipped from the cup. His eyes widened.

"Colonel, sir, this is truly excellent." Sipped again. "Frankly, sir, it is beyond words." His face softened, and he took another, longer swig. "I had no idea, sir," the private said.

"No idea of what?" Linh asked, vaguely annoyed by such innocence. The man was a child.

"Why, that a wine could taste so good," the Colonel said. "Most of our people drink their wine for the pleasure of intoxication. Excuse me, a hasty conclusion that sounds like a condemnation. Let us just say *some* seek a hurried escape from their toils, and so drink anything to hand simply to numb travail, never learning the joy of a wine that has truly achieved its potential. Intoxication certainly has its rewards, but there can be even greater pleasure simply in the experience of a wine's flavor, in that unique sensation that flows from first taste upwards to Mind."

"Never, never suspected." The soldier nodded his emphatic agreement and to the Colonel's clear amusement he tilted back his head and noisily drained the contents of the cup.

"He is a drunkard," Linh said disgustedly.

"A man on first meeting the nectar of gods, is all," the Colonel said, and refilled the private's cup.

"I must mind my manners," said newly promoted (Advanced) Private Nguyen, wiping wine from his chin, his eyes narrowed as though calling up reserves of temperance. Added, "And remember my place." The cup hovered indecisively, then slowly sank to the ground. Temperance had momentarily won. The private wore a slightly skewed smile. "I will always be indebted to you, Colonel," he suddenly gushed. "A pleasant day...I thought I would never see one again."

"And an *historic* day," the Colonel added. "Remember it, Advanced Private Nguyen." The Colonel spoke kindly, without trace of irony. "In this war there will not be many such days. Memory is a powerful antidote to the convulsions of our times."

"He will be in convulsions if he drinks one more cup," Linh said. "And his memory will be of headache and bile."

The Colonel waved his hand. "With such banter I could be sitting around my own table at home," he said delightedly.

30

THE SENIOR PATRIOTS AND OFFICERS, the Colonel said, had marveled at Bich Linh's accuracy, even in the face of such devil winds. He expressed surprise that Bich Linh had not quickly realized that new wind conditions were engineered into the test. *No pupil,* he said, fired on a windless day, for it was the winds, and not the distances, that *were* the test. Any pupil under his tutelage could shoot center target out to any distance; but could they shoot into the unknown? Could they master uncertainty? Were they truly *shooters*? Most importantly, were they *dragon*?

Unknown winds, unknown distances, proved the matter.

The Colonel related that small fortunes had been wagered, lost, won again and lost again even by the time she had fired at seven hundred yards. Complicated wagers they had been—on the target or off, a hand's width high or low, left or right of center, so close to an edge that the white disc would loom into the white field—and then the stakes truly rose. One of the wealthier patriots—wealthier, perhaps, though it must be remembered that all good communists were to be considered equal in socialist doctrine and regard—this wealthy patriot had suffered serious losses in convoluted bets at the previous distances. At eight hundred yards, this same officer in his desperation appeared to have gone slightly mad and given the others such favorable odds that none could resist. Three-to-one had been the wager on Bich Linh's success, though the contesting officers, realizing the bettor's dire straits and wishing to capitalize further, stipulated that Bich Linh's shot must land within an eight-centimeter radius of center. The officer agreed even to this further proviso, thereby presenting such terms that his adversaries were drawn in as though by riptide, and thus failed to safeguard their earlier winnings. (*Riptide?* Advanced Private Nguyen interrupted. The Colonel explained. *Ocean?* the soldier asked. Even the Colonel disbelieved his ears, but patiently drew the picture of bodies of water encircling the great land masses of the world. *I have heard of them*, the soldier said. *I had no idea*. He was sipping his rice wine again, lost in imagining himself alone on such a vast expanse. *I had no idea*, he repeated. The Colonel nodded and resumed.) Bich Linh proceeded to center her shot across eight hundred meters of hallowed patriotic soil. Eyes that strained through binoculars could not dispute her shot had landed within the indicated radius. The three officers were compelled to yield back their prior winnings. Three targets to go. At nine hundred meters, the losing officers were still bickering so bitterly with the victorious one at the moment of Bich Linh's shot that no new bets had been placed. At one thousand meters, full of himself and keenly aware of the erratic wind, the victorious officer now bet against Linh, again giving such benevolent odds (yet not so foolishly as he had earlier) that the remaining officers once more could not restrain themselves, seeing some small hope of redemption, even though to continue their wagering they placed years of their future earnings at risk as security. But Linh drilled this target, too, to the ample cursing of the losing officer. Now the winner became the loser, the losers the winners. All at some point during the wagering had forfeited noticeable gains, for which they had all eagerly arisen so early to be at the range that morning. None were happy, though none were any longer ruined, a fact lost on them. They rebuked the Colonel, making no sense, but not needing to, being senior officers and patriots. They were sorely discombobulated as Linh prepared for her final shot. When they saw her remove and destroy the telescope—*of course* the only means for scoring a hit on a target that distant—their final scheming fell to pieces, as what remaining reckless fool among them would now wager even a worthless piaster? Now the civilians, in true socialist solidarity with the officers, also inveighed against the Colonel, speaking wildly with even less sense. The Colonel quieted them by standing and removing from his pocket a roll of southern piasters and a large quantity of American military payment chits in dollars. He laid the roll and chits on the bench before the officers and said quietly that he believed in his student. Accordingly, even without the use of her telescope, he offered odds of three to one on an amount three times greater than what he placed as a token before them, that she would strike the black of her target at eleven hundred meters. Though it now meant risking years of his own future earnings to certain (so they thought) crushing indebtedness, by thus offering to make winners of them all (so they thought), the Colonel saved face for them and soothed their morning's wounds. They eagerly accepted his wager and turned rosy as highland flowers after a spring rain, even offering the Colonel a second cup of rice wine, which, given their recent displeasure with him, they expected him to politely decline, as of course he did. When Linh rose to her feet and made it clear she intended to fire from a standing position, the wealthiest officer otherwise equal in socialist doctrine seized the moment and stated that the principal of the wager was now doubled and didn't the Colonel agree? Though this too made no sense, the Colonel said, Of course, it is only fair, thereby extending (in the eyes of the senior patriots) the virtual certainty of disaster in his personal affairs an even greater number of years.

"But *Colonel*," interrupted Advanced (First Class) Private Nguyen, beside himself. This was a more wondrous story than riptides and the ocean, and by now his third cup of rice wine was nearly empty.

"Three chances to *one*. At *eleven hundred* meters, *standing, with iron sights*. Such a shot is not possible. I am new to this range, yes, but I have pulled targets now for months, recently at Tran Phuong Base, and before that in the reserve officer's training compound below Bat Trang, serving the Army's distance shooters. Not one shoots beyond seven hundred meters with iron sights, either with the Nagant or the Dragunov. At six hundred meters most fail. *Six* hundred meters, with rifle in the *prone* position. Even the best are inconsistent. And these all shoot the hand-tooled Mosin-Nagant, begging your pardon, Colonel, known as even more accurate than the new Russian Dragunov. And yet you wager three to one on a standing shot at *eleven hundred meters without a telescope*?" He shook his head, then threw it back and drained his cup again, held it motionless above him, stared into its empty depths. "Such excellent wine," he said into the cup. "No idea. I had no idea."

"A day to remember, soldier," the Colonel said, and filled the soldier's cup again.

Such a child, Linh thought, her irritation growing.

For the first time she really looked at the soldier who had tended her furthest target. Each target had a deep hole at its base, with steps carved into one side leading to the bottom, where the tenders could have been well protected during firing. Instead, but for the final target, the holes had been fitted with covers, and this Nguyen, like all the others, had been directed to stand there at devout attention, only meters away from the smallest error, his life so little regarded by the Army that he was required to risk it each time a target shooter fired. Such a child, she thought. Little more than a boy. A handsome boy though, now that she regarded him closely, slender yet sturdy from all his years in the field. A child that needed a *spanking*. In spite of herself she thought again of her husband's hand between her legs at the table, then his breath on her neck. And of lovers before him... *and none since...*

"Drink up, daughter," the Colonel said. "We run ahead of you." He poured himself another half-cup. But Linh remained momentarily lost in her memories, her nerve endings coming alive, old hungers rekindling, her monovision blurred but settled on the face of the target tender.

"Anyway," the Colonel continued. "I will not slander senior patriots by describing the ranting that attended that indescribable feat at eleven hundred meters with iron sights. Suffice it to say that we, all of us here, were accused, tried and convicted of gross bourgeois conspiracy to establish and manipulate games of fortune, to the discredit of the People and the blighting of the reputation of the Army. It was asserted, examined and concluded in the space of moments that we had all intrigued against them in a brazen farce of treachery culminating in the forgery of the final shot. *Which* they unanimously contended must have been fabricated by the willing complicity of Advanced Private Nguyen, who *must* have inserted a disc inside a hole that had never been made by the shooting candidate's rifle. Sentence was passed. Immediate assignment of all to forward units, in the vanguard of all upcoming attacks, with unmerited opportunity to expiate our crimes by heroic performance in the face of the enemy. Naturally I appreciated the leniency of their judgment and expressed this in full before they returned to their duties. Oh yes," the Colonel nodding, lowering his cup after another swallow, "on behalf of all, I thanked them most profusely, as you can imagine my position must dictate."

The fields around them were empty of human noise. In the distance something had offended a buffalo and it lowed its displeasure. With the triumph of broad sunlight insects had returned to the shadows and birds darted and clamored everywhere. Linh recognized the strange noise a reclusive toad made that many mistook for a certain water fowl. The sun was not yet to noon and the skies had gone piercingly blue. At heights beyond imagining the eyebrows of clouds arched in all directions. Linh wondered if this might be the last interlude of peace she would ever know. Warmed though it was by the wine and this interesting Colonel, and the stirring of memory, her being shied away from such moments. It was not peace she sought. Peace lulled, disarmed. The other, though, the stirring, *that* could be pursued. She turned her eye away from the target tender.

"And now?" she asked.

"Nguyen and I, we will serve together. A regiment forming up for a major offensive. You, daughter, will find a sapper unit where your talent and disposition will be given a better home. I would be honored to keep you in my command, but even in my command you would be remote from me, and I could not serve you well. That I favored you would only endanger you with the natural resentment of men overshadowed by women. A company of infantry would be a barbaric place for you and though other women may find it bearable, *you* must never accept such a fate. *Never*. For I do not see in you the gift of bearing a fool lightly, an omission which must lead to your undoing."

The Colonel took another swallow from his cup, pursed his lips appreciatively. "This much I can do for each of you. Daughter, the Dragunov is yours to keep, as long as you wish to bear its additional weight in the field. Though others will try to force a Kalashnikov on you, you will carry orders from me directing you to have the Dragunov as your sole offensive weapon and making it a punishable act to remove same from your possession. I am known among field commanders. None would countermand my order."

From behind him the Colonel produced a small pistol in a holster and extended it to Bich Linh. He nodded and Bich Linh accepted it. The holster held a spare magazine in an attached pouch. Red-hued copper cartridges shone dully beneath partly visible slats cut into the magazine's steel sides.

"And a second order authorizing you to carry for personal protection a nine millimeter Makarov, the pistol of officers, and now legendary shooters, too, with a similar discipline for attempting to confiscate it. Frenchmen from the Mekong to Dien Bien Phu fared poorly against my pistol. May you see to it that Americans fare no better. Keep it beside your head as you sleep, and that much more rely on yourself for good fortune. Nguyen."

"Sir!"

"You will be attached to my immediate command as my aide. You will stay in range of my voice night and day. Such is my confidence in you as my personal attendant that under no circumstances will you be further than one hundred meters from my person. My uniforms, my quarters, the order of my papers, billet and headquarters, will be your express duties. Additionally I may require you to carry orders that cannot otherwise be relayed than in person. May I rely on you?"

"Sir!"

"Very well. The details of the future we have settled, in the limited way mortals can. These are behind us now." The Colonel clapped his hands. "We celebrate one thing here this morning, and though inadequately, we will celebrate it. Soldiers! What is the condition of your cups?" The Colonel's eyes shined. He reached beside him and picked up the small plastic chest, set it down in front of him.

Linh squatted comfortably, her arms on her knees, her buttocks against her heels. The Colonel, formerly so grudging with words, now spoke sonorously, even melodically. A small trance had come over her as she listened, a spell that had begun as she stood behind the Colonel in front of her final target, looking at the white disc, dead in the center of the black circle. In that moment she knew she had not done this. A god had come to her, had held the barrel of her rifle as she bent backward, had adjusted the path of its flight with the wind of his own breath surging ahead and taming the wind of the world. Gusting into its gusts, adjusting, guiding. What the Colonel had said in front of her final target was the truth. *Mathematical.* Mathematics after all. The mathematics of the gods.

With surprise she noted her own cup was empty again. So it was not just the Colonel's words intoxicating her.

Nguyen, whom she had considered a typical country lout with little self-control, surprised her further. "Colonel," he said, "Respectfully, one more cup and I will be lost to my own legs and useless to the world."

The Colonel's eyes shone more brightly. "Prepare yourself for something different."

He opened the chest. Linh looked inside. It was full of ice. During the war the simple luxury of ice had become a rare thing in the countryside. Still plentiful enough in the cities, in recent times it had been almost unheard of in the valleys and highlands. Then it left the cities of the south again with the Americans. Now hard-nosed children hungry for barter and dollars pedaled strange little wheeled contraptions everywhere, even in the warring glens of mountainous reaches, seeking out American GIs, selling and trading cold concoctions packed in ice, many of the children sworn to equally hard-nosed Viet Cong masters. Linh considered the practice ridiculous. As if enough sweet liquid could raise enough money to bring America to its knees. Give them bullets, she had told the northern political officers. You have become ridiculous bourgeoisie. And they sent her north to the camps.

"We have all been witness to something no one will ever see again," the Colonel continued. "No one. Not ever. It is impossible. I would wager, if I were given to wager, that this fine intuitive shooter here right now, herself, could not reproduce the shot at eleven hundred meters, though she spent the rest of her life trying. But she will never need to. A miracle is itself, it is not an assembly line." He held the small chest aloft, his smile warm with irony. "And in recognition, a minimum ceremony allowed by the maximum of our resources."

The Colonel lowered the chest, reached in and swept a layer of ice aside, exposing a single red cylinder nestled in the depths. A breath of winter immediately cooled her cheek. Bich Linh had seen the cans before. In the stalls along street corners, in her rare visits to the cities. Crushed and empty in garbage dumps she dug up behind American soldiers traveling through the countryside, in her search for abandoned explosives, ammunition and other items of value. These were the same confections children peddled from their chests of ice on wheels. These and other such cylinders: orange ones, blue ones, many in different shades of green. But the red ones were most plentiful, and wherever she encountered the cans in any color Bich Linh had spurned them all.

The Colonel lifted the cylinder from its bed, brushed ice away and pulled a piece of silver from the top of the can. Air rushed out in a hiss.

"Soldiers, your cups," he said.

Wide-eyed, Nguyen moved his arm forward. Linh followed. The Colonel's own cup joined theirs. The Colonel poured. Inside the cups the liquid bristled and foamed. Colonel Trung went from one to other, pouring even the final drips equally, cup to cup. He dropped the empty can back into the chest and closed the lid.

"Colonel, what is it?" There was awe in Nguyen's voice as he watched the bubbles percolating on the dark surface. His hand tingled as the cold seeped through the walls of the cup.

"It is called 'Coca-Cola'," the Colonel said.

Nguyen tried repeating it. The words didn't work well in his mouth.

The Colonel raised his cup. "In honor of this true daughter of the country, who has done something that will never be matched, I retire from instruction in the long rifle a fulfilled man. I will teach no more. The senior patriots have only sent me where I now long to go. Let us drink to Bich Linh."

They did. The Colonel drank his in a long swallow. Bich Linh felt the rush of pleasure in her first tentative sip. Indescribable. The coldness startling. A sharp sweetness flavored with root of some kind. The liquid infused with a percolation she felt in her throat. She drank again, and again, and then it was gone, her tongue chasing it along the sides of the cup. Beside her Nguyen sat stunned, his mouth open, his cup also empty.

"Another oversight on the part of the senior patriots," the Colonel explained. "Forgotten beneath the reviewing stand. Unfortunately, there was just the one can."

"It is enough," said Bich Linh. "I have not tasted anything like it." She was already regarding the children driving their ice-bearing contraptions in a new light.

Advanced Private Nguyen was staring into his cup. "Did the gods make this?" he asked. Linh thought he sounded serious.

The Colonel made a noise like a chuckle. "Not gods. Devils maybe. Devils in America. But for the devil in all of us."

"I had no idea," Nguyen said. He was grinning from ear to ear.

"Say what you will," the Colonel said, "I think we can agree the senior patriots have excellent taste in beverages."

"Oh, they do." Nguyen giggled. Still slightly drunk.

If he smiles wider, his face will break, Linh thought.

"I love the Army," Nguyen said. "Colonel, I—"

"I know, soldier," the Colonel said. "You had no idea."

31

"AND HOW *IS* THE COLONEL?"

The officer with the polished sandals turned to face her, a meter away. Bich Linh noticed the soldier standing behind him for the first time, the man's Kalashnikov half raised, his eyes watching her darkly.

The officer, a junior grade lieutenant, said, "A wretch like you, a grotesque creature with half a face, does not inquire into the welfare of her commanding officer. A soldier does as ordered. And though you are a wretch, you are still a soldier, at least until your well-deserved punishment. For the last time, I order you to fall in and prepare to move out."

The officer turned to another soldier beside him. Linh noticed it was the soldier who had hailed her as she stood on the roof. She looked at him closely and recognition dawned. It was the simple peasant from the firing range months ago, the easily intoxicated tender of targets. The simple peasant's face still the face of a child. Still as handsome. It irritated her that over the passing months she had kept thinking about that face.

"You," the officer said to the soldier. He pointed to the motionless form of the American soldier in his narrow crater. "This American, this pet of the superstitious freak in a soldier's uniform, is alive for no good reason. He won't survive interrogation and we are not taking prisoners. Shoot him."

"Sir?"

The officer made a sound of disgust. He looked around him. "Where are the officers of this rabble? Who is in command here?"

No one answered. Someone finally said, "Officers dead, sir. All killed by the helicopter."

"Sergeants?"

"Here, sir." A soldier stepped up from the crowd.

"Do you need orders to assume command? Get these men formed up and moving. The route has not been changed. Are you not the vanguard for the regiment? Were you not briefed on this offensive by your officers?"

"We were all briefed, sir," the sergeant said.

"You know the route?"

"Up this street, sir, straight ahead. One kilometer to a known enemy concentration. At least, I think one kilometer, sir."

"Less. Mission?"

"Destroy the enemy where we find him, invest the buildings and surroundings. Kill the enemy if he counterattacks, hold until further orders."

"Well, fuck your mother, sergeant. Form these soldiers up and get moving. Destroy the enemy concentration before nightfall. Understood?"

"Sir!"

The sergeant saluted, stepped back smartly and began barking orders. Soldiers scurried into the remnants of squads. Bich Linh watched and prepared her mind.

"You," the officer said, pointing again at Bich Linh's former target tender. "Are you deaf? Or do you love the enemy?" The officer paused and looked at the soldier intently, eyes narrowing in recognition. "It's *you*. Servant of a traitor. His cowardice must have infected you. As I ordered, shoot this worthless American soldier. Do it *now*."

The target tender lowered his eyes. "Sir, I do not love the enemy. And I am no coward, and my Colonel is no traitor. This man is helpless, a soldier like any soldier dying. And, *sir*." He looked up. The eyes were anguished. Bich Linh remembered him talking with the Colonel inside the shade, childishly drunk, annoying in his innocence. And in the feelings deep within her that he had stirred. How many months ago? Or lifetimes?

And again, the stirrings. Here. By all the gods, even in this moment.

The target tender said to the officer, pointing, "Sir, there is *Lord Buddha* watching over him!"

The officer stared in disbelief, first at the idol, then at the target tender, and shook his head. "Superstitious idiots," he said. "I will have that worthless trinket melted into a boat anchor." Rivulets of sweat poured along his shaven cheeks. Over the smell of explosive that hung everywhere in the air Bich Linh could sense a cologne. Perfume. An insult to the river that ran through the holy city. And now an insult to Lord Buddha. Enough.

She stepped beside the target tender. Suddenly remembered his name. "Banh Nguyen! You will be coming with me, if you are stout enough." To the officer she said, "I am *Bich Linh*." She turned her back on him to show her contempt, then raised her voice so the soldiers now formed into small columns could hear her. "*Bich Linh*. I am from the south, where I have killed more Americans in my years than this regiment in its existence, as I killed the Americans on this street. I tell you again, you are all alive because of *me*. Look on the carcass of this dead helicopter and you know I tell you the truth. I am a free soldier and fight freely of my own will. I was brought north against my wishes and I was trained. I have now more than repaid this training in my service against the white devils. My unit is no more. It is dead. I alone survive. Having your lives in my debt,

I choose to leave this Army. I will return to the service of my own country and resume my duties there. I do so now, and this peasant child from the north comes with me, if he dares."

The officer's face, wet with sweat, turned red with anger.

"You will go nowhere but to your grave," he said, but before his hand could reach the holstered pistol at his side, Bich Linh spun around, removed the Colonel's Makarov and held it to the officer's right eye.

"Your perfume stinks," Bich Linh said, and fired.

32

THE OFFICER'S REMAINING EYE turned white with shock and rolled skyward. He wobbled dead on his feet and collapsed. Blood and grey matter dripped from the face and uniform of the soldier standing behind him with the Kalashnikov. In a swift motion Bich Linh punched the pistol into the soldier's chest, above his heart.

"The choice is yours," she said.

The soldier dropped the rifle and bowed his head.

She lowered the pistol but kept her gaze steady on the assembled soldiers. The dead officer's attendant did not move to recover his rifle. All the soldiers watched her silently. There was no defiance in them.

She said, "Banh Tan Nguyen. This man spoke ill of your officer. What has befallen the Colonel?"

The target tender hesitated, eyes fixed on the dead officer. "The Colonel," he began. Faltered. "The Colonel was arrested three days ago. For a week he argued against this offensive, knowing lives would be thrown away to no purpose, with no hope of victory. I was there when he suggested other, more useful attacks, but they would not listen. He has his enemies, generals he says are more politicians than soldiers. They accused him of cowardice. He mocked them, fully intending to lead the battalion though he opposed the orders. But they arrested him for their own ends and called him a *coward* and a *traitor*. He was taken away in chains, but it suits his enemies to pretend he still commands from Regiment, thinking his men will not know the truth. His men who love him. But the men know the truth. These men here know." Nguyen blinked, fought back tears. "When they came for him the Colonel stood proudly and said to me. 'Tell the men to do their duty as they can.' I made sure the subordinate officers received these orders. To me he said, 'You are released from my personal service. You have served me well,' he told me. 'You are a soldier. Fight well and die well, there is no other way.' And I have fought well, all morning. Against the *Yu-i*, against the Americans at the temple. They put me in the vanguard. I am not afraid to die. Though I would be ashamed to let the Colonel see me cry." He wiped his eyes with his sleeve. "And I won't cry!"

"You are a child," Bich Linh said. "Colonel Trung's honor will always protect him. Save your tears for the journey ahead, wherever it leads. Will you come with me or not?"

She watched the infantile wheels in his head turn. "They will say I deserted. They will say the Colonel's batman was a coward."

"Truth finds the truthful," Linh said. "The Colonel will know. Events of this day will travel beyond this army on the wind, since most here will be dead by morning." She put her mouth to his ear and said so only he could hear, "Do not deceive yourself. It is not your salvation I offer. If you come with me, you will be *my* batman. I am not your Colonel. You will do as I say, whenever I say, when I say it. I will use you for my own pleasure. Your body will be mine to command and its purpose will be to satisfy me. And in the end you will probably die at the hands of the Americans. Look at me before you decide. Look at this deformed face and only then make your choice."

But Banh Tan Nguyen looked away. "*Look,*" she hissed. He did, slowly. She met his gaze. He did not look away again.

"Now decide," she said. And then, "Sergeant!"

The sergeant stepped forward.

"I will speak one last time to your men."

The sergeant hesitated, then nodded.

Bich Linh spoke loudly. "*Soldiers*. You have your orders. You are soldiers. You have no meaning in this life other than what these orders give you. *Carry them out*." She moved among them as she spoke, Dragunov in one hand, pistol in the other, her small pack low on her back. "You have been commanded by a worthy officer. Do not dishonor him. Kill as many of the enemy as you can in the time you have left. Harden your mind to the pain that is coming and fight knowing you will die. There is no other way, as your Colonel would tell you." She stopped and gestured toward the horizon. "I am going south, to the mountains. I will fight the enemy there, in my own country, in my own way. I will die, too, but not with you. I die where I choose, free of *my* will, and as I enter the darkness I will be seeing the faces of the enemy I killed first. Such a vision I commend to you."

She resumed walking, looking at the columns of soldiers, forcing the men to look at her, at the dirt-smeared blood clotting her face, at the ruined eye, the dark scar-tunnels along her cheek. They all looked away. No candidates stood out.

"I can take two men with me," she said. "Two and no more. If you come, you serve me first. You take your orders from me. You obey without question. Expect to die, only somewhere else. But not tonight, and maybe not tomorrow."

She had walked back and now stood in front of the tender of targets.

"I will come with you," Banh Tan Nguyen said. He stepped forward beside her, looking straight ahead.

"One other," Linh said.

An older, haggard soldier stepped from the back of a column.

"I will join you," the soldier said.

"No, you won't," Bich Linh replied harshly. "You're a scarecrow. Your parents weaned you on paddy water and buffalo shit. Stay and die with the rest."

The man's mouth moved as though to argue. Went still. His shoulders slumped and he stepped back into line.

No one else spoke. There was a silence. Soldiers in the temple's plaza had heard the pistol and were watching. Linh could see the red-smeared collars of more junior officers looking and talking, some rallying troops from their hiding places, some pointing in their direction while others spoke frantically into radio sets. She felt the urgent need to move, to run. The shooting and explosions in other parts of the city approached. Colonel Trung's battalion must be broken and straggling, the various elements trying to maintain contact, fighting their way along as they came, forced to keep close to the American soldiers to keep the jets at bay, slowing their advance. But the jets would come. They would come here. The eyes of their forward observers, tucked behind the ruins of rooftops and watching them now from telescopes as they undoubtedly had for some time, would soon conclude there were no survivors inside the helicopter, none at the front of the temple. Then they would send the jets.

"An Trinh," Nguyen said. He walked away from Linh to the rearmost column. "An Trinh," he said again. Nguyen reached in and pulled a soldier from the column. He was a short man, another peasant by demeanor, young and solid looking. Plain of features but well-proportioned.

Nguyen dragged the man forward. In front of Linh he looked at the ground and said nothing, squeezing the barrel of his slung Kalashnikov nervously

"This is a good soldier," Nguyen said. "I recommend him to you, and I will see that he serves you well."

"No one can make another serve well, or at all. He must answer for himself."

"He is an excellent soldier," Nguyen repeated.

"And mute?" Linh said scornfully. "Did the Americans shoot out his tongue?"

"I can speak," the soldier said, suddenly animated. "I was reflecting. On many things. I have decided to go south with Banh Tan Nguyen, and with you. Serving you, as Nguyen has made clear."

"You serve me absolutely. You understand that?"

"Wherever a soldier serves, it seems to me he serves absolutely. Besides"—and Linh could hardly believe it, the soldier broke out in a smile. Lord Buddha, another *child*—"I have always wanted to travel!"

When she said nothing, he added, "Excuse me, a little joke."

Linh looked at the undersized soldier. Death everywhere, jets just waiting to fall on them, a perilous journey ahead, and here was a comedian.

"My father taught me, 'Find the joke in the sorrow, and never lose your smile,' " An Trinh explained apologetically. "I was still a boy, and he seemed so wise."

Linh sneered. "And did he teach you this wisdom as you plucked rice shoots from beneath buffalo shit?"

An Trinh looked at her, met her gaze. To her surprise she saw him appraising the damaged side of her face with interest, boldly, but without revulsion. "No, though I have done much of that. In the days of the French, someone accused my mother. Men came and took her away. They tortured and beat her for information she didn't have about one or another of the village elders. She died from this abuse. We were at the burial, just afterwards, when he first said those words to me. I remember the skies that day. Like today, and toward evening, as now. I did not see the joke that day. I try, but however I strive with laughter, I am not always sure what this joke might be."

Linh held him in her gaze. It was a nation of children, all of them pitiful. But these two would have to do.

"The next day, and in the years that followed, we pulled the rice shoots from below the shit. And the joke? Can it be that death is less to be feared than life? A joke on all of us?" An Trinh smiled again, into her sighted eye.

"Comedian and philosopher," Linh said. "Somewhere in between, I hope, a soldier."

"We will serve you well," Nguyen said. He looked anxiously back toward the temple. "Officers are coming."

Linh settled the Makarov into its holster at the hollow of her back, beneath her pack. "Sergeant," she said. The man tilted his head deferentially. "Make sure your men die like soldiers."

Without another word Bich Linh turned and ran. Surprised, the two men of her new army let her get five meters away before moving. A third man suddenly broke from his column and followed them.

She led them away from the road that ran beside the burning temple, the road that led to a fully alerted enemy, away from annihilation, from the banks of a river where only death waited. A stupid, unprofitable death. Death where there would be no white devils to close ranks with, none to drag into darkness with them. Death from the sky. From mortars and artillery, from the rockets and machine guns of helicopter gunships. But mostly from the Phantoms, from the bombs and cannons in their wings.

The voices of the officers behind her, ordering them to return. A quick look behind her and she recognized the older, scrawny soldier in pursuit. A pistol shot. Another. Angrily shouted orders, and the beginning of Kalashnikov fire. She ran with wings again on her sandals, her gift from the gods, the footsteps of her meager force outdistanced behind her. More concentrated AK fire and she heard a cry. Glancing back again, she saw the scarecrow lying twisted in a heap. Though refused, he had gambled against his fate and lost. But not, she reflected, himself. *I could have used such a man after all.*

She led them running as she loved to run, protected again by her mother the broken city, into the hulks of buildings and out into clogged and burning alleys, twisting through ruins and more ruins, heading first westward, then south, past the river and abandoned fields and broken roads where the wild reaches of this northern land waited, quickly turning their half-hearted pursuers into stragglers.

Once among the tall foliage of remote valleys, from inside their shadows, on and on they would go southward, moving at night, hidden at day, foraging as they must and sleeping where they could. Back to her home, or what she now called home. To the south, to the highlands. And to Thanh.

In the meantime, there would be the target tender.

Linh ran on, paying no attention to her tiny cadre, the two soldiers trying desperately to keep up. Faith born of certainty filled her, though certainty of what, she could not say. She ran and recognized a lightness of step she had not known since her days of fighting in the mountains. A lightness of being. A being in *Now*.

In space that once more belonged to her alone.

As she now understood she would always require.

The shackles of the army lay in the city behind her. She was not free of war, of service or of certain death, but she was free of masters.

Free enough.

Something flitted above her. The percussion of tiny wings caused her to lift her head. In and out of her monovision a sparrow tacked side to side, pacing her. Another small bird leaving the city, leading her on. She followed, confident she was being delivered.

Into the inwardly pulsing sun of the dying day, she ran. Sparks flew from her sandals as so much flint against stone. In the distance the darkness that had already overcome the east was settling over the west, engulfing all sparrows. Stars emerged and pricked the purple and magenta fabric of descending night until it bled ink. The moon increased and waxed fuller and brighter.

And she was gone.

There was still a ruby's reflection of light in the sky when the jets came.

IV

Kestermont

33

IT WASN'T MUCH OF A BOAT. You couldn't call it a cutter or tender, dinghy or launch. It hardly qualified as a skiff. Before decay and time and Navy scavengers gutted it, had it once been some builder's idea of a tug? What was it now? And what kind of boat commander lashes a battery of old tires to either side of a vessel's bow? Or keeps a rubber life raft inflated and sloshing around on the deck in monsoon rainwater?

Morning skies were darkening fast. The ocean bristled with restless wavelets beneath a stiff wind blowing away from shore. Kestermont leaned against a section of the rusted brass railing and then recoiled as it moved in front of him. He tried to focus on the horizon, but to no avail; he was hydrophobic and inside the devil's house, and demons rose for the torment. One moment he was looking out to sea, the next he was watching a black and white movie from some lost Saturday morning matinee unwind across his eyelids. Sails snapping in the wind behind him in a gale-force rain, Gregory Peck's obsessed sea captain clanked peg-legged across the deck, glared at the audience, then rode unrepentant beneath the waves, lashed by his own harpoon rope to the great white whale. Hardly the image Kestermont needed at the moment. Not with his own fate in the balance, roped by circumstance to the deck of this ugly duckling like Ahab to his monster. He gripped the railing as the boat stuttered along through gray patches of fog, low clouds and the wakes of real vessels like it was rowed by out-of-sync oarsmen. If he turned to look behind him, would the headhunter be standing there, oozing tattoos and sizing him up for dinner?

Not Queequeg, but a short, wiry marine named Johnson stood at the railing beside him and said, "It's a tub, sir. Old river junk. Not USA." Johnson spat into the oil slick. "It aint made for open water."

Johnson was shouting over the wind. They were both shouting.

"I don't care who made it," Kestermont replied. "I don't care if it came here with the French or Captain Cook. Just so it gets us there dry. And back. On time for that last bird."

To Kestermont the boat seemed to labor uphill. Had the ocean tilted?

And did the contraption have some hidden purpose? Was it a lifeboat conversion salvaged from some decommissioned naval graveyard, slapped into service here in the backwaters of the world? Maybe it had once been something exotic, something real but unbelievable. Like the remains of an ancient galley from a previous incarnation. Had it sought him out across the centuries?

And was his paranoia *always* necessary?

The short answer to that was simply that when it came to the ocean, paranoia necessary or not was out of his control.

Possibly there was no name for the thing that bore him out to sea. All he really knew was he didn't like it. Especially under skies fat with the threat of late winter monsoons, forerunner winds already whipping the harbor behind them into a frenzy of whitecaps. It had been the perfect morning for a helicopter. Chopper ride would've solved everything. But this was Vietnam. He was a grunt. He *needed* a chopper. So of course there was no chopper to be had.

Adding insult to injury, the chopper shuttle that did exist had still been visible against high black clouds when their truck finally rolled into the coastal LZ. Delay after delay in Da Nang traffic held them up just long enough to miss the morning's only scheduled flight to the hospital ship. Their driver made a hasty phone call, held up departure on an irregularly scheduled cargo run and thereby found them slots on a sea voyage. He wished them luck—*You'll need it if this storm breaks while you're on that bucket*—and dropped them off at a small inlet on the fringes of the harbor, two clicks south, a ramshackle neglected afterthought in the Navy's shore installations. Ten minutes away from the partially submerged dock and he was nearly hoarse. He didn't care. In fact, he was grateful the skipper had insisted someone babysit him and ordered Johnson out of the bush for the task. The distraction of talk was what he needed.

They slugged their way seaward, angled away from land. All around them, warships and tankers, trawlers, barges and patchwork sailboats of every description and state of decrepitude churned the waters of one of the world's busiest and deepest natural harbors, trailing fuel oils, cigarette butts, excrement and motley colored soda cans. Iridescent patches of petroleum scum rose on white-tipped swells and sank into increasingly deepening troughs. He knew there was irony in the claustrophobia he felt as endless expanses of water enveloped them. Dispelling the sense of suffocation was impossible; all he could ever do was hold it at bay. The horizon undulated on the waves. He willed his vision to chain it down, to fix the outer band of the ocean into a solid line, the way other people must see it. But anything like a true horizon fled from his gaze like the living from a doomed man.

Above them sea gulls rose and fell in patternless intervals, materializing suddenly beneath low gray cloud, miniature harpies hovering and crying, scolding and begging in the same monotone *skree*. Wheeling and circling they brayed their demands and cast searching glances at the craft and occupants, alert for the least sign of compliance. Finding none, they made the primary business decisions of their existence—*no action here*—and with loud last complaints let the wind carry them off. Kestermont watched the gray absorb them and reflected that if such creatures had been given gills instead of wings it would be just one more reason to stay out of the water.

Johnson turned a red eye skyward.

"What I'm hopin, LT, is we get there and get gone before them clouds open up. Sun's gone two days now it aint rained yet. Thing we're ridin in better come with buckets that sky opens up."

Johnson was from Georgia, some small town to hear him tell it never recovered from Sherman's march. Or forgot it. When he spoke you could hear the cotton burning.

Johnson went on, "Look at this rubber dolly slidin along the deck all aired up. What, this thing gonna sink any minute, you gotta keep a life raft ready for action? Don't exactly build confidence."

Kestermont moved aft, Johnson following. Kestermont tested the railing and steadied himself against a more rigid section above the gunwale.

The formula was simple.

Indifferent to the ocean when he wasn't near it, on its surface he felt stalked. Ergo, stay away from it. The farther the better. A simple syllogism that had never failed him. Yet here he was, a Marine officer that hated the ocean. A man who *dreaded* the ocean, to be more exact. A man who couldn't swim, aquaphobic to the bone, the all-devouring ocean only inches from his feet. Not smart to tempt a fate which earlier had proven benign, in that his battlefield commission had elevated him from the ranks and skirted officer's candidate school at Quantico, exempting him from what would otherwise have been mandatory training requirements for water survival. Without that exemption he could never have qualified. As a private in boot camp he had already nearly drowned twice during Wet Skills Testing. Drill instructors took him aside to berate him or stalked him as he floundered in the pool, pounding the catechism for staying alive in the event of shipwreck: *Use your natural buoyancy! Full lung inflation! Extreme relaxation, goddamnit, turd! Arms in an arc, slow movement! JAYsus Christ, go ahead and drown, maggot!*

There was no time in the training to bring incompetents up to speed and no patience anyway. He and a Nebraska farm boy stood to the side of the pool and took their landlubber's discipline, shouting out their squat thrusts (*one, two, three, four-EVER, sir!*) while the rest of the platoon treaded water or collided in laps with full combat gear. His dismal performance might have cashiered him in peacetime, but there was a war escalating that was being fought almost exclusively on land, no national draft, and the Marines needed bodies. So at the end of his failed water training the drill instructor sent him and the red-faced farm boy on a final 10-circuit punishment run around MCRD in lieu of expulsion. Exhausted at lights out, he nevertheless laid in his rack and was still smiling when he fell asleep: only moments before he and the Nebraska boy had been summoned to the duty hut and stood at attention while the platoon commander placed bald head and gnashing canines inches from their eyeballs and dripping his best drill instructor contempt informed them that they were officially *disqualified for life!—Turds!*—from sea duty. Tomlin shouted *Aye, aye, Sir!* at the top of his lungs, about-faced and flew from the hut. He couldn't speak for the recruit from farm country, but personally he was as happy as the proverbial rabbit thrown into the briar patch.

34

THE WHITE WHALE had left his mind's screen and taken Ahab to his watery grave beneath the waves; now Kestermont saw himself walking a tightrope over a wet coffin. He was headed to the heart of the sea—to Kestermont this was anywhere beyond the surf—in something that looked like Kon-Tiki with plywood sides and the semblance of a motor. A thing. A thing that slapped the water with the smallest wave and shuddered like a raft about to disintegrate. Thin wood between him and the ocean floor. Thin shield between him and the dream. And the laughing Numidian.

The two sailors hadn't said a word. The boatswain stood behind the wheel in his ragged little cockpit, the ember of his cigarette pulsing casual defiance against the darkening backdrop of sea and sky. His lone crewman perched on top of what passed for a wheelhouse, slouched in a makeshift chair that must have been bolted down to assume the angles it did and not fling itself and occupant overboard. The sailor did something with rope. It looked like the kid was practicing knots, bored if not serene, mindless of the ocean and the leaking contraption rolling on wave after wave, wind moaning low, sky blackening, storm coming. The wind was sharp and cool, but not unpleasant. In that country all wind was welcome until it rained.

To Johnson he said—shouted: "Hospital ship's headed for Cam Ranh tomorrow or next day, for sure by the end of the week. We're back in the bush tomorrow. So it was today or never, this boat or nothin. I owe him that much."

"I guess, sir. I don't know the guy."

"I sent him. I sent em all. Every godforsaken one of em. He's all that's left. I got somethin to say to him, is all."

"I don't think you owe anyone an apology, sir."

"That is most definitely not what I'm talkin about."

Johnson moved leeward of Kestermont and spat again. The wind drove his phlegm horizontal, drove it like a bullet. The sailor on the wheelhouse worked his knots, oblivious, the ends of his rope slapping like legs kicking.

"Sailors are crazy," Kestermont said.

"Sailors aint shit," Johnson replied.

"You're wrong there, Corporal. There's some damn good sailors. Hard corps. Your corpsmen. Doc Evers. Doc Mason. Lot of jarheads owe em big. Plenty of good men in the navy."

"They aint shit," Johnson yelled back. "Most of em okay, sir? Look at these two we got here. Run this tub across the water, work 8 hours, sleep in dry racks. Hot meals three times a day, women when they want em. Some of em shack up their whole tour. That aint right and they aint shit."

"That's green envy, Corporal. It's the boot camp jarhead in you talkin is what that is. You never met Doc Mason. I show you frogmen you don't say a word to. You're hard corps, you're hard corps. It don't matter what service and it don't matter what army. There's NVA out there half your size been carryin twice your weight in rice and ammo beggin Buddha for just one chance to put an AK round in your chest before they die. It don't matter what color cloth or skin you're wearin or flag you're wavin. Stars and bars, hammer and sickle, yellow star on red blood. It just don't matter. It's what's in you. It's what's in you that no one puts in you. It's in you or it aint."

The boatswain turned the wheel to counter a sideways skip from a sudden crosswind and Kestermont gripped the railing tighter, felt his heart quicken. *The sea's coming for me*. Foam leapt across the gunwales from small volcanic whitecaps. To keep his mind focused he kept talking. Shouting.

"I seen your jarheads get taken down. I seen em come apart. Poster boys. Big, beefy, corn-fed poster boys like you see in the recruit office. Seen em just come apart in the shit. Take some scrawny city boy, all the grunts laughin at this kid his first week in the bush. Pack weighs more than he does, they love givin him extra ammo, mortar rounds, illumination to hump. They don't call him by name, treat him like he's dead already. Detroit, they say. Hey, Chicago. New *Yawwk*. City boy don't say nothin. Straps the rounds on his pack, picks up the can of ammo. They hit the shit and it's this boy pulls his face outta the dirt and raises the flag. Dumps his pack and goes to work. Finds the M60, delivers the ammo. Gets the H E to the mortars. He's the one keeps fightin. Keeps fightin em till he runs that last magazine dry. Stops to reload magazines he's dead so he don't stop. All shot up himself he goes after em with a M7 hand to hand. Butt end of his rifle. Bleeds out swingin. He's fightin till the lights go out. I seen it. You don't know who somebody is until he shows you. And these two carryin our freight out to that ship? Didn't salute, aint said a word? It don't matter. It don't mean nothin. You don't know, Johnson. You don't know who they are. You never know till they show you."

"Well. Hell. All right."

"Like that one out there on that big boat. He showed us, only wasn't no one there to see."

"I guess, LT. I don't know."

"I know. I damn sure know."

"They say he walked point for Deering."

"He did. For him and Hardin both. For Deering on his second tour, for Hardin not three months ago."

They were both yelling louder now. Kestermont knew if he kept this up, he'd massacre his throat—something he'd done before, shouting at men during monsoon. There were things to say on that ship, and he needed his voice. But if he shut up, only the ocean would be talking. And he'd be listening.

"Don't know Hardin," Johnson said, leaning in closer to be heard. "I met Deering once. PX in Twentynine Palms. Thought he'd be bigger. Hero of Song Ba a bit on the skinny side, you ask me."

"Audie Murphy was a runt, Johnson. It's what's inside you, not the meat you pack around."

Unless the boatswain had changed course, the wind had shifted. Now it broadsided them, sending whitecaps racing to the horizon in rows of miniature snow-capped mountains. Johnson said something but any vibration from vocal cords was suddenly a tuning fork against a tsunami. The thunderclap broke so loudly Kestermont felt his eardrums move back inside his head. Concussion backhanded the boat, seemed to lift it from the waves.

Johnson sang out "Sweet *Jesus*, LT!" and fell to a knee, grasping for the gunwale, arms flailing. His sling slipped from his shoulder and the M16 clattered onto the deck and into seawater sloshing inside the separation of deck boards, Johnson right behind, face down, his swearing lost in a second thunder strike. Kestermont had his elbow hooked around the railing and when the boat lurched again his body slammed forward. His own rifle caromed off his back but stayed put. The railing gave outward and he felt his stomach heave. The black harbor sea foamed and hissed and reached for him and he thought he was overboard. The Numidian was laughing beneath the surface the way he always laughed, spear up and waiting, crooked finger beckoning him forward. But the railing held and stood back up. Kestermont stood up too.

"*I hate the goddamn ocean!*" He railed at the sky with all he had. "*You fuckin listenin to me?*" and to hell with his voice if it put God on notice, if in a single fell swoop of unfettered unfiltered distemper he could repudiate the obvious fear of his lifelong terror and raise himself above it and God too and if only the louder he yelled the more he convinced himself.

And then to Johnson, back-pedaling and embarrassed at his own outburst: "Ocean's been tryin to kill me since I was a kid."

Johnson didn't hear him, bent over on the deck under a fresh rush of wind and engaged in his own fit of swearing, the M16's magazine out and bolt open, salt water running out of the barrel.

Kestermont felt the cold nauseous hollow at the pit of his stomach. As far as he knew, he feared only death by sea. Not by the creatures of the sea. Not by teeth or barbs of sharks or eels or rays or any of the wet living things that mocked the world of man with insensible crude existence of slime and prehistoric pattern and vacuous eye through endless slaughter and pointless procreation. Death by man, death by fish, what was the difference. It was the cold swallowing vastness he feared, feared it worse than death itself, worse than a thousand tortures that left you begging for death. Depths that had no end, a void that masqueraded as matter, a void that could extinguish you so completely the living could doubt you ever existed, doubt their memory of you, think of you as an illusion, disbelieve your name even as they stared at it scrawled in the sidewalk or the family bible or between the lines of a birth certificate: *Did he really exist? No he did not. We dreamed him and we awakened* then shaking their heads and turning away as you kept sinking, sinking into that horizonless imploding space, hope deserting like rats from the burning ship in your dream, the door of your life closing, the echo of their denial by loved ones above you all that remains, they up there distancing, you down here descending, blackness everywhere, body temperature gone to ice, you alone as the seabed untold fathoms below and as foreign to its life as a bonfire to a grave. Entombed in oblivion. Encased. Erased.

Compared to this any death by war was a blessing.

Viewed in this light he was born to the infantry.

35 HELL, YES, KESTERMONT THOUGHT, sailors were crazy, living within cold easy reach of the merciless arm of the sea, subject to the ocean's caprice night and day. An ocean that brought nothing to the surface in him but dread and loathing. Or else it brought the dream. The anger in the dream. Anger at the humiliation. And then disbelief. And then nothing. Extinction.

Yet he admitted the ocean had never harmed him. Not that he knew of. He harbored suspicion but had no evidence. Only the images that came after him in the dark, sometimes not for years passing, sometimes twice a week. Images he had not shaken in the better part of two decades. The dream of the Numidian. The Carthaginian. Whoever.

As a kid he had instinctively known the intent of the ocean. He had never once entered beneath its waves, never given it a chance to sweep him away. When the family went to the beach, he stayed back in the dry sands or sat on the sea wall. His two brothers coaxed him, teased him. But he knew and resisted. In his exasperation his father once gathered him up in his arms to force feed him to the ocean, to sacrifice him like Abraham on the rock of the sea but he screamed and kicked and slapped his father for all he was worth and his father dropped him into the sand, stung by a pummeling he could not have believed possible from this thing he had procreated. Goddamnit alright, you don't have to go in the water, his father said. Crazy fuckin kid, it's your vacation. They left him alone after that. He sat on the sea wall and watched the rest of them tempt fate in the tides, every trip in every summer month. His older brothers stopped bothering him, abandoned him as something unnatural. His sister came sometimes and sat beside him on the wall after she tired of swimming and being splashed and dunked by his two brothers. There's nothing wrong with you, she said. Just cause you don't like the ocean. I know that, he said. It's you and them are crazy. Maybe that ocean gets you but it won't get me. There's nothing wrong with you, his sister said, as though he hadn't spoken. You just don't like the ocean. Yet it was years after they'd moved down south, away from the ocean, when he hadn't seen or thought of the sea again in those many years, that the affliction of the dream descended.

Back at the railing beside him Johnson was shouting. Kestermont looked up. Out of the pewter wall of sky loomed the hospital ship. ***HOPE.*** The stark black lettering unadorned and intermittent through the mist against the white hull. The throbbing of the diesels changing pitch as the boatswain approached. The bottom of the boat staccato against the waves, setting his teeth to clattering. Two stories of steel hull. Halfway between the railing and the water a square of hull opened and two men in oilcloth began running a steel ladder out of the ship's side. The young sailor pitched down from his loft above the wheelhouse and moved aft, slid a door open inside the wall of the fat gunwale and removed a pail.

"Wear these, lieutenant. That ladder comin down from that hole rusty with scale cut you open you're not careful."

The pail was full of gloves, thick with rough rubber. Kestermont fished around for a pair that weren't missing fingers or thumbs. Johnson did the same.

"Hole's meant for cargo," the sailor said. "Not passengers. Whole thing's juryrigged. What you get for missin the chopper, sir."

The ladder was hinged somehow. It bent from the horizontal ninety degrees and began descending. Kestermont couldn't tell if it was motorized or if the men above were operating some kind of pulley.

The sailor held the ladder like a horse to be mounted. "Climb it from the back," he said. "Once you're both on they raise you part way till the first man's level with the hole, then kick out a tray you can walk in on one at a time but sir don't let go the sides of that top rail till you're inside. You fall you'll be wishin you hit water but you won't you'll hit this boat or that one. Seen it happen, didn't help the poor bastard a damn bit this is a hospital ship. Survived Khe Sanh, killed fallin from a ladder. When you come back down they harness you. No harness going up."

The boatswain was saying something. Shouting. The wind took the words but the sailor said, "Chief's here to pick up two discharges missed their chopper too. Says he's leavin in fifteen minutes max or soon as they're aboard. That storm's gonna break, Lieutenant, and we don't want to be too far from shore when it does. You and your man gotta be fast. Chief don't wait for no one in waters like these. Those discharges a minute late Chief'll leave them too."

"I won't be long. Just don't shove off without us."

The sailor shrugged. "Chief he don't wait on generals. You can leave your guns here."

"You won't goddamn leave us," Johnson shouted. "And they aint guns. They're fuckin *rifles*. And we don't leave the fuckin rifles."

The sailor shrugged again. "Get ready. Keep away from the steel ends of this ladder, they'll plunge in these seas drive right through your foot. Grab hold and time it. Get a boot on a rung right away. Move fast and don't look down, I seen men freeze halfway up you practically have to pry their hands loose."

Kestermont was already moving. He kept his eyes off the ocean, found a ladder rung and swung himself onto the back of the ladder,

Johnson crowding behind him. The ladder bobbed and hitched, slipped side to side and back to front like a living thing that resented his foreign presence and meant to buck him off. He didn't think and he didn't look down. As he came level with the hull entrance a steel plank exited the side of the ship. He held on to an overhead railing, twisted around and walked himself along the metal tongue until a sailor on each side took hold and pulled him in and past a folding wooden fence, then did the same with Johnson right behind him. One of the sailors hooked the accordion fence to the bulkhead. A flight of metal stairs built above a cargo ramp led to a landing, made a left turn and disappeared into the bath of light tumbling from the opening in the deck. The wind howled past the hull opening, angered by another escape.

"On up, gentlemen," the shorter of the two sailors said. "Ship host right outside the stairwell. He'll take care of you. Lieutenant, this place is like Dodge City. They're gonna want you to check your hardware. We got a locker here to put em in."

"I'll check the hardware when I check outta country," Johnson said.

"You aint met the head nurse," the sailor replied. Behind him the tall sailor laughed.

Kestermont threw the rubber gloves into a five gallon bucket hanging from a nail and left Johnson to argue their cause. He took the stairs two steps at a time because time was running out. The last scheduled chopper was mid-afternoon, way the hell the other side of Da Nang and if the company moved in the morning and he wasn't back the skipper would take 2nd platoon himself and when Kestermont showed up on the next bird take his head off in front of everyone.

It was like the gunny told officers half the gunny's age, and as Kestermont had already observed to be no exaggeration: *Do what you're told, gentlemen. Do exactly what you're told. Cause doing what you're told might get your head handed to the enemy but it aint gonna hurt like it will if Captain comes for it.*

36

EMERGING ON DECK HIS EYES ADJUSTED from the gloom inside the stairwell to the lesser gray of daylight. It was another world. Recuperating soldiers and marines in red- or blue-striped hospital whites and flip-flops looked like colorful prison inmates. Unlike inmates they lounged against gunwales and deck furniture in tourist fashion, heedless of wind and skies and smoking and talking, arms and legs in casts, heads swathed in gauze, armpits perched on crutches. An amputee crouched on the surviving leg in his wheelchair and spun himself expertly in circles like a human gyroscope. Three men poised on crutches and canes stood in a triangle, the wheelchair at the center making a pyramid, the men lofting a volleyball over the amputee's head. As the man spun he threw up one hand then the other, trying to knock the ball away. They were all laughing, the amputee the loudest with the most conviction. For such men the war was over or grievously interrupted and what point remained in foreshortened adulthood if not to resurrect childhood. To laugh now before sacrifice was forgotten and bitterness dulled the fleeting sheen of glory. To buffer however briefly mutilation's coming years. To gallop this mortal moment loud and blind into the waiting maw of time.

Above the deck a pageantry of balloons and streamers bounced and twisted in the stiff breeze, a breeze stiff but lacking full authority, the wind less potent now assailing a true ship. A fanfare of brass and violin wafted past him. Young nurses in Red Cross white and blue with carmine markings on their caps held the caps in place with one hand and swung clipboards with the other. They moved busily among the lounging GIs, accepting their attentions good-naturedly, long uniform dresses dancing behind. Crew members lashed down deck chairs, a wheeled bar, racks of recreational tables, anything that could move in a storm. A man hobbled after a shuffleboard disc, swatting at the elusive disc with his cane as the ship slowly rolled. The fanfare subsided behind a tenor's croon. Kestermont recognized the voice, not the tune, the lyrics familiar because clichéd, not because he'd heard them before: *love undying, beacon in a mist, light through a maze*. Sinatra maybe, a voice from another world and another era, immediately reassuring, forget the lyrics, forget words, as though by treaty or grace or divine intervention the meaning resided in the sound not the syntax, layered inside a voice honeyed by fate and genes and imbued with the power to suspend time and alter reality provided reality wound you up here, provided reality wounded but didn't kill you. Heal you maybe, but not even the Lord of Hoboken could reverse a bullet or deflect the scythe of fragmentation.

Directly ahead of him a small shed had been grafted onto the wall middeck, the sign above the door announcing the destination for ARRIVALS. A middle-aged civilian in a pressed linen suit had him sign in and record the purpose of his visit, then appeared to struggle deciphering his handwriting and made a notation in another book. A plastic name tag across a broad lapel identified him as the HOST.

"Welcome aboard, Lieutenant," the host said, squinting again at Kestermont's scribbling. "I'm sorry, you're visiting who?"

"Last name Tomlin. Thomas A. US Marines. Lance corporal."

Johnson arrived and stood close to the shed, seeking anonymity. He removed his utility cap from a cargo pocket and put it on, snugging it against the wind. Adjusted it like a man preparing a disguise, his rifle slung barrel down, close to his side, an accomplice in deception. For all his caution he still managed an admiring eye at a pair of Red Cross girls walking past. He nudged Kestermont.

"That's some fine Donut Dollies right there, LT," Johnson said. "You know, sir, I believe I been wounded, been guttin it out for weeks now but just realized I might need to spend a day or two right here in sick bay."

"Easy, Corporal," Kestermont said. "They'll throw you overboard they catch you even lookin too hard. These Red Cross girls get protection wherever they go, especially from bush-crazy jarheads like you."

The man in the linen suit gazed up at a chart on the wall and frowned.

"Not sure that patient's cleared for visitors, Lieutenant. Still in Recovery middeck and been there a while from the entries. Weeks and weeks from the looks of it. I heard about this one. That's a long time, you don't mind me saying so."

"I won't be long. He'll want to see me."

"Well, you'll need to check in with the ward nurse or one of the Red Cross aides. Go along starboard here, 2nd hatch, down the stairs and straight to the office. Lieutenant, they'll have a fit if you take that firearm down there with you."

Kestermont unslung the M16 and handed it to Johnson.

"I know my weapon," he said. "Make sure I get the same one back."

"Shit, LT. I wouldn't trade peach delight here for Old Betsy. But she'll enjoy the company."

"That boat don't leave without us, you copy?"

"Copy."

Kestermont turned back to the chart. He found Tomlin's name.

"What room?"

The host looked again. "It says Recovery 3, but they wheel them around depending on who's coming out of surgery that day. He could be in any of them. The nurse'll know."

Kestermont made his way along the deck and ducked through the hatch. Descending the stairs he passed the nurse's office and scanned the doorways as he walked the passageway, trying to look without being looked at. Through the half-opened doors what he glimpsed could have been Central Casting for the mummy films of his childhood: men in gurneys, all of them wound in varying degrees of bandage, most sleeping, some reading magazines or paperbacks, others with legs in casts hoisted halfway to the ceiling. As he passed one room a nurse with short blonde hair glanced up at him and then resumed conversation with her patient, his face a mass of scars, one empty sleeve crooked at the elbow and pinned to his shoulder, one leg suspended, the cocked stub of a foot purple and unbound.

The hall ended in a small reception area in front of three closed doors. A magazine rack full of National Geographics separated miniature couches below a lithograph of Leutze's Washington. His Excellency poised on one leg while his rabble crew dodged ice floes in the river on Christmas Eve, in a boat that looked not much more seaworthy than the strange craft that had just delivered him across the harbor. Kestermont thought Washington might not look so confident crossing the Delaware in Kon-Tiki.

He opened the door marked Recovery 3. Three beds, all empty. A card on the door of Recovery 2 had three names, none of them Tomlin's. He opened Recovery 1, no names on the door, two beds, only one occupied. A single amber light above a stainless sink allowed him to see well enough to find a bank of switches a few feet from the door jamb. He flipped the first one and nothing happened. The second one and the fluorescents overhead blinked and fluttered and made clicking noises. When they came on they filled the room with droning, as if the ship secretly meditated.

Tomlin was asleep, swathed in cloth from torso to neck, one lone eyelid visible above a patch of purple tissue. His mouth was half open and his breathing came in small waves. The outline of a leg cast rose beneath the swirl of bedding. Bandages crossed the nose above a deep incision that bridged his lips. More stitches ran like canals down the triangle of his cheek. His head had been shaved; stubble crowded a crisscross of wounds. Bags of IVs hung from the stand by his bed; tubing ran from the IVs to a single needle taped high on the forearm. Below the needle angry red clusters guarded veins that refused further entry. One arm lay on top of sheets and a thin woolen blanket. At the end of the curled hand Kestermont noted the crusty red absence of the thumb beneath loose gauze.

Kestermont shook his head in wonder. When they stood beside the burning temple and watched the medevac disappear into the night, Doc said no one with those wounds would be alive when it landed. If anyone knew a ruined body it was Doc Mason. Yet here Tomlin was.

Torn envelopes jutted from the edges of a nightstand beside his bed. At the center of the table sheets of paper sprawled around a cup half filled with black coffee. Even from the foot of the bed Kestermont recognized the artful handwriting on the envelopes. Letters he had forwarded last week, from Tomlin's girlfriend. The battalion was in the rear, licking its wounds. He'd been thinking out loud at mail call, looking at the letter addressed to Tomlin, the woman's name in the corner of the envelope, when he said to no one, *What better healing than the tender words of a lover?*

Copy that, the skipper said, overhearing him, everyone in earshot nodding and agreeing.

Let the healing begin, said the platoon gunny, slumped nearby against a shattered stone column, the sarcasm as thick as the red mud he was carving from his boots with his bayonet. The gunny seventeen years old at Iwo Jima and old at twenty-three for the frozen retreat from Chosin Reservoir, with no more use for Kestermont than he had for any officer with only a single war in his resume. Kestermont ignored the gunny, went to the baggage hut and shuffled through Tomlin's pack again, this time alert for unopened letters. He discovered a small bundle bound in parachute cord, all the envelopes with the same name, same striking handwriting. Most of them pristine and untouched, one of them weathered and torn, inked with bloody fingerprints. A letter much traveled. He remembered Doc Mason removing an envelope carefully from Tomlin's fatigue pants when they'd cut his bloody rags off. Doc must have conscientiously added it to Tomlin's pack in the baggage hootch. Always the grunt's keeper, Doc Mason: the fearless, the sentimental, the late Doc Mason.

Kestermont combined the letters from Tomlin's pack with the one that had just arrived and expressly sent a man out on mail run aboard the next chopper. Special delivery was the least he could do. It was something. Made him feel good. Sort of.

Without hesitation Kestermont stepped up to the nightstand. The linoleum floor absorbed his bootfall. He picked up the nearest sheet and read the few lines:

Tommy,

You write me and I can't believe you've read my letters. Why don't you answer me? I can't go on like this. I won't. Please read my last letter. Or maybe I should say any of them.

G

Kestermont felt a little less rosy. He picked up another letter, this one two sheets of legal paper, white, not yellow. Unlined. A cornucopia of the beautiful handwriting, both sides. The envelope beneath it dirty brown, spotty with dried blood. The one salvaged by Doc Mason.

The voyeur in Kestermont could not be restrained once it started. He read:

Dear Tommy,

I'm writing from work because I can't wait any longer. I hate telling you this now because I never know where you are and it seems so horrible of me but I can't live with myself if I don't tell you the truth.

And when you do write me you don't answer me. Don't you get my letters or maybe you do but do you read them. So I'll say again what I've tried to say I don't know how many times. And for the last time. I can't go on like this.

I have a new love, Tommy. He's tall and skinny and kind of scraggly I guess, hair long like people are wearing it now. He's not beautiful, not like you are, but his soul is sweet and pure. He's smart and gentle and he's fierce against all this killing. The police beat him up in Chicago and threw him in jail. For telling the truth. For wanting to stop the killing. He walks with a limp now but he hasn't stopped speaking out. He writes the most inspired words about this war. He's waited for me a long time. He knows about us and understands and has never tried to persuade me about anything. I hardly knew him at all until my last year in school, but over the summer we became such good friends that now I know we are kindred spirits. As you and I could never have been, Tommy. Not anymore. Not since you left me for the killing. I tried, the best I could in the time we had, to give you something more than whatever was driving you over there. I tried giving you this child of mine for your own. It was selfish of me, really. I was trying to chain you to us with all the love I could wrap around you and at least in some way help replace what you'd lost. Though you never talked about that, did you. Another door you would never open. Why didn't you stay with me? Maybe it's best I never found out and maybe you never really knew yourself. I wonder if you know now.

And how do I say this but to say it. I'm on the other side, Tommy. I'm not blind anymore. I can't condone what I see so clearly. These corporations and politicians say this war is for us, they say it's all in the name of freedom, for our future, that we're helping the people over there. But Americans don't want to help people by killing them, destroying their homes, burning their children with bombs from their skies. Our parents didn't raise us to see other people die for money. These warmongers call themselves Americans. They may have been born here but they're not

Americans. I don't think they're anything but criminals. It doesn't matter how shiny their suits are.

You went there knowing what you would have to do. You could have refused. I would have stood by you forever. I told you I would. We could have lived in Vancouver or Montreal or even that silly little town where we spent that lovely weekend or anywhere and if we never came home so be it. You could have painted houses or played piano in a bar and I would have taken in laundry or worked in a shelter. Anything. Instead you chose the killing. The letters never say it but I know you're in it. You knew all along how I feel about this war but what I felt for you was the deepest love and it blinded me. How would we live together now? And yet I know you have sacrificed so much, I can only imagine. I don't know where you are, where you sleep, what your days must be like. Your gentle hands, so musical, now turned to so much violence. I don't understand it and you knew I didn't when you left that morning. Tommy, you didn't have to go. You didn't. Now I'm crying again, the stupid paper is all stained. These are my tears for you and me and us and for our time together and for what might have been except you left me for the killing when I asked you not to. I should have begged you on my knees and torn my hair from the roots but it would only have made your leaving worse when you left anyway.

I will always love you, Tommy. I hope in all the years that pass only good things will happen for you. I hope you get home soon and I hope if you have healing to do it will be kind and complete and happen swiftly. I see so many lost souls from over there, they pass through this new life of mine now, full of terrible stories and bitterness. Some of them are finding a new beginning from sharing and speaking out, but I fear many of them never will. Maybe in ten years we will meet again and we will both be so different, maybe the passing years will change us both in ways we could never imagine now. But I am lost to another, Tommy. He's not you and you would never be him but he's who I needed you to be. I hope one day you will see that. I can't write you anymore, it breaks my heart to tell you this now where you are but I can't do anything else and live with myself. Why did you leave me, Tommy? I wonder if I will ever stop asking that question. I will love you forever, but I can't love you now. Please take care of yourself. I know you're a good person, I know it so well. Please come home to your family. I don't know what that fine sweet brother of yours would do if he lost you.

Goodbye, Tommy. I don't know what else to say that I haven't already said. None of this was planned. This world just seems to be made of two things, love and war, and we have each made our choices.

And I don't even know if you will ever read this letter.

I know this is selfish too but when you come home will you send me a note saying you are safe.

Please don't hate me.

I'm sorry for everything.

Guinevere

Well, shit.

No good deed.

Nothing went unpunished in this country. He was numb from his good deeds.

The handwriting haunted him, forget what it wrote. He imagined a woman who could travel those ovals and form such capitals, so evenly space her words and then blur the resulting perfection with tears even when driving the knife. He couldn't see her face, but he imagined her form backlit by twilight reflected from a lake. Shadows across a bare shoulder. The evening star low in the sky. Castle on a hill, a king alone on a parapet. In the forest below, auburn hair redolent of sex mingled with earth, sweat, starlight. He imagined a Guinevere in the shadows with her new lover and Tomlin's loss in the same instant.

On the other hand, what the hell did she know about this war? Or for that matter what did she really know about Tomlin? Had he ever shown her, had she ever looked?

He put the letters down in exactly the same place, fiddled with them a moment to get the angles right. To place them with care as Tomlin had dropped them in...what? Despair? Grief? Resignation? Or was it relief? He fiddled with the two sheets, as if perfect restoration of their position would restore his own innocence.

As if anything could ever restore that.

37

AT THE FOOT OF TOMLIN'S BED he picked the clipboard from its hanger and scanned the sheaf of pages. An outline of a human body on the last page told the story. Words stippled along the margins, words he knew, words he didn't. Marks and scrawls all over the body. Doctors' handwriting worse than his. Near the neck, red ink circling a question mark. Tomlin already had two Purple Hearts; what Kestermont saw would make him eligible for another dozen. He should have been rotated out after the second wound (Kestermont tried, Tomlin refused), but even the infantry couldn't use him now. His replacement would already be en route. They weren't really discharging him so much as making him down payment on a new model.

When Kestermont looked up from the paper Tomlin's eye was open, the eyelid trembling from the effort. It looked like he was smiling, or trying to, an effort that started blood running from above the stitched upper lip and across the chin, trickling into a gauze landscape near his shoulder to form a small red delta.

"LT."

The voice weak but clear, as though spoken and heard in different rooms.

"Hello, Tomlin. Smarter man than me might not ask you how the hell it's goin."

"Goin all right, LT."

"You hurtin?"

"Naw. Got so much somethin in me all I do is sleep. Might fall asleep talkin. Or go back to the movies. Got movies playin twenty-four hours a day, LT."

"Morphine City."

"I think so. Makes for crazy dreams. Good to see you, LT."

"I heard a rumor they were sendin you home stead of back to the bush. Had to see for myself before I just sign off on losin another point man."

"War's over for me, LT. This is number three. I aint arguin this time. I'm gonna go get me that early discharge."

"I never figured you for a skater."

"I aint nothin but."

The door opened and closed behind him. Kestermont turned and recognized the young blond woman from the ward down the hall, wearing the Red Cross cap. She was young, pretty and angry. Her hands went to her hips and she leaned in, pointing her body at him like taking aim with a weapon.

"You can't be in here."

"Well, I'm here."

"You won't be long. I'll have you arrested."

"Oh Jesus don't do that. They'll bust me and send me to Vietnam."

"LT, this is Miss Raymond, a volunteer nurse from the States. She's helping me out. Miss Raymond, it's okay."

"It's not okay. This is post-op. No visitors. The doctor wants you healing. For you healing is peace and rest." Her voice softened just a bit.

"And morphine," said Kestermont.

The nurse's nostrils flared. She was pretty like a tiger lowering to spring was pretty.

"You don't rest when you're in pain. He has what the doctor says he needs."

"I like the morphine, LT."

"Course you do. I like it myself, only not enough just yet to go and get myself shot up halfway to hell and back."

"I want you to leave *now*."

"Are you sweet on this boy? Cause I aint here to compete with your charms. Just gotta give him some news, straighten him up a bit. Five minutes, darlin. All I need."

"I'm not your darling. I'll have the master at arms here in three minutes that's how much your darling I am."

"Miss Raymond, this man's an officer but that can't be helped. Officers forget there's places they aint in charge. He's a friend and I'm fine. Feelin much better. Once we're done talkin I'll sleep like a baby. Honest."

"You shouldn't be talking at all." She leaned over with a tissue from nowhere and daubed his lip and the blood from the little pool on his shoulder. "Look at you, bleeding again. When you talk too much those stitches start leaking. You'll scar. And you can hardly keep that eye open."

She looked at Tomlin and Kestermont saw the look. Not a bad looking woman at all. Standing behind her there was nothing not to admire. He felt a little bit better about the letters. She put her hand on Tomlin's forehead, made a show of feeling for fever through bandages.

"It's Maggie, okay? Not Miss Raymond. And I'm not leaving while he's here."

She walked over and sat in the chair against the bulkhead, removing the Red Cross cap with its crimson insignia. She crossed her legs and glared at him, putting him on notice that she was a full combatant in the matter of Tomlin's care.

He knew better than to speak out loud the thought that rose: *Nice legs, too*.

"*Five minutes*," she announced.

"Little chaperonin never hurt anyone," Kestermont said. He felt a whole lot better.

To Tomlin he said, "You know what happened back there?"

"Not too clear on that, LT. Couple sky pilots passed through with this story and that, probably didn't give me the straight skinny but I pulled out of em what I could. I knew about Debro without them tellin me, and I figured it out about the rest of em."

"There aint much else to tell. We're workin our way up, takin incomin the whole way, then run into what looks like Tail End Charlie for beaucoup NVA. They pin us down but good. Heavy machine guns we can't get a fix on their location. Phantoms everywhere but FOs won't do shit. Some chopper pilot gets out the word you're haulin someone on your back and he's goin in, identifies you by name and how he reads your dogtags from a hundred feet in the air maybe you tell me someday. Some oak leaf flyin a desk somewhere orders him out of the air space but he goes on in. Last anyone hears from him. We get some help from Lima Company mortars and disengage and get movin again. By that time chopper's down there's no word from anyone aboard. FOs call in the Phantoms from whatever holiday they been on where the hell were they when I needed em. Now here they come friendlies or no friendlies in the line of fire. Lost my temper on the radio they liked to court-martial me but I couldn't stop my mouth or those fast movers either. We were still three blocks away when the jets came and when they left there was nothin left alive halfway to Hawaii includin three companies of NVA got smoked. It was dark when we got there. Bodies everywhere I never seen the like of it, not even at Song Ba. You were the only thing livin on that street and we only found you cause the place was lit by fire and here was this gold Buddha half buried shinin like a trip flare in the flames burnin down this big temple. Right there by him stickin outta the ground a hand missin a thumb. We dug you up outta brick and stone I swear a foot thick and I only know one other man got raised from the dead."

Kestermont paused and watched Tomlin's eyelid as it vibrated involuntarily. For a moment he thought Tomlin might be dying.

"Tomlin, you there?"

The eyelid went still and closed over the bloodshot eye, but Tomlin's chest moved in a discernible rhythm. Kestermont relaxed.

"Here, LT."

"Don't you go fadin on me like you thinkin about buyin that farm. Now I came here to tell you two things you don't know or maybe you do. One's about Buddha. That little statue is solid gold and I mean solid, got a ruby the size of a small egg stuck in its forehead and gold and rubies is the least valuable part of it. You know what I'm talkin about I say gold Buddha?"

"I do, LT. Sorta. Wasn't sure if I was dreamin him."

"Not unless everthin's a dream. That Buddha's twenty-four pounds gold and dreams don't weigh nothin. He aint just gold neither. That little statue's got a history. Some kind of national monument goin back centuries got a pedigree like a racehorse and strictly between us he's been liberated, headin stateside not long after you do. Hell, he may rotate before you do. There's a fair penny waitin for us once he finds a new home."

Tomlin's eye remained closed. He breathed more evenly, quiet so long Kestermont thought the morphine had carried him off.

"Tomlin, you copy?" Another long moment.

"LT."

"Yeah?"

More silence. Tomlin's thumbless hand twitched as though reaching to pull Kestermont to him, then went slack in defeat.

"LT, go on and leave Buddha here. Wrap him in a blanket, orphan him to some temple. Put him in a basket the dead of night and set him down the river. Anythin. Let some of his own kind raise him."

"That's a negative, Lance Corporal. Can't do that. Buddha's already travelin. Anyway, there's no temple left in that city to leave him to and that river's no place for a man much less a god. Tomlin, here it is. Buddha was the target. Everybody's target. NVA had sappers in that temple lookin to didi with him. We had some of our own midnight boys after him too and they must've met each other goin in and comin out and didn't none of em live to tell about it. Both sides must've got the same skinny at the same time on Buddha's coordinates, sent in teams didn't expect each other and didn't no one on either team of spooks know a damn thing about the rest of the NVA's plans for that day. Nothin else makes sense. Big clusterfuck absolutely but things don't just happen. Everthin movin got steps on the way, maybe you know em maybe you don't. Somebody set the parts to movin. What parts we talkin about? Who the hell knows? Air Wing, artillery, Battalion? Regiment? United Nations and Ho Chi Minh for all I know. You and Debro and the rest, just one of them parts along one of them steps. Somehow. Some way. Everthin movin and didn't nobody on the ground know a damn thing but the steps got laid down. Somebody laid em down, somebody knew em. It don't matter who, or who they didn't tell, includin me, includin you. Buddha can't go home, Tomlin. The steps are still layin down, parts are still movin. They're lookin for him. He stays here, they'll find him, cause whoever they are, they're used to gettin what they want."

"Don't matter, LT. Leave him here. Take him outta the city. Plenty of temples left other places. It's only gold."

"I'm tellin you the gold aint what's gold about that Buddha. It's outta my hands, Tomlin. Buddha's travelin."

"Nothin good gonna come of it, LT."

"You're wrong there. You'll see when you're stateside. You got a share comin."

Tomlin's eyelid fluttered but the eye didn't open and went still.

"I can't even make this fuckin eye work, what's Buddha gonna do for me. I don't want nothin to do with it, LT. It comes to that, Debro has a baby daughter, lives with his mother. That's where it goes. See to it, LT. All I ask."

"I copy that, Tomlin. I got Debro's address. Nothin's gonna be lackin for any little girl of Maurice Debro, I give you my word. His mother neither. We'll talk about you later, way later, stateside. Now I've told you half what I came to tell you."

Before he could continue the nurse was standing beside him. "I don't know what you're talking about and I don't care." And then pleading, "Please, Lieutenant. Everything isn't in those charts, if you've been reading them. Your time's up."

"Time's almost up," Kestermont said, as kindly as he could. "Just a few more minutes, miss, I'll be done. Tomlin. You listenin?"

"I am, LT." The eye stayed closed.

"This is the way it is, and it aint no other way. It's hard but it's true and I'm sayin it the way it is now cause who knows a damn thing about later. You hearin me, Tomlin?"

"I am."

"Here it is, then. Didn't nobody put a gun to your head when you chucked bein a college boy out the window and joined up. That sweet summer day you tossed your draft deferment aside and set your legs to walkin down that post office hallway they were goin where you sent em. When you strolled through that recruit office door into the arms of that smilin jarhead in the dress blue trousers waitin on you spider to the fly and signed papers that was *you*. Didn't no one but you wind you up in the infantry. If a beautiful woman couldn't talk you out of it who could. You aint here cause you weren't smart enough to find the Canadian Rockies or cause some juvenile court judge sent you to Parris Island to save the county some reform school money. You here cause of your own choices, Tomlin. You here cause of *you*. Choices *you* made got you here on the receivin end of this fucked up war and my fucked up orders. Now I reckon them choices didn't include runnin away, refusin duty or throwin up your hands and beggin for mercy, otherwise one of them things is what you woulda done. No, here you are now, thanks to your own damn self, shot to hell, blown up again this time but good, can't even feed or shit yourself and you're damn sure no more use to this green machine."

All fight gone, the nurse seemed about to cry.

"Lieutenant, that's enough. *Please*."

She tried pulling Kestermont toward the door, but her hands only slid across a network of scarred and crusted skin that cracked and flaked. Her hands were small and moist, as if they were crying too, but they felt cool against his arm, distantly reminiscent of other places, other people, other hands.

Kestermont said, "Almost done, miss, don't you worry." He placed a hand on hers as gently as he could.

"Now I sent you on this mission, Tomlin. It was me got you wound up here in swaddlin clothes half crippled and blind and everbody else dead spite of everthin you did or didn't do out there. That's the way it is and it aint no other way. I sent you and you damn sure better know I don't regret it. If I had to send you again I would. I won't spend one minute bein sorry about it, not if I live to the end of time. It may have been the stupidest fuckin thing I ever did or the worst goddamn order I ever gave but I gave it. I had the duty to give it and I gave it cause orders don't always come with reasons and duty don't ask for em. Let anyone knowin in advance he's givin bad orders square it with his own conscience. Now you had the duty to take that order and carry it out and you did it. You did your duty and I did mine and everbody dead did theirs and that's all needs be said about it, now or anytime however many days or years either of us got left. I'm proud of my goddamn duty and you better be too cause that duty is all you have and all you ever will have till Time or the Almighty or the sons of Ho Chi Minh turn out your lights tomorrow, the next day or a long way down the road. Aint no one who aint been where you been knows a goddamn thing about any part of this war and that includes any woman no matter what love does or doesn't have to do with any letter that woman wrote. Aint nobody knows nothin about that street on that day in this dogfight but you and there aint nobody knows nothin about Debro and the rest of your squad but you and let me tell you right now Lance Corporal *there never will be* no matter how many years you live or women you know and leave or they leave you or how many pasty-faced reporters say what they say or college professors write what fuckin history books. And won't nobody care neither, not 10 minutes after they make you a civilian again. They'll forget you faster than the VA's gonna forget what size crutches you need or when your pissbag needs emptyin. You best believe that right now. You get straight on that. It was your choice true to the rest of your choices got you sent to this ship and you did it and I sent you and I am goddamn proud of you and all the rest of em and honored fuckin honored to have been the one sendin you and the hell with the rest of it. Just the *hell* with it. Now that's the fuckin truth. And I tell you what, that night we dug you outta that street and I stood there disbelievin you were alive in that grave even with that one eye starin up at me and Buddha flickerin his red eye in a gold fire over you, I said to the Lord if I did wrong sendin you or you did wrong goin Lord strike me dead right here right now for givin you that order and let's be done with it. Those were my words and I said em fuckin loud too so He couldn't mistake hearin em Doc Mason is my witness. And seein as here I stand and there you lie and He aint seen fit to smite either of us in His fury, Tomlin, I rest my case. Cause it aint complicated, Lance Corporal. They called you, you answered the call. They sent you, you went. While in this place right or wrong you did your duty. Nothin more, nothin less. That's all there is to it. Do you copy?"

"Copy, LT. I do."

"Well all right. Now I've said it." But there was something else, some remaining damage to address. Kestermont felt suddenly tired. The hell with it, he'd said enough. What could words do now? He took a long breath. "I'll be seein you stateside, Lance Corporal. You won't be expectin me the day I show up."

Kestermont turned to the door and the nurse moved immediately closer to Tomlin and spoke but Kestermont couldn't hear her. At the door he stopped and hesitated, hand on the door lever. Shook his head and turned around. The nurse ignored him. She sponged another trickle of blood from below Tomlin's eye, then used the same tissue to wipe her own cheek.

"Tomlin."

"Yes, sir."

"There's one more thing."

Tomlin's head turned in his direction, but the unbandaged eye didn't open. Kestermont could sense the frustration in the gears shifting behind the eyelid.

Kestermont said, "I run you down with that lecture cause I looked over that file at the foot of your bed. They got a picture there showin just where and how you took your licks." He paused and shook his head. "Wasn't gonna do this, but hell. What aint I said by now, what aint I done."

"Lieutenant, you could just *leave*," the nurse said.

"Go on, LT."

"Here's the rest of it. Lance Corporal, you aint the same man you were day I gave you that mission and you aint never gonna be that same man again. Now that's a fact. You're not careful, that fact gonna kick your ass the rest of your life. Cause they tore you up good, Tomlin. There aint much left of one knee and you are gonna limp, jarhead. You might be good for a sack race in some county fair Fourth of July in Hicktown Texas but that knee and a AK round that burrowed on through a shoulder blade gonna keep you from playin outfield in the big leagues. That eye aint gonna grow back and missin a thumb you damn sure aint gonna be hitchhikin round the world left handed. Hell, you got a testicle missin too left or right the chart don't bother to say and seems the jury's out you ever gonna be able to bring any little jarheads into this world. Shrapnel and bits of stone all down one side my guess that's from a Phantom they're gonna be pickin that outta you for years and damn if there aint a few pieces right there snugged against the heart. Top it off, looks like they aint quite had time to figure out how to pull that piece of mortar round outta the back of your head. Some doctor got a nice question mark circled in red ink right there by the picture of your head to make sure they don't overlook that little detail. I don't think they ever seen the likes of you, Tomlin. That's probably why they're takin their time, wheelin you in and outta these rooms, hell, maybe fightin to take turns doin the wheelin. That's a fact, Tomlin, and gettin to the point, you been *rearranged*. Enemy done some of it, Air Wing did their share, now the doctors. And from the look of your charts that pack of bonecutters aint done with the rearrangin. Frankly I think these doctors are keepin you down here cause keepin you alive is makin them famous. I know you damn sure impressed me."

The nurse seemed about to object further, but by now they were practically a family. She made a face like a child turning away from a father hardened against its pleas. Placed her small delicate hand gently on Tomlin's ruined one, as if to prepare him for the next blow in the world's injustice.

Kestermont dove in for the kill.

38

KESTERMONT SAID, "Here it is, Tomlin. Runnin down that list of missin and wrecked body parts it seems to me a man who aint quite sure of did he or didn't he make his own choices might start wafflin a little bit, get convinced by some smooth talkin rear echelon motherfucker who don't know shit and can't do shit that he *aint* the end result of his own choices, that it *wasn't* him did that walkin down that post office hallway, it was mommy and daddy or the first grade teacher or moonbeams, brain cells or a broken heart set him in motion. Man a little bit foggy on the subject might start listenin, might start lookin for someone to blame, take that first baby step on that long road to hell and if there's any devil in hell it's the man preachin that bullshit. Nothin here but facts, Tomlin, facts like napalm at sundown. So what I want to know is, you gonna be all right? You straight on this shit? Or is what we got here the beginnin of a lifetime of *whinin?* I been disappointed before, jarhead, and that's a fact too. Tell me now and I'll lay it to rest. You gonna disappoint me, Lance Corporal?"

Tomlin lay quietly, the eyelid unmoving. His chest was in fitful motion and the fingers of his thumbless hand twitched. The nurse looked at Kestermont and he read the entreaty in her eyes: *Please please go.* Kestermont thought how noble of him to reply: *Least I can do after all I've done.* But he said nothing, fresh out of nobility after eleven months in the bush. He waited. Tomlin remained silent and after another moment Kestermont gave it up and nodded to the nurse. He turned to leave but stopped when Tomlin finally spoke.

"LT."

"Still here, Lance Corporal."

Tomlin's eye opened like a living thing breaching the ocean's surface. The lip formed its quarter-smile and a small rivulet of blood instantly formed on the banks of an incision that ran from beneath the gauze along his forehead and across the bridge of his nose. The blood paused, swelled and lay poised in equilibrium, glistening and static and restless, like an army at the borders of another country waiting for scouts to return and orders to advance.

"LT."

"Here, Tomlin. You goin under or comin up?"

"Morphine's tuggin, LT. Sendin me to the movies night and day. Crazy shit shufflin by inside my head. Ceilin looks like it's breathin. But I'm *lookin*. At least I'm lookin. And there's somethin to say. Hell, I got a couple somethins." The smile suddenly broadened and the rivulet plunged across the borders, streaking his chin. Kestermont instinctively caught the nurse's arm and interrupted its journey with the tissue.

"Here's one of em, LT."

"I got a notebook open. Go ahead."

"This aint the first time."

"What aint?"

"This. All this. A fucked up war. Debro. Me. You. The rest of em. The rest of my fine boys dead to a man. Dressed in green or red. Or blue. Or gray. Sick green light in a hospital. Hospital or tent, boat in the ocean, patch of dirt, what's the difference. Shot up, cut up, full of arrows, half a head missin, spear in the back, cannonball in the chest. All there in the movies, LT. Leg gone below a knee, arm at a shoulder. Thumb from a hand. A thousand kinds of morphine. A girl. Girl like this beauty here. Another one ugly as dirt. Someone peelin your boots off what's left of your legs, someone rakin the dirt out a hole in your guts. Other times me where you are and you lyin here. Like the hands of a clock, LT. Round and round. Nothin changin. Only names. Places. Faces. What we use to do the killin. Not the killin."

"You say so, Tomlin."

"I do, LT. I say so. I know."

"Well all right."

"I want somethin different this time, LT. Somethin besides the killin."

"Well all right."

"That's what I'm gonna get, LT."

"That's all right."

"Somethin else to say."

"Notebook's open."

"This body got rearranged don't mean nothin. It don't mean a damn thing. You like music, LT? You know rock and roll? The blues?"

"I do, for a fact."

"Yeah?"

"Hell, I aint always wore camo, Lance Corporal. You believe it, I seen the King, man, what about that. Still a kid and crazy for the music I was hearin on the radio. One summer I got mad at the old man like a kid gets and stole away from home the way a kid does, gone for days, hitchhikin and sleepin in fields and old barns, back of old pickups, lyin to people givin me rides. Livin on Wonder bread and peanut butter. One day sundown just about over and night fallin I'm passin through some little town outside Texarkana on the Arkansas side I hear this music comin from a beat up old honky tonk. *That* music. No one watchin the doors so I sneak inside followin some drunk cowboys and there he was, man, him and Carl Perkins, out on some private road trip, just hootin and hollerin and livin it up."

"You never did, LT."

"Hell I never did. That bar was *wild*, let me tell you. Two guitars no drum, no bass no amp, nothin. Just the two of em and some local guy bangin on a table with a pair of big wood-handled forks. People gettin up and leavin, rednecks yellin at him and throwin beer, their girlfriends screamin and dancin and tearin their shirts half open. It was a sight a kid never forgets, let me tell you. I knew right then what I wanted to do. And it aint what I'm doin now."

"That's somethin, LT."

"That aint all. Jerry Lee Lewis, seen fire leap from his fingers practically burn the stage down, little dump in Alabama my senior year in high school, helped him put that fire out after the show with a six-pack of Pabst Blue Ribbon. Soul? Otis Redding, Wilson Picket, James Brown, saw em all, year I finished college up in Lexington and before anyone ever called that music by that name. Went on a pilgrimage, Tomlin. Seen more pickers and harp players than I can count, used to piss off the highway patrol racin an old Studebaker down country roads to Memphis and Knoxville. Over to Chattanooga. Over to Asheville seen em all the time, seen so many bluesmen. Willie Dixon, Howlin Wolf, others you don't know their names but one day you will. I aint always babysat a bunch of adolescent marine grunts, Tomlin. Wasn't half bad drunk or sober with three-bar chords on an old Harmony f-hole myself. Played a little harmonica, had a band almost a year, left it when duty called nothin I can do about that now. That surprises you I say you don't know who someone is till he shows you."

"Hell, it does surprise me, LT. All this time thinkin you were somethin unnatural, anyone could send people out in the shit day after day, watch em saddle up and leave, half of em you never see again, you just write those letters home and somehow stay glued together. Sleep and eat and laugh like any job any day of the week Sundays too. Look us in the eye and send us back out next mornin."

"It don't mean nothin, Tomlin."

"It does, LT. You can do that it means you believe in somethin."

"I believe in you."

"Then you'll be comin to my shows, Lieutenant. My little brother's got a band and they're waitin on me. Them boys can play and wait till I get back to the World and tune em up. They're waitin on me, LT. I'm gonna put this body back together and you know what? I get back I'm gonna be the best one-eyed, gimp-legged, nine-fingered honky tonk piano player missin half his family jewels you ever fuckin heard."

"You say so."

"I say so. I damn sure know so. I aint gonna disappoint you, LT."

"Well all right. That'll do for starters."

The nurse freed her arm from Kestermont's grip, wiped the blood from Tomlin's face. Tomlin kept smiling. The red stream blanched, reddened and ran again.

"Feels good. Maggie."

"I know."

She bent and whispered something. Tomlin's smile didn't fade.

"Maggie, think it over. Every kid in Texas gonna take one look at me, think Halloween's come early and run like hell."

"I won't run away from you. Not ever."

Kestermont cleared his throat. "Well, I best be going, Lance Corporal. There's people out there need killin whether you found religion and this fine woman or not. And I got a chopper I damn sure better not miss."

From the door he said, "I'll be showin up when you aint expectin me. Like I said. Stateside or anywhere else."

"You got less than 2 months left, LT. Look me up in San Antonio when you get back. We're in the phone book, aint but a couple of us Tomlins. There'll be a forwardin address wherever I am. You're short now, you gotta pay attention out in the bush. Might just be somethin different waitin back home for you, too, LT. Hell, my band could use a harp player now I think about it. So you pay attention out there. You pay that short-timer attention. You copy, Lieutenant?"

"I copy, Lance Corporal."

"Now it's me has one last thing."

Kestermont waited. Tomlin paused and Kestermont recognized it was for effect.

"And?"

"You know what that is?"

"Go on and say."

"It aint rainin, LT."

Kestermont shook his head. "Not all that original, Lance Corporal. But if you say so."

"I do, LT. I damn sure do."

"Well all right."

"San Antone, Lieutenant. Two months."

"See you at the Alamo, then."

"Already been to the Alamo, LT."

"Copy that."

The nurse nudged Kestermont to the door and he had a hand on the doorknob when Tomlin added, "And guess what else, LT."

Kestermont turned around. Tomlin smiled up at him. His face was flushed and he seemed to glow. Droplets of blood hung from the stitches across his forehead like tiny ornaments.

Tomlin said, "This aint my first Alamo, Lieutenant. We meet again, maybe I tell you where we first met." His smile widened. "Maybe I tell you why I always hated climbin ladders."

39

KESTERMONT CLOSED THE DOOR behind him and saluted as he passed Washington where the artist had left him, balanced for eternity mid-river on his boat ride to ambush the British, the unborn centuries heavy on His Excellency's shoulders, the full content of the weight to come unimaginable to him. From the Delaware and Trenton to Hue City and the Perfume River a long way.

Boat ride of my own coming up, thought Kestermont.

He wasn't halfway along the hall when he heard someone rushing down the stairs, footsteps clanging on metal. The host appeared around the landing, jacket flung open as he spun from the railing, hair in centrifugal disarray. The coat was rumpled and wet, tie ends going in different directions. Seeing Kestermont he slowed to a canter, adjusted his glasses and ran his fingers through his hair.

"There you are, Lieutenant. I'm afraid you're needed up top immediately. There's a most frightening situation has developed."

"Hell's going on?"

"It's your man, I'm afraid." He bent over to catch his breath, hands on his knees. He sounded apologetic when he added, "Well, there's also a sailor that has complicated matters. Do hurry, Lieutenant. Our master-at-arms has a very short temper."

They were out of the stairway and through the hatch. The skies were a battleship gray though it was still morning. The deck was wet with intermittent rain but the storm had yet to break beneath the canopy of black clouds threatening everywhere. Salt filled his nostrils and an occasional raindrop driven by the wind slapped him hard. Ahead he saw the reason for the host's panic. He recognized Johnson grim in front of the cargo passageway, one rifle slung, the other one in full reaction mode, shouldered, barrel trained at the feet of a marine sergeant in equally poised condition not ten feet away. The master-at-arms wore a red armband and held a .45 automatic in both hands directed knee-level at Johnson. Had they been duelists, this was the crossed-sword opening ritual before someone offered the first thrust to parry.

Kestermont stopped ten yards away, then moved forward cautiously. The host disappeared inside his shed. Two dozen onlookers balancing on crutches and canes held onto their caps in the wind and watched with keen interest a respectful distance away.

"Stand down, Corporal, goddamnit. You too, Sergeant. Lower weapons both of you."

Neither man made a motion to comply. A figure leaned against a bulkhead nearby, face in shadow but not concealing the look of amusement.

The master-at-arms said, "This is my ship, Lieutenant. Your man's out of line. He's my prisoner on his happy way to the brig. In these waters on this ship what I say is law."

"Law your ass," Johnson said. "This damn ship's run by civilians. It aint no government property."

"The ship aint. But you are. And all government issue on this vessel I don't care two-legged or any other kind answers to me."

"I said stand down, Johnson," Kestermont repeated. "You will remove that buttstock from your shoulder or I will do it for you."

"Sir, this man aint holstered that .45. I aint gonna be shot down like a dog."

"Hell, I'm gonna take this man's pistol and shoot you myself for insubordination and you'll be just as dead, dog or dogshit. I aint tellin you again."

"*Hell*, sir. Yes, sir."

Without taking his eyes from the master-at-arms Johnson let the barrel of his rifle drop toward the deck.

"Safe that weapon and sling it, Corporal."

Johnson did.

"Now you, Sergeant. Let's get the matches away from the fuse."

The master-at-arms didn't move.

"Sergeant, whatever happens now you won't need that firearm, I promise you. Put the weapon away. Personally I have found heads in this country run cooler with empty hands."

The master-at-arms contemplated Johnson a moment longer, then engaged the pistol's thumb safety and slowly holstered it.

"This man's under arrest, Lieutenant. Nothing changes that."

"Arrest your ass," Johnson said.

"Shut up, Corporal. Who wants to tell me what in hell's goin on?"

"That would be me, Lieutenant."

The figure emerged from the gloom behind them. It was the boatswain that had ferried them across the harbor.

"This jarhead must think he's fleet admiral, Lieutenant. I'm tryin to get to my boat and get underway before this storm breaks and he blocks the gangway down. Orders me to stay off my boat. *My* boat. When I tell him to pound sand he puts his rifle to my head. You can't do that last time I flipped through naval regulations and I believe the master-at-arms feels the same way."

"He was gonna leave us behind, Lieutenant. Row-your-boat peckerhead wasn't gonna let me round you up before he left. I said 'You will goddamn wait on my LT'." Johnson patted the side of his rifle stock. "That didn't make the necessary impression so I introduced the petty officer to peach delight here."

Kestermont shook his head. "Johnson, if you're not a disaster on two legs. Sergeant, while I didn't specifically authorize the employment of armed confrontation, this man was in fact following my orders. I did tell him to be sure that boat didn't leave without us. I assure you he's under control now. We'll leave your ship and you'll never see us again."

"That discipline doesn't satisfy, Lieutenant."

"Well, now, Sergeant. There's enough discipline comin to satisfy anyone, you included. Take Corporal Johnson here, the object of your understandable ire. His platoon's been under half complement most of a year. I've known him three months, he's had three squad leaders. Now he's squad leader. I promoted him so a private wouldn't be runnin a squad. We leave in the mornin for more of the same and we got men waitin on us and a chopper to catch that explains his short fuse and lack of manners and for a short fuse you should meet the skipper. You want this man disciplined? Victor Charlie and the NVA out there are lookin to do just that and chances are damn good one of em will by the end of the week. It don't please me to say it, Sergeant, but why don't you leave discipline to Charlie? Cause what discipline you think is waitin on a man crazy enough to fight to get back to the bush? We aint all got sea duty, is part what it comes down to. And we aint who we used to be, is the rest of it."

"I got a tour behind me, Lieutenant. Spent a year in the Arizona. I humped my ruck, took my own medevacs, got my own sad stories no one wants to hear. I paid for my sea duty, hard money on the barrel."

"I'm sure you did, Sergeant. I know it's all true. But that aint what we're talkin about here."

The master-at-arms looked at Kestermont, shaking and nodding his head in one motion.

"What do you say, Sergeant?"

When his head went still the master-at-arms said, "Hell of a day, sir. Hell of a day. Why don't you just take Wyatt Earp here and the two of you get the hell off my ship and we decide that's enough discipline to satisfy military decorum? And I aint bannin either of you for life but if you come aboard again, you *will* leave your firearms at the point of entry. What about it, sir?"

"As you say, Sergeant. We accept your authority in this matter. I commend your judgment and appreciate your lenience. Johnson, let's go."

Johnson didn't budge. He stared at the master-at-arms. "Hell's a 'dakorum'? I aint got no idea what I just got handed."

"I got a dictionary down in the ship library, jarhead," the boatswain said and strode past Johnson. He stopped at the landing and added, "Just aft of the lounge and the lava lamps, in case you get lost." He turned away into the stairwell gloom and disappeared, followed by a hard look from Corporal Harold Johnson.

40

KESTERMONT SHOVED JOHNSON to follow the boatswain. Out of the corner of his eye he noticed Tomlin's nurse step from the middeck hatch and cross to the railing. Johnson had unslung Kestermont's rifle and was handing it to him but Kestermont pushed it away. "Go on down, I'm right behind you."

By the time he reached the nurse she was leaning against the railing, smoking and staring into the blurred gray of sea and sky. The ember of her cigarette glowed in the wind as it tossed her short hair and flattened her skirt against her side.

"I didn't thank you in there," Kestermont said. "I am now, for all you're doin for that young marine. I wanted to tell you before I left."

When she looked up at him he could see she'd been crying. "I'm breaking all the rules," she said. "Smoking in public like this, staying up too late…getting *involved*."

She took a drag and her cheeks darkened where little caverns formed as she inhaled. She exhaled slowly, then bent and ground the cigarette out with her shoe and slipped the butt into her pocket.

"The head nurse oh she'll just frown at me for days if one of the girls reports me. I don't care. I don't even enjoy smoking. I just do it. More some days. Like today."

"Well." Kestermont paused awkwardly, then said, "I just wanted to thank you. Anything you ever do for that lance corporal you have all my gratitude forever. That aint much maybe but you have it."

"This ship full of gratitude wouldn't make any difference, Lieutenant. Full of miracles, maybe."

"Why, I know he looks bad, miss. But he's tough. He wants to make it. You heard him. He knows the score and he'll make it."

She put a hand to her mouth to stifle her crying. Tears rolled and ran into the hollows between her fingertips. She swallowed, wiped her cheeks and composed herself.

"I'm sorry, but it's you that doesn't know the score."

She blew her nose, folded the tissue and slipped it into her pocket to join the cigarette butt.

"He's going to die, Lieutenant. It doesn't matter what he wants or anyone else wants. We have the best surgeons in southeast Asia on this ship. After two weeks and a thousand x-rays they swallowed their pride and brought in the best surgeon in Hawaii. Not one of them alone or together know what to do. It's that metal in the back of the head. It's—" She paused, took a deep breath, found another tissue and dabbed at her eyes. "It's inoperable. They say it's lodged against all these nerve centers, all these critical places with these big Latin names, deep—impingement, they always say—and getting at it will do too much damage. The explosion sterilized the metal so there's no infection or only a little and they can keep that under control but the heat on entry fused things together or something. Always something. They go on and on. I don't understand half of what they say when they get to talking, how it's all attached or connected and they can't move it. They don't dare touch it. They don't dare move him to a shore hospital. They don't even know how he's still alive. But they can't just leave it. It keeps sawing inside, keeps him bleeding internally, building up pressure inside his head. They keep draining it, it keeps coming back. It's like he's got a knife slowly sinking inside his brain. If you breathe on it the pain's unbearable." She pulled new tissue from her pocket and blew her nose again. "That trouble with his eye just started. He's begun slurring his words."

"He spoke pretty good just now."

"Yes, today he did."

A pair of seagulls dropped suddenly from the overcast, nearly invisible against the low slate clouds. They hovered at a distance, arched their heads and regarded Kestermont and the nurse with equal parts hope and resignation. In another moment they looked at each other and rose back into the sky and disappeared.

The nurse watched the dull skies swallow up the gulls. "This gray day," she said. "This stupid war. Would be nice to be a bird. Even a hungry bird." The wind tossed her clipped hair. "I love the wind. I wish I could fly." She turned sideways to face him. "So thank you for your kind words, Lieutenant. But in the end we're going to need that ship full of miracles."

"One miracle's come and gone," Kestermont said. "He's here. He's alive. You're the other miracle."

"Don't say that."

"You are. It's why you're here."

"Please don't say that."

"You love that boy."

"Yes. I do."

"Do you know why?"

"I don't know why. All I know is what I feel."

"From the moment he arrived?"

"Yes."

"Not knowing who he was?"

"I don't know who he is."

Kestermont was silent a moment. "You remember what he said?"

"About what?"

"He said this wasn't the first time."

"I didn't understand any of that, Lieutenant."

Kestermont shrugged. "I'm not sure I do. You should ask him about it sometime. Cause you're the miracle and don't know it."

"I wish you'd stop saying that. What can I do?"

"You love him."

"I told you I did."

"Then you take that seed of love and plant it deep as you can. You water it and keep it growin. Night and day, you water it. Let it cushion that damaged head of his and all the rough handling he's gonna get from these doctors no matter they come from Hawaii or Hell cause I don't care what they say, one day soon they're gonna have to open their black bags and take out their scalpels and dig that piece of mortar round outta his head. That pride you mentioned gonna make em do *somethin*, they aint gonna just stand there and watch him die. They're gonna pick up that knife and when they do and no matter how desperate they feel remember this, there's things they don't know and don't believe in but are the only reason anythin they ever do works anyway. That boy wants to *live* and here you are beside him wantin him to live too. You just turn up the volume and you keep his amplifier cranked up and that miracle's gonna ride in on a white horse and you and that boy can go on and take up residence in San Antonio or whatever part of the world suits you. Now I seen young men live or die just because they believed one way or the other. I seen it. I seen it too many times to know otherwise. And right now it aint about believin it's about *decidin*. All I'm askin you to do is what I'm doin. I am *decidin* that man's gonna live. I aint acceptin any other outcome. Not from nobody or nothin. I want you to join up, miss, in this army of two. Army of you and me. In this crusade. I need your help. You love him so just love him. You decide he's gonna live and love him hard. Add your reason for livin to his. Don't hold back cause you might be hurt for losin him. That's all, simple as a love song. A love song, not the blues. There's a time for the blues and this aint one of em. This jukebox is playin a love song, corny as the one I heard first steppin boot aboard this ship. Now do you understand that, miss? *A love song*. Do you copy?"

"But I don't know what I can do."

"Why, what I just said, miss. Nothin else. And it's gonna happen forget how your mind gets in the road. You couldn't stop yourself carin if you tried could you but for a miracle you gotta throw everythin in. Maybe this happened to you before, maybe this aint the first time just like he said. Maybe you already had your heart broke. Once, a dozen times. For all I know that's how come you to be out on this wild ocean right now stead of back home raisin babies. That don't matter. It don't. Give this everythin you got night and day and no matter what happens you won't ever look back with anythin like a broken heart. You won't have nights lyin awake wonderin did you do everthin you could. I wouldn't ever want that for you, miss, not for a minute. So you love him with everythin you got, like there aint no tomorrow and there aint been a yesterday. It'll all work out, miss. One day that miracle arrives. When don't matter cause when's got nothin to do with it. You know what I'm sayin is true. I know you do. Do you copy?"

She was silent a moment, eyes fixed on the sea and sky. He thought she seemed too young to stare so hard. To look for proof there was a horizon somewhere in the gray. Or that a sun shone behind the clouds. But what did he know about this girl? The answer was always the same: he only knew what anyone showed him.

She said, "Nothing makes any sense."

"What we're talkin about don't answer to sense."

Now the cries of gulls surrounded them, but the birds were nowhere to be seen. The sea was wrinkled and dark, restless and surging. Massive and gray with indifference. Kestermont looked toward the bow and watched the ungainly craft that had brought him buck fitfully against the side of the hospital ship. The tires tied to the bow crushed as they cushioned the impact. He understood the tires now and the boat commander too, at least that much more. Sometimes no one showed you. Sometimes you had to look.

A light rain was falling. He felt the increasing raindrops sideways in the wind. The sky above him, the sea before him, storm coming. Between him and the sanctuary of land. Of the bush.

The Numidian rose from the depths. Kestermont pushed him away and fought back the dread.

And then the rain stopped, ominously. The wind picked up and so did his paranoia.

"LT!"

Kestermont looked over his shoulder. Johnson was back on deck, his arms outstretched in a gesture of panic. The wind had long since taken his utility cap.

"I best be goin."

Before he could move the nurse took his hand, the wind gusting at her back, her short hair moving staccato across her forehead and cheeks.

"Okay, Lieutenant. Okay. I copy. I'll do what you say. I'll throw it all in. I won't hold back. I won't hold back for *nothin or nobody*." She laughed and hugged him and filled his nostrils with a blend of youth and nicotine. For a moment he felt her wet cheek against his own. The warmth in her tears startled him.

"Outstanding, miss." He squeezed her gently at the back of the neck. "That'll do for starters."

She laughed again, pushed herself away and wiped her eyes, then reached up and brushed her tears from Kestermont's face.

"Take care out there, Lieutenant. I need your help on this. Army of two."

"We have us a deal, miss."

"Maggie. I want you to call me Maggie. I want you to think of me as Maggie. Not as 'Miss' or 'the nurse' or 'that Red Cross girl on the ship'. I'm Maggie."

"I copy that. Maggie." He smiled. "We're a team. Now you go on and get outta the way of this storm comin."

Kestermont turned and ran toward the ramp, ducking below the low entrance, Johnson clattering down the stairs after him.

"Damn, LT. You gonna give me a heart attack. Another minute I'd still have to shoot that swabbie sumbitch. Hell's 'dakorum' anyway? I keep thinkin about that damn word."

At the landing halfway down Kestermont stopped. "Chrissakes, Johnson, it means doin what's right under the damn circumstances. Like givin me my weapon and getting your ass down these stairs, down that ladder and back onto that boat before that sailor strands us in the middle of the ocean."

Johnson handed him the rifle and then vanished down the stairs, Kestermont on his heels.

41

THE SAME TWO SAILORS STOOD at the opening in the ship's side, one watching as the other hauled the fence across the opening and latched it. When Johnson pulled up in front of him, the sailor at the fence said, "Sea's gone bad, marine. Chief signaled shut it down. We're bringin the ladder up."

"Bring it up your ass," Johnson said and pushed the sailor aside and kicked the gate open. He scrambled along the extended metal plank with suicidal abandon, pirouetted and threw himself down the ladder.

"*You need gloves!*" the sailor shouted but Johnson's head disappeared below the plank just as Kestermont arrived at the gate. The ship was rolling and the sky flickered ghost white a millisecond before thunder crashed so hard it was all Kestermont could do to override his first instinct to throw himself to the deck, only this time the deck would be the ocean. He felt bile in his throat and his stomach heaved like a separate creature prostrate with terror *Christ that's the ocean down there fuck am I doin here?* but he slung his rifle, gripped the overhead railing furiously and forced himself out to the end of the plank and into his descent. He heard the sailor shout *Lieutenant the harness and you need the gloves!* but Kestermont could no more pause in his actions than fly to dry land and it was with both of them him and Johnson on the ladder descending with speed in the hammering wind and the rolling and pitching seas and the gray gone almost to night that the rain fell from a sky of upended barrels and struck him a thousand furious blows at once, a heavy rain with no outlier warning of drops or sprinkles just the fists arriving en masse and driving through the cotton shield of his jacket punching and gouging, a monsoon burst a burst that exploded like an ambush that could put an eye out mistakenly turned heavenward but he knew better and he wouldn't look up he needed both his eyes and he kept descending one foot on metal after another and the ladder suddenly bucked and he knew intuitively that Johnson had left it and from unloading Johnson's weight it had more energy now to come after him and it slammed him from side to side so that he had to lock his feet against the sides of the ladder and absorb the hammering as though he rode some wild beast or machine gone totally mad with desire to obey the storm's single intent to fling him wide into the ocean where the fathoms waited to absorb and vanish him and for a moment he was lost to Reason and Will and he could not find himself and he could not move or unclench his hands from what felt like nails driving through his palms and he would never have moved or unclenched his hands but for the stormmuffled pleading he heard of his name or what passed now for his name *ell-tee! ell-tee! ell-tee!* coming from below and though the ladder shook and beat front to back in renewed attack the distant sounded drumroll of the nonsense syllables of his nonsense life like a soldier's tattoo calling him to quarters calling him home calling him in from the fury of the moment unbuckled him from paralysis and he moved again and with three steps slammed his body downward as the gunwale of the boat rose on the heaving seas and slammed upward into the ladder's two spikes and splinters flew in the wind and the impact was like the detonation of a buried grenade to take another marine's young life from his parents and bride and children but he knew where he was now and with the terror full in his mouth he loosed his grip and fell back into the boat Johnson waiting to break his fall and collapse with him into the rising sea of monsoon rains flooding the boat's deck there to lie, the two of them, bodies limp in exhaustion, eyes closed against the pound of the heavens but alive, alive and disbelieving, the water already up to their chins, the loose rubber life raft caroming from their bodies and the smell of the sea in their nostrils, a smell like a mortal sentence passed and due yet waiting to be carried out.

But when he could register thought again, Kestermont exulted.

And why not?

Cheated the sea! By God hadn't he? He may be wet, soaked like some despised and abandoned wayfarer maybe, but he wasn't in the water, was he?

"*Fuck the ocean! Fuck the Numidian!*"

"Sir?" Johnson's voice was weak and watery.

"Nothin."

He sat up. His back hurt where some part of his rifle had found audience with his vertebrae. Above him the fogged contours of the ladder disappeared from view and a face appeared. It was the young deckhand, the knot-tier. Rain cascaded from the sailor's slickers, his face almost completely in silhouette, but Kestermont knew the dull glare of teeth when he saw them. The sailor was laughing and shouting and shedding water from his oilskin hat as he yelled, "Now I've not ever seen that before, not *ever*. Damn if you aren't lucky, Lieutenant, damn if you aren't the both of you. You oughtta be drowned dead or neck-busted comin down like that this ocean barin its teeth the way it is. Cargo handler throws the gate on the hatch I'm untyin ropes next damn thing I know here come two crazy bastards (no disrespect sir) hangin off that tin ladder in heavy seas and the Chief never saw you neither was reversin throttle but the engine died and that mighta saved your life but for sure it was your good luck it kept us in one place long enough for your man to land like a lump of cargo and you not far behind and *damn,* sir meanin no disrespect but you jarheads must want to get somewhere *bad.*"

Kestermont twisted himself to his knees. Kept one hand on the deck for balance.

"We hate disappointin people," he said, keeping his eyes shut against the rain.

Nothing felt broken. His hands stung for some reason.

Beside him Johnson lay flat on his back, motionless. Kestermont couldn't see well enough to see if he was still breathing or was stone cold dead. The rain drove sideways now like artillery adjusted for elevation, striking with renewed force. The ship's motor coughed and wheezed, then leapt back into life with a diesel *boom!*

"*Johnson!* You okay, Johnson? Anythin busted?"

Johnson pushed himself onto his side, kept his face down to protect it from the onslaught and yelled, "I think I drove peach delight halfway up my ass, LT. Other than that I'm good unless standin up says different. Damn sir, travelin with you is workin out to be one hell of an adventure."

"Copy that, corporal. You just lie there soakin wet on the boat deck and rest easy now. Adventure's over."

The boat throbbed and vibrated as it moved away from the hospital ship. The boatswain suddenly gunned the engines and swung the craft seaward, sending Kestermont and Johnson sliding on the rain-slick deck and slamming into the gunwale. Even the young sailor was taken off guard, lost his balance and sprawled onto the deck beside Kestermont, driving a leg into Johnson's side, Johnson responding instantly with a string of curses, saying, "How the hell this bucket get engines to move like that?"

Bewildered, Kestermont sat up and found himself laughing, and then laughing harder. And as abruptly as the storm had pounced, it retreated. While they lay crumpled against the gunwale, the rain diminished to scattered drops, single large globules playing a wet percussion on wood and metal surfaces. The wind kept up but seemed to change direction. A band of sunlight tore through the murk and stabbed the ocean. Kestermont blinked when it ricocheted from the peak of a whitecap and struck him in the eye. It was monsoon season, unpredictable as the sea.

The boatswain held the boat steady in a long, slow arc, still mostly seaward, so long and slow that Kestermont felt a panic rising that the boatswain intended deep water rather than the harbor.

But the *hell* with it.

He had taken the ocean's worst, at his most vulnerable, and here he was. The *hell* with it. He *won!* It was over! Even the rain had collapsed at the feet of his victory. The boatswain hit the top of the arc and now they ran parallel to the harbor entrance and he knew that when his feet touched ground again his triumph would be complete.

And then he was staring at a rush of pink water racing inside channels between the irregular slats nailed to the deck. He knew blood when it mixed with rain on flat surfaces: a muddy trail, a boat in the ocean, no difference. But it was always, whose blood?

Johnson was pointing at him and shouting something over the thrumming of the engine but all he could do was stare at his hands. Blood rushed from gaping holes in the center of his palms. His fingers were shredded. Red globules hit the wash in the bottom of the boat and rippled in circlets indistinguishable from the intermittent rain drops but for color.

"Well, damn," he said and sat back against the gunwale, irritated. *Hell, I was winning.*

The young sailor had a compartment in the gunwale open. He removed a pair of small green towels and a roll of gray tape. Over the diesels he yelled, "That damn ladder, Lieutenant. You cut yourself good. Let me wrap those hands."

As he had watched wounded men do many times, the more mortal the wound the more incredulously, now Kestermont did the same, rejecting the offer of aid, forgetting where he was, reflexively and irrationally denying the injury he could see full well he had sustained. He stood and raised his hands and stared at the blood pouring down his wrists and forearms. At that moment the boatswain gunned the engine again to swing further out of his arc and toward land and Kestermont took one off-balance step backward, threw his arms out to steady himself and instead hit the gunwale at a gap in the railing and went overboard.

42

HE SANK FAST DESPITE HIS FLAILING. Kestermont kicked but only sank further, adding to his confusion. He had never learned to swim, but didn't swimmers kick their feet when they swam for their lives? The water grew colder by degrees, his eardrums built pressure, salt water stung his still bleeding wounds. The rifle on his back constricted the rage with which he floundered. His boots turned to lead. A certainty of the pointlessness of resistance spread almost instantly, perfect root for his emanating terror of the endless deep. He crushed its upward movement by unleashing anger at the irony. So many other ways to die, but now *this*. And to have it happen this way. To *him*, who had made a religion of avoiding even puddles after rainfall. And only moments before, the cusp of victory. The anguish so bitter he could taste his own bile.

It made no sense, but by forcing himself to *stop kicking* he slowed his descent. Now he only floated downward, retarding the elevator ride. Oxygen combusted and his head grew lighter, as though his head were a closed garage, car engine running, clock ticking.

The fire already burning in his lungs.

His sister saying *You won't learn to swim sitting on that wall.* Ponytail and a tongue purple from candied ice.

A first wave of understanding passed over him. The ocean was tricking him. It feinted with a frontal attack—a rolling barrage of the Fear of Immense Depths—when really it sought out his flanks to break him internally: to force his lungs open and so complete the irony of his life and death by making him invite the ocean in.

Of course.

He was *meant* to inhale those depths, in an act of near sentience on the part of the sea. Sinking into the cistern of the depths was just a by-product of its strategy. Depth was irrelevant. The ocean intended to replace every last molecule of his being with itself, at whatever fathom. To extinguish and convert him long before his progress downward might end. *Matter can be converted it can't be destroyed* and there was the high school chemistry teacher, name forgotten over the years but image in full view as though they'd spoken yesterday: the eternal cocked bowtie, the limpid sprouts of hair, coke bottle glasses. Paper spit wads flying in the back of the room.

And then the second wave of understanding: Awareness that all his thought was sideshow now and vanity too, a passing entertainment, so much advertisement for The End.

Think what you like, can a thought save you?

I think not.

He was on his way Down. Forever.

And beside him, grin on full display, one hand locked on Kestermont's sword hilt, the other on Kestermont's throat, black eyes wide open even in salt water, rode the Numidian, the short tip of his slender spear buried beneath Kestermont's war tunic.

The fire in Kestermont's lungs exploded in a final, searing white wave of understanding.

Some dream was memory.

But which was he seeing now?

The colors never so bright or the water so near. How many times had these images imposed themselves unbidden? Uncountable, but never like this. His hands felt the weight of sword and shield. Leggings chafed his raw skin. The familiar discomfort of a damaged helm. Men yelled and cursed and he recognized voices, knew the name of the ship, where he stood his watch and the names of the constellations in the night sky. His mind knew faces, the curve of *her* breasts, the last time he awakened beside her. Odors were as familiar as his name: *Marcus Selvii Gracchus*. He *knew*. Information *crackled*. There were aged and unhappy parents, a despicable father's hands hard against a loving mother, brothers dead from war and disease. A sister in dull grief abandoned by a lover, shamed and living in squalor. A child of his own he had yet to meet in eleven years but the light of his world nevertheless. He *inhabited*.

And just then he inhabited a ship. Someone was talking. It was a voice he knew and disliked profoundly.

"Look at Valerius up there," the voice said. "He doesn't know whether to shit or go blind."

The fool Avienus has opened his mouth again. I don't choose to look. Valerius should be worried. We should all be worried, since we are all going to die. And in the loathsome sea, where a soldier has no business. It is only a matter of when, as Reolus has confided in a whisper, and as all the veterans know anyway.

Typical of a boorish farmer like Avienus to make fun of a good officer. A man like Valerius, the bravest among us, a poet and as skilled with the lyre as he was with the sword.

Beside me, Reolus lowers his scutum, reaches across and slaps Avienus. Hard. I can see two arrows already embedded in Reolus' shield. The deed done, he immediately returns the shield overhead.

"Dacian idiot," Reolus says. "What do you know? Valerius will get the blame when we're all dead. And him with a wife and two kids. They'll get

treated like shit the rest of their lives and no one to return and tell them this disaster is no fault of his."

Avienus really is an idiot. Nothing sinks in, even now. He starts to retaliate and I tell him if his arm passes in front of me I'll hack it off.

He sulks for a moment and says, "You'll pay for that, Reolus Tiro. We're ashore and I'll thrash you good, city boy!"

As if Avienus could thrash his own grandmother. As if anyone is ever going to set foot on land again. Land even like the barren coastal hills that trace the southern horizon.

From above us Quintus Labeo brings the pommel of his gladius down hard enough on Avienus' upraised shield to buckle his knees.

"Shut up and keep your eyes outboard, idiot!" he roars. Quintus has the cohort warrant to kill the insubordinate, the defeatists, the undisciplined. We've all seen him exercise it, and Avienus is all three. Avienus goes quiet as a tomb with Quintus one sword stroke above him.

Around us arrows fall. They make different sounds striking masts, water, shields and bodies. The bodies either fall into the sea or, to clear the decks, are pushed overboard. That makes a different sound, too.

Fire arrows are coming. We all know that.

The Numidian craft that sweep by are nothing we have ever seen before. Shallow of draft and narrow of beam, they row easily around us whether leeward or windward, assisted by short movable sails their crew adjust continuously. Dark-skinned sailors and marines wear no armor or even leather vests. They look underfed, like emaciated children in headdresses and painted faces.

Our own galley is refitted and recently out of drydock. The oarsmen are all enlisted citizens, not a slave or captive among them. The corvus is broad and thick, ready to fall on the enemy, the ship's ram extended below the waterline. Minerva rides at the prow. We have left Misenum with the best omens and reach Africa in record time. As augured, there to meet us is a full moon in daylight. We think we are swift and invulnerable. But these light Numidian craft with only two banks of oarsmen and those short moving sails have put the lie to "swift and invulnerable". Their archers have done the rest. Three of our ships burn already, one boarded in her death throes and everyone living put to the sword, the oarsmen slaughtered at their benches without mercy. We alone are not yet in flame.

But we are next, and Valerius knows this better than anyone.

Our useless single sail has been struck long ago. Our oarsmen turn this way and that, but we can't get close to any of the nimble little enemy craft. The corvus is useless too, an upright torch waiting to be lit. The enemy galleys close and open their distance at will. We'll never ram and we'll never board. Retreat is unthinkable and we couldn't outrun them anyway. Our own archers are dead. A few infantry try their hand with dead men's bows, but they couldn't hit a senator if they were standing in the Forum. They fall to enemy arrows as soon as they lower shields to bend the bow. The oarsmen below decks must know by now what their own fate will be.

"Fire!" someone announces. It's spoken without fear. Fear is an emotion for those with a semblance of hope; it's pointless when Hades is certain. We are angry, nothing more, nothing less. To die in the sea without even the chance of combat. To sink into a grave without boundaries. No tomb, no mourners, no ancestral rites. Nothing but conversion into the feces of fish. As the flames rise, rats drop into the sea, preferring one death over another.

"He's gone," Reolus says. Now I do look but I know he means Valerius. The pedestal is empty. I turn away and there is that sound as Valerius is added to the sea.

And there are sharks, of course. I see the first fins circling the remains of Hydra, where we watched the enemy massacre the oarsmen. The sea around the hull is crimson.

The Numidians maneuver around us, two craft on either side of the ship. There is a respite in the barrage of arrows overhead. But not for long. Closer now, their archers change tactics. They take their time and fire directly at us. Men fall from the boarding stations on both sides of the ship. Beside me Avienus has spoken his last idiocy. A dart catches him in the throat. Blood spurts from between his clutched hands and he falls into the sea. Reolus and I both kneel to make smaller targets. The sea shields are small and round for boarding and offer little protection, but they stop their share of arrows. Before long we alone remain at the starboard station. Only the gods know why.

"I'll move forward, you go aft," Reolus says. "An honor, Marcus Gracchus, to campaign with you."

"Honor mine, Reolus Tiro," I respond, not for the first time, but clearly for the last.

We move to opposite ends of the station, as our training requires. Romans do not die alongside each other like frightened children. They take the battle to the enemy, split the enemy's concentration. The arrows diminish, then cease. I stand up and watch the two small enemy craft as they maneuver to broadside and plow toward us along their port hull, hitching and bobbing as only the starboard oarsmen strike the sea. I have to admire their skill. These children are all grown up. They move their ships steadily sideways without the slightest deviation bow to stern, masterfully in motion with the drumbeat.

They are close enough I can see their leaders conferring. They speak excitedly, nodding their heads and throwing their arms about, yes, like children, but children who fight like men, arguing now for inclusion in the boarding party. I realize our arrogance first doomed us and now prepares us for humiliation.

On this side of the ship it is just Reolus and myself, Reolus now standing too, both of us waiting. I can hear flames behind us. I would consider mortality but I will wait until the moment descends of its own, as I have also been trained to do.

They intend to board us, fire or no fire. The archers have retired, denied the prize; their marines hold short spears, teeth bared for the obvious game: Who kills the last men standing? To whom the honor and the bragging rights, to whom the trophies?: Roman shields and helms, the booty of swords and rings.

"Come on, children!" Reolus taunts. He slashes his gladius in front of him. His war-laugh is at full volume. With Valerius gone, the seniority is Reolus' and it is his example to set. He sets it, so I follow and issue the refrain.

"Come on and die, little ones!"

We are the lucky ones. We meet the end fighting.

"'We who are about to die send you first!'" Reolus loved the old gladiator parody and he has never sung the line better. In the old days it has been our marching song. Reolus would break out in the melody while everyone else stumbled along in the dust, Valerius would throw his head back and join in and before long the rest of us would come to life. A song so irreverent the centurions banned it and thereby enshrined it forever among the legions.

"For Valerius!" cries Reolus.

"Valerius!"

"Fuck Caesar!"

"Fuck Caesar!"

Now I'm laughing too, trying to match Reolus. The Numidians are a horse-length away. I can smell them. I can smell my own death.

"Fuck Rome!"

"Fuck Rome!"

The oarsmen below deck cannot hold the Numidian craft off and the sides of our ships meet. I counter the first swipe of blades. The Numidians are ecstatic, jostling each other at their own gunwale to strike first, parrying their own blows in their competition, never more than now like a tribe of excited barbarian youth from some Gallic forest. Then they clamber onto the flat debarking station midships. A column rushes each of us. I do not hear Reolus die; the Numidians fill the sky with their bloodlust. I knock aside one final mass of blades from the ship and turn to meet my lead attacker. He thrusts the short spear but I shield-block it and then raise his head as I sweep back with the scutum. His dark unprotected belly is exposed and I sink my sword hilt deep, the fury in me singing the last line from the old marching song:

"'To Hell with Caesar! To Hell with Rome! And Legions, to Hell with you!'"

I can't count the number of spear strikes that find my legs behind the armor as the Numidian ship slams into the side of our own again and recoils. That pain is nothing. I can feel the heat from the flames now and my nostrils come fully to life: the smell of burning pine and bodies, of my own sweat and frenzy and again, stronger now, the odor of my own dying to come. I shake the agonized Numidian off my gladius toward the sea and before I can recover another spear strikes like a serpent through the vacuum my turning has left, finds the space between my breastplate and tunic and slips inside. Why it should be so I'm not sure but instantly my knees fail me and I begin my fall. At the last instant I pull myself forward and up the shaft of the spear and grab my enemy and pull him with me and as we hit the water in the narrow space between the ships and descend into the sea I see the Numidian's face with its teeth bared in triumph and feel his fingers around my neck as he drops my sword hand to take hold of the spear and drive it deeper and twist it side to side, eyes wide open and fixed on mine so I will know his victory over me before he finally pushes away and kicks upward toward the pool of light between the silhouetted bottoms of our ships. As I cease to struggle I realize I am still holding the gladius. I ask myself, why, then, did I not strike with it while we were locked together? The answer is my arm cannot move it; the hand cannot even yet release it, much less rid this body of the anchor of its armor or these entrails of the strange little spear.

The last sight that I have of this world is blurred in the poet's wine-dark sea. But these seas have never been wine-dark, they are as blue as the eyes of my eleven year old son, the light of this world; as Valerius explained in his recitations beside years of campfires, the blind poet took his liberty with the language, used it where its rhythms suited his verse whether colors were right or wrong. But maybe the poet knew of

times like these: wine-dark when sinking into it and one's own light is fading. That last sight is the child-body of my enemy being hauled from the ocean, suddenly ejected into the sunlight, as though thrown to the surface by Poseidon Himself.

No, not the last sight: the outline of the first shark passes below the Numidian as his body leaves the water.

Poseidon does not return for me. Of course the sharks will.

No matter. I am gone to find Valerius.

43

THERE IS NO TIME OR SPACE between these oceans. An ancient one ends. Another begins.

The ocean claws at his throat. A beast claws him from behind and he spins and wrestles and tears it from his back. The beast is his rifle. He signals his hand to open, to send the rifle into the depths but the rifle does not fall. His hand does not respond. While his hand struggles to release the rifle the ocean claws harder, its design to open his throat and rush inside him.

To colonize him. He sinks no further. The ocean has him as deep as it wants him. *Here's where I convert you,* the ocean says. Bright stars flash behind his eyes, colors without form punctuate the suffocation that intends to explode him.

For no reason he can articulate Kestermont still resists. He hears *ell-tee! ell-tee! ell-tee!* As though from a desert, where the voices are thousands, the language foreign but his understanding complete.

Someone is calling him.

His hand opens and the rifle is gone.

Convert your ass, Kestermont says as the last of his oxygen burns in a pyre of purest heat.

It is no room he has ever entered before, or he has been here a thousand times. Either condition seems identical. He knows he is inside a house of learning. What else could it be? An amphitheater, or half of one. Red seats rise in circular rows around a large plain desk on a tall dais with no steps. No one sits in the wingback chair behind the desk. The ceiling is a skein of dark beams, a thick lattice of wood gridwork above insets of myriad bronzed plates. The bronzed plates look sinister, retracted into their grainy caverns like some malevolent species. There is writing on the plates. The writing resembles deformation more than the letters of an alphabet and from this distance he can make no sense of the crude scratching. A domed skylight weeps a gauzy brilliance through the dimly lighted interior. The dome is oddly placed, not in the center of the huge room as would be proper, but off to one side, directly above Kestermont where he sits at the far end of the highest row of seats. A tiny seahorse dances above what he recognizes as an aluminum canteen cup floating in front of him. The off-center placement of the skylight skews the room and distorts the dimensions of the bronze plates in the ceiling. This is wrong. *Bad architecture,* he announces. The seahorse prances away, leaving little white deposits. *Bad architecture,* Kestermont insists.

As if in response, now there is someone sitting in the huge chair on the dais below him, outlined by a wash of overhead lighting. The figure rises, takes a familiar hat from the desk and spins it on a fist. In a flash of supremely controlled motion the smokey is on his head. Beneath the stage lighting everything about the drill instructor glows. His skin is white but not Caucasian white. The hat and his entire uniform is white, too. Snowflake white, if a snowflake burned from within. The white of the sun, if eyes could survive to describe it.

Bad architecture your ass, the drill instructor says.

He adjusts the smokey artfully forward into a perfect boot camp cant, walks from behind the desk and stands at the forward edge of the dais, rocking on his toes in a brief ritual. The room darkens as the spotlight narrows to encircle him. The brilliance in the drill instructor's form pulsates.

Kestermont sees in that brilliance a perfection like the marble of Michelangelo's David and recognizes the pulsing as the rhythm of his own heartbeat.

The drill instructor places arms akimbo and stares up at Kestermont.

I'm not going to rant and rave like your prototypical DI, he says. You can relax. But you'd best be paying attention.

Kestermont rises from his own seat in the auditorium. I'll come down front and center, he says.

Stay where you are.

You'll get a crick in your neck talking up at me like this.

The drill instructor smiles. My neck, you say. I think we're here on account of your neck. Stay right there. You're where you are for a reason. And I get damn tired of a worshipful audience in all these front rows.

Yessir.

I'm going to make this short and sweet, private. I aint got all day.

Yes, sir.

The drill instructor looks at his watch.

Damn. Never enough time. If it's not one place it's another. He looks up at Kestermont again. I got less than three minutes, private. I'd say two. You got less than that.

Yes, sir.

Listen up. The news has been bad on all fronts but one for too long now. Let me recap the same riot act you just got done reciting at near-nauseous length up top to one of your own. It aint no secret but you damn people keep acting like it is. Here's the deal, pure and simple: *I am not the Grand Master of this parade.* Now whatever else you do for as long as you got left, will you kindly contribute your voice to this message out there in the wilderness? There's a few I can hear now, one in particular, but too damn few overall. Hell, it's bad enough when a bunch of interbred knuckleheads across the centuries only have access to stones and knives, but now the same mental midgets got their paws on little things like fission and ICBMs and worse stuff coming down the pike I'll spare you the gory details. Now I need some assistance, private. In exchange for a way out of your current fix, which, by the way, I am also not responsible for, you can damn sure make it your mission to let the rest of your two-legged kind in on the news: *I am not the Grand Master.* Or Inquisitor, for that matter. Copy, private?

Copy, sir.

All right.

The drill instructor looks at his watch again. Shakes his head. *Jesus,* he says. Shakes his head again. Listen to *me*. Now *I'm* callin out the names and passin the buck.

Sir?

Never mind. Kick.

Sir?

Kick. You deaf, private?

No, sir.

Then kick. Kick your feet. Start, damn it! That's it, now how hard is that? And remember the deal. What's the message?

You are not the Grand Master.

Correct. You just joined the team. Continue kicking.

Yes, sir. But that leaves the obvious question.

You're the one's got the answer. Kick.

Kestermont feels foolish, kicking his feet in mid-air now, or rather in suspension, since there is neither air nor water. The drill instructor raises his arms from his waist. He holds them straight out to the sides, drops his head and rolls his eyes. He smiles wryly. Private joke, he says, and disappears. The room goes dark just as the walls and ceiling implode and send thousands of bronze plates streaming and tumbling from the gridwork. *Some joke,* Kestermont thinks as now the jet-black ocean rushes in to engulf him.

Kestermont kicks. Hard. His lungs want to burst. The ocean resumes prying his mouth open. He fights back. And *kicks*. He rises into that odd column of gauzy mist from the misplaced skylight, the one that should have been centered in the room, not over his head. Only it was where it should be. *You're where you are for a reason…*

He is half-way up the muted trail of light from the dome above. He understands the architecture now. He needs the dome, the dome is his salvation. But he knows he can't make it to the dome. He kicks but the propulsion is inadequate. He has an order to obey so he keeps kicking. The ocean is telling him it's pointless now. He knows it's pointless now. He knows he can kick exactly three more times, though how he can predict this he does not pause to wonder. He's furious, to come this far and not reach that dome. All around him the ocean waits, gloating, raising its tides unbidden, sowing whirlpools inside its currents, rejoicing in its undertows. The ocean regards him as an evening meal. He kicks *one*. The top of the dome is still out of reach. The ocean places the dinner napkin in its lap. He kicks *two*. Hardly any closer. The ocean rubs knife and fork together. He kicks *three*. No movement at all. The ocean reaches for him but something grabs him by the waist first.

The voice is the sound that waves make rushing along the beach to the limit of high tide.

Well, I wasn't going to intervene, says the voice. But if I do it for a Numidian, I guess I can do it for a Roman.

Kestermont looks down into a face like a statue's: graven visage, coils of grey hair, eyebrows like coral reefs, a ring of stone through one ear. Beneath the face, robes flow into the sea, trailing phosphorescence. Poseidon rides a trio of monstrous dolphins.

He draws a huge trident from its scabbard. This is gonna feel a bit…*special,* he says, leaning over and dropping the trident out of sight behind Kestermont. He thrusts upward and the massive central tine pierces Kestermont's rectum. Kestermont screams, spooking the dolphins. Poseidon makes soothing noises as he calmly works the reins.

The ocean has been watching and prepares to rush inside Kestermont's opened mouth.

Dinnertime.

Not to worry, Poseidon says.

A massive looping tube hangs from the base of the trident's shaft. Poseidon takes the elastic loop between thumb and forefinger of one giant hand and stretches the tube until he grasps the shaft at its upper junction with the curved bar of the outer tines.

Here's proper hand control, Poseidon says, and releases the shaft.

Kestermont's head is bent backward as he streaks upward beneath the G-forces, carrying the unasked question with him as he prepares for impact with the gauzy dome: *Then who is the Grand Master?* No answer comes. He hits the dome at terminal velocity only to find the dome is the reflection of the moon on the ocean's surface. The reflection shatters in a kaleidoscopic geyser. Not in nighttime but in broadest daylight he travels up, up, and up, through clouds and bands of ice crystals and serrations of cosmic dust in countless colors not part of the visible spectrum and so without description. Somewhere in space's gravitic balance between day and night he comes level with the moon. He slows and returns to a familiar suspension, spinning slowly, watching the panorama of the galaxy swing past him. When he finally comes to a stop he realizes he is looking at the side of the moon that faces away from earth. The side that no one has seen. That he is the first to see. The gravitic balance shifts and Kestermont feels the tug. Where did the moon get such a gravity? Down he goes, accelerating. It's useless to resist so he drops his head and brings his hands to his sides, palms in. Space hurtles through the holes in his hands, adding propulsion. He streamlines his body to increase his aerodynamics. In this configuration he exceeds terminal velocity. The moon's surface is dark but colors appear in the perpetual night as he approaches. Penetrating the darkness are the thousands of bronze plates in the room he has just left, only now they are scattered everywhere, transformed into billboards, giant television screens, electronic banners that trail behind ancient biplanes, light-emitting posters on the sides of skyscrapers, multiple lengths of teletype rolls streaming from the windows of public conveyances, a multitude of buses, trains, taxicabs, helicopters. Bicycles stream the image from their handlebars. Bronze pennants fly from lamp posts. Robots walk back and forth across intersections, dressed in sandwich boards, all displaying the bronze plates. Other robots hawk bronze newspapers or magazines or plaster the plates onto theater marquees. The bronze plates are everywhere, the only brightness in the inky night. The single image at the center of each plate is a pill, of which there are two versions, one a capsule, the other a tablet. Their color variations are innumerable. The capsules and tablets glow. They radiate a warmth that penetrates the lunar chill. Actors in Times Square advertisements fix the world in endless loops of bronzed neoprene smiles as hands deliver pills to mouths without pause. Kestermont marvels at his own speed. Approaching the surface he recognizes his trajectory is aligned to impact dead center of a rectangle of dark ground. At the same moment his velocity suddenly converts to slow motion and he sees that the rectangle is the center of an ink-black metropolis, the emanating point for the bronze plates. It is itself a bronze plate, black and bronze at the same time. The buildings are arranged as though they are monstrous letters typeset in an alphabet of no language he knows, some tongue primitive and bestial. There is a dim glow, circular, in the center of the metropolis. Circular like a moon is round, white like a putrid growth. It exerts an influence like gravity or magnetism, drawing him to it, dragging him downward beside tall black buildings, unbelievably tall, buildings that rise from the black granite of the rectangle and disappear in a cloud base of black crepe. Each building is a charcoal monolith as broad as a city block, countless stories high. They extend in all directions, rising and falling into the distance over uneven ground, black silhouettes against a blacker horizon. His blood chills and the old claustrophobia descends. He resists the pull of that moon-like glow. He resists looking. He doesn't want to look, not down toward the outline of the moon. *He doesn't want to know.* He wants to shield his vision but can't. Wants to look away from the buildings, but now something has control of his head. Something like hands. Firm hands. They arrest his further motion downward toward the slime-white circle and at the same time prevent his eyes from turning away. With his last bit of strength he closes them instead.

You need to *look,* the familiar voice says. What do you *know?*

Nobody knows nothin, Kestermont says.

Look. What do you know?

The question exerts a force stronger than the gravitic field of the moon, stronger even than the hands that have laid hold of him and suspended his descent into the rectangle.

He knows something.

There is no escape from it. You can labor all your life to forget it, you can hire professors to contest it, you can bury your head in sand or a vault of books. You can invent philosophies against it, wage wars in protest of it, seek refuge in a life of dissolution.

You can run, but you can't hide.

How he knows it he doesn't know, but no amount of savagery or deceit, treachery or legerdemain inflicted against his mortal being—by himself or anyone else—can any longer dispute or deny it.

No eye can stay closed and never see it.

He knows he still has *Choice.*

He knows what is right, he knows what is wrong.

Only because of this does he open his eyes and *look.*

The metropolis rising from that black rectangle is the inner sanctum. There are ghouls everywhere. Ghouls that once were human, now foul beyond description. In the streets, on the balconies, inside storm drains beneath curbs, hanging by their feet from unlit lamp-posts, straddling window ledges half in and half out of buildings, faces deformed and grim, sacks hanging by chains from their necks. The ghouls all do the same thing. Monotonously and lifelessly they grind rocks into powder with mortar and pestle and empty the pots into the sacks.

But the noise and façade of activity above have disappeared, lost in the blackness. The beehive of advertising is gone. His descent has punctured the veneer. There are no more colors, no pulsating lights, no smiling actors. Beneath the color, only darkness. Has he entered Hell? If this is Hell, and these misshapen brutes are goblins, where is the Devil? Where is His Majesty?

He looks closer.

At the base of the black buildings, forms take shape in the darkness. He can see them now through the ink. Citizens stand in long lines, entering the buildings through many doors. Rows of windows rise from the sidewalk and encircle story after story until they disappear out of sight countless floors overhead. In the multitude of windows the sight is the same. Bronze posters hang from the walls with slogans clawed into the surface in that demonic script: ALONE I AM NOTHING/WITH THE STATE I AM ALL and WAR FOR PEACE IS NOT WAR and MY NUMBER IS MY FREEDOM. Technicians in gray cloaks peel capsules and tablets from tiny bronze squares and hand the pills to people admitted through one door and shunted to another. In building after building, room after room, the same three elements are present: technician, citizens, pills. Some people hold the pills in their hands and stare at them despairingly before swallowing them. Others take them without a second thought. The lines move between doorways as if on a cog railway. Children look up at their parents. Children of all nations and races, all dress and language. The parents nod and the children take the pills. The technicians dip lollipops in bowls of red liquid and hand them to the children. Kestermont knows the red liquid is human blood. When a child takes a pill small horns rise and fall from the heads of the technicians. They knead their webbed hands together and the line moves. Flames surge from the bronze posters on the wall.

Inside one room a man protests, steps in front of a child. Instantly a door opens at the back of the room and two orderlies dressed in black enter, club the man to the floor and drag him away. Kestermont watches as they strap him into an oversized metal chair in the small adjoining room and place a bowl on his head. An orderly kicks the door shut, the lights dim in the metropolis and there is an odor of singed flesh in the air. The technician in the gray cloak smiles expectantly at the next citizen in line. The citizen presses a child forward, and the line resumes moving.

No more, Kestermont says. Having seen, he looks away.

I would *never* slaughter my own child, the voice says. No matter *what* rumors are abroad. And I *damn* sure would never do *that*.

I believe you, Kestermont says.

You just saw all the Devil there is.

Yes sir.

In all the Hell a devil needs.

Yes sir.

And just what in hell are you going to do about it?

Get me a team, sir.

It's not the politicians.

No?

It's not the State.

No?

Hell, it's not even the wars.

Not the wars?

That all comes after. They bring the wars. They degrade the State. They peddle their pills and their machines, their fear and their tripe to the politicians and call it science. To the bankers and call it profit. To the people and call it help. It's *them*. They built this dark city. They always build a dark city.

Yes sir.

And remember this. I am not the Grand Master.

Then who is?

Work it out. Work it out, all of you.

All goes black again around him, but asphyxiation floods his head with color and the lunar landscape with water. The hands of the ocean resume tearing at his mouth. That dim round glow at the center of the rectangle has disappeared, releasing the magnetic field, but he panics and cranes his neck, looking upwards for a sign of life. There is a glow above him now, faint inside the darkness. Far above him. A glow that might be a moon, but not the same moon. The bright side of a moon, a side toward earth. A harvest moon. As far away as salvation. Beckoning. A moon to walk beneath? To live and not die beneath? That reflects sunlight, not flame from a dark city? Yes, he realizes, the dim glow must be salvation again. Or might be. Or seems to be. Does he know nothing, or something?

Asphyxiation stalks him. Why not concede? Why not? How simple. To allow his being to be torn apart. The sea to enter. To colonize him. *Nothing easier.*

Attaboy, says the Ocean.

But Kestermont knows something, and there is no escape from it.

Even now he still has Choice.

Well, *hell.*

He *kicks.*

44

KESTERMONT BROKE THE SURFACE in a froth of flailing and choking, his head just high enough above the water to explode poison into the atmosphere and avoid inhaling the ocean. He barely heard Johnson shouting *el-tee!* over the vacuum of his lungs instantly and violently expanded with the elixir of air. He was instantly intoxicated. Too intoxicated by raging air sacs to sense the dorsal fin as it slid past him. He felt the cold draft of its passage just as a ring of yellow canvas struck the side of his head. That sobered him. There were more dorsals criss-crossing the distance between him and a rubber raft bobbing nearby. These he saw.

"Fuckin sharks, LT! Fuckin swim sweet Jesus!"

Over Johnson's yelling and the throbbing in his own head he could hear the roar of a diesel engine pushed to its endurance.

Kestermont couldn't swim but he could climb rope.

He thrashed about and his arm identified the rope attached to the lifesaver. His hand closed on the rope and hand over hand he pulled himself along, the pain in his wounded hands part of the engine that drove him, for all his external panic resigned to the inevitable crush of primordial teeth, hearing what seemed like an old refrain: *It is only a matter of when…*

Above him the bow of a boat flared against the side of the rubber raft toward which he traveled and rose and sank as the whine of the diesels abated. Through gaps in his saltwater exertions he recognized the boatswain standing on the gunwale, feet locked beneath the lowest rung of the railing, face grim and bearded and focused like Ahab come to life or Poseidon taken human form. The boatswain pressed his body against the upper rail and leaned outboard, the 12-gauge trench gun exploding again and again, each explosion sending nine pellets of .33 caliber buckshot bunched like tiny asteroids inches from Kestermont's head. He heard the rounds meet flesh and more flesh and the boiling waters augment in confusion and rage. Then there were hands beneath his armpits and grasping his web belt and Johnson shouting, "*Kick, LT, kick fuckin HARD!*"

Everybody wanted him to kick.

He did. Hard, as directed.

His feet launched him from the flesh-dense sponge of a shark's body. The shark lunged, but with two sets of hands pulling him Kestermont rose just enough to foil the shark's timing. A vise of stiletto teeth crashed together on air and sea foam and the prehistoric head slammed into his body and thrust him into the bottom of the raft. The boatswain fired twice more and the shotgun went quiet, instantly followed by the sound of shotgun rounds clicking into place as the boatswain reloaded. Kestermont kicked himself to his knees and looked up into the perpetual smile of the young sailor, who clapped his hands in delight. Johnson knelt beside the sailor, caught his breath and dripped saltwater.

"Now damn aint that *some*thin!" the sailor said. "I *won't* be forgettin that!"

The sailor reached up for the railing of the boat, pulled the raft alongside. "Come on, sir, those bastards are stupid but they'll breach and board this rubber bitch in a heartbeat."

"Wait one," Kestermont said. He shook Johnson and the sailor off.

In a moment he had himself composed enough to pull his barely responsive body from the raft over the gunwale and onto the solid wood deck on his own power, the sailor leading, Johnson following. Kestermont fought off the urge to collapse on the deck. The boatswain remained on the gunwale like a living figurehead on a pedestal and finished reloading the shotgun. They all watched silently as a half-dozen smaller sharks tore into the bodies of two large ones and turned the waters crimson, the big sharks still alive but helpless in the center of the carnage.

"Engines, seaman," the boatswain ordered. The young sailor went forward and disappeared inside the cockpit.

"Damn injectors can't take a hard braking," the boatswain said.

The sharks disappeared into the ocean with the sinking carcasses. Chunks of gray flesh littered the red surface. Already there were gulls circling.

After a few moments, Kestermont said, "Damn fine shootin, Chief, and I thank you for it."

The boatswain shook his head and lowered himself from the gunwale.

"Credit's not mine, Lieutenant. Fact is, I fucked up bad. I've been seeing packs of these sharks more and more lately. Think the weather's stirring up the sea bottom, pushing up the food fish. I should've known better but I let your man in that rubber floater get too far from the boat with my bow wrong way to. Saw that first dorsal coming full steam and did what I could but fast as that fish is I came around too late. Those were makos, sir, fastest shark in the ocean, competing for whatever was bleeding and frankly you should be dead. Even the juveniles are killers when they swarm like that. Those two big fish, I watched each of them swim right past you, one of them I swear looking you in the eye. I got their attention, Lieutenant, but whatever saved your hide, it wasn't me."

The diesels turned over, complained and roared back to life.

"You got a chopper to catch, sir," the boatswain said. "Let's get underway."

On the ride across the harbor Kestermont leaned against the railing and watched the coastline magnify. He felt a calmness he could not name. He had no urge to talk, to distract himself from the ocean, but for some reason his silence didn't surprise him. Where did fears go, when they left? He could look at the ocean now, all the way to the horizon, straight into its eyes, and see no enemy. That didn't surprise him either. Maybe nothing would ever surprise him again.

He did have a question. Johnson stood quietly beside him, yet somehow he knew Johnson had something to say. Kestermont spoke first.

"Think careful on this before you answer, Corporal. How long was I under the water? Exact as you can work it out."

Johnson took his time out loud.

"Well, sir, things happened kinda fast. It's a damn good thing the swabbies keep that rubber lady sloshin around on the deck after all. You hit the water and that young pup sailor had the raft overboard I would say less than half a minute. Me to commandeer it, so to speak, get in and get my bearings and paddle to where I figured you went down, maybe a minute. I saw that first big shark, then all them others right about that time. Hell, sir, like they knew you were comin. I'd say you come up right after that."

"You're sayin two, three minutes? I go overboard and you see me come up?"

"Not three, sir. Maybe two."

No, there would still be things to surprise him.

The storm had passed into the volatile sky. The sun was momentarily out above broken and scattered clouds, making it look briefly like a summer day after a morning shower. Kestermont watched the approaching shoreline. A wind lingered but he hardly noticed the chill through his wet fatigues. His hands hurt as if from a distance and he paid them no attention. The dilapidated dock had just come into view when another light rain started up, random drops that cratered the ocean's surface and winked back at the sky. The raindrops landed on his shoulders and bare head like fingers tapping to get his attention. He looked into the distance. Above the mountains, where they would be scrambling from helicopters tomorrow, he noticed the full moon.

Johnson said, "Devil's beatin his wife."

"What?"

"What Grandma said. About the sun shinin and it rainin at the same time. Used to sit on the porch with her when I was a kid. Me leanin up against a post, her in a squeaky old wood rocker talkin soft about things like fireflies and walnuts, summer nights and turnin leaves. Her voice wrappin me in a blanket, LT, sweepin me away. When she went on like that it was somethin special. I remember this day me and her on that porch late afternoon it rained and the sun came out from behind the clouds but it kept on rainin. Just like now. I remember her sayin that. 'Devil's beatin his wife.' She meant it, too. Serious when she said it. 'Devil's beatin his wife'. Aint thought about that in all these years. Her in that old basket-weave rockin chair rockin away and sayin that."

Kestermont stared into the shore, at a small figure standing motionlessly at the end of the dock, as if patiently awaiting their arrival. Beyond the first line of mountains he saw a second horizon of purple highlands, more distant and more jagged. Jagged as shark's teeth.

The sun disappeared again behind clouds. The drizzle continued. Now there was just the moon.

"She ever see a full moon in broad daylight? Say anything about that?"

Johnson was silent a moment.

"No, I guess not. Nothin I remember anyway."

"Well."

"LT?"

"Yeah."

"Are you a religious man, sir?"

It seemed suddenly strange to Kestermont that no one had ever asked him that before—not his teachers, his parents, or any of his friends. Certainly no one in the military. None of the many pastors of his youth. It hadn't even been on the application for seminary school, at least not so directly.

"If it's yes or no, I guess I am."

"I don't know if I am or not," Johnson said. "Maybe nobody knows nothin after all."

"Copy that."

"What do you know about it, sir?"

"About what?"

"Well, about God, I guess, sir."

Kestermont hesitated but not because he didn't have an answer. He knew the answer. His gaze was fixed on the solitary figure at the end of the dock, still too distant to identify. It could have been a statue in a starched black uniform, unimpressed by the rain. Or sun.

Or the moon.

"I only know one thing, Corporal," he said finally. "I know He aint the Grand Master."

Epilogue

I THEY MOVED QUICKLY among the bodies sprawled across boulders, woven into bushes or crumpled in the trail, removing personal effects and the bounty of war: loaded M16 magazines from rifles, bandoleers from bloody chests, grenades from pockets, watches from wrists, wallets from trousers. Everything went into the basket, half-filling it. They ran a pole below the handle and Nguyen assigned the two new arrivals to carry it, sending them on ahead. Two more soldiers gathered rifles and a machine gun while another strapped on a radio that almost certainly had been damaged beyond use. He knew she would be angry about that.

Nguyen performed his routine check of the corpses against the faded photograph and saw no convincing likeness. Privately he held the opinion that all the white foreigners looked alike, particularly in death, but he had accustomed himself to rendering definitive judgments that there was no match among the dead to the face in the photograph. One of the dead men's helmets had a solid black bar inked crudely into the helmet covering. Nguyen removed the cover and stuffed it into his trouser pocket.

They did not talk. Nguyen pointed to An Trinh and held up two fingers. Trinh nodded and set to work. He selected the two American bodies at the end of the column, laid his rifle on the ground and adjusted the bodies to his satisfaction. Taking the strangely shaped enemy grenade from his satchel, he pulled its pin and inserted it between the ground and the shoulder blade of the first body. Repeated the booby-trapping with the second body, only this time placing the grenade in a small depression below the corpse's boot. He recovered his rifle and carefully stepped over the bodies. By the time he was done the rest of the ambush team was formed up and waiting at the top of the trail. When An Trinh passed by him, Nguyen, the last to leave, held up his hand for silence and bowed his head, concentrating. He heard the approach of helicopters, but still some distance away. They had opened the ambush by killing the radio operator, but any other nearby American unit or patrol below would have identified the firefight in progress—the AK-47's language was as different from their own rifles as Vietnamese was from American. Getting no response on the radio, they would have come to the obvious conclusion and called for the predictable reinforcement. He made another motion and the little column stepped briskly up the trail, Nguyen following.

She was sitting in shadow on a small boulder to the side of the trail, her rifle across her lap, only a hundred meters from the ambush site. He was surprised to see her and spoke quietly to An Trinh, leaving him in charge and telling him to move directly to basecamp. He approached Bich Linh, who paid no attention to any of them. She was looking through a large opening in the highland trees at the distant valley and rice fields below, cut in half by the late afternoon shadows of the mountains. The thin ribbon of river was not yet in darkness.

"That is the Song Ba," she said. "In the valley where you see it there, though, the river has another name. But it is the same river." She looked up at him. "How many?"

"Nine," he said. "All Americans but one. An ARVN."

"Tell me we have no casualties."

"There are none."

"Any prisoners?"

"There was one badly wounded. He would not have lived. We shot him."

"I saw the radio. It's ruined."

"We shot the radio operator first, carefully. The damage was from random firing during the ambush."

"I knew I should have come earlier. Train these children until they understand how badly we need a radio."

"They know that. The Americans were grouped together and fought back without surrender. We had limited time. It was unavoidable."

Linh made a mocking noise and stood up.

"Do you have anything of actual value to report?"

"There was an officer." He pulled the helmet covering from his pocket and showed it to her. She took it and studied the single black bar.

"Junior grade. Hardly value at all."

"How often do we find officers on their patrols? This one carried the map. There were papers in his pockets. It could be important."

"The maps mean nothing. Common as flies. We have many of them." She stood and slung the Dragunov. "Let me know what you find in the basket when I get back. Send the papers to the translators." She held out her hand. "The photograph."

Nguyen handed her the photograph, now back in its protective plastic cover. Bich Linh took it and placed it inside a small folding hard case, and then into her own pocket.

"No match. Nothing close."

"Then we keep killing them," she said, which was what she always said. She stepped out of the shadows and into the sunlight. When Bich Linh spoke looking away from him, the ruined side of her face gave the impression that she talked without her lips moving.

"Where are you going?" Nguyen asked.

"You hear the helicopters now. Where the trails below converge in a small clearing there is room for only a single helicopter. When it lands, I will be waiting."

"There will be gunships above the helicopter. I could come with you."

But Linh had already turned and left. Nguyen watched her as she stepped along, disappearing where the trail fell away. She moved gracefully, even with the ungainly Dragunov slanted across her back, the rifle nearly as tall as she was. The vision of her leaving him always nicked his heart, but by now this was what life had become. Moments linked to days in a calendar of sorrow that had no larger increments of time and no discernible relation to the rest of life. And one day Time would end. But Life? He did not know what that would mean for Life.

When she had not returned by evening, and still not yet deep into nightfall, he took third watch on the rock ledge and stayed most of a fourth. A bleary-eyed An Trinh finally arrived, fumbling with his shirt.

"You did not wake me properly," he scolded.

"Don't worry. You didn't fall back to sleep. I didn't wake you at all."

An Trinh laid his rifle down and swung himself onto the outcropping beside Nguyen, letting his feet dangle above the sheer drop to the stream below as he buttoned his jacket. They sat quietly, watching the night sky, its multitudes of stars, the clusters and countless pinpoints, searching ritually for the brief flash of meteorites, commonly held to be the passage of dragons. To see one meant good luck and gave a warrior invulnerability in any battle the next day. A light wind rose along the cliff face, balanced between chill and warmth, strong enough to move their hair in the starlight. When they spoke it was in their nighttime voices, inaudible an arm's length away.

An Trinh knew what was bothering him. "You worry too much," he said. "She will be back soon. Or late. Or tomorrow. She keeps her own schedule. She may be back now, while you've been on watch."

"She is a strange bird in this world," Nguyen said. He would only ever speak what he felt to An Trinh. "She has no fear of anything, least of all dying."

"She is in love with vengeance, that's why," An Trinh said. "As my father was, after the French killed my mother. He changed forever after we buried her, though the change came slowly, a little at a time so that I hardly noticed it until he was no longer the same father I had always known. He was a farmer, nothing more, with no hope of ever realizing the justice he sought. At first he sought refuge in philosophy and the ancestors, but as the years passed he gave in to bitterness until he was lost to us. To me and to the village. He rarely spoke of her, but I could tell what thoughts consumed him. When I left for the army he told me the sadness he felt at my leaving was in contest with a joy that I might kill enough of the enemy to avenge my mother's death. I feel sorry for him, alone in his small house, with his heart in such a state."

"You have killed many of the enemy. You did today."

"It is necessary, but it does not bring me joy."

"Necessary is enough," Nguyen said.

A meteorite blazed. They both reflexively pointed and it was gone.

"So we live tomorrow," An Trinh said.

"We do."

Above the passing of the meteorite they could see the lights of an enemy jet crawling across the heavens, connecting the dots of stars. Across the valley and the rice fields on an opposing hilltop a Korean compound pulsed in green tones.

"She is in love with vengeance, and you are in love with her," An Trinh said. "And stranger still, she keeps you with her at night when she really thinks only of that monk Thanh. If she can love anyone, he is the one."

"He is not a monk, though it is true he seems to have little interest in women. You don't know him very well. He is as strange as she is, in a way that is very different, but somehow her equal. Maybe that explains something. I don't know. I sometimes think he is not of this world, but has lost the trail back to his own. Or has been sent to show us a better way, maybe as the price of his return."

"You make too much of very little. He is just a strange Northerner. All of us Northerners are strange. I'm the only exception."

"Well, keep alert while you bask in your private glory," Nguyen said. "And I have stood most of your watch. I will wake your replacement on my way in."

The moon was down but the starlight was adequate as he followed the narrow little path down to the basecamp. He woke the soldier who had the first watch for his second stint, staying with him long enough to be sure he was fully awake. At the entrance to his cave he saw through the darkness that the hammock was empty, thinking she hadn't returned, then noticed the slight form in the leaf-filled mattress below the hammock. If he lived for anything anymore, it was this sight: to find her on the mattress rather than in the hammock, inviting him beside her. He brushed aside the mosquito netting, ducked his head beneath the low overhang and entered, setting his rifle in its place. He removed his clothes quietly. Naked, he slipped onto the mattress and below the single blanket. She stirred and turned away from him onto her side, allowing him to press himself against her.

"In the morning," she said. "And your body is so cold."

"It will warm quickly. Sleep well, darling."

He was prepared to fall asleep when she spoke again.

"The helicopter came." She did not turn to face him. When she spoke at night, half asleep, she had a lovely voice. "A Sea Stallion, full of marines, with one gunship. They landed and soon I heard the grenades explode. There must have been casualties. The transport helicopter rose immediately, abandoning the broken vessels where they lay, while the gunship opened fire stupidly everywhere. A medical helicopter and a second gunship arrived for the dead and wounded. I did not interfere with these. I wanted the transport helicopter. One of the gunships remained until the first helicopter came back for the rest of the marines. I was in a tree. I did not have a shot at the pilot but as the helicopter turned in front of me I had an easy target at its back gate. This one fell from the helicopter as it rose and the helicopter never returned. They may not have missed him until after they landed. Can you imagine their confusion?"

"They will have no idea what happened."

"Perhaps they will think he fell from the sky."

"They will be completely bewildered."

"I found the body impaled on the limbs of a dead and broken tree. Broken by their artillery. Thanh would call that justice."

"Was it him?"

"No. I will keep killing them."

"You should sleep, darling. You stayed out late."

She placed a hand behind her and gently stroked his leg.

"Wake me before dawn," she said.

There was a river that changed names before it entered the valley below. Where it rushed out of the side of the mountains far to the south, fed by myriad underground streams and aquifers and perennially refreshed by monsoons, the current was irresistible and shoals and rocks made the river unnavigable. It wound much farther along, from the base of the mountains bend to bend and through the descending countryside before it finally exited into the valley by a steep turn, after which the river broadened, slowed and carved itself deep into fertile, ageless soils. Here the plains and terraces and rice fields pacified it and so changed it in nature that generations of farmers past had given it another and kinder name. But at its source in the mountains, where the river raged through clefts of granite in narrow channels, and along its course before it turned toward the flat land and the valley at its eastern extremity, the river was called Song Ba. The Song Ba finally widened and slowed enough to be passable, and there was one long stretch of waterway where the shoals became a series of fords during the dry season, some of which were shallow and tame enough to sustain the passage of large numbers of soldiers with packs and weapons, even flat bottomed boats carrying military equipment and supplies. But these fords were chameleons. Their locations shifted from dry season to dry season and there were sections in some of the fords where abrupt, invisible and treacherously deep channels appeared and shifted also. In his time in the south Nguyen had still never seen the Song Ba. Yet he had heard of it before he ever left the north or had met Bich Linh, from returning veterans and instructors during his basic training. It was the site of a terrible disaster, the candid among them said. An entire regiment decimated by an attack force of American jets. Here the more timid veterans would avert their faces, some would leave the room. But the others would continue their story, telling it together as one person, keeping their voices low. The government would never admit it, they said, and history would never write it, but it was one man. *One man* and a single machine gun that prevented the lead battalion from crossing that ford. There were guides, local guides, who knew where the shallows were truly shallows and which of these were unblemished by the sudden underwater drop-offs. The Army blamed the guides. The Army said they were southern traitors who led the lead battalion blindly into an ambush. But in hushed voices the veterans said it was all bullshit. They said the guides argued against passage on a cloudless night beneath a bright moon, going from officer to officer, telling of their many enemy sightings in recent weeks, pleading with them to wait until the moon was down. But the guides were scorned and berated and told to lead on. They did as ordered, choosing the right fords, away from the deep water, avoiding the hidden channels. But on the other side of the river a small American force awaited them. Six men, maybe less. Was it chance? Bad luck? Were the Americans a reconnaissance patrol that fate had brought? A lost detachment from a larger unit? No matter. It was not possible that a battalion of regulars could be defeated by half a dozen men. Only it was, and they were. In the course of the battle the army must have eventually killed all the enemy soldiers but one, yet that one last man and a machine gun kept fighting, his weapon operating without pause, his supply of ammunition seemingly endless. How does any earthly contrivance sustain such a rate of fire without malfunction or its barrel melting? Or its operator remain unscathed by so much return fire directed at a single white-hot flame? Was the weapon made in heaven? Had ancestral gods abandoned their children? Was the enemy soldier himself a god, protected by armor no earthly missile could penetrate? These are things no one can know. Yet this we do know but cannot say too loudly. Waist-deep in a strong current inside the middle of that ford, wave after wave of attacking infantry, revealed as they were by moonlight, could not extricate themselves from the river to silence that last man and that machine gun. And the regiment, its two remaining battalions thus balked at moving forward and huddled in confusion on the opposite shore, with no plans for such a contingency and no permission to withdraw, found itself in the open at daybreak. When dawn came, the dual pins of the operation, surprise and speed, were lost along with the cover of night.

And then the jets came.

And then the gunships.

Bodies washed downstream for days. The jets and the gunships chased a broken regiment back into the mountains, slaughtering them as they ran. The Army removed the regiment from the roles, court martialed surviving officers and blamed the guides, all of whom perished in the river and were unable to defend themselves or prove their loyalty.

There is a woman, one of the veterans said. The wife of one of the guides and the mother of his children. They were with the guide mid-river when the Americans opened fire.

What happened? Nguyen asked.

The guide and the children were killed. The woman was wounded by exploding ordnance and found half-dead downstream on the river bank the next day, horribly disfigured and blind.

Why were the woman and the children with her husband on this operation?

Excellent question, private. Would the government have used a family as hostages, to ensure proper performance of southern guides? What do you think, private?

I could not believe such a thing. Did she live?

The veteran said, They say she is among the living dead, in the mountains above Song Ba. That she lives only to kill Americans. That she has a photograph of the American with the machine gun and hunts him with the obsession of the damned.

Where would she get such a photograph?

It is just a story.

That's a sad story.

No, private. That is the story of your country. Do not believe your government, and never underestimate your government's belief in harvesting and harnessing the power of vengeance to win this war. You are still a child. You have not been south. But on the day you leave you will learn that nowhere is the belief in vengeance stronger than in those who plan war but do not fight it.

He lay beside her as she slept, the way she did when her mind was quiet. He did not judge her. He never asked about her past. Instead he waited for the day when Thanh might exercise whatever power over her that he had, to convert her, though to what Nguyen did not know, unless it was to that same confidence and peace that seemed to emanate from Thanh. He did not believe that he himself would survive the war, but until the day of his own death he would simply do his duty.

To love her and to protect her. All that he could. This was all he knew of life, all that he cared to know and all he felt he needed to know.

He had long since decided it was enough.

He awakened her and they made love in turn tenderly and fiercely in the complete blackness, then fell back to sleep. When he awoke again, she was gone, as was her habit. His arms missed her. The tips of the tallest trees were just turning red above the untouched darkness in the basecamp below. It was hardly daybreak and the watches were already coming in from the night stations, shuffling by his quarters, looking forward to their own few hours of morning sleep. He wondered when leaving their stations at the first hint of daylight had become a practice and made a mental note to instruct squad leaders to direct them all not to leave their posts until fully half the sun had cleared the eastern ridges.

After he set the small fire to burning for his tea, he arranged the simple bed and noticed the small notebook she kept under her pillow, the notebook Thanh had left her the morning of their reunion in the hidden village, in the first days of their arrival from the North. In the half year since that time, the notebook was steadily decomposing. The scribbled name of its original American owner had long since faded and the contours of the bullet hole in the center were lost to decay. The glued binding was failing, pages had come loose. At some time the little binder would simply disintegrate in spite of her care. Nothing fragile survived the monsoons. After its inevitable demise he imagined she would place the notebook's remains in a container and keep it with her like ancestral ashes.

When he examined it he found many of the pages at the front and back had turned to pulp. The last entries appeared in the middle pages, these few remaining largely intact and legible despite the rot at the notebook's borders. On days and nights when storms turned the caves to riverbeds and drove them to refuge on higher ground, she would lie beside him beneath the stone ledge and read the poem or recite it from memory, always telling him it was the last Thanh intended to write, however long he lived, and how he had composed it for her, sitting at her bedside as she slept. Whenever he told her he did not enjoy the poem, she scoffed and called him a sentimental child.

His tea was ready and he poured the battered American canteen cup full. Letting steam from the metal cup warm his face, he moved closer to the small opening of the cave. There was now enough light filtering through the forest canopy that he could just read the lines, formed in neat rows of handwriting small and regular, presuming to retain their precision through time and humidity like a sculptor's chiseled strokes on stone.

But these, too, would one day be gone, long before the war was over. As he knew he would be gone as well. And so many others.

The few words that he couldn't make out, his own memory supplied. The poem had no title and cried out for verses, but the poet had turned a deaf ear. The lines simply rushed unbroken to their unhappy end. Reading it again, he felt he understood why at its completion Thanh had vowed to write no more poetry. The poem filled Nguyen with a sadness not just for Bich Linh and his country but for the human race. Thanh's last work was surely a brief history of all the ages of the world, but if it were also prophecy, the world was doomed.

All Thanh had ever said, smiling, was that it was an exceptionally bad poem.

Into the inwardly pulsing sun of the dying day she runs
Sparks flying from her sandals as so much flint against stone.
Stars emerge and prick the magenta fabric of descending night
Until it bleeds ink
Engulfing all sparrows.
And she is gone.
There is still a ruby's reflection of light in the sky when the jets come.
As they once came above the river
They come again.

Beneath the moon.
A special moon.
A moon loosed from daylight's chrysalis
Wings spread and waxing fuller
Cradling darkness in its folds.
The moon crosses the ocean.
It rolls like thunder from west to east
Mocking daylight
As if the sun could set backwards
As if the moon could reverse the course of the sun.
An ancient moon.
Unrestrained.
Craters gorged on blood. Moonbeams falling like razors.
Poised in its orbit to harvest the years ahead
To shred innocence from the last nations on earth
To rain copper from acid skies and bleach the tomb of millions.
And then to be forgotten.
Until risen again.
And again.
And again.
A vampire moon.
A full moon.
Full malice.
Full auto.
Full metal.

II

IT WAS A BEAUTIFUL DAY.

There was a gloriously warm breeze and the skies were alive with competing noise from the harbor's variety of seabirds. She watched the birds from her sanctuary at the railing. They were like orchestra members practicing scales feverishly in the moments before the conductor stepped to the podium to raise his wand and prepare them for the opening unity.

The morning was passing swiftly. She had finished her last rounds and knew she could get away before Tommy's friends had to leave but something held her back. Instead she had climbed the stairs to the upper deck and walked out on the small midship promenade, where only a few patients in a small huddle lounged against the railing above the deck below. She watched crew members manhandling the piano into place on the dais and placing chairs into their rows. Someone wrestled with the microphone stand. A few early arrivals flopped into chairs as soon as they were unfolded, laid crutches or canes aside and drank the watered-down beer and talked while they waited.

The patients at the starboard railing nodded courteously as she moved to the front of the promenade, respecting her obvious desire to be alone. The men passed burning cigarettes to each other in a chain-smoking ritual, rocked easily on their crutches in their thin cotton robes and chatted away about the things recuperating soldiers talked about: home, girlfriends and wives, officers they respected and those they didn't, cars, how long each had left in-country, the first thing they would do when they got home, usually involving wives or girlfriends. She could hear them but it was easy to tune them out and lose herself in her own thoughts against the backdrop of a perfect summer day. She thought briefly about a cigarette herself, but not seriously. For some time now the need had left her.

His three friends had been model visitors. When they arrived and greeted Tommy, she had been on her early morning chores. Tommy was improving daily and had been making consistent progress in the weeks following the final surgery. Still, she worried that it was too early to be reliving old emotions and experiences, which she feared would be unavoidable in a meeting of old comrades. But her concerns proved groundless. In the hours after their arrival and introduction, throughout conversation in which she had mostly sat quietly and not participated, she observed new color coming to his face, his animation and liveliness escalate, his laughter change in ease, vitality and naturalness. She marveled that she was really seeing *him* for the first time, the person he must have been before that last day of war, maybe even before the aggregate burden of a year of war threatened to alter him forever, as it appeared to have done to so many of the wounded patients she tended.

The truth was, she stood against the railing now and hesitated rejoining Tommy and his friends below for only one reason. She resisted falling in love with any more young men. In the sense of that love in which you saw an innocence of such fundamental decency and goodness in so many otherwise completely different people that you could not fail to recognize the true nature of the human race and that They were You. In the sense that the loss of any one of these innocents to the world was equally your own, making it impossible that any of these men were natural enemies to any other men of any nation or color. And so it must be true of all young men everywhere. True of the same young men whose elders nevertheless succeeded in bringing them to hate, oppose and kill each other.

It was the news that the three men brought that affected her so profoundly. Just in the way they delivered it, first making sure that Tommy was ready to hear the story. And then, by no other means than their presence and their voices, helping to dissolve the pain of the loss in the natural pool of healing their camaraderie provided.

They did not do this by attempting to spare him. They told him everything they knew about how the young lieutenant had died. On patrol high in the mountains. An ambush. No survivors. The lieutenant with less than two weeks left before he was due for rotation home. The makeshift squad on a reconnaissance patrol and no one the lieutenant felt with the experience to lead it, so he had taken charge himself. They named the dead, Tommy nodding at each recognized casualty.

"Who was on point?" he asked.

They said a name. Tommy shook his head.

"Where was Johnny West? Or Morgan?"

"Down in Cam Ranh, both of them. Johnny with malaria. Morg took RPG shrapnel day after leavin Hue. Lucky to be alive and luckier still, that cowboy's goin home."

The tall, lanky marine asked if Tommy knew Harold Johnson. Tommy shook his head again.

"Came over from 5th Marines. LT promoted him after you medevaced and gave him a squad. He was tight with LT and volunteered for the reaction team with Two Bravo. Disappeared. They don't know what the hell happened, think maybe he fell out of the chopper on the way back. Never found him. Gone like a ghost."

The short dark-haired marine handed him an envelope, addressed by typewriter simply to Thomas A. Tomlin, L/Cpl, San Antonio, TX.

Below that line, scribbled hastily in ink, was Tomlin's last known address: *SS Hope, Da Nang Harbor, Republic of South Vietnam.*

"Clerk in the rear at HQ found this in LT's locker," the marine said.

Tomlin opened the letter and read it silently, then aloud:

Tomlin—

I hear that big boat decided to drop anchor after all and stay put a while. I have no idea if you're still aboard or not but wherever you are I know you're going to be okay. Not that it matters much, but if you've rotated on back to the world, it would please me if this letter catches up with you somewhere.

Well, getting right to it, you reading this means I bought shares in that short-timer farm and I'm out there somewhere shoveling manure or feeding chickens. It's been on my mind to tell you this so if I don't make it to the Alamo here it is.

I think you're right. This isn't the first time.

And there must be someone, somewhere, who knows something.

I'll leave it at that.

Give my best to Maggie. What a lucky jarhead you are.

Kestermont

"What's he mean?" the skinny marine asked.

Tommy put his hand on hers.

"Look at this lady, Timmy. He means I'm lucky."

"I have more rounds to make," she said. When she rose they all stood. The three marines removed their utility caps and they shook hands warmly. The one who was clearly the ringleader gave her a hug and said something about how he was going to go and get himself all shot up just to get sent to the hospital ship like that *skatin* Tomlin, get her attention and steal her away. They all laughed, Tommy the hardest. She kissed Tommy on the cheek and left.

In the stairwell at the back of the mid-deck wards, she cried into a towel to muffle her sobbing. Tommy had introduced each of his three friends, but at the moment the only name in her mind was that of the young lieutenant who had died in the mountains. She cried harder before she composed herself, listening to Kestermont again out on the deck the day she met him. After a few moments she blew her nose and dried her face and went on her rounds. A number of young men asked if she were okay, and once she had to step outside the wardroom to cry again. Fortunately the hallway was empty. She returned and steadied herself with the routine of her nurse's aide chores: bedpans to empty, wound dressings to change, Eye-Vee bags to monitor. She read letters to soldiers bandaged head to toe. In the critical ward a soldier's wounds were bleeding again while he slept. She got the doctor on duty and helped him change the dressings on the stumps of the soldier's legs while the doctor chattered away about early season baseball. The soldier stared at the bulkhead and never said a word. When they closed the door the doctor looked into her red eyes and said, "It's healing slower than we like but there's no infection. He's going to be okay. Give him time."

"Sure," Maggie said. She didn't cry.

At the promenade railing the breeze helped. The ocean air and the wind never failed to lift her spirits. It was useless to despair. Young men were resilient. Already she was receiving letters from patients transferred months ago expressing gratitude, affirming their improvement, detailing future plans, rarely even mentioning the ghastly wounds they had suffered. She knew many of them were in love with her and she always responded, promising to visit whenever she was in Chicago, Sioux Falls, Tallahassee, or a dozen other towns, cities, or RFDs. She loved them, too. All of them.

But that morning there was just no more room inside her to risk falling in love with three more young men. No more room to add new layers to heartbreak. More faces in the twilight before sleep.

Even her memory seemed to begrudge further space for names. So instead, recognizing her limitations, she watched from her refuge on the upper deck as the three marines matched Tommy's pace on his crutches and they made their way toward the ramp that led down to the little cargo launch.

"That's him," said one of the patients at the railing.

"The tall one? That skinny guy?"

"No, the one in the middle. Guy without a cap. Taking his boots off. Hell's he doing that for?"

"That guy got a Navy Cross? Don't look like John Wayne to me."

"He might, you on the receivin end of a machine gun."

She watched as the one who had hugged her finished removing his socks and stuffing them inside his boots. Laughing heartily, he tied the boots together by their bootlaces and draped them around the neck of the quiet, dark-haired marine, the one she suddenly remembered Tommy had introduced as Danny. Tommy was leaning on his crutches, shaking his head but smiling. The tall marine was speaking earnestly but having no effect on the grin of the bootless marine as he next removed his utility jacket and tossed this too to Danny, who looked disgusted. Barefooted and now shirtless, the marine shook hands with Tommy, gave him a punch on the arm and jumped up on the ship's wide gunwale, then turned to face them naked from the waist up and gleaming in the morning sun, arms brown from elbows to wrists, torso white as marble. Even at that distance she could see the scars engraved on his chest. A silver peace medallion hung from his neck on green cord beside what looked like a bullet cartridge. He weaved for a moment getting his balance and sunlight flashed from a simple coil of bracelet in motion with his arm. After a quick look behind him, he spread his arms wide and with a rebel yell pushed off and disappeared from view in a beautifully executed backward dive.

She ran over to the starboard railing on the promenade, joined there quickly by more patients in a clatter of canes and crutches. The marine's head broke the surface and he immediately backstroked from the ship, looking up at them as he windmilled away. She could hear him laughing again and calling up to his comrades, who were being crowded at the gunwale by an influx of new arrivals. Word traveled fast on a ship.

The marine in the water was saying something, but she couldn't make out the words. With a final wave he turned and began swimming toward the launch as it rolled beneath gentle swells at right angles to the hospital ship. A sailor on the launch already had a black-bottomed orange life raft in the water and was clambering in. Above the raft in the cargo launch a number of newly discharged patients leaned against the railing like children watching a sporting event. The ladder from the opening in the ship's hull seemed to rise and fall as the little boat rocked.

The life raft approached the swimmer and the sailor threw a yellow canvas ring attached to a rope. The instant it landed the swimmer grabbed it, turned his back on the raft and backhanded the lifesaver like a discus. The sailor in the raft jumped to avoid being hit as it landed against the side of the raft, sprang straight upwards and dropped inside. The swimmer waved one last time to the ship and resumed swimming to the launch.

"Crazy bastard," the soldier beside her said. He smoked a cigarette through narrow lips caked in blisters. She couldn't identify the rest of the speakers.

"Was that him?"

"Same one."

"That's a long way down."

"Sharks all over this harbor. See em all the time."

"I guess you don't have to look like John Wayne."

The blistered soldier flicked the butt of his cigarette overboard.

"And that's the moral of *this* story," he said.

"I'm sorry they couldn't stay for the music." She leaned against him lightly and watched the launch glide toward shore on the mirror-flat sea.

"They have a helicopter they better not miss," Tommy said. "Afternoon chopper leaves too late."

"That's a funny way to leave a ship. Why did he do that?"

Tommy shrugged. "He gets an idea, there's no changing his mind. Said something about doing it for LT."

"Your friend Danny seemed upset."

"Danny spends most of his time worrying. Phineas is just the opposite."

"You better go. They're waiting on you."

She handed him his crutches.

"I won't be needing these forever."

"I know." She squeezed his waist and he smiled. The eyepatch only made him more handsome. His hair had grown and covered the incisions at the back of the head. There would always be scars but they softened and receded when he smiled like that. And at night, in the shadows on the promenade deck, in his arms, she could tell *that* was working.

He kissed her on the cheek, letting the kiss linger. They were showing their affection more openly, and she knew the head nurse would eventually succeed in having her transferred. It didn't matter. Tommy was in no hurry to go anywhere as long as she was there. The doctors were satisfied with his progress and the ship loved him and what he did for the patients—the Captain particularly, who was the only man on the ship who could hold his own with the head nurse. They would keep him as long as he cared to stay. Or he could ask to leave anytime, and to whatever naval hospital they sent him, she would follow. Oak Knoll, Balboa Park, wherever.

She was a Midwest girl. After the baby died and the divorce and the sale of the cottage, people were kind but she felt stranded and suffocated by the immense tracts of countryside stretching in all directions, barriers as limiting as if they were walls outside her window. She withdrew the application for night shift at the hospital and her first job as a nurse ended before it started. They all said she needed time, but after enough time passed she felt the tug of the ocean and distant lands. For movement anywhere but inside her walls. She left home to look for her healing, or to forget, whichever came first. Somehow in finding the truth, she found both. The truth was simple. It wasn't time that healed, it was love. It was being kind to others, helping them. Seeing beyond your own troubles. Self-pity infected a wound, love healed it. Sometimes it took a lot of love. End of wandering. End of quest.

Her morning rounds were over. She took her seat in the audience and watched as he made his way to the middle of the ceremony deck, used the crutches as poles and gracefully vaulted himself onto the little dais the ship carpenter had hastily built. There was scattered applause. He took his seat at the piano and played a quick scale. The small audience of bandaged and stitched faces chattered inside a forest of canes and crutches. A growing band of opportunist gulls were already circling.

There would never be a better stage, he had told her. She loved seeing him turn into a showman.

She knew her duty. How simple, too, after all.

To love him and to protect him. All that she could. This was all she knew of life, all she cared to know and all she felt she needed to know.

The hardened of the world would mock her simplicity. She would just love harder.

That was enough for her.

Unbidden, the image of the young lieutenant came to her. He stood on the deck again on a day full of gray storm and said to her, *That'll do for starters…*

"Some brave soul out there throw me a Beatles tune," Tomlin said, adjusting the microphone. "Free beer to the first soldier, sailor, airman or marine who stumps me."

"Hell, the beer's free anyway," someone shouted out.

"This way there's no sore losers. Cause none of you have stumped me yet. My nine-fingered honky tonk rides supreme."

The catcalls and applause increased and from the noise he heard the first challenge.

"Stand up," he said. "Come on, soldier."

A man stood in the middle of the audience and balanced on a cane and the back of a chair.

"Okay, then. Name, rank and outfit, soldier. Spill the beans."

"Specialist 4 Jimmy Bell, sir. 9th Motor Transport, 4th Armored."

"Your nation thanks you for your service, soldier. It'll be a race to see which of us throws these walkin sticks away first."

"Yes, sir."

"Now don't go callin an enlisted jarhead 'sir', Specialist. We aint that bright and we're already confused enough."

"Yes, sir."

The soldier shook his head. More laughter.

"Well, guess I'll just have to thank you for the promotion. Now what's that tune, soldier?"

"'Drive My Car.'" Whistles, shouting and more applause.

"Specialist, you got me worried. Let's see. I need a little help on this one. Where's my barber shop boys?"

Four men rose from the front row and turned toward the audience.

"You know the chorus for this little ditty?" he asked.

"Free beer if we don't," one of them said.

He played the intro and sang the first verse, pounded the last chord and the four men pounded the simple car noise refrain with gusto, to cheers and clapping. Another verse and refrain, and the quartet bowed and took their seats.

"Nice try, Specialist Jimmy B. No cigar but enjoy the beer. Next brave soul."

"'Day Tripper'!"

"Oh, *please,*" he said.

He knocked the microphone aside, launched furiously into the keyboard intro and played the melody against the chords flawlessly, his index finger surprising him daily as it learned to think of more and more ways to stand in for his missing thumb. The shoulder limited his range on the keyboard and with the knee he wasn't as sharp on the pedals. But he was managing. The audience picked up the beat and clapped or slapped crutches and canes against the deck while a young soldier in the back row followed along credibly with a jew's harp. It was the first Beatles tune he had ever driven his mother half-crazy with on the living room piano.

"'A Hard Day's Night'!"

He played.

"'She Loves You'!"

The quartet jumped up and joined him in song. Someone threw a small tomato. One of the quartet caught it and heaved it back at the assailant to loud cheering.

He played on. Many times. Some he sang, some he didn't know the lyrics for or they were in some key unsuited to his voice and these he didn't. Someone shouted out a Rolling Stones song. He played 'Satisfaction.' A crew member leaned on an upper deck railing and called for one by Buffalo Springfield.

He waved up at the man. "Okay," he said into the microphone. "But a deal's a deal. You're sendin me all over the map. We stick with the Beatles after this one."

Tomlin slowed the song down just enough to turn it into a ballad. He sang as he played and brought down the house with a minute's worth of 'For What It's Worth'. Near the end an officer at the back with his arm in a sling and a leg in a cast struggled to rise. He shook off the aid of the soldier beside him. The officer's face was scarred and red above a swath of bandages woven around his lower jaw. Even on a hospital ship it was a face that other patients looked away from in narrow passageways. Shiny grafts of skin stretched across his forehead in delicate mismatched flesh tones. One ear was mutilated above a mass of crusted welts that ran from the pulp of the ear down the neck into his loose collar. He balanced himself against the chair in front and waited patiently for the last chord and the applause to end, then removed his peaked cap, revealing a maze of stitches in deep blue trenches. He closed his hand over the dull brass of the cap's single bar before he spoke.

"I have a song," he said.

He paused for a moment, his throat moving beneath the bandages.

"Yes, sir," Tomlin said. "What's your song, Lieutenant?"

"It's not really *my* song," the officer said. "But it's in my keep for protection now, the way things have worked out. You know how that can be? How that can come about?"

"I think I do, sir."

"It's for them that I'm asking you to play. For all my boys that aren't coming home. This was their song, and they taught it to me. And they could sing, sir, they surely could. I never heard anything like it. They could stop a tank in its tracks and didn't I see them do that very thing. Me now, I can't sing a lick but they had me singing along anyway, once they knew I was there for them, that I wasn't some boot officer trying to make a career on their dead bodies. That where I was sending them I was going too. Only where we went, all those times, this time it was only me for some reason got back. Platoon strength already down to seventeen one morning and before noon the same day it's down to one. Only one of us comes back. I wake up a thousand feet in the sky and I think it's just me and the medic and the door gunners and green bush out to the horizon. Then I see one of my boys there with me, but he's gone by the time we land. Why me, I could ask you. But no one can say."

He paused again, eyes brimming. In the silence someone said, "That's the bush, sir. That's not on you. That's the bush."

"There it is," someone else said.

The officer held up his hand. No one else spoke.

"My arm's shot up and my knee's a mess. I've got a quarter pound of shrapnel in me they haven't picked out yet. I look in a mirror I don't think good things. But I'm here. I'm going home one day. I'm going to have a warm fire in winter and be there with my wife when our child comes into this world. We here, we're all going home to a better life one kind or another. They aren't. No, sir, my boys aren't. Not one of them. Not one. I would appreciate it if you could play it, sir, with respect for the dead. For my boys, and for *all* the boys, and I mean to say I don't goddamn care anymore what uniform, what skin color or what country. Or what damn war. For them all. For all the dead boys. Would you play their song, Lance Corporal?"

"If I know it, sir. I surely will."

"You know it."

He did. Like most of the songs, he had not played it in years. Some of them he had never played. He didn't know all the words but he knew all the melodies, and music came to him on the fingers of thought, as long as he knew the melody. It was the gift of his dead father, a drunkard genius of a musician, a singing cowboy who could make music slapping the dashboard of a rusty pickup and taught his sons to do the same.

He knew the first verse by heart and he remembered the way Lennon's voice cracked on the last line of the song, a sound a heart breaking might make. There was irony behind the lyrics, but there was sad truth behind the irony. He imagined the officer's infantrymen singing the song at the end of the mud-drenched day, its meaning changing after their numbers were whittled away, then restored with new faces, only to be whittled again. And again. Until the day came when men, song and irony were all gone altogether, the whittling complete, leaving only their officer behind. Abandoned to whatever fate chance or fortune or the killing radius of fragmentation had wrought. To whatever nights the long years would bring, whatever thoughts and memories that now would never be shared in homes or hotels where reunions would never gather. What remained of his family would be collected from the jungle floor, shoehorned into dark bags and shipped home in dark caverns, the first stop in their native land a fluorescent warehouse. Their names and numbers would be checked and sorted and their containers separated and staged, then wheeled, railroaded or flown to different plots of ground and different receptions, where after ceremony and sermons and folded flags and tears, their pictures would be removed from unopened caskets and their journey finally end in silence inside the earth. They would not hear the weeping above them. Darkness to darkness, and however long in between the light. Seasons on end would come and go and they would move inexorably into the footnotes of history, dots of black ink in the pages of books rarely opened, the shapes of their earthly forms now rendered as faded or piously maintained white crosses erect against a field of manicured lawn. Lawn as green as the wild matted jungle once turned crimson with their blood. As though the earthly forms of these crosses in their mirror rows had never fallen saying *See how proud we stand*. As though meant to evoke vestigial memories inside strangers there for other ceremonies or reflection. Yet as all soldiers did and the human heart required, they would grow old in their graves and pass away a second time, even in parents, siblings and lovers, even in these for whom the stone of grief is last to be commuted by the dull buoyancy of time. So it has been. So it must be. In the memory of one man, though, his soldiers would never age any more than they had ever really died, either as symbol or as flesh. They would travel alongside their officer, this proud warrior crying unabashedly in front of him, their laughter and sorrows and joys unabated, in the full bloom of their beauty and youth and disfigurement, singing their song beneath a foreign sky he would carry forever within him. They would live as long as he did and die the last time when he died. In the end they would all be buried together. Darkness to darkness, and in between the light.

No match for Lennon's voice, Tomlin let his fingers seek the same depth of sorrow and beauty and left the irony to the audience as it chose to recognize it or not. As he played, the images of the ones he had known rose before him, some dead, some living, some in between. Like them, he, too, had been cast out. However long it took and however his body recovered, it could never bear that load again. He could never rejoin the three friends who loved him like family, loved him enough to risk court martial and discipline, even jail time, for going AWOL, just so it would be his family and not some stranger that added another lost brother to the private vaults of his memory. His family was *out there* and he would not be with them. They would leap from helicopters in the morning onto soil where none of them belonged, to fight an enemy no one had ever understood, in a war no one wanted. He knew now why so many kept coming back, despite doubling their odds of never going home again. All the war had left them was each other. Maybe it was all war ever left anyone. Tomorrow when the last chopper rose from the earth, and the last gunship circled a last time and then turned away, they would be alone and he would not be there with them. There would be one less grunt pledged to their mutual survival, one less pair of eyes to watch for movement in tall grass or ripples in the darkness after dusk. Above all, as he struck the final chord, he realized he grieved for that.

The last notes hung in the air and an image from nowhere recognizable startled him.

Under volcanic red skies he stands naked and knee-deep in the surf on a wild and desolate beach so prehistoric sand has not yet formed. The beach is strewn with razor sharp stones and immense coils of black seaweed that strangle the life from sea creatures trapped in their tentacles. Bladed outcroppings of rock rise along the shore and far out into the sea and bleed the underbelly of low clouds. Waves that blot the muted sun from the sky roll in and crash into the wrack with enough force to scatter boulders and form craters. The wind rages and howls and slashes through towering heights of dense vegetation growing right to the edge of the jagged shoreline, filling the air with alabaster spray torn from the froth of thundering breakers. An onslaught of sound, of the ocean, sky and earth, an immense and incontestable power of energy beyond reckoning nearly deafens him as a furious weight presses against his back. Bowed at the waist, his legs failing, in all the world he is alone and abandoned. He knows the sea smells blood and is coming for him. He twists his tormented shoulders and drops his head into the wind's fury and sees there beneath him a shelled creature, thrashing half-in, half-out of the foam, flailing crude articulating sections of its hinged body toward the shore. Nature's raw engineering has armored it with ridges of spiky horn to ward off attacks by the ocean's boundless predators, many of the horns broken above fleshy scars and open gashes from past incursions. Tomlin watches as the ungainly creature pumps saltwater frantically from openings in its shell, then gasps for air through the same holes. Water out, air in, struggling to find the controls. Timing is everything. The surf recedes and hisses back into the primeval water, tugging Tomlin seaward too. A fresh wave rolls in with an enthusiasm not much removed from malice and the creature hastens to seal its tubes tight and brace itself before disappearing again beneath the surface. Tomlin feels the determination surging from that strange little life form in its contest against the sea. It wanted the land and it was fighting back, a tiny, unremarkable David against an antediluvian Goliath.

No, he wasn't alone.

"We're a team!" he shouts.

The ocean redoubles its efforts and claws at him relentlessly. With renewed faith, he stops resisting just as his feet are swept from beneath him. He feels himself rise, and a weight like a tree falls from his shoulders.

The image vanished. After the piano's last vibration, the world went silent.

Leaving only LT. Somewhere, and with only one thing to say.

You here cause of your own choices, Tomlin. You here cause of you.

It was simple after all.

There was no time left for grieving. And no point in it.

They had all made their own choices.

Himself and Debro.

Doc and Swede.

Bender.

Red Man.

All of them down the line.

So this world cared nothing for the dead and the mangled, the ruined and the oppressed. So it specialized in heartbreak and had no definition for justice or mercy. Maybe it was all true. Maybe you ran the world's gauntlet from your first breath to your last and as the blows rained down the world heard no pleas, issued no pardons and took no prisoners. You made one wrong turn or stumbled in the least, it pounced with drawn sword or bared fang.

That was a tough one.

And just what were you going to *do* about it?

Like Debro said. *You gotta cowboy that shit up.*

Leave second-guessing the mission to history. Leave regret to the conscience of politicians and to the warmongers the anchors of their own crimes. All that evil did, evil repaid. Forget what the world despised or paid homage to, tomorrow or in years to come. Didn't matter either way. In the end no one escaped his own deeds, and no amount of opinion good or bad would change them. The deeds mattered, not the opinions. These deeds were what they were. They were *exactly* what they were. Only the deeds to come could make a difference now.

Therein lay anyone's salvation.

Yes, country had called, but *he* had answered. The country had sent him, but *he* had gone. While in that place, rightly or wrongly to the rest of the world, he had done his duty. Nothing more, nothing less.

To deny his own choices would leave him buried in the middle of that street with a head wound forever. To affirm them was a starting point for the rest of a life.

A resurrection.

What other value it had he wasn't sure, but it was not nothing.

That was enough for him.

And he had learned to *look*.

Tomlin had no idea how long he had been lost in thought. The audience sat quietly. There was no applause and no one spoke, as if each had momentarily left on his own private journey and not fully returned.

There were birds everywhere, birds in flight as far as the eye could see. In the weeks of wandering in and out of twilit fog from surgery after surgery, clumsy on his crutches and barely able to use his voice, a time when even to think exhausted him, the birds had given him somewhere to go, a place to escape the clamor and tyranny of his ravaged body. He had sat in the little ship's library and learned all their names and life dramas—born here, followed this current, mated, migrated or wintered there—then spent wordless hours leaned against the railing studying their patterns and daily routine. On occasion a wild creature startled him with a nearby landing on a perch of wood or steel, flicking saltwater from its wings and ignoring him completely, though he might have reached over and touched it. For some reason, it gave him comfort to see how little his presence registered in its life or disturbed its momentary leisure. Possibly some primordial kinship underlay everything despite ages of combat among species.

Now broad-winged seagulls and black-hatted terns circled and hovered from the lifeboats out to the horizon. A family of migrant storm petrels walked in their curious way across the water or leapt gracefully into the wind from wavelet to wavelet, snaring smaller fish unseen by the gulls at their greater heights. Occasionally a tern folded its swallowtail and plummeted into the sea, barely disturbing the surface, while in the distance a band of gulls escorted a trio of pelicans skimming the ocean's mantle in perfect formation. When sunlight played from the wings of the gulls it looked like little candles burned in the sky. All nature seemed to be present and in tune, like a piano itself.

He had the odd sensation that he had been playing for an eternity, and that the audience had been with him all along, in that place or any other place. That the birds and the ocean and the sky had always been there and they had all known one another since the beginning of time. The railing on the superstructure was crowded with patients and doctors, nurses' aides in their Red Cross caps and bearded ship's crew and officers, all silent too. Silent as a family witnessing childbirth. Above his audience and above the world, through thin, gray clouds drawn above each other like lines in sheet music, the sun burned and reflected from the tears on their cheeks like notes of the staff. There were no other clouds, no rain and no moon to be seen anywhere.

It seemed something was expected of him, and it was not an encore. Some words, as though in conclusion. Something to break the silence and to make sense of it all. A benediction. For himself, and for them.

For all of them.

He said the first thing that came to mind, and he said it without irony.

"God bless America," he said. "God bless this life."

Glossary

Ahab: See *Captain Ahab.*

Afro: A hair style characterized by usually a large volume of tight curls, cut in a rounded pattern, as worn by Jimi Hendrix in the late 1960s.

AK47 (AK-47): Military designation for the primary assault rifle used by the Viet Cong and North Vietnamese Army during the Vietnam War. The AK47 was developed by Russian designer Mikhail Kalashnikov after World War II and has become the most widely produced automatic rifle in the world. Durable and inexpensive to produce, the AK47 has become an inevitable presence wherever there is conflict between nations.

Arizona, the: An approximately two hundred square mile area of South Vietnam in Quang Nam province, in central Vietnam (northern South Vietnam, during the War), also referred to as "the Arizona Territory". A US Marine Corps area of operation and site of fierce fighting during the Vietnam War.

Armageddon: In Christian theology, the prophesied battle at the end of time between good and evil.

Armalite: Another name used for the M16 rifle at the time of the Vietnam War, from the name of the corporation whose chief designer, Eugene Stoner, invented the rifle.

ARVN: Army of the Republic of Vietnam. A soldier in the South Vietnamese army was frequently referred to as an "ARVN".

Attila: Also known as Attila the Hun, the Huns being one of the confederations of people that formed an empire in central and eastern Europe during the 400s A.D. As ruler of this empire, Attilla made it his business to wage war on his neighbors, including the Roman Empire, destabilizing western Europe for the twenty years of his reign.

Avenues, the: Local name for a residential district in San Francisco in the northern part of the city, north of the Haight-Ashbury district (See *Haight-Ashbury* below).

AWOL: Absent Without Leave.

Axe: Musician slang for "guitar".

Balboa Park: A reference to Naval Medical Center San Diego, located within the grounds of Balboa Park in San Diego, established in the years following World War I.

Ball ammo: A bullet designed with its softer metal inner core (usually lead) encased completely by a harder metal outer surface, traditionally copper or steel; also known as *full metal jacket* ammunition.

Ballistic: Relating to the science of ballistics, a wide-ranging field encompassing ultimately the physics of projectiles in motion, with emphasis on conditions and peculiarities that affect accuracy, distance, performance and impact.

Bandoleer: A sash containing ammunition in its various pockets, worn around the chest. A marine infantryman invariably carried loaded rifle magazines in the pockets of the bandoleer; very rarely just the ammunition itself, which was useless to him in combat unless preloaded inside a magazine. The marine bandoleer was simply the same cloth or synthetic sash used to contain the packets of his cartridges. The cartridge packets were emptied, the cartridges placed inside magazines and the magazines back into the bandoleer. The bandoleer with ends tied was draped around the shoulder and chest. In any typical photographic image of infantry in Vietnam, the bandoleer is prominent.

Battle dressing: A sterile bandage for treating combat wounds carried by US infantry during the Vietnam War, commonly carried by troopers attached to helmets with black rubber bands.

Beaucoup: French word meaning "very much or very many", normally used as slang when speaking English.

Beelzebub: An ancient name in a number of cultures for a demon. In Christian theology, another name for the devil.

B40: The B40 recoilless rifle—a type of "bazooka"—used in Vietnam was either made in North Vietnam or in China and was based on a Soviet design. These early versions did not use rocket fuel as later ones did, but conventionally oxidizing small arms powders.

Blitzkrieg: German for "lightning war", and designating primarily a German strategy of warfare in World War II based on rapid armored movement (tanks and artillery) through war theaters supported by massive coordinated aerial attack. Blitzkrieg was intended to demoralize opponents, shorten time in combat and particularly to avoid protracted struggles between opposed armies, as had become the primary mode of warfare during World War I.

Boatswain: Pronounced "bosun" and often spelled that way, a boatswain is historically the most senior rating (enlisted man, as opposed to commissioned officer) in charge of various functions and overall readiness and condition of the physical components of a ship's deck. At times, in small vessels lacking large crews and used primarily for workhorse duties, a boat's commander may have an enlisted rank rather than commissioned status. In the novel, the cargo boat's commander is by military specialty a naval boatswain, whose traditional duties include the receipt and delivery of cargo.

Bogarting: Taking more than one's share to the detriment of others.

Bolt: A working component of any rifle that has the primary duty of inserting unfired cartridges into and removing fired cartridges out of the chamber (back end of the rifle's barrel). The bolt is the hard-working part of any rifle, particularly an automatic or semi-automatic rifle.

Boonies: Another name for the *bush* (see in Glossary).

Brain housing group: The skull.

Bulge, the: Reference to the Battle of the Bulge, most common name for a World War II battle in which German armies launched a massive and desperate final attack against invading allied forces. The attack in mid-December 1944 involved over 400,000 German troops and most remaining German aerial and armored resources, surprising the Allies and achieving some early success—producing the "bulge" in the battle line as German troops advanced—but ultimately failing under stubborn Allied resistance and counterattack. In the five weeks of the German offensive, American forces suffered their greatest casualties of any military action in the war.

Bush: In Vietnam, the bush was any area of operation outside secure military bases where the enemy might be found, whether valleys or mountains, lowland terrain or triple canopy rain forest.

Buy the farm, Bought the farm: Vietnam War era expression among infantrymen, meaning "to be killed in action", or "was killed in action".

C-4: A plastic explosive from a class known as Composition C-4, the military grade formed into rectangular blocks and carried in the field by infantrymen. C-4 had many uses other than demolition, from brush clearing to heating rations or boiling water for coffee and cocoa, the latter for which it was greatly valued by the grunt in the field.

C-ration: Combat ration. The basic field ration of the US infantryman during the war.

Cam Ranh: Short for Cam Ranh Bay, a seaport on the coast of South Vietnam, and here referring to the army hospital that troops of all branches in Vietnam needing advanced care could be sent for treatment and recovery. Also the site of major naval and air force bases throughout the war. One of the finest deep water harbors in southeast Asia.

Canteen run: On Marine operations in the field during the Vietnam War, a trip to any local water source by a handful of designated marines, some carrying the canteens of an entire unit for refilling and later redistributing on return, others providing rifle security for those lugging the water.

Captain Ahab: A reference to one of the main characters in Herman Melville's novel *Moby Dick*. Ahab, the captain of a whaling ship in the 1800s, pursues revenge with pathological devotion against a white whale that has previously crippled him. His obsession with the whale leads him to his own death.

Captain Cook: A reference to James Cook (1728 – 1779), renowned British sailor who explored the Pacific Ocean extensively before meeting his death in the Hawaiian Islands during his third voyage. On its return home, his crew sailed past the coast of 18th century Vietnam and may have anchored in Vietnamese waters during its journey.

Carl Perkins: Musician (1932 – 1998) who heavily influenced early rock and roll, and a contemporary of Elvis Presley.

Carpe Diem: Latin phrase, literally "Seize the Day." Urging a course of action that makes the most of the present and takes advantage of present opportunity.

Carthaginian: An inhabitant of the city-state of Carthage, traditional foe of ancient Rome, located on the Mediterranean shore of northern Africa. The Carthaginian empire included much of the coastline of northern Africa, parts of southern Spain and a number of islands in the western Mediterranean.

CH-46: The Boeing Corporaton CH-46 Sea Knight was the Marines' workhorse assault and troop transport helicopter during the Vietnam War and for decades afterwards.

Charging handle: A lightweight, slender rod at the back of an M-16 rifle used to pull the bolt to the rear, either to load a first round from a recently inserted magazine, remove a round from the chamber of the rifle or verify that there is or isn't a cartridge in the chamber.

Charlie: Slang name for the Viet Cong during the Vietnam War, from the military alphabet code words ("Victor Charlie"), meaning "Viet Cong".

Chief: Chief Warrant Officer. A Chief Warrant Officer receives a commission from the President of the US like any commissioned officer. Lower grades of warrant officer do not. They get a "warrant", a simple decree authorizing their officer-like status.

China Beach: A white sandy beach on the outskirts of the city of Da Nang, frequented as an in-country R and R destination (see R and R in the Glossary) by American servicemen.

Chosin Reservoir: Major battle of the Korean War, in which surrounded and outnumbered US Marines and other United Nations troops fought their way to safety against Chinese troops, sustaining and inflicting heavy casualties.

Class As: Reference to the Marine Corps Service Uniform "A" (basically a semi-formal uniform), one notch down from the highly recognizable and formal "Dress Blues" most commonly worn by Marine recruitment personnel and seen in recruitment posters. The Service "A" uniform includes a green coat, green trousers and a khaki web belt.

Click: 1. One graduated movement of the turret of a telescopic scope, moving the crosshairs of the scope internally a minute, highly precise and regular amount. 2. In military topography, slang for one kilometer.

CMOH: Congressional Medal of Honor.

Cobras: Helicopter gunships, typically armed with rockets, machine guns and grenade launchers, providing fire support for transport helicopters and ground troops.

Cohort: A tactical military unit in the ancient Roman army, composed of approximately 500 men and roughly equivalent to an infantry battalion. Actual size over time varied with the era of Roman history and the function of the cohort (infantry, cavalry, archers, etc). 10 cohorts at one period of time formed a Legion.

Cook: See *Captain Cook.*

Copy: Military radio jargon meaning, "I have received and understood your communication."

Corps, hard: See *hard corps.*

Corpsman: An enlisted medically trained sailor serving with marine infantry.

Corvus: An elaborate mobile ramp attached to the deck of a Roman vessel, capable of rotating at its base for lowering onto enemy ships, a hallmark of ancient Roman tactics in boarding enemy ships for hand to hand combat.

Cow Palace: A large indoor arena built in 1941 in Daly City, California and hosting a multitude of varied sports, entertainment and political events. It has been a popular venue for rock concerts since the 1960s, when the Beatles played their first American concert there in 1964.

Dacian: An inhabitant of ancient Dacia, occupying land in modern eastern Europe, including portions of Serbia, Romania, Bulgaria and the Ukraine. Eventually conquered by Rome, the kingdom of Dacia remained hostile, and to call another Roman a Dacian was to insult him.

Da Nang: A coastal city in South Vietnam, with major US military installations in the era of the Vietnam War. One of the main points of arrival and departure of American military personnel during the war

Dak To: Grueling three week battle in the Central Highlands of South Vietnam, November of 1967. American and Vietnamese soldiers alike suffered heavy losses and showed great courage in what appears to have been part of the strategy encompassing nearly suicidal personal loss by the North Vietnamese leading up to and characterizing the Tet offensive of 1968 (see *Tet Offensive* in this glossary).

Delaware: A reference to the Delaware River, crossed during a bitterly cold December by General George Washington and American troops en route to a surprise attack on German mercenaries in the town of Trenton in what is now west central New Jersey. See also *Trenton*.

Di di: to leave, go away, make yourself scarce.

Di di mau: "Go now", "Go fast", "Get lost"; the basic idea is to move quickly away from where one is, or to direct another to leave quickly.

Dien Bien Phu: A city in northwestern Vietnam. Most known for the hellish 57-day siege and defeat in 1954 of French forces by communist Vietnamese, resulting in the expulsion of the French from Vietnam and the partition of the country into North and South Vietnam.

Dinky-dau: As phonetically translated into English from the Vietnamese sounds, this means "crazy" or "insane".

Doc: Colloquial and short for "doctor", the title given without exception to every corpsman who ever served with marine infantry.

Dodge City: A town in Kansas, USA, which, during the heyday of the American Old West (1860s – 1870s), and after an early period of colorful violence, enacted strict laws enforcing an ordinance that residents could not carry firearms out-of-doors, and all visitors, particularly cowboys entering the town from cattle drives, had to place their guns in designated locations for the duration of their stay. Armed persons within town limits were subject to being shot on sight. Neither were cattle any longer tolerated on raised board sidewalks nor horses above the ground floor of a building; both practices were also outlawed by town legislators. Such notable figures as Bat Masterson and Wyatt Earp enforced these regulations.

Donut Dollies: See *Red Cross girls*.

Draft deferment: During the Vietnam War, a condition or status which legally exempted one from entry or postponed entry into the armed forces corresponded to any of a number of "draft deferment" designations. Being a currently enrolled college student in good standing qualified many a draft-age American male as "2-S" and absolved him from military service.

Dragunov: A sniper-grade rifle adopted by Communist-bloc countries beginning in the 1960s. While it has a rudimentary iron sight system, the rifle was always intended to be used with a telescopic sight. Many variants exist. The Vietnam-era model sacrifices some accuracy for reliability and relative light weight, but with attention by knowledgeable gunsmiths and the addition of improved telescopes, this original version can be extremely effective beyond the range of its standard design parameters.

Dulce et Decorum Est: Originally a line written by the Roman poet Horace and published 23 B.C. Although Horace's poem exhorted young Roman soldiers of the day to be ready to meet the threat of a contemporary war emergency, it also summarized the prevailing Roman view of the proper soldier's attitude. The full line "*Dulce et decorum est pro Patria mori*" is translated most commonly as "It is sweet and fitting to die for one's country." There was no irony in the Roman poem. It was intended as instruction:

> It is sweet and fitting to die for one's country.
> Yet death chases after the soldier who runs,
> and it won't spare the cowardly back
> or the limbs, of peace-loving young men.

Compare these lines to those from the most celebrated poem of World War I, by the poet Wilfred Owen, who was killed in action one week before the signing of the Armistice ending the war:

If in some smothering dreams you too could pace
Behind the wagon that we flung him in,
And watch the white eyes writhing in his face,
His hanging face, like a devil's sick of sin;
If you could hear, at every jolt, the blood
Come gargling from the froth-corrupted lungs,
Obscene as cancer, bitter as the cud
Of vile, incurable sores on innocent tongues,—
My friend, you would not tell with such high zest
To children ardent for some desperate glory,
The old Lie: *Dulce et decorum est*
Pro patria mori.

81s/82s: Referring to the diameter in millimeters of two distinct crew-served but ultimately portable mortar systems. 81s were American mortars; 82s were based on Soviet designs and copied by Chinese and Vietnamese suppliers. The 82 could utilize captured American mortar rounds.

11Bravos: Soldiers in the Unites States Army whose military occupational specialty (MOS) is that of Infantryman.

E Pluribus Unum: Latin phrase "One out of Many", as found on the Great Seal of the United States, inscribed on the scroll clasped in the beak of an eagle. Motto of the United States dating from the Revolutionary War.

ETA: Estimated Time of Arrival.

EU ST: Initials of the name of Eugene Stoner, designer of the Armalite rifle, the basis for the M-16, the earliest version of the generally similar current US infantry rifle, now in service for over half a century (see *M-16*).

Eye-Vee bags: Liquid filled plastic containers, filled with medicine or nutritional supplements dripped intravenously by tube and needle into a patient's arm.

Farm: From the expression "bought the farm", meaning killed in action.

Fastmovers: Infantryman's name for jets.

Fighting holes: Called *foxholes* in the US Army, in the Marines, the similar excavations dug by infantrymen into the ground, usually large enough for 2 or 3 marines, as a position from which to engage in expected fighting during combat operations or routinely at the end of a day's march for protection from bombardment or other unexpected assault.

Fire for Effect: A direction to an artillery unit to fire its weapons without reservation on the target just established, often after having first fired a number of "spotting rounds" (which see) to establish the exact point of impact.

Five five six (5.56): 5.56 mm is the caliber (width in millimeters) of the bullet for the standard issue American rifle, both at the time of Vietnam and modernly.

Flak jacket: An armored vest worn by infantrymen. At the time of the Vietnam War the jacket worn by marines weighed ten pounds and consisted of compartments sewn into the garment containing shrapnel-resistant synthetic plates. The flak jacket was effective only against low-velocity particles and was easily defeated by a rifle round from an AK-47.

FO: See *Forward Observer*.

Force Recon: Short for *Force Reconnaissance*. Designating marines trained in special high-risk or esoteric weapons and skills and usually performing clandestine information-gathering or combat missions requiring such special skills and weapons.

Forend: Loosely defined, the forward part of a military rifle where the shooter supports the rifle as his remaining hand operates the trigger. On a Vietnam-era M16, the forend consisted of two removable, triangular plastic guards toward the front of the barrel that provided a stabilizing grip on the weapon and also protected the shooter from the heat of the gas line encased by the guards.

.45: This is the caliber, or barrel diameter (.45 inch) of the primary US sidearm at the time of the Vietnam War, expanded in nomenclature to refer to the weapon itself.

Forward Observer/FO: An officer who served in forward combat units on the ground and directed attacks by aircraft providing support for ground operations.

4-F: A designation in the US Selective Service System for procuring military draftees, assigned to those who fail to meet minimum moral, physical or mental standards for entry into service in the armed forces. Most widely used among Vietnam War era servicemen to refer to those who failed the physical examination at an enlistment processing station.

FREQ: Short for Radio Frequency.

Gallic: of Gaul, ancient territory above ancient Rome, now primarily modern France.

Gas guards: Located behind the front sight of an M-16, a pair of Vietnam-era triangular plastic sections that enclose and protect the gas tube that provides force to operate the bolt of the rifle. They protect the shooter from the heat of gas operation and provide a grip and rest point for a shooter's hand in aiming and firing the weapon.

General Giap: Nguyen Vo Giap, prominent military strategist and commander of North Vietnamese forces that defeated the French at Dien Bien Phu (see in Glossary) and opposed American forces during the Vietnam War.

Ghost sights: A type of firearms aiming system, mostly installed on rifles and shotguns, with the rear sight composed of an opening inside a small steel circle and the front sight of a simple upright steel post. The shooter indexes his target with the tip of the front post centered in the rear sight's circle. This method of acquiring a target comes naturally to the eye, and this basic sight system is common to many past and present US military service rifles.

Giap: See General Giap above.

Gladius: Roman sword, hallmark weapon of Roman infantrymen in varying lengths and blade design for seven centuries.

Gore, Lesley: Female American pop singer of the fifties and sixties, whose version of "It's My Party" became a #1 hit in America in 1963.

Ground One: Fictional name in the novel for a two-man team (one of two teams) whose mission involved the novel's Buddhist temple.

Ground Two: Name in the novel for the second of two teams that are part of a mission involving the novel's Buddhist temple. Ground Two contains three members.

Grunt: Slang word for "infantryman."

Gunny: Nickname often given the individual of the rank of gunnery sergeant, a higher enlisted non-commissioned officer rank in the Marine Corps. At one time historically, a Marine sergeant was promoted to Gunnery Sergeant according to his personal skill in weaponry, including his ability to repair firearms under battlefield conditions.

H E: High explosive, referring to a type of mortar or artillery round designed to wound and kill by fragmentation of its projectile into lethal and jagged high-speed particles.

Haight-Ashbury: District in San Francisco, famous for its colorful stores, building fronts and history as both birthing movement and gathering place for the hippy era of the late 1960s.

Halozone: Referring to a water purification tablet used in field conditions throughout the war. It added a distinctive, unpleasant taste to the treated water.

Handset: A combination microphone and speaker in a small, rounded-edge receiver, attached by cord to a field radio carried on his back by an infantry radio operator. The handset had a lever on one side. In the lever's default position, the handset was a speaker; when the lever was pressed, the handset acted as a microphone for the radio transmitter.

Hard corps: A term used in military circles to describe fearless, fearsome and dedicated action, attitude or combat servicemen and their groups, including the enemy.

Harmony f-hole: A guitar made by the Harmony Company, once the largest instrument-maker in the US, founded in 1892, closing its doors in 1975. An f-hole guitar has shapes resembling the letter f cut into its soundboard.

Ho Chi Minh: Influential 20th century revolutionary and Communist leader in Southeast Asia over a long career in Vietnamese politics. President of North Vietnam for a quarter century. His life's goal, not realized before his death in 1969, was to unify North and South Vietnam into a single communist nation. Known affectionately by North Vietnamese soldiers and less reverently by US troops as "Uncle Ho".

Hootch: A term used by Vietnam era Marines to describe any small structure primarily used for sleeping or storage, such as the plywood-floored tents used at many military installations, an improvised lean-to in the field or the small thatched huts commonly used for habitats by South Vietnamese civilian farmers.

HOPE: SS *Hope*, built in 1944 and entering service as a US Navy hospital ship (USS *Consolation*), it was donated in 1958 to the charitable organization Project HOPE for worldwide travel in providing hospital services and preventative medicine. On one of its eleven voyages, *Hope* provided medical services in Vietnam.

HQ: Headquarters.

Hue (Hue City): City in central Vietnam, formerly the seat of imperial Vietnam's government, in the modern era site of one of the longest and bloodiest single battles of the Vietnam War, lasting nearly a month with heavy casualties on both sides.

One of the main battles of the Tet Offensive of 1968. (See *Tet Offensive* in this glossary.) Also the site, during the battle, of the massacre of civilians, prisoners of war and political opponents, in much greater numbers by the North Vietnamese but also by South Vietnamese troops in revenge in the aftermath. The exact numbers are contested, but the death toll is generally estimated to be in the thousands.

Huey: A nickname for a family of helicopters originally designated the HU-1 by Bell Helicopter Corporation. By the time of the Vietnam War the designation had changed to UH-1 but the nickname stuck. This was the primary troop transport helicopter used by the Army in Vietnam (but not by the Marines, whose workhorse transport helicopter, the CH-46, was made by a rival helicopter corporation)

Hump: Military slang meaning "to march", or "a march," and intending to convey the grinding, often exhausting movement of infantrymen under grueling conditions in the "bush" (see in Glossary).

Hush puppies: from Hush Puppies, a brand of footwear best known for comfort and leisure wear, widely prevalent in American culture of the 1960s.

Icon Nine: Code name and call sign for the commander and pilot of the Huey helicopter described in the novel's action.

I Corps: A military zone of the Republic of South Vietnam, from the 1960s until the conquest of its territory by the North Vietnamese Army in 1975. I Corps was one of four such military zones, consisting of northernmost South Vietnam and including its border with North Vietnam. Hue City was in I Corps.

Illum: Pronounced *ih-loom,* and short for *illumination.* Refers to narrow, handheld canisters used to provide nighttime illumination for infantry. The cap of the canister contains a fixed post that acts as a firing pin. The cap is fitted to the base of the canister and struck on a hard surface or slapped with the heel of the hand, firing the illumination material from the canister to ignite in the night sky. The parachute of material floats slowly earthward burning brightly. Carried by infantry and used if under attack or in need of observation of the environment.

India: There are four rifle companies to a marine battalion. In the novel's action, the companies are India, Kilo, Lima and Mike, each named for a corresponding military code word for sequential letters of the alphabet ("J" is omitted in a marine battalion because its international code word is "Juliet").

India Two: Second platoon, in the rifle company designated "India". At the time of the Vietnam war, a marine rifle company had four platoons, three rifle platoons and one "weapons" platoon, consisting of machine guns and mortars. Traditionally weapons platoon assigns crew members to individual rifle platoons for longer or shorter duration.

Iwo Jima: Island in the Pacific and site of a major World War II battle between US Marines and Japanese soldiers.

Jolly Greens: Vietnam-era helicopters (model HH-3E) designed by the Sikorsky Aircraft Corporation. A heavy-lift and transport helicopter originally used by the Air Force in recovering downed pilots. See *Sea Stallions* for more information.

Kalashnikov: Soviet officer and World War II veteran Mikhail Kalashnikov designed the AK-47. In former eastern block countries, the AK-47 is commonly referred to by its creator's last name, a Kalashnikov.

Key the handset: To press the lever on the side of a portable radio's handset, thereby activating the voice transmission capability of the radio.

Khe Sanh (Khe Sanh Combat Base): Site of a months-long major battle of the Vietnam War at a US Marine base in the northernmost portion of South Vietnam. US forces, though under siege and constant attack, were never overrun, but later abandoned Khe Sanh due to its long-term indefensibility. North Vietnamese troops occupied the abandoned base, raised a flag and declared victory.

KIA: Military acronym for "Killed in Action"

Kon-Tiki: Reference to a crude raft constructed in 1947 by Norwegian explorer Thor Heyerdahl, designed to test his theory that prehistoric people from the coast of South America could have sailed the ocean in prehistoric times and settled the islands of the Pacific. The raft was constructed according to available information about the existing facilities and materials of that early time. The sailing expedition proved successful, and the raft is now on display in a Norwegian museum.

Lance Corporal (LCpl): A service rating two promotions up from entry level (private). In the US armed forces, the title is unique to the Marine Corps.

Leon Russell: Popular rock vocalist and pianist during the time frame of the Vietnam War.

Leutze: Emanuel Leutze, German-born American artist, whose famous work *Washington Crossing the Delaware*, painted on canvas over 12 feet wide and 20 feet long, is displayed in the New York Metropolitan Museum of Art.

Lima: Code name designation of one of the rifle companies in a marine battalion containing companies I, K, L and M (India, Kilo, Lima and Mike).

Lord of Hoboken: A reference to Frank Sinatra, who was born in Hoboken, New Jersey, USA.

LT: Nickname often given in the field to an officer of the rank of Lieutenant.

LZ: Landing Zone

Magazine: The detachable steel or aluminum device that stores and holds cartridges inside a rifle during the process of loading and firing.

Makarov: A service pistol of Warsaw Pact and communist nations during the era of the Vietnam War.

Mama-san: From English and Japanese and first coined by American serviceman in post-World War II Japan, during the Vietnam War used by American GIs to refer to an older Vietnamese woman, most typically as encountered in rural areas during combat operations.

Marathon: Pivotal battle of the ancient world (390 B. C.), near the town of Marathon on the southeastern shore of Greece, in which outnumbered Greek infantry decisively defeated the forces of a massive Persian invasion fleet.

MCRD: Marine Corps Recruit Depot. There are two training centers for the Marines, one in San Diego, California, and another on Parris Island, South Carolina.

Medevac: A helicopter serving to extract wounded soldiers or marines from combat zones for needed medical care. Also, to so extract wounded personnel.

Mekong (Mekong Delta): A historically important wetlands region at the southern extremity of Vietnam for trade, fish harvesting, agriculture, and transportation. During the Vietnam War, the site of significant wartime activity between US and communist forces. The Mekong River flows through the delta.

Mephistopheles: In German folklore, a demon subordinate to the Devil. Used in modern times as another name for the Devil himself.

MIA: Missing in Action.

Midnight boys: Slang term for intelligence agency operators in combat zones.

MI KA: Initials from the name Mikhail Kalashnikov, designer of the AK-47 (see *Kalashnikov*).

Mike: The title of the fourth company of the third battalion in a regiment of Marine infantry, derived from the military code word for the letter *m*.

Mike 60s: Slang designation for the 60 millimeter (2.36 inch) caliber portable mortar system used by American forces from World War II through the Vietnam War.

Misenum: An ancient Roman city on the coast of southwestern Italy and the site of its most powerful naval base.

Mitch: Referring to Mitch Miller, an entertainer with a popular television program at the time of the Vietnam War called "Sing Along with Mitch", in which lyrics appeared on a television screen to assist audiences to sing while they watched. Part of the graphics included an animated bouncing red ball, which moved from word to word in time with the music.

Mosin-Nagant: A versatile and rugged bolt-action rifle designed in the late 1800s as the primary service rifle for Russian infantry. Though mediocre in accuracy without significant gunsmith work, by the time of the Vietnam War the rifle nevertheless had a history of successful use as a sniper rifle in eastern Europe and Soviet Russia.

Mother Teresa: Roman Catholic missionary and nun, known worldwide for her charitable work on behalf of the poor and severely ill. She received a Nobel peace prize in 1979 and was recognized as a saint two decades after her death.

M7: Military designation of the bayonet designed for use with the M16 service rifle.

M16 (M-16): The military designation for the automatic combat rifle issued to the American infantryman during the latter part of the Vietnam War.

M60: Military designation for the primary field machine gun carried by American infantrymen during the Vietnam War.

Mortar tubes: The tube of a mortar is its barrel. A mortar is basically a simple cannon. Its cartridges are dropped by hand into the barrel. The force of gravity is adequate to cause the cartridge to fire when its base contacts a fixed firing pin inside the base of the tube.

MP: Military police.

MPC: Military Payment Chit or Certificate, a substitute for American paper currency in making payments to GIs in foreign countries, beginning after World War II and ending shortly after the Vietnam War. Never a perfect system, the MPC was subject to black market activities and profiteering at the expense of local economies.

Navy Cross: The second highest decoration for valor in combat awarded in the US Navy and naval services, which includes the US Marine Corps.

Net extraction: A military helicopter technique of evacuating troops inside hostile territory by dragging a net across the ground. The troops leap onto and cling to the net and are thereby extracted.

Nochem: A word created by the novel's character, meaning "night", coined from the Latin word for "nocturnal".

No. 10 cans: Cans used for food storage worldwide, measuring 7 inches tall with a diameter of approximately 6 ¼ inches. The No. 10 can was a popular size in military food services in the era of the Vietnam War.

Numidian: Inhabitant of Numidia, an ancient country of Roman times, located on the Mediterranean coast of northern Africa, in the region of modern Algeria and Tunisia.

NVA: Acronym for the North Vietnamese Army, as used by its opponents. (The North Vietnamese soldier thought of himself as PAVN: People's Army of North Vietnam).

Oak Knoll: Reference to Oak Knoll Naval Hospital, built in Oakland, California, USA, in the early years of World War II, which provided treatment for military casualties of American wars in eastern Pacific lands, including the Vietnam War. The hospital closed in 1996.

Oak Leaf: Colloquial, slightly pejorative term for either of two officer ranks in the U. S. Marine Corps. If the insignia (a stylized oak leaf) is gold, the rank is Major; if silver, the officer is a Lieutenant Colonel. Both ranks are typically staff officers (with planning, command and logistics duties) and not usually found in the front lines of combat areas.

Okinawa: An island in the Pacific containing an American military base and serving as a departing point for marines headed to combat zones in South Vietnam during the Vietnam War.

Old Betsy: A name given by Davy Crockett to many of the rifles owned over his lifetime, in honor of his favorite sister Betsy Crockett, including the rifle now on display at the Alamo in San Antonio, Texas.

0300s: Marines assigned a military occupational specialty (MOS) in one of the infantry (03) categories, such as Rifleman (0311), Machine Gunner (0331), Mortarman (0341). In the Marines' system, the first two digits represent a general field, the last two the specialty within that field. "0300s" designates the Infantry in all its specialties.

0331s: Numbers designating marines with the military occupational specialty (MOS) of an infantryman further trained in the operation of machine guns.

Pabst Blue Ribbon: A brand of American beer first introduced in 1844. The brand was near the height of its popularity during the period of the Vietnam War.

Parris Island: Marine Corps Recruit Depot. There are two training centers for the Marines, one in San Diego, California, and another on Parris Island, South Carolina

Patton: George S. Patton, colorful senior General in the US Army and commander of tank forces in Europe and Africa during World War II.

PAVN: Acronym for People's Army of Vietnam; during the Vietnam War, it designated the armed forces of North Vietnam. The same title is now used for the single country of Vietnam. The abbreviation "NVA" for "North Vietnamese Army" was primarily a US military designation to distinguish between northern enemy (NVA) and the southern insurgency, the Viet Cong (VC). PAVN, however, considers the Viet Cong to have been a branch of PAVN.

Perfume River: A river in central Vietnam that runs through Hue City. It is named for a seasonal aroma from flowers that fall into the river during the autumn months and float downstream.

Petrel: See *storm petrel.*

Phantoms: American jets during the Vietnam War era. Also known as F-4s, or F-4 Phantoms.

Pogue: A derogatory term with a long US naval history reaching back to days of sailing ships. During the Vietnam War a "pogue" (to the infantryman) was any noncombatant, rear echelon personnel performing any duty other than combat duty. The pogue typically never entered the fighting and lived a life of relative ease.

Point: 1. The position at the front of an infantry squad as it moves through its area of operation. 2. The infantryman who is walking this position. His responsibility is to lead his squad along a designated route safely while observing, avoiding and alerting his squad to potential hazards such as booby-traps and ambushes. "Walking point" is a dangerous assignment and generally given to a highly experienced and proven member of the squad.

Poseidon: In Greek mythology, the god of the seas. Often depicted in statues and paintings carrying a trident as the equivalent of a king's scepter.

Prick 25/PR-25: Military designation and slang for the Portable Radio-25 carried by American soldiers and marines during combat operations in the Vietnam War.

P38: A small can opener issued for use with C-rations ("Opener, Can, Hand, Folding, Type 1" as it is lovingly described by the US military) often worn around the neck on the same chain that held an infantryman's identification plate ("dogtags"). A vital part of an infantryman's gear.

PX: Post Exchange. Known by various titles in different branches of the US Armed Forces since the Vietnam War, during the Vietnam War the common name for the retail store (exchange) operated by the military for its base (post) personnel.

Queequeg: Character in the novel *Moby Dick* by Herman Melville, ferocious-looking and tattoed South Sea native who becomes a whaling ship sailor. An unrepentant cannibal in his home environment (though eating only the bodies of enemies slain in war), he becomes a close friend of Ishmael, the novel's central character, and survives after the destruction of his ship by the white whale through clinging to a coffin he had earlier fashioned in the belief he was destined to die.

Que Son mountains: A mountain range in Quang Nam province in modern day central Vietnam (northern South Vietnam during the era of the Vietnam War). Both mountains and the Que Son valley below saw frequent combat between US Marine and North Vietnamese forces.

R and R: Rest and Recuperation. After a certain amount of time in-country, an American serviceman became eligible for a week's vacation at a number of destinations, including Honolulu, Hawaii, Bangkok, Thailand and Sydney, Australia, depending on flight reservations available at the time of his selection for R and R. Known more colorfully among American troops as *I and I* (Intoxication and Intercourse).

Rear, back in the: In a war zone, located in an area that is at a distance from combat operations and considered safe from hostile action. The *rear* is anywhere behind the *front* lines where the enemy can be contacted.

Recon: Short for "reconnoiter" or "Force Reconnaissance," a highly trained group of combat specialists within the Marine Corps.

Red Cross girls: During the time of the Vietnam War, as in many wars before, young women under the auspices of the American Red

Cross volunteering to serve in a number of capacities in combat zones, including hospital care. Known affectionately as "Donut Dollies", Red Cross girls trace their service to the military back to the Spanish-American War.

Red Skelton: Popular American comedian popular at the time of the Vietnam War, one of whose skits included mimicking a seagull by use of comical movement of his arms folded and hands placed beneath his armpits.

Reset the trigger: Refers to a careful shooter's technique, after firing, of easing a trigger forward under its own internal pressure until it "resets", meaning it arrives at a position where it has advanced mechanically enough to be ready to fire again. Usually accompanied by a clicking sound and discernible also in the trigger finger. Proper trigger reset, along with other components of manipulating a trigger, is indispensable to precision and accuracy in firing.

Re-up: to re-enlist. A seasoned infantryman was valuable at the end of his tour. During certain periods of the war, attractive bonuses and other inducements were made to entice veterans into returning for further duty.

Re-up money: A reference to a bonus offered to American veterans completing a tour of duty in Vietnam in exchange for re-signing for a further tour of duty, usually following a brief leave of absence.

Riki-tik: Phonetic pronunciation of Vietnamese for "very fast, quickly".

Rotate: To leave Vietnam on completion of one's tour of duty, early in the war, of thirteen months duration, and later, of twelve.

Rotor: The propeller of a helicopter that allows it to overcome gravity in providing lift and forward motion.

Round: A term used interchangeably with bullet and also for an unfired cartridge. An unfired cartridge is improperly referred to as a bullet, the bullet being the actual projectile that leaves the barrel of a weapon.

Round Eyes: Non-oriental people as regarded in oriental lands.

RPG: Rocket propelled grenade. In the novel, the RPG launcher is actually a shoulder-fired recoilless rifle and not a true rocket launcher as later generations of this weapon came to be. Infantry did not distinguish between the two when confronting either in the field and used the generic term "RPG" to describe both.

Rubber Lady: An inflatable air mattress for field infantry (*Mattress, Pneumatic, Nylon Cloth*), if an infantryman cares to hump its weight in the field. Highly susceptible to leaking, puncture and subsequent discarding.

Sansui: The name of a still operating but largely diminished electronics company that manufactured highly regarded high end audio components during the time of the Vietnam War and for some years afterward.

Sappers: During the Vietnam War, communist soldiers engaged in disruptive operations against American and allied forces, often in advance of major offensive infantry operations. These were elite commandos greatly respected by fellow soldiers in both NVA and VC forces.

Scutum: Roman word for shield.

Sea Stallions and Jolly Greens: Two Vietnam-era helicopters, both designed by the Sikorsky Aircraft Corporation and sharing design features. The Sea Stallion (CH-53) was the Marine Corps' heavy-lift and transport helicopter while the aircraft that evolved into the Jolly Green Giant (HH-3E) was originally used by the Air Force in recovering downed pilots.

7.62: A reference to the width in diameter, in millimeters, of the bullet used in the primary weapon of communist forces during the Vietnam War, the AK-47 (see in glossary).

Short: A description used of and by a US infantryman getting close to his rotation date, or end of tour of duty, as in "I'm short, man."

Short Timer: During the Vietnam War era, a serviceman in a combat zone whose tour of duty was approaching its end.

Six, that takes care of our: In this context, "six" refers to the area or environment behind the speaker.

Skater: Derogatory term for a marine who intentionally avoids personal danger or excessive effort in a combat zone, often by feigning or exaggerating injury.

Skating: The action of arranging circumstances to avoid personal danger or risk of injury, as by feigning or exaggerating injury or illness. When used as an adjective, intended to describe someone accomplished in this action.

Skinny: Slang word for "information".

SKS: A rugged military carbine that fires a more powerful cartridge than most carbines historically have, widely used as a transition weapon among Soviet-influenced European and Asian nations. Replaced as a primary infantry weapon by the AK-47 in most of these countries by the early 1950s, it remains in many armories in various capacities and saw extensive use in the Vietnam War.

Sky pilots: Military chaplains.

Slick: Vietnam era term for the Bell Corporation family of UH-1 helicopters, the primary transportation and attack helicopter of the US Army (but not Marines) during the war.

Smedley Butler: Colorful and celebrated Marine officer of the late 19th and early 20th centuries, winner of two Medals of Honor and many other awards and citations. In his day the most decorated U. S. Marine in its history, upon leaving the Marine Corps after 34 years of service with the rank of Major General, he became an outspoken critic of civilian use of the military for corporate and banking interests. His book *War is a Racket* called for an end to war and major reforms to accomplish it.

Smokey: Colloquial name for the hat worn by both U.S. Army and Marine drill instructors and many other military and service organizations, a design dating back to nineteenth century cavalry troopers and formally known as a campaign hat. Called a "smokey" because the US Forest Service's mascot and character "Smokey the Bear" wears such a hat as he reminds each generation of Americans that "Only you can prevent forest fires."

Spooks: A vague and vaguely pejorative term referring to military or paramilitary operatives with connections to intelligence organizations.

Spotting rounds: Projectiles fired from large bore infantry support weapons such as mortars or artillery with the primary purpose of fixing the relative position of the projectile's strike from the intended target in distance and direction so subsequent rounds can be accurately adjusted onto the target.

Squat thrusts: A physical exercise in which a person drops first from the standing to a squatting position, then thrusts the torso and legs out behind him, returns rapidly to the squat position, rises upright and then repeats the motions until done exercising. At the time of the Vietnam War, this exercise was common in Marine Corps basic training and used as discipline as regularly as it was for exercise.

Steaming pile from shinola: A variation on the mainly military colloquialism used in reference to someone who doesn't "know shit from shinola." Shinola was a wax shoe polish at the time of the Second World War, when this particular witticism became popular. A "steaming pile" refers to a deposit of fresh manure.

Storm petrel: A generally deep-ocean, small seabird of many species, some with distinctive plumage, with wide distribution throughout the world's oceans. The white-faced storm petrel is known for its unusual "walking" ability as it forages near the surface.

Swabbie: Marine Corps slang term for naval enlisted men, from the sailor's historical duty of "swabbing" the decks of a ship.

Tern: A slender, fork-tailed seabird whose distribution and breeding is worldwide. Most species have grey and white plumage with black "caps" that vary in size and density.

Tet Offensive: The historical military setting for the novel, the Tet offensive was a major, country-wide attack by North Vietnamese and Viet Cong forces against American and South Vietnamese troops, launched in late January, 1968, at the beginning of the celebration of the Vietnamese New Year (Tet). While unsuccessful militarily for the North Vietnamese Army, which took years to recover from the devastation and subsequent lowered morale inflicted on its forces, the size and ferocity of the campaign resulted in unprecedented American casualties. The Tet Offensive is considered to be the point at which US public opinion against the war strengthened, leading ultimately to peace negotiations and eventual victory for North Vietnam.

Texarkana: A twin city with one metropolitan area in Texas and the other in Arkansas, both named Texarkana.

Thirty caliber: A diameter, in hundredths of an inch, of a particular firearm's bullet, whether pistol, rifle or machine gun. There are weapons in each of these categories that fire a bullet of .30 (thirty/hundredths of an inch) caliber.

Thumb safety: A mechanical safety lever installed on the frame of a M1911 service pistol, left engaged when the pistol was loaded and holstered during normal combat duty to prevent positive motion forward by the cocked hammer of the weapon if accidentally struck or dropped.

Time in grade: Period of time that a serviceman has held a certain rank, sometimes useful for determining seniority in a group of servicemen of otherwise equal rank.

Trenton: Currently the state capitol of New Jersey, during colonial times in North America a small town and site of a pivotal battle of the American Revolution, in which General George Washington crossed the Delaware River on Christmas Eve and launched a successful surprise attack on German mercenaries. The victory at Trenton, Washington's first, was valuable in reviving American spirits against what to that point had been a string of notable, even humiliating defeats.

Trip flare: During the Vietnam War and since, a grenade-sized device carried by infantrymen on operations in the field, enclosing a combustible core that burns brightly when its spring-actuated hammer is released and fires the flare. The trip flare was heavily used defensively in Vietnam by infantrymen "digging in" for the night as protection from infiltration. It is firmly secured in a selected location and one end of a nearly invisible plastic filament is tied to a pin holding the hammer in place and the other to a nearby object or plant. Enemy soldiers "trip" the flare on disturbing the filament, thereby exposing themselves to hostile action, often from weapons already in place and sighted in on each trip flare location.

Twenty-five Buddhas: A reference to the belief of some sects of Buddhism that Gautama Siddhartha was preceded in Enlightenment by twenty-four others, known collectively as "Buddhas", with an appearance yet to be made of a final (twenty-sixth) Buddha.

20 mm: Twenty millimeter, the diameter of bullets used in one of the rapid-fire weapon systems of the Phantom F-4 jet.

Twentynine Palms: A reference to a large Marine Corps training center near the city of Twentynine Palms in San Bernardino County, California, established during the 2nd World War.

Two Alpha: The first squad of the second platoon in a Marine rifle company.

Two Charlie: The third squad of the second platoon in a Marine rifle company.

Uncle Ho: See *Ho Chi Minh.*

Unload: In the context used in the novel, slang meaning "to fire a weapon".

VC: Viet Cong (Vietnamese Communist), the primary guerrilla combatant opposing the South Vietnamese government.

VD: Venereal Disease.

Victor Charlie: Military alphabet code words for "V" and "C", meaning "Viet Cong".

Viet Cong: See *VC* above.

Viet Minh: The political organization and revolutionary armed forces of communist Vietnamese during the 1940s and 1950s that assumed control of North Vietnam following the defeat of the French at Dien Bien Phu (*see in glossary*). The Viet Minh as a political force lost popular support due to brutal land reform policies and was eventually disbanded and effectively replaced by the Viet Cong (*see in glossary*).

Villain of the piece: Used figuratively, an idiom referring to someone considered to be the person responsible for something bad or wrong or who, in fiction, is the main enemy of the hero.

Wait one: Radio jargon for "Wait one minute and I will get right back to you."

Wasted: Killed.

Web (or webbed) belt: A type of belt common in the military, made without traditional holes in a belt end, using instead friction applied to belt material in a box-like buckle that adjusts belt length to waist size.

Wine-dark sea: A reference to the ancient Greek poet Homer's description of the Mediterranean Sea. Some scholars believe the analogy is used not for descriptive accuracy (the Mediterranean being an exceptionally blue body of water) but as artistic license for convenience. Being the center of the ancient world, the Mediterranean is frequently referenced in *The Iliad* and *The Odyssey* and the Greek words for "wine-dark sea" fit the Homeric poem's meter and cadence well. Other scholars contend that under stormy skies, clouds and heavy rain, the Mediterranean does indeed look dark, that in such conditions the sea would naturally impress itself more strongly on the poet's imagination, and therefore the poet did indeed intend the analogy to be accurate. Homer is not here for the professors to consult.

Wonder bread: A popular brand of commercially processed bread, widely sold in American markets at the time of the Vietnam War.

Yellow-seven: A fictional location in the novel where a prearranged exfiltration of the helicopter troops that stormed the Buddhist temple was to occur. No one ever makes it to Mark Yellow-Seven.

www.ingramcontent.com/pod-product-compliance
Lightning Source LLC
Chambersburg PA
CBHW030419310726
48979CB00009B/1530/J

* 9 7 8 0 9 9 7 8 7 7 5 1 9 *